A KILLING FROST

**DAW Books presents the finest in urban fantasy
from Seanan McGuire:**

*Coming soon from DAW Books

SEANAN McGUIRE

A KILLING FROST

AN OCTOBER DAYE NOVEL

DAW BOOKS, INC.

DONALD A. WOLLHEIM, FOUNDER

1745 Broadway, New York, NY 10019

ELIZABETH R. WOLLHEIM

SHEILA E. GILBERT

PUBLISHERS

www.dawbooks.com

First Printing, September 2020
1 2 3 4 5 6 7 8 9

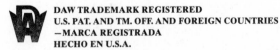

DAW TRADEMARK REGISTERED
U.S. PAT. AND TM. OFF. AND FOREIGN COUNTRIES
—MARCA REGISTRADA
HECHO EN U.S.A.

PRINTED IN THE U.S.A.

For Manda.
For cake and support, but most of all,
for her car's heated seats.

ACKNOWLEDGMENTS

Here we go again. Every time I get to write one of these, it gets a little harder to come up with something new to say, and a little more amazing, because so few urban fantasy series—or series, period—will ever make it to book fourteen. Fourteen volumes of October's adventures! How is that even possible? It doesn't seem like it should be, and yet here we are, moving blithely into a misty future, still fighting our way through the brambles and briars of an often-hostile Faerie.

I am so, so grateful that all of you are still here. As I'm typing this, my home in Washington State is under lockdown as we fight to win out over a global pandemic; these are frightening times, and being someone who tells stories for a living can be hard when it feels like reality weighs more than the atmosphere of the entire world. Biggest of thanks to everyone who's supported and tolerated me through this process, including my D&D group (We blend! We really do!), the Machete Squad, the entire team at DAW Books, and the cast and crew of *The Lightning Thief: The Percy Jackson Musical*, who helped me to celebrate one of the best birthdays of my life. Thanks to Kayleigh and Betsy, for Broadway ridiculousness, and to my little sister, whose first Broadway show got canceled by the shutdown.

Thank you to my dearest, most darling and beloved Amy, who has finally agreed to meet me in the corn; to Vixy, who stands up against an onslaught of email with compassion and grace; to Jude and Alan, who keep the doors open and the fires burning despite endless obstructions; and to Dr. Gawley, for her incredible veterinary medical care. Thanks to everyone who hosted me when travel was still possible, especially Scotchy and Marnie, whose incredible driving made the second half of 2019 infinitely easier, and to

Geralyn, who went well out of her way to help me find a dance machine. Thanks to Shawn and Jay and Tea, to Margaret and Mary and a whole list of people, all of whom I adore utterly.

My editor, Sheila Gilbert, makes so many things possible, as does the patient work of Joshua Starr, who emails me to nag when I let things slip. Diana Fox has finally learned how to use Discord, while Chris McGrath's covers just get better and better. All my cats are doing well: Elsie, Thomas, and Megara all thrive on my being home constantly, and spend most of their time glued to my side. Finally, thank you to my pit crew: Christopher Mangum, Tara O'Shea, and Kate Secor.

My soundtrack while writing *A Killing Frost* consisted mostly of *The Lightning Thief, Beetlejuice: The Musical, The Musical, The Musical, Instar,* by Nancy Kerr and the Sweet Visitor Band, *The Hearth and the Hive,* by Talis Kimberley, endless live concert recordings of the Counting Crows, and all the Ludo a girl could hope to have (eternally waiting for a new album). Any errors in this book are entirely my own. The errors that aren't here are the ones that all these people helped me fix.

Let me show you what's waiting down by the edge of the water. I think you're going to enjoy it.

OCTOBER DAYE PRONUNCIATION GUIDE
THROUGH *A KILLING FROST*

All pronunciations are given strictly phonetically. This only covers races explicitly named in the first fourteen books, omitting Undersea races not appearing or mentioned in the current volume.

Aes Sidhe: *eys shee*. Plural is "Aes Sidhe."
Afanc: *ah-fank*. Plural is "Afanc."
Annwn: *ah-noon*. No plural exists.
Arkan sonney: *are-can saw-ney*. Plural is "arkan sonney."
Bannick: *ban-nick*. Plural is "Bannicks."
Baobhan Sith: *baa-vaan shee*. Plural is "Baobhan Sith," diminutive is "Baobhan."
Barghest: *bar-guy-st*. Plural is "Barghests."
Blodynbryd: *blow-din-brid*. Plural is "Blodynbryds."
Cait Sidhe: *kay-th shee*. Plural is "Cait Sidhe."
Candela: *can-dee-la*. Plural is "Candela."
Coblynau: *cob-lee-now*. Plural is "Coblynau."
Cu Sidhe: *coo shee*. Plural is "Cu Sidhe."
Daoine Sidhe: *doon-ya shee*. Plural is "Daoine Sidhe," diminutive is "Daoine."
Djinn: *jin*. Plural is "Djinn."
Dóchas Sidhe: *doe-sh-as shee*. Plural is "Dóchas Sidhe."
Ellyllon: *el-lee-lawn*. Plural is "Ellyllons."
Folletti: *foe-let-tea*. Plural is "Folletti."
Gean-Cannah: *gee-ann can-na*. Plural is "Gean-Cannah."
Glastig: *glass-tig*. Plural is "Glastigs."
Gwragen: *guh-war-a-gen*. Plural is "Gwragen."

Hamadryad: *ha-ma-dry-add*. Plural is "Hamadryads."
Hippocampus: *hip-po-cam-pus*. Plural is "Hippocampi."
Kelpie: *kel-pee*. Plural is "Kelpies."
Kitsune: *kit-soo-nay*. Plural is "Kitsune."
Lamia: *lay-me-a*. Plural is "Lamia."
The Luidaeg: *the lou-sha-k*. No plural exists.
Manticore: *man-tee-core*. Plural is "Manticores."
Naiad: *nigh-add*. Plural is "Naiads."
Nixie: *nix-ee*. Plural is "Nixen."
Peri: *pear-ee*. Plural is "Peri."
Piskie: *piss-key*. Plural is "Piskies.'
Puca: *puh-ca*. Plural is "Pucas."
Roane: *row-n*. Plural is "Roane."
Satyr: *say-tur*. Plural is "Satyrs."
Selkie: *sell-key*. Plural is "Selkies."
Shyi Shuai: *shh-yee shh-why*. Plural is "Shyi Shuai."
Silene: *sigh-lean*. Plural is "Silene."
Tuatha de Dannan: *tootha day danan*. Plural is "Tuatha de Dannan," diminutive is "Tuatha."
Tylwyth Teg: *till-with teeg*. Plural is "Tylwyth Teg," diminutive is "Tylwyth."
Urisk: *you-risk*. Plural is "Urisk."

ONE

October 11th, 2014

The third day comes a frost, a killing frost,
And, when he thinks, good easy man, full surely
His greatness is a-ripening, nips his root,
And then he falls, as I do.

—William Shakespeare, *Henry VIII.*

"WE'RE GOING TO HAVE to discuss dresses eventually, October," said May, holding up a bridal magazine and waving it at me like a weapon. "Something pretty. Something lacy. Something—and this is the part I can't stress enough—that you're actually *willing to wear.*"

"It doesn't matter what I wear to the wedding, we both know it's going to be completely covered in blood before we reach 'I do,'" I said scornfully. "Do purebloods even *say,* 'I do'?" Having never been to a pureblood wedding before, I was woefully uninformed about their customs. Thanks to my mother, my wedding knowledge is much more romantic comedy than formal fairy tale.

My sister—technically my retired Fetch, but that's not a relationship that's easy to explain, and she's family either way—rolled her eyes. "Of course not," she said. "That's a Christian thing, which means it's a human thing. Purebloods don't do Christian wedding vows."

"Got it," I said, even though I didn't. I didn't "got" any of this.

May snorted before pushing her hair, currently streaked in electric blue, out of her eyes and dropping the magazine onto the pile that had come to dominate our coffee table. "Liar," she said. Like most of our furniture, the table had originally come from Community Thrift, and like every other flat surface in our house, it had been immediately covered in a thick layer of junk mail, books, and generalized clutter. We're not tidy people.

It doesn't help that we have a constant stream of teenagers flowing in and out of the house, which is huge by San Francisco standards. We have a dedicated living room *and* a dining room, and four bedrooms, most of which are in use on any given afternoon. Tybalt and I share one, despite his occasional protests that it's inappropriate for us to cohabitate before the wedding; May and her live-in girlfriend Jazz, share a second, which is far enough down the hall from mine that we can all pretend to be untouched paragons of virtue.

The third bedroom belongs to my squire, Quentin, and will until the day his parents call him home to Toronto to take up his place as Crown Prince of the Westlands, which is what Faerie calls North America. We steal human words with gleeful abandon, but we don't like to use their names for things when we have any other choice in the matter. We're sort of like the French that way.

The fourth bedroom is currently a guest room and plays host to a rotating cast of people with nowhere better to spend the day. Usually, it's either Quentin's boyfriend Dean, who prefers to sleep alone, my friend Etienne's daughter Chelsea, or my friend Stacy's middle daughter Karen. Like I said, a constant stream of teenagers. Tybalt's nephew Raj is in Quentin's room what seems like three nights out of five, and I continue to hold out hope that my own daughter Gillian will eventually decide she's tired of hating me and take her turn at using up all the hot water. I like having a full house. It feels safer than the alternative.

Although that might be an artifact of my childhood. When I was alone with my mother in her tower, that was always when things got bad. When I was with Uncle Sylvester and my friends in Shadowed Hills, I was safe, and fed, and cared for. For me, home never happened in the building where it was supposed to live. I guess that's why I'm so determined to keep my doors open, and to keep the kids who tumble through my life as safe as I can. I want to be the kind of friend to them that my uncle was to me, back before he became my liege, back before I understood what we really were to one another.

Growing up doesn't mean getting over everything that happened to us as children. It just means calcifying it and never letting go.

May grabbed another bridal magazine, flipping it open to a picture of a bride who was wearing so much lace and beadwork that it was a miracle she could stand under her own power. Wait. Maybe she wasn't standing. Maybe the dress was doing it for her. It certainly looked stiff enough.

"How about this one?" she asked.

"If you want to open a bakery, I won't stop you, but I'm not walking down the aisle looking like somebody's grandmother's prize meringue," I said.

May wrinkled her nose. "You're no fun at all."

"If you want a dress with its own zip code, *you* get married."

To my surprise, she sighed heavily, turned the page in her magazine, and said, "I want to. Jazz isn't sure."

I blinked. "Why isn't she sure? You're amazing. Any girl would be lucky to marry you."

"Try telling her that," said May. She put the magazine down on the table and stood, stretching. "I think I'm done with this for the afternoon. I'm going to go bake some cookies."

"That's your answer to everything."

"Better than your answer to everything." She made an exaggerated stabbing gesture. "There's a reason I don't go through as many pairs of jeans as you do."

"Brat."

"Proud of it." May cracked a smile, although it lacked her usual intensity. "I'd bake your wedding cake if you hadn't promised the job to Kerry when you were six."

"She'll do an amazing job, and you know it."

"I do," May agreed. "But my buttercream is better."

"Questionable."

She laughed as she walked out of the living room, leaving me alone with a pile of bridal magazines and the two geriatric half-Siamese cats sleeping on the other end of the couch. I gave them a worried look. Cagney and Lacey can sleep through virtually anything these days. They're cats, so sleep was always a strong suit of theirs, but for the last few years, they haven't wanted to do much of anything else.

Age comes for everything mortal. Everything except for me, assuming I can play my cards right.

My name is October Daye because my mother should never have been allowed to name her own children. My mother should never have been allowed to *have* children. She's a Firstborn daughter of Oberon, absent Lord of Faerie, and nothing about her is human. She used to pretend she was, once upon a time, and that's how I happened, because my father was as human as they come. I'm what we call a changeling, a blend of two worlds, magical and mortal at the same time. It's an awkward place to stand since we don't belong anywhere, not really. We have to fight for our place every day of our lives, and it can be exhausting. A lot of changelings break under the strain.

Sometimes, I'm not sure I haven't. I spent my childhood as my mother's shadow, dogging her heels and trying desperately to make her love me, even when it was clear she didn't really want to. I didn't know it then, but I wasn't the daughter she wanted to have. No, that honor was reserved for my missing sister, August, who had decided to play the hero and go looking for our grandfather.

She didn't find him. She lost herself in the act of trying and stayed lost until I went and brought her home. But nothing in Faerie is ever that straightforward. I'm the daughter of a fae woman and a human man, and I'm holding onto my humanity by my fingernails. One day it's going to slip away, and I'll be immortal like my mother, my sisters, and my daughter.

I'm not ready for that. I can't hold it off forever but giving up my mortality feels like betraying my father, who never asked to get swept up in any of this.

August's father is as fae as they come. He's a man named Simon Torquill, twin brother to my liege lord, Duke Sylvester Torquill of Shadowed Hills. He's also the man who turned me into a fish for fourteen years and destroyed the life I'd been trying to build outside of Faerie. He did it to save me from something even worse, because fae don't think about time the way humans do—as a pureblood, spending a decade or so as a fish would have been inconvenient, not devastating. It took me a long time to forgive him. Part of me never will. The part that will always be human, no matter what my blood says. The rest of me says I wouldn't have what I've got now if I'd stayed where I was. I didn't choose to lose my human fiancé, or my then-mostly-human daughter. I would never have chosen that. But I also wouldn't go back if someone could offer me the choice. Not now.

Now, I'm a knight errant and a recognized Hero of the Realm, thanks to Queen Arden Windermere in the Mists, who was able to reclaim her family's throne and get her brother back because of my chronic inability to mind my own damn business.

Now, I live in a house that I own free and clear, thanks to Sylvester, who gave it to me when it became apparent that my squire needed to come live with me. Houses are a weirdly extravagant gift in human circles, but the fae amass land the way some people amass little ceramic figurines. If Sylvester divested himself of his real estate holdings, he might actually crash the Bay Area markets. For him, giving me a house was a small price to pay for knowing I was safe behind a locked door and not at the mercy of a mortal landlord.

Again, purebloods think differently than changelings or humans do. They're so far outside the flow of time that it doesn't matter as much to them. It doesn't have to. There are exceptions, of course.

Younger purebloods, like Quentin, may have eternity in front of them, but they're still living within the limits of a mortal lifespan where experience and opinions are concerned. Their thoughts follow lines I can understand, and they're as baffled by their elders as I am. Being the larval stage of something doesn't mean you comprehend it. Maybe that's why I have so many teenagers in my house. Or maybe they just figured out that I'm willing to feed them. The jury's still out on that one.

May is technically a pureblood, but since she was created when a night haunt consumed my living blood, she has my memories up to that point, and some of her own memories from the person she was before. I'm not sure how deep those older memories go, but I know they're less real to her; she's May Daye, now and forever, mixed mostly with Dare, the girl whose face she wore before mine. We're on much the same level most of the time.

And then there's Tybalt. A man I never expected to call friend, much less anything more. But he loves me as much as I love him, and that's a rare and precious thing in this world. He's my best friend and my favorite person to talk to and the reason I'm letting May subject me to her increasingly questionable taste in wedding gowns. Although that may be partially her trying to mess with me, since she knows I don't like dresses that are bigger than I am; she just wants me to pick something.

Some people seem to think my disinterest in the planning process comes from a secret desire not to get married. That couldn't be further from the truth. If Tybalt would agree to it, or if it wouldn't cause a massive diplomatic incident, I'd drag him to the courthouse tomorrow and get married in jeans and a tank top, since those make up the majority of my wardrobe. He fell in love with me without finery or billows of lace. I'd be happy to marry him the same way. It's just that my life is chaotic and I'm something of a magnet for people who want to kill me, take me apart and use me for my magic, or ensnare me in incomprehensible plans for world domination.

It doesn't matter what my wedding dress looks like because by the time the actual ceremony rolls around, I'm going to look like the lead in a high school production of *Carrie*. We should start out by rolling me through an abattoir since there's no way we're getting around it.

I've learned not to be too attached to plans. They never survive contact with reality when I'm around.

Groaning, I stood, leaving the couch, the cats, and May's pile of magazines behind. There was a time when I would have been horrified by the thought of my wedding dress getting so drenched in blood that it was ruined; these days, I'm more resigned. My mother, who is not a very nice person, raised me to think I was Daoine Sidhe, descended from Titania, and that the reason I found blood alluring and revolting at the same time was because my magic wasn't strong enough to handle it.

Thanks, Mom. She's not Daoine Sidhe, and neither am I; there's nothing of Titania in my veins. We're Dóchas Sidhe, and while our magic is still tied to blood, it's not the same. For us, there's nothing else, no flowers, no water.

All we get is in the blood.

It was about six in the evening, and May and I were alone in the house. Quentin was at Saltmist spending time with Dean, who's been over less since our collective visit to the Duchy of Ships back in May, where we'd helped the sea witch keep her word by bringing back her descendant race, the Roane, from the verge of extinction. It turns out that suddenly reintroducing a long-lost type of fae to the Undersea, while removing most of the Selkies at the same time, was a little destabilizing, and as one of our coastal nobles, whose mother is a Duchess in the Undersea, Dean had been spending a lot of his time dealing with the fallout.

Better him than me. Of the two of us, he's the one who actually speaks "diplomacy" with something other than a knife.

Jazz was likewise absent, since the small antique store she owned and operated in Berkeley didn't close until seven. With wedding planning done for the day, Tybalt off at the Court of Cats, and May busy baking, I was free to go upstairs, take off my bra, and do nothing for the rest of the afternoon. Paradise is real.

I was halfway to the stairs when the phone rang. The landline, not my cell. I stopped, blinking at the sound. It continued ringing.

"You going to get that?" called May.

If someone was calling the landline, it was probably a client of mine. Just what I wanted. I'm technically still a private investigator, although I don't have nearly as much time as I used to for tracking down cheating spouses and untangling complicated paternity cases. I swallowed a sigh, walked over to the end table, and hooked the receiver out of its cradle, bringing it to my ear. "October Daye Investigations, October speaking," I said.

"Aunt Birdie, you need to listen to me."

I froze. "Karen?"

So far, two of Stacy's children have shown an unexpected talent for soothsaying. Karen can see the future in her dreams; Cassandra can read it in the movement of air. When they order someone to listen, listening is the only reasonable response. I caught my breath.

"I'm listening," I said.

"You're going to learn something soon that makes you unhappy. I don't know what it is because it didn't matter to what I saw. You're going to go looking for someone you've lost, and you're going to want to take everyone you can with you. But you can't do that. In my dream, when it went the way you wanted it to go, you had May and Quentin with you, and sometimes Spike, and no one else. Do you understand what I'm saying?"

"I think so." I was going to go on another quest, and Tybalt wasn't allowed to go with me. Oh, that was going to go over well.

"You're going to go to the place where the bad lady is sleeping, and you can't wake her up. Promise me you won't wake her up."

Evening. There was no one else Karen would refer to as "the bad lady." She'd been too close to Evening once, and like the rest of us, she'd learned not to use her name. It wasn't safe. "All right," I said.

"Promise me."

"I promise."

"I believe you. I'm sorry, Aunt Birdie. You can't take Uncle Tybalt with you, or people will die. I don't want anyone to die. Be careful."

The line went dead.

I was still staring at the receiver in my hand when someone knocked on the front door. Slowly, I turned to face it.

"May," I did my best to keep my voice as level as possible. "Did you order pizza and forget to tell me?"

"No," she called back from the kitchen. "Why?"

"Someone's at the door." Someone at the door almost never means anything good outside of Girl Scout season. The people who live with me, whether intermittently or full-time, don't bother to knock; they just charge in whenever they feel like it. The people I answer to in the hierarchy of Faerie don't usually come to the house.

Any chance of a quiet evening at home that had survived Karen's call slipped away as I reluctantly approached the door. I didn't have my knives on me, but I had the baseball bat in the umbrella stand if I needed a weapon, and I had May, who had come into the kitchen doorway and was standing there with a rolling pin in her hand. If someone had come looking for a beat-down, they were about to have a lucky day.

"I'll get it," I said, and reached for the doorknob.

We don't usually bother to lock the door when we're at home. Anyone who could get through the wards we have on the place wouldn't even be slowed down by something as simple as a deadbolt. With a simple twist of my wrist, the door was open, and I was braced for trouble.

Trouble, in the form of one of the tallest men in San Francisco, looked down at me and blinked before raising one thick eyebrow. "Tobes?" he rumbled. "There a reason you look like you're getting ready for an MMA cage match?"

I relaxed, realizing as I did how much adrenaline had just been dumped into my system by the one-two punch of a ringing phone and a knock on the door. I may be under too much stress. "Hi, Danny," I said. "To what do we owe the pleasure?"

Danny McReady is a San Francisco cab driver and the owner of the world's only Barghest rescue. There's a good reason for that, since Barghests are hostile and venomous, with tails like scorpions built on a canine scale, and most people don't consider them good pets. Danny's not most people. He's a Bridge Troll, with skin that's literally as hard as granite. It's also the color of granite when he's not wearing an illusion designed to let him pass for human. I did a favor for his sister a long time ago, and he's basically pledged himself to help me whenever I need it as a consequence.

"Your kitty-cat sent me," he said. "Said I should ask you to put on something nice and not *too* bloodstained and get in my car. Hey, May. You're looking fetching as always."

"Oh, stop," said May, before both of them laughed at his joke.

I didn't. Tybalt doesn't usually send people to get me; he prefers to come get me himself, using the Shadow Roads for transportation. Maybe I was being paranoid, but given the last few years of my life, I'd earned a little paranoia. I took a step back, gesturing for Danny to come into the house.

"Shut the door and drop the illusion, please," I said.

Danny didn't look surprised. He's known me for a while. Instead, he closed the door before making a sweeping gesture with his right hand. His human disguise wisped away with the faint but distinct scent of fresh-mixed concrete and ripe huckleberries, revealing his true face. Gray and craggy, like a boulder that had decided it would be a good idea to put on jeans and a San Francisco Giants hoodie and go wandering around the city. He seemed to get taller, and broader at the same time, until it looked impossible for him to have fit through the door. He grinned at me, exposing square, craggy teeth.

"Do I pass inspection, princess?" he asked, in a voice like rocks being tumbled in a barrel.

"Sorry, Danny," I said. "You know how it is around here."

"I do, which is why I ain't mad. Just get in my car, and we're square. Only maybe change first, so the kitty doesn't take it out on me."

"I'm making cookies," said May. "Come on, Danny, you can have one while you wait for Toby to make herself decent."

"Never gonna happen," he said and guffawed as he followed her into the kitchen.

I rolled my eyes at both of them and turned for the stairs. If

Tybalt wanted me to wear something nice for some reason, that was exactly what I was going to do. And I *wasn't* going to look like a meringue.

My room is warm and dark and comfortable, with blackout curtains on the windows and clothing usually strewn across the floor. Neither Tybalt nor I are much on putting the laundry away, and with as often as I get bled on in the course of my duties, I throw out as many shirts as I wash and fold. We make an effort to keep sharp things off the floor, since neither of us cares for blood on the sheets, and that's good enough. I flicked the light on and was greeted by a chirping grumble and the sound of rattling thorns as Spike, our resident rose goblin, rose from where he'd been sleeping curled in the center of the bed.

"Hey, buddy," I said, pulling my shirt over my head and tossing it into the mess on the floor. "Karen says I'm going somewhere, and you can come with me. Does that sound good to you?"

Spike rattled again, sitting down and beginning to groom one paw.

The bra I was wearing was pretty all-purpose, and so I left it on as I made my way to the closet, where my meager store of dresses hung, waiting for another night of disuse. Well, the joke was on them for once. I started rifling through them, looking for something that fit Tybalt's definition of "nice" while still leaving me free to run, fight, and draw my knives if necessary.

Leaving the house without making sure I'm equipped for a knife fight is a good way to guarantee I wind up *in* a knife fight because the universe likes nothing more than making me regret my choices. Scowling at my closet, I pulled out a simple sleeveless dress in dark green, with a lace-covered bodice giving way to a knee-length velvet skirt. It pulled on easily over my head, with no zippers I'd need anyone else to help with, and that made it ideal despite its lack of pockets.

My knife belt and silver knife were on the nightstand next to my bed. I fastened the belt around my waist, where the illusion I'd inevitably need to cast to make myself seem human would hide it, then slid my knife into the sheath at my right hip. The left side remained empty. That's where I used to carry an iron knife, back when I was more human and iron wasn't quite so painful. Faerie comes with costs.

It only took a second to shimmy out of my jeans and step into a pair of black flats, and then I was heading for the bathroom—the nice thing about owning the house and having the master bedroom is the attached en suite, even if I mostly only use it to shower and pee without someone hammering on the door and telling me I'm taking too long. Tybalt said to put on something nice, not to make myself fancy, so I just ran a brush through my stick-straight brown-and-blonde hair before giving myself a critical look in the mirror.

There's not much point to makeup when I'm going to be spinning a human disguise. Illusionary eyeliner is always perfect, and I've never jabbed an illusionary mascara wand into my eye. Considering that, I looked pretty put-together. My hair is easy to tame, thanks to its utter lack of curl or body, and the blonde streaks I've been developing ever since I started shifting my blood more toward fae look like intentional highlights. The pointed tips of my ears poked through, as usual; another thing for my illusions to hide.

Much as my hair has changed, my eyes are still the grayish, washed-out color of fog rolling across the bay in the small hours of the morning; they still look like mine, and I'm oddly grateful for that. I don't want to look in my mirror and see someone else looking back at me. I took a deep breath, blew it out, and reached one hand toward the mirror in a beseeching gesture, snapping it closed as the smell of cut grass and copper rose in the air.

"'Twas many and many a year ago, in a kingdom by the sea," I said, tone as light as I could make it. "Where there lived a maiden whom you may know, by the name of Annabel Lee. But she moved and she didn't leave a forwarding address, and I have no idea what happened to her after that."

My magic gathered around me, growing heavier and heavier until it finally popped like a soap bubble, leaving me draped in the almost invisible glitter of a human disguise. The woman looking out of my mirror wasn't a stranger, although her eyes were darker than mine, gray blue instead of blank fog. Her hair was the same, but her ears were rounded, and the bones of her face were softer, making her cheekbones, chin, and eyebrows seem gentler, less likely to cut anyone who touched them. I'm not as angular as a pureblood, but I don't pass for human the way I used to.

Also, she was wearing mascara. And her eyeliner was perfect, and she wasn't carrying any weapons.

I turned away from the mirror and left the bathroom, the faint smell of my magic clinging to my skin. Spike was in the middle of my pillow, stretched out with its thorny belly showing. I smiled at it and stepped into the hall, heading for the stairs.

May and Danny—now back in his human disguise—were still in the kitchen, the latter holding a napkin full of fresh chocolate chip cookies. He beamed when he saw me.

"You always clean up good," he said. "New dress?"

"Not really," I said. "Jazz brought it home from her shop. I think it's as old as I am, and I was born in 1952."

"Baby," scoffed Danny. "Come on. Your chariot awaits. Good cookies, May."

"Have a nice time wherever it is you're going," said May, beaming at me. "Here's a tip: if someone tries to stab you, duck."

"Oh, ha ha, I never thought of that before," I said, and grabbed a cookie off the rack cooling on the counter before I followed Danny into the hall, to the front door, and outside.

His cab was parked in the driveway. One more luxury of the house we live in: we have a driveway. I could rent it to desperate tech workers for fifteen hundred dollars a month if I wanted to, and there have been times in my life when the temptation would have been almost irresistible. From the outside, Danny's car was a standard yellow cab, the sort that crops up in most major American cities. I was relieved to see that there were no Barghests in the backseat.

"I ran the vacuum yesterday, so you don't need to worry about your dress," he said, gesturing for me to take the front passenger seat. "An' the kitty said not to stress about getting home, he'll take care of it. So it's cool that you're leaving your car."

"Not sure how I'd bring it along, since I don't know where we're going." I climbed in and fastened my seatbelt, first checking to make sure there was no one lurking in the back. It's happened before, and a one-person car chase isn't as much fun as it sounds.

Several strange charms and bundles of herbs dangled from the rearview mirror. One of them appeared to be an elaborate knot made from bright green hair. I squinted at it, inhaling gingerly as I tried to feel out the magic behind it. All the charms had been enchanted by the same person; they smelled, distantly, of engine grease and coal dust. I leaned back in my seat, rubbing my nose in an effort not to sneeze.

Smelling magic, even when it's old, faint, or distant, is another Dóchas Sidhe party trick, although it's part of what makes me terrible at parties. I'm constantly getting distracted by things no one else can smell, although almost all fae can pick up on the broad strokes. When I was younger, I thought everyone got as much detail as I did, and I was always very confused when people didn't know what I was talking about. Just one more thing to add to the list of ways my mother made my childhood miserable.

If I ever find a therapist who works with changelings, I'm going to send Mom the bill.

The car dipped as Danny climbed behind the wheel, sliding into a space too big to fit into the apparent size of the frame. Magic again, making his life a little easier. And why shouldn't it? We live in a world that was never designed for us, where iron lurks around every corner and where hiding from the humans is both increasingly difficult and of paramount importance.

There used to be places we could run to when the mortal world got to be too much to take. Worlds other than the Summerlands, places like Annwn and Emain Ablach, whole realities tailored to the needs and natures of the fae who occupied them. But the deeper lands of Faerie were sealed when Oberon disappeared, leaving us stranded in only two worlds, one of which is actively hostile to us, the other of which is too small to contain all of Faerie comfortably. The Summerlands are the only other realm we can get to now, and while they welcome us, they're not *home* to anyone but the pixies.

Sometimes I wonder whether Amandine would have followed in the footsteps of her older siblings if Oberon hadn't vanished right after she was born, spinning a world of shimmering spires and endless brambles, perfectly suited to the magic and desires of the Dóchas Sidhe. But then I remember that it would be a world that owed its existence to my mother and decided I wouldn't want to go there if it existed.

Danny pulled out of the driveway, driving with the speed and safety of a man who not only got paid to do it, but had excellent reason not to want to be pulled over by the human police. He could always cast a don't-look-here if he had to, to keep them from seeing how unreasonably large he was, but that wouldn't necessarily fool a dashboard camera, and those are becoming more and more common.

"When are you going to tell me where we're going?"

"When I absolutely have to," he said jovially.

I folded my arms and glowered at him. He laughed.

"Try relaxing for once," he suggested. "Me and the kitty aren't going to hurt you, and you know it."

"I do, but I didn't become a detective because I liked people having secrets," I countered. "Please, a hint?"

"You've been there before."

He was heading for the 101. We were clearly leaving the city; I just had no idea why. I huffed. "You people."

Danny laughed again.

We kept driving for almost twenty minutes, leaving San Francisco proper behind us. When we passed the sign for the Brisbane city limits, I turned and gave him a stern look. "Are you taking me to the airport?"

"What? No! That would be ridiculous. I didn't tell you to get your ID." He turned on his turn signal. "Hold tight, we're almost there."

I leaned back in my seat, folding my arms again. Wherever we were going, I was going to be getting there already mildly annoyed.

Danny pulled off the freeway and onto surface streets, driving through three intersections before he turned again. "Do you ever lighten up?"

"Not habitually."

He turned onto a winding driveway, which vanished ahead of us into a patently artificial copse of trees. I sat up straighter, finally recognizing our destination. "You could have told me Tybalt was taking me to dinner."

"Nope. Promised him I wouldn't."

I turned to glare at Danny. "I'm the hero here. You should be more afraid of me."

"Tell it to the boyfriend," he said. We passed into the trees, and a low brick building appeared in front of us. It was quaint looking, like something from an old Disney movie. Ivy clung to the walls, and roses covered the trellises out front. Danny pulled up in front of the valet station, gesturing grandly to the restaurant.

"Welcome to Cat in the Rafters, Tobes," he said. "Now get out so I can find a paying fare."

"I could pay you."

"Nope. I keep telling you, your money's no good here."

I laughed as I opened the door and got out of the cab. "Then go. Make money."

"Have a nice date, don't get stabbed!" Danny drove off as soon as I closed the door, and I turned to face the restaurant, and the terrifying prospect of a normal dinner date.

TWO

CAT IN THE RAFTERS isn't the best, most exclusive, or most expensive steakhouse in the Bay Area. It is, however, the only steakhouse owned by a Cait Sidhe changeling, a man named Jason Thomas. He's chosen not to live with the Court, preferring to master the fine art of exposing meat to high temperatures and putting it in front of hungry people. He was waiting in the foyer, dark gray hair at odds with his generally youthful appearance. He smiled when he saw me, which was a nice change from all the nobles who look faintly sick when they see me, like they expect me to start throwing knives at people immediately and without provocation.

"Miss Daye," he said, a note of relief in his voice. "We greatly appreciate you joining us to dine this evening."

"I wasn't given much of a choice," I said. "I think this is technically an abduction. I want to speak to your manager."

The corner of his mouth twitched upward as he tried and failed to suppress a smile. "You're about to have dinner with him. I'll be sure to pass along the fact that you dislike his company."

"I can handle it," I said. "How'd he rope you into this, anyway?"

"He made a reservation," said Jason mildly. "I may not choose to spend my days in a dusty room full of cats and ancient mattresses, but I *am* Cait Sidhe, and he *is* my King. When he calls, I'm compelled to answer."

"Huh. The feudal system has a lot to answer for." I shrugged. "Better take me to my fiancé before he decides you're trying to seduce me and comes out here angry."

"Is he that much of the jealous sort where you're concerned?" Jason beckoned for me to follow him through the door into the main dining room.

"Not usually," I said. "He knows he's got nothing to worry about. But you're Cait Sidhe and only sort of under his command. If he's going to get snitty at anybody, it's probably you. Sorry about that."

"No need to apologize, just . . . try not to give him the impression he needs to be 'snitty' about anything." Jason shuddered delicately.

The dining room was surprisingly devoid of customers. It was early in the day, but reservations at Cat in the Rafters are hard to come by; according to Stacy, who actually has to make a reservation when she wants to eat there, people book tables months in advance. I gave Jason a curious look. He shook his head.

"When certain luminaries wish to dine with us, they notify me, and I give the mortal staff the night off," he said. "You and my King aren't the only ones dining here tonight, but you'll have few dinner companions, and all of them fae. You can release your illusions, if you'd prefer."

"Aw, but I'm not actually wearing mascara," I said, in a tone that made it clear I didn't care, and waved a hand dismissively, releasing my human disguise. It burst with the smell of copper and fresh cut grass, and Jason shot me an amused look.

"If you think my King will care, you haven't paid as much attention to his preferences as we've all assumed."

"No, he knows what he's getting."

The steakhouse décor was best described as "rustic," with rough-hewn redwood walls and quaintly mismatched tables, each topped with a candle burning in a jar of thick red glass. The windows were stained glass portraits of cats, black and tabby and colorpoint and calico. Unlike many of the steakhouses I'd seen, there were no antlers or taxidermically preserved birds on the walls; the lighting came from chandeliers heavy with warm yellow bulbs that mimicked candlelight well enough to make my skin crawl but didn't flicker. If they'd flickered, I would have run.

I don't care for candles. They always seem to get me into trouble.

We crossed the empty dining room to a smaller door, which Jason opened to reveal Tybalt standing at attention next to a table set for two. The expected candle centerpiece was conspicuously absent, replaced by a bouquet of flowers, which, in typical Tybalt fashion, couldn't have come from a local florist, since I doubted any of them would have out-of-season arbutus, or arbutus at all.

Jason murmured a pleasantry I didn't quite catch and retreated, closing the door behind him and leaving the two of us alone. I started toward my fiancé, my annoyance at the way he'd brought me to the restaurant melting away at the sight of him.

Faerie has more than its fair share of beautiful men. Beauty is the specialty of the Daoine Sidhe, and of basically anyone descended from Titania, whose children have always been as striking as they are cruel. In the great annals of Faerie's beauty, Tybalt barely even ranks. But as far as I'm concerned, he's the best of them, and always will be.

Tall, slender, well-muscled, with brown hair banded in streaks of tabby black, and eyes the color of malachite, a dozen shades of green warring for position around the cat-slit ovals of his pupils. He looks less feline than many of his subjects, with only his eyes, hair, and the faint stripes on the skin of his back betraying the fact that he's not secretly Daoine Sidhe. His ears are pointed, but more like mine than an actual cat's, and he has the face of a classical sculptor's masterpiece, strong and flawless.

There was a time when I thought he was out of my league. I still sort of do, if I'm being completely honest, but since he doesn't agree, I try not to argue with him.

He smiled as I approached, and my chest tightened the way it always did when he looked at me like that, like I was the only thing in the world that mattered enough to smile for. "You came," he said, and the relief in his voice was evident.

"You didn't give me a lot of choice," I said. "Danny wasn't taking 'no' for an answer. He got May on his side just by offering to take me out of the house."

"Well, if I'd been less forceful in my request, would you have come?" Tybalt took a step toward me. He was wearing a white button-down shirt and brown leather pants. Most of his pants are leather, either because he likes it, or because he knows how much *I* like it. Not the most comfortable material in the world, but the things it does for his ass should be illegal.

"Maybe," I said, before admitting, "Probably not. I got a weird call from Karen just before he showed up, and I was going to go upstairs and try to relax."

"You can relax with me instead, over a lovely dinner, and I'll carry you home after we're done, to enjoy less gustatory pleasures of the flesh." He wrapped his arms around my waist and pulled me close, planting a kiss on my chin. "If I'd asked you on a date, you would have laughed in my face, or told me you'd be happy ordering pizza. Again. For a woman with a penchant for grand, romantic gestures, you have the least interest in actual romance of any lover I've ever had."

"Yes, please tell me about your former lovers while trying to convince me to stay for dinner," I said dryly. "That always helps me get into the mood."

He kissed me again, more languidly this time. "Ah, but you are in my arms, and those past loves are long gone from my life, some to the night-haunts and others to their own designs, and none of them shall warm my bed again. That pleasure is reserved for you and you alone."

I laughed as I pulled away. "Sometimes your tendency to talk like a romance novel is less confusing than others. Let me see these flowers."

"Ever the practical one," said Tybalt approvingly, and let me go.

It was a nice bouquet, if non-standard, mixing common flowers with things he must have gone hunting for. "Arbutus, I know," I said. "That means 'my love is yours alone.' Orange blossom's for eternal love and marriage. Little on the nose, don't you think? And then ivy, that's for wedded love, friendship, and fidelity. Getting ahead of yourself there, aren't you?"

"I know you're faithful, as you've never come home covered in another man's blood without telling me about it, and I can't imagine any lover of yours getting close to you without someone bleeding at least a little," said Tybalt, natural smugness showing through. He circled the table, easing out a chair for me to occupy. "Still, I applaud your sense of caution. I'm 'getting ahead of myself' only because of the interminable length of our engagement."

"It's been less than two years!" I protested, laughing. My amusement turned to ashes in my mouth as I saw the hurt in his expression, brief but obvious. "Tybalt. You know I want to marry you. You know I'm *excited* to marry you. I'm not stretching this out to be cruel."

"I also know you're mortal, sometimes horrifyingly so, and every day you and I remain unwed, I worry something will happen in your human world that keeps me from your side." He stepped back from the chair. "So I bring you roses, for love, and stephanotis, to remind you that happiness awaits us on the other side of the ceremony."

"I'll still be mortal after we're married," I said, easing myself into the chair and watching him with concern. "I don't know when I'll be ready to let go of what's left of my humanity, if I ever will be." But I had been once, hadn't I? When Tybalt had been elf-shot, and I hadn't been sure we'd be able to wake him up? I'd promised to strip the mortality from my blood in order to still be there when he woke up and came back to me.

Was it selfish of me to hold onto my humanity, when there were people who loved me whose lives were going to be so much longer than mine if I didn't let it go?

Tybalt looked at me gravely as he walked around the table to take his own seat. Then he smiled, chasing away the shadows in his eyes, and said, "And I'll love you regardless of how human you remain, as I have done so far, as I have promised to do forever. But you must allow me my anxieties about the length of our engagement."

"Things are moving," I protested. "May and I were talking about dresses when Danny showed up to collect me!"

"I see." Tybalt raised an eyebrow, picking up a carafe of water and tipping it over my glass. Normally, that would have been the waiter's job. Given that we had the dining room to ourselves, I was betting the standard of service for the evening had been set to "leave them alone, for the love of Oberon, or they might decide to eat you." His own glass was already full. "And did you come to any conclusions that will please me?"

"Well, no," I admitted. "Most of the dresses May thinks would be suitable wouldn't survive five minutes on me. Lace and blood are not friends."

Tybalt sighed. "Are you so determined to bleed on our wedding day?"

"No, but I'm also a realist, and blood is going to happen," I said. There was a breadbasket on the other side of the flowers. I pulled it toward me. If this was a dinner date, I was going to have a pretzel roll. "I mean, at least we know no one's going to kill me with a little casual stabbing."

"Yes, because that makes the thought of you bleeding on your wedding dress when I've just confessed to the fear of losing you *so* much better." Tybalt pushed the butter dish across the table before slumping in his chair, rolling his eyes. "If I didn't know you as well as I do, I would suspect you of going out of your way to torment me."

"Luckily, you do know me," I said, and buttered my roll. "I love you. I want to marry you. There's not much in this world that I want more than to call myself your wife. Although we're going to have to discuss last names at some point. I hope you don't expect me to take yours."

"Why would I?" he asked, sounding honestly baffled. "I stole it from a man who was very special to me, but whose bones have long since gone to dust in his grave. William would have been glad to make it a loan, I think, but would never have expected me to keep it forever. Your last name remembers a father who was dear enough to you that you still cling to his mortality, even now that you have no intention of leaving Faerie behind. I'll be glad to wear it on my sleeve for those times when a surname is required by the mortal world."

I blinked, slowly. "Most human men aren't that cool about the idea of taking their wife's name," I said.

"Then it is a good thing for you that I am not a human man," said Tybalt, and smiled.

He was still smiling when the door opened and Jason stepped back into the room, a stack of menus in his hand and a tall man following him, pushing a dark-haired woman in a manual wheelchair. The polished hardwood floor offered no unwanted resistance for her wheels, which rolled with an almost imperceptible whispering noise. The man's shoes, in contrast, were new enough that his heels clicked with every step.

Jason walked them to a table some distance from ours, but with a clear sightline, and handed them their menus before walking over to offer us the same. "Will you be wanting the wine list this evening?" he asked.

"No," said Tybalt.

"I don't really drink anymore," I said. "My body clears the alcohol out too quickly for it to be worth the trouble."

Jason smiled. "Indeed," he said. "Well, then, I'll give you a few minutes to look over your menus before I come back to take your orders." He went into a quick recitation of the night's specials, all of which sounded perfectly delicious, and none of which sounded like a good enough reason for him to still be talking. I looked at him flatly. He finished describing the mushroom risotto, smiled, and walked away, leaving us with our menus.

I looked across the table to Tybalt, who was struggling to contain his laughter. "I'm sorry," he said. "You simply looked so *offended* by the recitation of market price fish and clever ways of preparing lamb."

"We're at a steakhouse," I said, picking up my menu. "I'm going to eat a steak, not a scallop salad or a creative vegan facsimile of a chicken. A steak and probably a potato of some kind, I haven't decided."

"You know, it wouldn't hurt you to broaden your culinary horizons," he said, opening his own menu.

"Are you sure about that? Because Mom says she can taste the death of trees when she eats maple syrup. I already have to get my steaks well-done to avoid the ghosts of all the dead cows I've swallowed from appearing in my head. Broadening my culinary horizons might hurt me. It might hurt me a *lot*."

"My mistake," said Tybalt, sounding distinctly amused.

I scowled at him for a beat before I returned my attention to my menu. The steaks at Cat in the Rafters really *were* excellent— enough that I didn't mind having them cooked more thoroughly than I would once have preferred. The side dishes were even better. Thanks to this being the only local restaurant owned by one of the Cait Sidhe, this was where Tybalt and I tended to end up on our rare date nights—although that made it sound uncomfortably like a Denny's. No one *goes* to Denny's. People just end up there.

There was a faint scrape of wood on wood as one of the other diners pushed back their chair and rose, followed by the tapping of shoes against the floor, which told me who was approaching even before I looked up. If Duchess Lorden was using her wheelchair, she didn't currently have legs, and if she didn't have legs, she didn't have shoes. That meant her husband, Patrick Lorden, was making his way to our table. That didn't make an enormous amount of sense. The Lordens have about as much trouble getting away for private time as Tybalt and I do, and I would never have taken time out of my date to interrupt theirs.

But then, I'm a Hero of the Realm, not a person who needs to call upon a Hero of the Realm on a regular basis. It's sure fun to have a job with nebulous and intentionally ill-defined duties. I lifted my head and turned, directing a smile at the approaching Daoine Sidhe.

Tybalt wasn't being as friendly. He was also looking at Patrick, but he was scowling, and if his ears had been more feline, they would have been pressed flat against his scalp. Someone did *not* care for interruptions.

Well. It wasn't like his possessive streak was anything new, and it wasn't like Patrick was coming over to try stealing Tybalt's fiancée, although he might have a job for me. When he was close enough that I wouldn't need to shout, I tilted my head and said, "Duke Lorden. To what do we owe the pleasure?"

"My apologies for interrupting your evening," said Patrick, mild Boston accent stronger than usual, possibly due to nerves. He turned his attention to Tybalt. "You have my assurance that I'm not planning to disrupt things more than absolutely necessary. My wife is very interested in the salmon, and she might do me material damage if I got in the way of the meal I've promised her."

"I lack her authority to harm you, so I would have to throw myself upon her good graces if you were to break your word," said Tybalt, in a tone that implied he would *absolutely* ask Dianda for permission to harm her husband if Patrick spent too long at our table. "Pray, continue."

Patrick nodded before turning his attention to me. "I felt it appropriate that I offer congratulations on the impending occasion of your marriage," he said. "I remember my own wedding fondly."

It was starting to feel like I needed to hurry up and get married just so people would stop trying to *talk* about it. "Yeah, we're pretty excited," I said. "I think Tybalt might tie me up and drag me to Toronto if I don't agree to a date soon."

"Toronto?" asked Patrick politely.

"The High King and Queen have requested the honor of hosting the celebration, and we could not in good conscience refuse them," said Tybalt. "It answers the question of where to conduct the ceremony, since we cannot wed in the Court of Cats, and my lovely lady wife-to-be is currently estranged from her liege. Queen Windermere would have been willing to host, but the fear of giving insult to Duke Torquill would still have loomed troublingly over the event."

It was public knowledge that I was currently persona non grata at Shadowed Hills, and had been ever since I'd convinced Sylvester to wake his twin brother, Simon, who had been in an enchanted sleep thanks to elf-shot, and then lost him. Simon, not Sylvester, although in a way, I had lost Sylvester, too, in the moment when his brother—now spell-mazed and unable to remember all the progress he'd made toward becoming a good person again—had turned on his temporary allies and disappeared.

Sylvester might have been able to forgive me. His wife, Luna, was not. As far as Luna was concerned, I was responsible for every ill that had befallen her house since I was born, and having me around the knowe was nothing more than a reminder that her life, so carefully constructed and designed, was falling apart around her. So I stayed away. I waited for the moment my liege lord, the first person who had ever treated me like I might matter despite being the unwanted changeling daughter of a local woman who didn't even belong to the political structure enough to have a minor title, would remember that I was his responsibility and call me home. He might not want me around right now, but I would be loyal to him until the day I died.

That didn't make me happy about the reminder of my current outcast status. I kicked Tybalt's ankle discreetly under the table and was rewarded with a slight flinch, followed by an apologetic look. He was annoyed, but he knew he'd overstepped.

"So no date has been settled upon?" asked Patrick. "I assume that means invitations have yet to be delivered?"

So that's what this was about. I relaxed marginally. "Don't worry," I said. "You're on the list. You and Dianda both, and Peter, of course. Even if we weren't friends, there's no way Quentin would let me get away with not inviting Dean, and if I invite Dean and not his parents, that's sort of a slap in the face, right? I know you may not be able to attend—Toronto is pretty far away, and I'll understand if Dianda doesn't want to leave Saltmist unattended—but you'll be receiving invitations."

"I wasn't concerned for myself," said Patrick uncomfortably. "Is it safe to assume you'll also be inviting your father to the event?"

I blinked, surprised by the cruel thoughtlessness of the question.

I hadn't been expecting that from him. "My father is dead," I said, in a sharp tone. "He died a long time ago, believing I was dead, that I'd been killed in the house fire Uncle Sylvester started when he gave me my Changeling's Choice. I can't invite a dead man to my wedding, even though I wish I could."

Humans don't join the night-haunts. There's no reason they couldn't; changelings do, which means mortality isn't anathema to them. I can ride the memories encased in human blood, and as far as I can tell, that's what the night-haunts thrive on. But human bodies rot and decay, while fae bodies don't, and that puts humans outside their purview. More's the pity.

"You should go now," said Tybalt, tone suddenly formal in a way it hadn't been before. He set his own menu aside and pressed his hands flat against the table, fingers flexed just enough to show the points of claws beneath his human-seeming nails. Oh, he was pissed. I knew I liked him for a reason.

My father would have liked him, too, if he'd been able to see me grow up and fall in love. I didn't remember him well enough to make many sweeping statements about how our relationship would have been when I reached adulthood, but I was absolutely certain he would have liked the man I was going to marry.

"I'm sorry, but you misunderstand," said Patrick, seemingly oblivious to the danger he was putting himself into, which was ridiculous—the man was married to Dianda Lorden, whose first response to any situation was trying to figure out how she could most efficiently punch it in the throat. Not every situation has a throat, but that's never stopped Dianda.

I narrowed my eyes. We hadn't ordered yet, which meant Jason hadn't brought out the steak knives, but I always bring my own. Maybe a little light stabbing would make Patrick drop whatever this was and go sit down. "Was there something else you needed to say?" I asked coldly.

Patrick took a deep breath, standing up so straight that it looked as if his spine had been starched. "I was referring to your *legal* father."

I stared at him, aghast. "You're talking about *Simon*?"

"He was, and presently remains, your mother's husband," said Patrick. Then he stopped, looking at me, clearly waiting for me to connect the lines he was drawing.

Unfortunately for me, I could. I just didn't see why it should matter. "Simon was gone before Mom met my father. He has nothing to do with me."

"He has everything to do with you," Patrick patiently corrected. "Under fae law, since he remains married to your mother, and humans are not recognized as viable spouses, he is legally your father, and always has been."

"I know all that, but she left him when he went all dark side and started working for Evening!" I countered.

"She left him. She didn't divorce him. She *couldn't* divorce him, as your sister wasn't there to agree to the proceedings. A pureblood divorce requires approval from all children involved, as they declare for their chosen family lines. It keeps inheritance from getting complicated."

"Because this isn't complicated *at all*," I said sourly.

"I repeat my question," said Patrick. "Will you be inviting your father, who is very much alive, to your wedding?"

"Since he currently wants to kill me on behalf of the nasty-ass Firstborn he works for, and who he's probably trying to wake up right now, which is something I do my best not to think about more than I have to, and there's nothing I can do to stop him short of elf-shooting him again, and that would require *finding* him, which no one's been able to do—no, I wasn't planning to invite him to my *wedding*," I didn't try to keep the frustration out of my voice. It would have been a losing battle. "And I frankly don't appreciate you interrupting my date to ask about it. I thought better of you, Patrick."

"And were we discussing any other man, I would never have brought it up," said Patrick. "You realize you must invite him, or the wedding can't proceed."

I blinked. "I realize no such thing, and I'd appreciate it if you'd go back to your table now and leave us the fuck alone."

Tybalt didn't say anything. He had gone pale and was staring at Patrick, pupils reduced to thin slits against the banded malachite-green of his eyes. I scowled, looking impatiently between the two men.

"Is this where you reveal yet another way in which Faerie is planning to screw me over because I got too complacent?" I demanded. "Because if it is, I'd really, really like you to just walk away. Don't say anything else. Let us order our dinner and eat in peace. Please." Not that there was much chance of that. Based solely on the expression on Tybalt's face, we had already missed the window on "peace" for the evening.

"Yes, it is," said Patrick. "And for what it's worth, I'm sorry. I didn't know how many holes there were in your education. I'd say I thought better of your mother, but it would be a lie. I never once in all my days thought better of Amandine. And no matter how poorly I've thought of her, she's continually found ways to disappoint me. Truly, that woman is an artisan of letting people down."

"Normally, I'd be thrilled to sit around trash-talking my mom," I said. "Right now, not so much. What are you trying not to say to me right now?"

Patrick sighed heavily. "That's the problem. It's nothing you'll want to hear, and I hate to be the one to say it to you."

"Then why say it at all?"

"Because it wasn't his idea," said Dianda. She had wheeled herself over while I was focused on her husband, and was looking at me levelly, her hands resting on the curve of her wheels. Like Patrick, she was dressed in date night finery; unlike Patrick, hers ended at the waist. Since there were no humans here, she wasn't bothering with the blanket I'd sometimes seen her drape across her legs, leaving the jewel-toned sweep of her tail exposed. Merrow are basically the classic human idea of mermaids, and Dianda Lorden is a perfect example of her breed.

She took her hands off the wheels and leaned forward, resting her elbows against her own tail. Her fins twitched at the pressure, not quite slapping the floor. "Patrick and I were discussing Dean's excitement about your upcoming wedding when we realized it was entirely possible your mother had never bothered to explain to you what it meant that she'd been married when you were born. That sort of omission is Amy to the bone. But if we could realize the problems that could cause for you now, others could realize it as well. People who'd be less inclined to help than we are."

"So far all you're helping to do is ruin my evening," I said. "How did you know we were going to be here?"

"Dean mentioned that your fiancé was planning to take you out for a private evening, and there aren't many places where a King of Cats and a Hero of the Realm can do that," said Dianda. "I doubt we'll be able to get a reservation after this."

"No," said Tybalt, voice barely above a growl. "You won't."

"Can everyone please stop talking around the problem and tell me what the hell is going on?" I demanded. "I'd like to salvage what I can of this evening, if you don't mind."

Dianda shook her head. "This is land custom," she said, and looked to Patrick.

He took a deep breath. "When two purebloods marry, they can't divorce without consent of their living children—including any changelings or merlins born outside the marriage bed."

"Patriarchal and weird, but okay," I said. "At least the kids get a say."

"Yes, but it meant that when your sister disappeared, her parents—*your* parents—were no longer able to separate in the eyes of Oberon, because she couldn't declare whose house she belonged to, and neither could you. Hence their being married when you were born, and still being married today."

"Not that Simon would ever decide to leave his wife," interjected Dianda. "He loves that woman the way the moon loves the sea, not that I understand why. She's never done anything but betray him to serve her own interests."

"Di," said Patrick. "Be kind."

"Oh, I am being kind," she said. "If I were being unkind, I'd be saying something much worse about her, that self-centered, deceitful, treacherous—"

"Mother to the very patient woman who hasn't stabbed either of us yet, despite us giving her plenty of reasons to find the idea appealing," said Patrick, cutting her off and earning himself a brief but vicious glower. "October, because Simon is currently married to your mother, making him your father in the eyes of any chain of inheritance, if you fail to invite him to your wedding, you're offering him a public insult too large to be ignored. Any relative of his could claim the right to see it satisfied." He paused to emphasize his next statement. "His relatives *or his liege.*"

I stared at him. "Bullshit."

"Yes, but still true."

I turned to Tybalt. "Bullshit," I repeated.

"I wish I could agree that this claim has no bearing on our upcoming nuptials, but I do my best not to lie to you, as you find dishonesty personally insulting," said Tybalt.

"Bullshit," I said a third time, this time speaking to no one in specific.

Supposedly, Faerie has only one Law, handed down by Oberon himself before his untimely disappearance some five hundred years ago: no one's allowed to kill a pureblood. Of course, the Law doesn't apply to humans or to changelings, meaning we can be slaughtered with impunity by anyone who decides we're looking at them funny, but that's Faerie for you. Only fair as long as it suits the people in power.

But despite our lack of other formalized laws, a complicated system of manners and etiquette governs everything we do. Giving someone insult is one of the worst things possible, aside from violating hospitality or otherwise transgressing against traditions that date back to the days when our King and Queens still walked among us. Once someone has been given insult, they can demand basically any recompense they like, as long as it doesn't result in someone winding up dead. Imprisonment, involuntary service, material payment, it's all on the table.

Not giving a pureblood the excuse to say that I'd given them insult had been one of the major motivations of my youth, and if I'd lost sight of that in the last few years, well, that was on me, wasn't it?

"Oh," I said faintly.

"Yeah," said Dianda. "Oh. I'm sorry we interrupted your dinner. But I'm sure you can understand why it's important that you find Simon Torquill and bring him home as soon as you possibly can. Patrick?"

"Yes, dear," said Patrick, and moved to stand behind his wife, gripping the handles of her wheelchair and turning it nimbly around before wheeling her back to their table.

I looked at Tybalt. Neither of us said a word.

THREE

JASON DIDN'T SEEM to notice the charged atmosphere in the room when he returned to take our orders. He approached our table with a polite smile on his face, stopping at a respectful distance, and asked, "Well? Have you had a chance to look at the menu?"

Tybalt actually flinched. I was a little surprised when he didn't hiss. Then he thrust his menu at Jason and said, "The fish of the day, with shrimp risotto."

I blinked. We were eating after all? Well, all right. Jason turned to me. I managed to muster a smile as I handed him my menu and said, "I'll have the filet mignon, well done, baked potato with everything, and a house salad with blue cheese."

"Very good," said Jason, managing to suppress his moue of disapproval at my steak order. I'd been to the restaurant often enough that both he and the chef understood why I needed my steak just a few steps shy of becoming a charcoal briquette, much as it pained everyone involved. "Will there be anything else?"

"Not right now," said Tybalt.

Jason might be practicing his best customer service obliviousness, but he was still Cait Sidhe, and he could hear the unhappiness in his King's voice. "I'll get your orders in," he said, and fled.

Good. I wanted this next part to be semiprivate. I looked across the table to Tybalt. "You *knew*," I accused, and he flinched away from the bitter betrayal in my voice. "Don't try to pretend you didn't. You're a pureblood, you knew Simon was legally my father, and you didn't tell me this could happen. How could you keep something like this from me?"

"As long as you had no idea of the implications of your relationship to him, you had a defense against him making any claim of offense," he said. "You could argue that because you were raised human, human law had a greater authority over you, and he had no right to demand niceties you had never been taught. Queen Windermere would have been able to rule in your favor."

"An argument the Lordens just blew out of the water," I said glumly. "You know how much I hate people keeping secrets from me."

"I do."

"Yet you did it anyway."

He looked down at his empty plate. "Will it help to say that I had only the best intentions, and meant no harm?"

"Sylvester lied to me with the best intentions and look how that turned out." I tried to force my anger aside. It wasn't budging. "What the hell would make you think it would go differently this time?"

"I love you?" he ventured.

"Love isn't going to be enough if we're lying to each other."

Tybalt sighed. "What Sylvester did, unfair and cruel as it was, was of no benefit to you. He kept secrets solely to benefit himself, to salve his own feelings of betrayal over how things had ended between his brother and your mother. I withheld information because it was the only means of protecting you—and ignorance *is* a valid defense. Every time I have personally witnessed a charge of offense being refused, it was because the one who had given it could successfully argue that they didn't know. Arden would be inclined to take your side, especially if you had the truth behind you. I would have told you *after* we were married, when the offense had been given and forgiven, and your ignorance was no longer protective."

I wanted to believe him. I just wasn't sure I could. "You know how I feel about people keeping secrets from me."

"And you know how I feel about your safety. I will always protect you if I have it in my power to do so. Even if it may cause us problems afterward."

I narrowed my eyes, glaring at him. "And how were you planning to deal with situations like the one we're in right now?"

"I wasn't. Simon has so few friends left, I never anticipated one of them ambushing us like this."

That was putting it mildly. Simon was practically public enemy number one in the Mists, and Patrick might be the last person in the Kingdom who gave a damn about him. Patrick, who was going to have a lot of groveling to do to get back into my good graces. Dianda would have to do slightly less, but only slightly, and only because I knew this hadn't been her idea. I sighed. "No more secrets. No more lies. Agreed?"

"Agreed," he said, with some relief, before looking up again and saying, "It seems the time for another quest is come upon us."

"There's no 'us' in this one," I said. "You haven't stepped down from your throne yet, and that means wherever I have to go to fix this, I can't take you with me."

"You can't go alone," he said, tone imperious. "I will not abide it."

"Gosh, you bounced back fast from pissing me off. That was a good choice of words. Dangerously close to 'I won't allow it,' which you know would get these flowers thrown at your head, but you managed to swerve at the last second." I snagged another roll, trying to keep my expression as mild as possible. There was no point in being doomed *and* hungry. Might as well fix the one I had some ability to deal with. "We knew I was going to have to go looking for him eventually. The Luidaeg made me promise, and Karen called earlier tonight. She said she had a dream about me going on a quest with Quentin and May, but not you. If I bring anyone else, I fail. You can't come with me."

"I don't care for your niece's gift of prophecy being turned against me so."

"And I don't care for being lied to, so let's call it even for right now, okay?" I glared at him across the table. He met my eyes for a few seconds before sighing and turning his face away.

"As you say," he said. "I have one further concern. You can find his body without too much trouble, I'm sure; I have faith in your ability to locate things that have been lost. What about his heart?"

"That's . . . going to be more difficult," I admitted.

"Indeed."

Simon was a lot of things. At the moment, he was a villain, lost in the darkness and unsure of how to find his way back. Maybe incapable of finding his way back because—once—he'd been something a lot closer to a hero. Heroes run in the Torquill family, after all.

He'd originally turned to dark paths in an attempt to find his daughter, August, and bring her safely home. What he hadn't known was that August had traded her way home to the Luidaeg for a path she believed would lead her to Oberon. She'd been hoping to find him and bring him back to Faerie, making herself a greater hero than her uncle had ever been. Making herself more of a legend than our mother. She'd failed.

She'd failed, and in the process, she'd managed to get so lost that she couldn't find her way back on her own. Without Oberon to redeem her way home, she couldn't recognize the landmarks of her own heart, and her father's face might as well have belonged to a stranger. And Simon—poor, sweet, overly devoted Simon— had exchanged his own way home for hers, so she could be reunited with our mother while he took his turn wandering lost through a world turned suddenly strange and unforgiving.

Stripping away Simon's way home had also taken everything he'd done to break free of Eira Rosynhwyr—also and sometimes better known as Evening Winterrose, Firstborn of the Daoine Sidhe. She'd been the one to convince Simon he could find his daughter if only he'd allow himself to be tempted into more and more acts of unnecessary cruelty. I wasn't going to call him my favorite person, but the Simon Torquill I'd glimpsed without her influence had been a kind, thoughtful man who protected pixies for the sake of his friends and doted on his wife. He'd been doing his best to survive in a world that didn't always consider kindness a virtue.

And if I wanted to get him back, I might have to find Oberon himself. No big.

I reached for my water glass, only aware that my hand had started shaking when the contents sloshed over the lip and onto my fingers. Tybalt was looking at me with open despair in his eyes. I forced a smile.

"Hey," I said. "It's okay. Like I said, the Luidaeg already told me I had to do this. It's not news."

"Yes, but you were meant to do it with me beside you, to keep you *safe*," said Tybalt. "Not on your own. Not leaving me behind."

"I don't think I could do this on my own if I wanted to," I said. "There's no way May and Quentin would let me, even if Karen hadn't seen them in her dream. The only reason Raj won't insist on coming anyway is that he's stuck here, learning how to be King for after we get married. No matter what else happens, I won't be doing this alone."

Tybalt didn't look as reassured as I'd hoped he would. If anything, he looked even more miserable, slouching in his seat and reaching for a pretzel roll, which he began ripping into smaller and smaller pieces, until they were barely large enough to be considered crumbs. He let them fall onto his bread plate, watching his own hands as he worked.

Finally, I leaned across the table and put my hand over his, stopping him before he could mutilate the poor bread any further.

"Stop," I said. He raised his head and looked at me, eyes wide and wounded. His pupils had expanded again, drowning his irises in darkness. He had never been more handsome. This was the man I was going to marry. This was the man I was going to spend the rest of my life with, and raise my children alongside, whenever we decided it was safe enough for us to risk having them.

More importantly, this was the man who'd learned to open up to me when he was confused or frightened or lost, telling me what was in his heart and trusting me to tell him what was in mine. I had never had that kind of relationship before. I'd loved Gillian's father enough that I'd been prepared to leave Faerie behind for his sake, loved him enough that I'd found the strength to walk away from the only Home I'd ever really known, but we'd never *talked*. Not the way Tybalt and I did.

If we had, he might not have been so quick to have me declared dead and replace me with another woman when I disappeared.

"That bread didn't do anything to you except for tempting you with its deliciousness," I said gently, and removed the remains of the roll from his hand, dropping it back into the breadbasket with a soft thump. "Look at me, okay? Just at me."

Tybalt swallowed hard, eyes still locked on mine. He gave the very slightest of nods.

"Remember when you hated me?"

"October, be fair. I never *hated* you. I thought you were a distraction to my adopted niece, who needed to devote herself more cleanly to the Court, and I believed your mother had been fairer with you than she ever was." He swallowed again, folding his fingers around mine. "I thought there was no possible way she could have left you ignorant of your family history, and that you raced through our world like a wrecking ball because you didn't care, not because you didn't know."

"Okay, so remember when you thought the worst of me and never bothered to ask me so I could tell you what was really going on?" The door opened again as Jason returned and approached the Lordens, who were blessedly staying at their own table. Tybalt flinched, starting to turn. "No, don't look at them. Eyes on me, kitty-cat, until I'm done talking at you."

"I . . . my apologies," he said, voice gone thick and tight with a combination of fear and amusement that I recognized more clearly than I wanted to. "I will do as my lady bids me."

"Awesome." I squeezed his hand. "And remember how we got to know each other better, and you learned you'd been wrong about me, and I learned I'd been wrong about you? It took a long, long time, didn't it? Longer than it would have if we weren't two of the stubbornest people in Faerie. We had to figure out so many of the places where we were standing on the wrong assumptions before we could even start moving toward each other."

"I remember," said Tybalt softly.

"And do you remember how many times it could have all gone wrong? How many times we should have missed each other? Hell, how many times I could have died before my magic got strong enough to make that virtually impossible?"

From the way his hand clamped down on mine, he remembered all too well. "I do," he said, voice suddenly stiff.

The way he was crushing my fingers hurt, but it wasn't going to do any lasting damage. He would have needed to start chopping pieces off of me for that, and even involuntary amputation didn't guarantee he could do anything I couldn't recover from. In the last few years, I'd bounced back from breaking every bone in my body, having a knife jammed through my heart, and having an actual chunk of my physical spine yanked out of my body. Jin, Sylvester's resident Ellyllon healer, had been unnervingly delighted about that last incident, making a house call after Quentin told her about it, so she could verify for herself that the missing bone had grown back. Pain is pain, even if I know it's going to be fleeting. I still didn't try to pull away.

"We both lived," I said. "We both lived, and you told me you loved me, and I was smart enough to get out of my own way and tell you I loved you back. We've navigated so much already, what's one little quest that you can't help me with? We've got forever, you and me. We're going to be together, and we're going to meet our kids, and they're going to be amazing. There's no way they could be anything else."

"And your mother will never be anywhere near them," said Tybalt.

"Not ever, not once," I agreed. His grip on my hand began to loosen. "They'll grow up surrounded by Torquills and Cait Sidhe and my weird collection of teenagers, and they'll think of Raj and Quentin and Chelsea and Dean and Karen and all the others as siblings. Which means, much as we might both want to right now, that you can't gut Patrick Lorden. He's going to be an uncle to our children, and he didn't make the laws."

"No, but he was happy to make sure you couldn't claim ignorance of them," said Tybalt bitterly. "I hope you won't think less of me for holding that against him, because I'm going to. My forgiveness will take time and effort on both our parts."

I nodded. "I understand, and I love you, unforgiving as you are."

One corner of his mouth quirked upward in the beginnings of a smile. "I'm a cat," he said. "Being unforgiving is a part of my job description."

"Well, then, Mr. Cat, I hope you're not too dedicated to your work." I reclaimed my hand. "I like it when you forgive me."

"Fickleness is also a part of my job description," said Tybalt. "You shall always find forgiveness in my eyes. Others will not. Others have not pledged to be my wife."

"Hey, hey, hey, is this some Cait Sidhe thing where you expect me to share?" His mood was clearly lifting. If teasing could help that continue, I was all in. "No second wives for you. I'm a greedy girl."

"And I am not Oberon. We shall share our home with family, but not our bed." Tybalt's smile was real this time, and I allowed myself to finally relax. We were going to be okay.

The next time the door opened, it was Jason returning with our dinners, which he placed in front of us before withdrawing from the dining room. I picked up my fork and steak knife. Tybalt watched. I raised an eyebrow.

"Yes?"

"You have a knife. I find it best to pay attention when you feel the need to arm yourself."

I stuck my tongue out at him and commenced cutting up my steak. The food, as always, was excellent, and all conversation stopped for a few minutes while we enjoyed our meals.

I was considering using the last pretzel roll to sop up the meat juice on my plate—too dark to be considered bloody, but still delicious—when the whisper of wheels against the floor caught my attention and I raised my head. Tybalt was already looking toward the sound, eyes narrowed and pupils hairline thin in his irritation.

"Hello, Dianda," I said wearily. "Do you have some other horrible point of Faerie law to bring to my attention? Because I'm sure you can understand why I don't really want to hear anything else you have to say right now."

"No, and I'm sorry to interrupt you twice in one evening," she said. Focusing on Tybalt, she added, "I'm not trying to make you uncomfortable."

"You're doing an excellent job," he said.

Dianda sighed. "See, this is one of those times when I wish the Undersea way of doing things had become the dominant way for the rest of Faerie. If we were at home, you'd punch me in the stomach, I'd kick you in the face, and then we'd move on. Instead, you're going to be mad at me for days, if not weeks."

"I was thinking of years," said Tybalt.

"And if we could just punch it out, this would all be a lot easier, on both of us," said Dianda. She shifted her focus to me. "I get that you're pissed, and you have every right to be. When Patrick and I decided to get married, it felt like everyone in Faerie had an opinion, and everyone's opinion was 'no.' If not for Simon and King Gilad, I don't think we would have made it."

"Gee, that's an inspiring story," I said. "Thanks so much for sharing! Good thing I'm marrying a literal king who doesn't have to get permission from anybody, and I'm still a changeling, which means there aren't that many people willing to claim the responsibility of telling me what to do."

"For once, your humanity serves a purpose," said Tybalt direly.

Dianda rolled her eyes. "Please. If you think I came back over here to tell you I don't approve, you don't know me as well as I thought you did. I approve. Not that my opinion matters. I came to say that all the resources of Saltmist are at your disposal on this quest. Whatever you need, you only need to tell me, and I'll do my best to provide it."

I blinked at her. As a noble of the Undersea, Dianda technically lives in another realm, meaning Arden designating me as a hero of the realm in the Mists doesn't mean anything in Saltmist. Arden would also supply me with whatever it was reasonable to need for a quest to bring one of her Kingdom's wayward nobles and greatest criminals home. But I hadn't been expecting the offer from Dianda.

"I, uh, that's very kind of you," I said, fumbling my way around the urge to thank her. No matter how much time I spend in Faerie, I'm a child in the human world, and humans thank each other when they do things that are unexpectedly kind. "Why is this so important to you?"

"Patrick and Simon were like brothers once," said Dianda. "If not for Simon's devotion to your mother, things might have gone very differently for all three of us. He refused to believe any ill of Amy, and when the woman we knew as Evening Winterrose attempted to interfere with my engagement to Patrick, Simon intervened. I've always felt that was the beginning of his downfall. She would never have been able to get her claws into him as deeply as she did if we hadn't opened the door for her manipulations." She looked, and sounded, genuinely sorry for any part she might have played in Simon's downfall, and some of my anger melted away like frost in the summer sun.

"They were still brothers when Patrick came with me to the Undersea. Your mother . . . she wasn't as bad then as she is now, but she was getting more and more unreasonable, and Evening had begun to make demands of Simon that made us very uncomfortable. We were trying to convince him to leave his wife when your sister disappeared." She paused expectantly.

I picked up where she clearly hoped I would. "Meaning divorce was impossible until August was found," I said.

"I'll admit, when he first went looking for her so *vehemently*, we half hoped it was because he'd seen sense and wanted her to consent to his leaving her mother. We were willing to delude ourselves if it meant we weren't losing him, and I was still adjusting to life in Saltmist with an air-breathing husband, and we allowed our attention to waver more than we should have. That's our regret to carry.

I won't say we could have stopped or saved him, but maybe we could have done more than we did, and you've suffered because of the actions of a man I still have cause to love dearly. And then the earthquake came, and everything got too complicated to walk away from." Dianda looked at me, dark eyes dry and solemn. "Bring him home. Whatever you need to make that happen, you'll have it from us; you know you will."

"There are things you can't give me," I said. "But I'll remember that you offered. Good night, Dianda."

She nodded, accepting my dismissal for what it was, and wheeled her way back to the table where Patrick was waiting. I turned and looked across the table at Tybalt.

"I don't feel much like dessert, do you?" I asked.

He shook his head. "I find that for once my sweet tooth has deserted me. Shall we return to the safety and comfort of home?" He held his hand out to me.

I took it as we both rose. "Don't we need to wait for the check?"

"We're not getting paid for dining here."

"I meant—you have enough interaction with the human world to know what I meant, you dork. Don't we need to pay for dinner?"

Tybalt looked at me like I'd never said anything more foolish in my entire life, something we both knew wasn't the case. "We granted my subject the honor of feeding us," he said. "Why would we need to compensate him further?"

"Silly me," I said, and picked up my bouquet, tucking it under my arm. "I guess that means we're ready to go."

"Indeed." In a single motion he had swept me off my feet and up into his arms, holding me against his chest as easily as if I were made of straw. He dipped his head toward Patrick and Dianda, more out of politeness than any sincere farewell, I was sure, and strode across the room to the nearest patch of deep shadow.

The shadows pulled apart as he approached, parting like curtains to reveal even deeper darkness beyond. I took a deep breath, screwing my eyes shut against the cold to come, and he carried me onto the Shadow Roads.

FOUR

THE COLD WAS A SHOCK. The cold of the Shadow Roads is always a shock, no matter how often we travel this way. Every kind of fae has their own innate talents and skills; Cait Sidhe, like Tybalt, can access the Shadow Roads, one of the old conduits through the Summerlands. They allow for faster, more efficient travel than should really be possible. Only problem is that while the Shadow Roads are cold and airless for the fae who can natively access them, they're freezing and suffocating for the rest of us. If I tried to inhale, my lungs would collapse, because there was nothing there for me to breathe in.

I huddled against Tybalt's chest instead, focusing on the steady, reassuring beat of his heart as I shivered. He would see me safely out of the darkness he'd carried me into. He always had before. And then I would throw myself right into another kind of darkness, as I went searching for the man who'd been my personal bogeyman, only to show a certain sort of stunted heroism in the way he lost himself again.

Why can't anything ever be easy?

My lungs were starting to burn from the strain of holding my breath when the dark outside my eyelids bloomed into bloody red. I opened my eyes, blinking away the ice coating my lashes, and beheld the brightly lit walls of my own kitchen. May wasn't there, but the scent of sugar cookies lingered in the air, telling me she hadn't been gone for long. She hadn't baked this much when we first moved in together. We hadn't played host to an endless parade of rotating teenagers back then, either.

May and I both remembered what it was like to be young, hungry, and unsure that there were any safe places left in the world. We'd never discussed it openly, but I knew she was as focused as I was on making sure the teens who trusted us would never need to feel the way we'd felt at their age. Not as long as we had the power to keep them safe.

Tybalt swung my feet to the floor, keeping his hands on my waist for a beat longer than necessary. I blinked through the melting ice, offering him a shivering smile. He laughed and plucked the flowers from under my arm, holding them up for me to see.

"A little refrigeration is good for a bouquet," he said, and turned to take a vase down from the top of the cabinets. "These will keep nicely, I think."

"They're really beautiful." My dress, which had been so appropriate for a dinner out, felt overly fancy for my kitchen. I pushed my hair back with both hands, glancing at the door. "I need to go find May and tell her we're going hunting for Simon. Do you want to come with me?"

"No." He suddenly scowled. "If your heart is set on going without me, I'd best practice letting you race off on your own."

"It's not my heart, it's Karen's vision, combined with the political reality you've worked so hard to drum through my thick skull," I said. "You know I'd take you with me if she hadn't already told me it would mean failure, and if it wouldn't make everything harder for you. And for Raj. Poor kid already puts up with enough."

"He is compensated for his suffering," said Tybalt. "He's a Prince of Cats. He'll never want for anything in his life."

"Except for freedom, right?"

Tybalt grimaced. "Except that," he admitted. "I only hope his heart is better behaved than my own, and that it fixes itself upon something easier to keep and protect than you."

"You've basically raised the kid, and the only reason he's not officially my squire is because the politics of dragging him into the peerage of the Divided Courts might cause someone's head to actually explode," I said. "I think the ship of Raj being well-behaved and obedient to Cait Sidhe law has well and truly sailed."

Tybalt made a pained expression, clearly trying to hide the fact that he was fighting not to smile. "A perfect representative of his kind, he may never be, but he'll do as he's told enough to take and hold the throne."

"I'm really going to enjoy seeing how much he listens to you or does as he's told once he's King of Cats," I said, and blew him a kiss as I made my way to the door.

The downside of having a big house is that sometimes you have to go looking for people. When we shared my old apartment, I knew where May was at all times; she literally couldn't go to the bathroom without me knowing about it.

Okay, maybe most of having a big house isn't such a downside after all.

May wasn't in the living room or the dining room, which eliminated the downstairs from contention. I turned to the stairs, starting upward into the gloom. Her bedroom door stood open, which meant she wasn't doing anything she'd get mad at me for interrupting. I still paused to knock before sticking my head inside.

My style of housekeeping is best referred to as "benign neglect." I don't have a lot of *stuff*, which is the only reason there are any visible flat surfaces in my house. If not for Quentin's desire for tidiness leading to him constantly straightening things up in his wake, we would have lost the dining room to the slow march of spiderwebs and junk mail a long time ago. I'm not *filthy* or anything—I wash dishes, do my laundry, and don't let the bathroom garbage overflow—but I'm messy.

May takes messiness to the Olympic level. Looking into her room is like looking into the Cave of Wonders from a retelling of *Aladdin*, with costume jewelry, makeup in brightly colored containers, and heaped-up piles of jewel-toned clothing everywhere the eye can see. I swear she emptied out all the drawers of old, weird, unsalable silk scarves at the local thrift stores and used them to build decorative heaps in the corners. Her bed is a sea of pillows, blankets, and the kind of handmade quilts that wind up in those same stores when someone's grandparents die and their worldly goods get donated because it's too much to deal with. In short, it's beautiful, but it's a lot.

May was sitting on the edge of the bed, brushing her blue-streaked hair and humming an old English folksong under her breath. She looked up and smiled at the sound of my knock, putting the brush aside. "Hey. How was your date?"

I stepped fully into the room and leaned against the doorframe. "More eventful than either Tybalt or I would have preferred, but no one got stabbed, so we're okay. Where's Jazz?"

"Out with her flock for the evening," said May. "Something about family time. I didn't ask too many questions. She doesn't like explaining herself, and to be honest, it's none of my business."

"Ah," I said. Jazz is a Raven-maid, a skinshifter, who possesses a feathered band that allows her to transform into a raven and keeps her tied—sort of literally—to Faerie. Now that the Selkies are largely gone, there aren't many skinshifters left, just the Ravens and Swanmays. Maybe that was why Jazz's flock had been asking for more of her time lately, sometimes going so far as to land in the front yard and caw until someone came out to ask what they wanted.

Somehow, they never thought to knock on the door or ring the doorbell. It was like we were good enough to yell at, but not good enough to talk to. Jazz was the only member of her flock I'd ever seen in human form. That was interesting, and dwelling on it right now wouldn't do me any good, not with May watching me with wary, slightly narrowed eyes.

As my Fetch, May has my memories up to the moment of her "birth"—inaccurate, but more correct than "creation," since she was a night-haunt for centuries before borrowing my face and yoking herself to my survival. If I'd died when I was supposedly meant to, she would have winked out of existence and been lost forever, leaving the rest of the night-haunts to miss or mourn her. As it stands, she found a family and got to keep it, which is more than any Fetch before her could say. It may never happen again. She's unique in all of Faerie, and she knows me too well to be fooled when I get flippant.

"All right, since you're clearly not planning to volunteer the goods, what do you mean when you say 'eventful'?" she asked.

"I mean Patrick and Dianda Lorden also dined at the Cat in the Rafters tonight, and they came over to our table to make sure I was aware that if I got married without inviting Simon, his family, or his liege—that being Eira—could claim insult against my household."

May's eyes widened. "They did *what*? Why would they do that?" She fell backward on the bed, groaning. "Pureblood marriage law is *so stupid*," she said. "I knew that, I *knew* that, but I never thought anyone would care enough to make sure *you* knew that."

"You and Tybalt have been banking on my ignorance throughout this whole process, and now your reward is that you have to go with me to look for Simon Torquill, and Tybalt can't come," I said dryly. It was impossible to think of Karen's vision and the visit from Patrick and Dianda and not see the two as connected. "So I guess you got a pretty quick 'don't keep secrets from Toby' reminder here. Are there any other fun points of fae law that you'd like to remind me of, so we don't get fucked unexpectedly?"

"Um." May pushed herself up onto her elbows. "There's a decent chance I'm legally your kid, so you and Tybalt may not be able to divorce unless I let you? I don't think anyone's ever tried to nail down exactly where a Fetch falls in the chain of inheritance."

I raised an eyebrow. "Okay, that's . . . special. And probably good to know. But I'll fight anyone who tries to say you're not my sister."

"If I'm your sister, then I also have to sound off if Simon ever wants to separate from Mom," she said, matter-of-factly. "Not that he will. I remember enough from lives before this one to know he thinks the sun sets in her shadow and the moon rises in her eyes. Their love story may be terrible and bad for everyone around them, but it's going to last a long, long time."

"That's not what Dianda's hoping," I said. "She seems to think if I bring Simon home, she can talk him into leaving his wife."

"Is 'talk' mermaid for 'threaten'?" asked May.

"I don't know. It seems more likely than the alternative." Whatever that was. I couldn't think of anything. "So okay, you're my sister every way but legally because we don't need to make this shit any more complicated than it already is, fine. I still need you to come with me."

"Why me?"

"Karen called and told me she'd seen you going with me in a dream, which means it definitely happens. Tybalt has to stay here and keep kinging, Raj can't come, Walther will literally laugh in my face if I ask him to go on another wacky, potentially fatal quest right now, and I'd leave Quentin if I thought he'd let me get away with it. You're literally unkillable—even more so than I am, since I can die, I just get better. You can't die."

"Why does that being a selling point make me so uncomfortable?"

"You're smarter than we look."

"Damn right I am." May stood. "Okay, so what's the game plan here? We go to the Luidaeg and—"

"No," I said. "We go to Luna."

May blinked. "You can't be serious."

"I am."

"But she *hates* you and, by extension, hates *me*."

"I know."

Slowly, her look of shock became a scowl. "The Luidaeg would be, and I can't believe I'm saying this in a serious, non-ironic manner, easier."

"I know that, too." The Luidaeg is the eldest daughter of Maeve, one of Oberon's two missing wives. She's one of the oldest people left in Faerie, and they call her "the sea witch" because there was a time when she was the only witch of the water in the entire world. She's my mother's sister, making her my aunt, and her magic is essentially boundless—which *is* ironic, because it's been pretty tightly bound by Oberon's *other* wife, Titania.

The Luidaeg can't lie. She can't harm anyone descended from Titania, even if they're trying to harm her. And she can't say "no" when someone asks her to use her considerable magical powers to grant their heart's desire. All she can do is set a price so high that no one with any sense would be willing to consider paying it.

It's still surprising to me, even after everything I've been through, how many people think that when her prices are so high it hurts, it's because she's being cruel, and not because they're asking for something they'd be better off leaving alone. The Luidaeg will give you anything. She doesn't have a choice. She gets to decide how much you'll have to pay, though, and she uses what little choice she has left like a surgeon uses a scalpel. When she cuts the flesh of your desires, it bleeds.

August had gone to the Luidaeg, looking for a way to find Oberon and bring him back. The Luidaeg's price for giving her a chance had been her way home: her memory and ability to recognize anything and everything that anchored her to the life she'd had before her quest began. To save August from the consequences of her own actions, Simon had traded his way home for hers, and I'd stood powerlessly by and watched it happen. The Luidaeg had been able to see that he was clawing his way back to being a good man. She hadn't wanted to do it. She hadn't been able to refuse. Not once he met her price. Unless he found Oberon somehow, he was a danger now and would remain one.

I was direly afraid that if I went to her for help, even if I did my best to play my cards close to my chest, she'd turn her previous order to find Simon into an order to *kill* him—an order I wouldn't be able to refuse. I didn't know why she'd want him dead, but I didn't know why she'd wanted him found in the first place, and the risk wasn't something I wanted to take. He had been redeeming himself. He had been doing his best to come home, before August's choices, combined with his own, had taken that option away from him.

I'd already lost my father. I wasn't going to be the reason she had to lose hers as well. And I know that being a hero means I'm supposed to put Faerie first, always, but there are some costs that are personal, and too much to pay. I wanted to find Simon. I wanted to come home and get married.

And yes, I actually wanted him to be there when I did that, if it was even remotely possible. I had little enough family who could realistically be in attendance. If Faerie was going to make him my father, he could damn well act like it.

Technically, bringing Simon home might still mean killing him, depending on how he responded to the attempt. I wasn't ready to think too much about that yet, just like I wasn't ready to commit to giving up my humanity yet. Somewhere in the muddle my life had become, I'd wound up dealing with things that were much bigger and more terrifying than anything one changeling from San Francisco should be expected to contend with. I wasn't going to do it until I had to.

"You're worried she'll make the cost something impossible," said May.

I nodded. "I am."

"I'd never let you make a bargain like that. I'd take the price first."

"We don't even know what it might be, which is why we're going to Luna first," I said. "Karen's vision implied that the Rose Roads would be the way to get to him, and Luna's tied to the Rose Roads. She can get us there. The worst she can say is 'no.'"

"And if she refuses to help?"

"Then we'll think of something else," I said. "We're good at that. Will you help me?"

"Of course," said May. "Just let me call Jazz while you change into your work clothes, unless you were planning to wear your nice shoes to Shadowed Hills."

"Not tonight," I said, and smiled, before leaving her room and heading to my own. She would have said something if Quentin was home already; we'd have to stop at Saltmist and pick him up before we crossed the Bay, unless I wanted to spend the next year being yelled at for leaving him out of a quest.

Spike was still asleep on my pillow when I stepped into the room. I paused to tap it on the head and say, "Hey, get up. I have to go to Shadowed Hills. You want to come?"

It opened its vibrantly yellow eyes and blinked before clambering to its feet and shaking vigorously, resulting in a sound like someone rolling a barrel of maracas down a hill. Then it chirped, the sound interrogative and sharp.

"Yes, I know Luna's mad at me," I said, heading for my dresser. "It doesn't matter. This has to be done, and she can be mad at me while I'm there just as easily as she can be mad at me from a distance." More easily, maybe. I've been told I'm an irritation that lingers, but everyone who said that was mad at me at the time, so I don't know if I can call them objective observers.

Spike rattled at me again as I pulled off my dress and dug a tank top out of the drawer. I glanced over my shoulder at it. "Are you willing to come or not?"

I've never been sure how intelligent rose goblins are or aren't. Not human-smart, I don't think, but closer than the cats. Spike— the rose goblin I interact with the most—seems to understand speech, or at least, responds as if it does, and that's generally been good enough for me. It doesn't always come when called, but neither do I. If we're going to measure intelligence based on obedience, we're all going to be very disappointed.

It rattled its thorns a third time before jumping off the bed and trotting over to sit next to my ankles. I smiled at it.

"Awesome. I appreciate it, buddy." Technically, the prohibition on saying "thank you" doesn't apply to fae animals. Technically, pixies are considered animals, but they have their own magic, customs, and society. It seems safer to assume everything in Faerie is fully capable of understanding me and holding a grudge if it decides it wants to.

Getting dressed didn't take long. It never does, since my taste in clothing is more practical than decorative. I like interchangeable jeans, tank tops, and sensible shoes. Everything I own is going to get bled on at least once, so why not make it easy to replace things when necessary? I had to remove my knife long enough to refasten the belt over my jeans, but apart from that, it was remarkably easy to reach the point where I was ready to leave the house. I paused for a long moment before opening my nightstand and removing a braided metal key. The last thing I did before heading for the door was grab the leather jacket hanging off the chair beside my bed. It settled across my shoulders like the armor it represented, well-worn and comfortable and conforming to the shape of my body more accurately than any other piece of clothing I owned.

It wasn't always mine. Unless something is custom-made for you, nothing can ever be said to have "always" belonged to anyone, but this jacket's provenance is a little more specific than "I bought it from Sears." Once upon a time, before I was even willing to admit we were friends, this jacket belonged to Tybalt. He'd handed it to me because I was cold, and somehow I'd just never quite gotten around to giving it back.

It was mine now, no question. With as much as I'd bled on the leather, it was probably technically a member of the family. I shoved the key into my front pocket, pushing it down until there was no chance it would fall out. This was one thing I really didn't want to lose.

May was in the hall when Spike and I emerged. She'd changed her own clothes, going for jeans with brightly colored cotton patches on the knees and a neon-green peasant blouse that looked like it had been stolen directly from the 1980s. I stopped, blinking. She beamed.

"Like my new shirt?" she asked. "I dyed it myself."

"It's clashing with your hair," I said. "How is it clashing with your hair? Blue and green are supposed to be friends."

"I'm very good at color theory," she said.

I shook off the stunning color mismatch in front of me, turning toward the stairs. "Come on. We need to go ruin Quentin's date."

"He won't thank us for that."

"His manners are too good for him to thank us for anything,"

I said. "But if I don't get to have a nice time with my boyfriend, neither does he."

"See, this is why I don't have a boyfriend," chirped May, following me down the stairs. Spike stuck to my ankles the whole way, like a very well-trained dog. He only paused occasionally to rattle. "You don't feel the need to crash my dates."

"I don't understand your dates. 'Let's visit every thrift store in San Francisco' doesn't feel like high romance to me."

"It works for us," said May. She brightened as we stepped into the kitchen and she spotted Tybalt. "Hey, kitty-cat! You clean up good."

"I could say the same of you, sweet Lady Fetch," said Tybalt.

May looks like me, but she's old enough that she finds Tybalt's occasionally archaic manners and patterns of speech charming, not confusing. She dimpled at him, miming a shallow curtsy, before asking, "What do you think of the blue? It's a new brand of dye that's supposed to be more resistant to being stripped out by saltwater."

"It's lovely," he said. "Are you planning a trip to the beach?"

"No. I live with Toby, and blood and saltwater are basically the same thing." May shrugged. "She plans for her clothing; I plan for my hair."

"Indeed," said Tybalt, with a flicker of amusement. He turned his attention on me. "Do you have everything you need?"

"We're going to head over to Goldengreen and get Quentin, and then we're on the road," I said. "We're heading for Shadowed Hills first. After that, we go wherever the trail takes us. I promise to call if there's anything you can do to help."

"Or if you find yourself in danger of a type you cannot navigate on your own."

"Oh, come on," I protested. "I call for help when I need it! I've gotten so much better about that over the last few years. I hardly wind up ambushed and alone at all these days."

May slung a companionable arm around my shoulders, beaming at Tybalt. "Trust the lady, kitty. You're about to be stuck with her forever, and she's a lot more stabby than you are."

"I do trust her," said Tybalt, and sighed, stepping forward and brushing his fingers against my cheeks, leaving them lingering there, barely touching me. "I trust her to be wild and impulsive and bold and self-destructive when it means someone else might be saved. I trust her to be the month she was named for, cold and kind by turns, endlessly storming, so that nothing can stand in her path but risk being blown away. I trust her to be *October*, and what I've learned, what's done nothing to stop my heart being given to her care, is that to be October is to be constantly in the path of destruction and not always to have the sense to step aside. I'm uncomfortable not because I don't trust her, but because I trust her too well."

"I love you, too, you ridiculous man," I said, turning to kiss the palm of his hand. Then I stepped away, out of reach. "We'll be back as soon as we can. Feed the cats, please."

Tybalt actually laughed at that. He was still laughing when we stepped out of the kitchen and into the cool darkness of the San Francisco evening. It's never truly dark here, not the way it is in Muir Woods, or even in Pleasant Hill, where Shadowed Hills is anchored. The glow of the city lights forbids true darkness from slipping past its defenses, turning the world into eternal twilight.

Is it any wonder that the fae flock toward human cities, even with their iron and their dangers, when they turn the mortal world into such a lovely reflection of our forever twilit Summerlands? I unlocked the car, checking the backseat for intruders before sliding behind the wheel. May did the same on the passenger side.

"You know, anyone who watches the two of us get into a car has got to think our parents did a number on us," she commented.

"Didn't they?" I asked, jamming the key into the ignition and snagging a handful of shadows from the air, working them between my fingers like bread dough, until they turned stiff and crumbly. "Humpty Dumpty sat on the wall, Humpty Dumpty had a great fall, which was clearly suicide, since the man was a goddamn egg."

My magic rose and crashed down in a wave of cut grass and copper, leaving us unchanged. May raised an eyebrow.

"Don't-look-here?" she asked.

I nodded. "Better to hide the car than the passengers. Means I don't have to recast when we pick up Quentin."

"Smart. Try not to have an accident."

"I always try not to have an accident, and I'll thank *you* not to lecture me about driving safety." May doesn't drive, mostly because she remembers learning how, but doesn't have the muscle memory necessary to turn any of her memories into reality. Her few attempts to reconcile the two have ended . . . poorly.

Everyone is safer if May stays off the streets.

I pulled onto the street, paying closer attention than usual to the cars cutting through our residential neighborhood. With the don't-look-here on the car, no one would pay much attention to us. We weren't truly invisible—no one was going to casually drive into us, either—but we were hard to see, disinteresting and obscure. That was how we needed things to be.

Goldengreen used to be held by Eira Rosynhwyr, back when she was pretending to be Evening Winterrose, the intimidating but ordinary Daoine Sidhe. She lost control with her "death," and didn't take it back when she revealed she'd been alive and hiding the whole time, like the terrible person she was. As one of San Francisco's original nobles, she had established her own holdings solidly within the city, and it wasn't a far drive from my apartment to the San Francisco Art Museum, the low, modern building that served as the mortal side of the knowe. There were no charity events going on tonight; the parking lot was empty, save for the cars belonging to the night watchman and the janitorial staff. At this point, there was no way they didn't think the place was haunted or something, with as long as they'd been surrounded by the fae.

Oh, well. It's not like anyone was tormenting them on purpose. Goldengreen was mine for a while, before I passed it on to Dean, and as I parked the car and got out, breathing in the salty, eucalyptus-scented air, I couldn't help feeling a little like I was coming home. I'd passed the knowe on voluntarily and as quickly as I could; I wasn't ready for the responsibility when I'd been handed it. That doesn't mean I didn't miss the place sometimes.

I don't miss the title that came with it. If there was one thing I didn't need, it was to be called "Countess."

May got out of the car, shooting me a look of wordless under-standing, and together we started across the parking lot, swerving to avoid the front as we approached and tromping into the weeds and brush growing around the back, tangling around an old main-tenance shed that had never been used by the human maintenance crew in all the years I'd been visiting the knowe. It was flanked by two massive oak trees that shouldn't have been able to thrive so near the edge of the cliff. The fact that they were was a testament to the woman who had planted them, damn her eyes.

Strange whispers rose out of the grass as we approached the shed, accompanied by rustling in the nearby bushes. Under normal circumstances, the warding spells intended to keep the unwary from stumbling into the knowe would have long since faded or been replaced by Dean's own defenses, but these were the work of a Firstborn, and they were lingering.

I reached the shed before May did, and reached for the doorknob, grimacing as a bolt of static lanced through my palm to warn me off. Pain is never going to be my favorite thing. The door swung smoothly open, silent despite the rust caking its hinges.

"Still better than jumping off a cliff," I said, and stepped into the dark inside. May followed close behind me, pulling the door shut with a soft click.

FIVE

THE QUALITY OF AIR changed the instant the door closed, turning sweeter, cleaner, untouched by pollutants. The room seemed to spin, a dizzying dip and whirl like a carnival ride on the edge of breaking down, and the darkness disappeared, replaced by a dimly lit hallway lined with small tables and bookshelves, the walls softened by hanging tapestries.

Goldengreen hadn't always looked like that. When Eira had held it, it had been cold, unwelcoming, and virtually unlived-in. It had looked more like a showroom or a theater set than a place where people were allowed to be. Dean had changed that.

Dean had changed a lot of things. I let my fingertips trail against the wall as I gestured for May to follow me down the hall toward the kitchen. The stone was warm and the air was sweet, and it was good to be back, even if this wasn't home for me anymore.

I've always believed knowes were alive. They just don't exist at the same speed people do, probably because there's no need when you're an immortal faerie building existing partially outside the rules of normal geometry. With that in mind, it made sense that Goldengreen would be glad to see me. I'd always tried my best to do right by it, and that's more than I can say of a lot of landholders.

"You don't look as off-balance as you used to when you made that transition," said May. "You feeling okay?"

"I'm not as human as I used to be, either," I pointed out. Moving between the human world and the Summerlands is disorienting for humans, which means it's also hard on changelings. Harder when they're using a door that isn't opened all that often, which used to apply to literally every door into Goldengreen. "I feel fine. I just want to get this over with so I can go home and reassure Tybalt that I'm not going to throw myself willy-nilly into the first wood-chipper I see."

"You'd probably get better," said May.

"I don't think 'probably' is going to make him less tense about the whole situation," I countered. As we got closer to the kitchen, the light got brighter, until the hall was almost at what I would consider normal levels of illumination. I didn't hear anyone. I frowned and raised my voice, calling, "Marcia? Are you here?"

She didn't answer. Instead, there was a sound like someone ringing a hundred jingle bells, and what looked like an entire flock of pixies burst through the kitchen door, multicolored wings chiming with every motion. They swarmed around us, wings tickling our cheeks, and settled on our arms and shoulders, or tangled themselves contentedly in our hair.

"Hello to you, too," I said. They could understand me, even if they were too small and their voices too high-pitched for us to understand them. "We're looking for Marcia. Do you know where she is?"

One of the pixies—male, about six inches tall, glowing a deep cherry red, like cough syrup in sunlight—launched himself off my shoulder and hung in front of my nose, an imperious look on his face. He snapped his wings together with such force that the sound was more like a thundercrack than a bell, something I hadn't known pixies could do, and shook his head.

"Oh," I said. "Are you saying you don't know where she is, or that you won't take us to her?"

He scowled at me and shook his head again, harder this time. I sighed.

"I'm sorry," I said. "You're too small for me to understand, and I'm too big to understand you. We're really here for Dean and Quentin, so if you'd lead me to them . . . ?"

The pixie shook his head again. This was getting annoying. May put a hand over her mouth, visibly concealing a grin.

"Don't help," I snapped at her.

She laughed. "I'm sorry, but you should see the look on your face," she said. "They're pissed because you haven't come to see them. They feel abandoned. You should be able to understand that, even if you can't understand what they're saying. You start to feel abandoned when one of us goes to the store for too long."

I focused on the pixie, rather than giving in to the urge to yell at my Fetch for knowing me too well. "Is she right? Are you messing with me because you're mad?" I asked. "I'm sorry. This isn't my knowe anymore, and you know how it is with the big folk. We get territorial and weird sometimes."

"That doesn't mean you're unwelcome," said a voice. The pixies scattered as I turned. Marcia was standing in the hall behind me, arms folded, looking at me with bland amusement.

Marcia. A thin-blooded changeling, barely a quarter—and that was if I was being generous—with bottle blonde hair that was none-theless completely natural so far as I could tell. She was casually dressed in jeans and a long tunic-style sweatshirt, the arms of Goldengreen pinned to her collar like a badge of honor, which technically I suppose they were. Marcia is the only thin-blooded changeling in the Mists to stand as seneschal to a noble court, even if many people would argue that Goldengreen only counts as a noble court on a technicality.

She was my seneschal before she was Dean's, and she was my friend Lily's handmaid before she worked for me. She has always been, unfailingly, kind. If there's a person in Faerie who personifies doing their best, it's Marcia.

"I know," I said, and smiled at her. "I'm here for Quentin."

"I don't suppose I can talk you out of that, can I?" she asked, her own smile fading. "Dean's going to be spending the next week hunting kelpies along the coast—they've been breeding faster with-out the Selkies there to keep their numbers down, and until things stabilize, they're a problem. He really needs a little quality time with his guy."

"Sadly, no, you can't. Dean's parents decided to remind me of some of the finer points of pureblood marriage law, and now I need to take Quentin on a quest neither of us is going to enjoy."

"Can't it wait a few hours?"

I wanted to say yes, and that was the problem. Karen's dream aside, Tybalt was already worried about me trying to delay our wedding on purpose. If I allowed an actual barrier to us getting married to exist until I felt like it was the right time to tear it down, he was never going to forgive me. Oh, he might say he would. He might even think he would. But I know rejection, and I'd seen the pain in his expression. This would eat at him if I didn't do every-thing I could, as quickly as I could, to make it better.

Besides, the very vague outline of a plan that I was formulating was absolutely terrifying, and terrifying things don't get easier when I put them off until tomorrow. "I'm sorry, but no."

Marcia frowned. May stepped forward, shrugging broadly.

"Dean knew what he was doing when he got involved with a squire in active training," she said. "If Quentin's knight calls, he has to answer. That's the deal. Just like if there's something wrong in Goldengreen, Dean has to handle it no matter how inconvenient the timing is. It's lousy, but it's the way things work. Where are they?"

"Follow me," said Marcia, and sighed as she turned and walked down the hall. May and I followed. It wouldn't have made sense to do anything else.

Marcia led us to a door that had appeared after I gave up the knowe, adding further credence to my belief that knowes are alive. It had recognized Dean's need for a private way to spend time with his parents, and it had provided what everyone now referred to as "the receiving room." She opened the door, revealing a stone stair-case winding down into a cavernous, well-lit room. Gently glowing abalone shells were set into the sides of the stairwell.

"They're on the beach," she said. "I really wish you wouldn't do this."

"Your objection is noted," I replied, and stepped past her, start-ing down the stairs.

Marcia and I usually get along pretty well, but she's protective of Dean, and for good reason; he needs someone to be protective of him. His parents love him. They also spend most of their time in the Undersea, where they can't intervene if anything goes wrong, and Merrow don't believe in coddling their children. Dean's half-Daoine Sidhe. He could do with a little coddling.

The stairs grew damp underfoot as we descended, but never became slippery. Magic has its uses. When we came around the last curve of the stairway we beheld the receiving room itself, large enough to have qualified as a ballroom if it had had a dance floor, half the floor covered by a redwood deck that wouldn't have looked out of place behind a fancy restaurant, the other half covered in unstained white sand, sloping gently downward until it reached the water. Dean had his own private cove down here, blocked from the sea by a wall of unyielding black stone. When Dianda and Patrick wanted to visit without it becoming a big diplomatic to-do, they could just swim under the wall and have easy, discreet access to their son.

It was a perfect arrangement, and so far as I knew, the knowe had taken care of everything without any outside input. It had recognized a need and filled it, which implied a level of awareness and interest that was surprising even to me. For the people who thought I was weird for believing knowes were people, it was probably mind-blowing.

Then again, many purebloods still can't accept that changelings are people. Asking them to believe it of the place where they keep all their stuff is probably a step too far.

Quentin and Dean sat side by side at the edge of the redwood deck, facing the water, hands clasped and Quentin's head resting on Dean's shoulder. It was a lovely scene. For the first time, I asked myself whether Quentin was going to be angrier at me interrupting him than he would at being left behind.

It didn't matter. He was my squire, and Karen had seen him with me on this quest. His training meant it was my responsibility to bring him along whenever I decided to do something potentially fatal. Doubly so if leaving him behind could mean failure. And if that was selfishness, sometimes it's okay to be selfish. Selfish keeps the lights on.

I trotted the rest of the way down the stairs, not making any effort to muffle my footsteps, and hit the floor as hard as I could, letting my heels thump down on the wood. Quentin raised his head as both of them turned. There was a moment of shared confusion on their faces, melting into resignation on Dean's and surprise on Quentin's.

"Toby!" he exclaimed, letting go of Dean's hand and scrambling to his feet. "I thought you and Tybalt were having date night tonight!"

"Okay, seriously, did he tell literally everyone else that I had dinner plans without even bothering to *ask* me about it?"

"Yes," said Quentin and Dean, in unison.

I wrinkled my nose. "Don't do that, it's creepy. Also, get your things. We have a quest, courtesy of pureblood law and *somebody's* parents hearing where I was having dinner tonight."

Dean had the good grace to look chagrined. Quentin, on the

other hand, looked confused, looking from me to his boyfriend before asking, "Dean? What's she talking about?"

"I, um, told Dad he couldn't come over tonight because I knew you'd be free," said Dean. "I didn't want anyone interrupting our date. He asked how I knew, and so I . . ." He trailed off, looking even more embarrassed.

"So you set him up to go and interrupt mine," I concluded.

Dean nodded. "I didn't mean to. It wasn't a secret from anyone but you, and it's not like my parents are enemies of yours. I didn't think they'd bother you. Did they bother you? Do I need to call them and yell?"

Thanks to April, the cyber-Dryad daughter of the Countess of Tamed Lightning, phone service in the Summerlands and Undersea has gotten much more extensive and reliable over the past few years. I sighed.

"No," I said. "But maybe in the future, don't volunteer where I'm going to be unless it's been announced in public, not told to you in private? Your parents aren't my enemies, but a lot of people are."

That was putting it mildly. I seem to collect enemies the way May collects gaudy necklaces these days, and some of them are pretty damn dangerous.

Dean nodded again, more vigorously this time. "Of course. I'm so sorry."

"Don't worry about it. You're getting punished the same way I did: with the interruption of your evening." Quentin was watching me worriedly. I shifted my attention to him. "How much do you know about pureblood marriage laws?"

"Enough that if I weren't going to inherit the throne someday and need a legitimate heir, I'd never be willing to get married," he said. "They seem simple until you start looking into them, and then you find all these little snares and pit traps of tradition buried in the middle of the cake. It's awful."

"Yeah, I wouldn't be surprised if Eira had something to do with creating a lot of those 'traditions,'" I said. "Apparently, not only can I never divorce without the permission of my children, I can't actually get married unless I at least attempt to invite my parents. *Both* my parents."

"Um, wasn't your father human?" asked Quentin. "Isn't he . . ." He trailed off awkwardly. He's more comfortable with the concept of death than most purebloods his age, but he's still functionally immortal. Unless something comes along and kills him, he's never going to die.

"He's dead," I said bluntly. Both Quentin and Dean winced. "He died a long time ago. I leave roses on his grave every Christmas. But because legally, in Faerie, Simon Torquill is my father, if I don't invite him to my wedding, he can claim offense against me—or someone else can do it on his behalf."

"Who would do that?" asked Dean, horrified.

"Who wouldn't? Eira, if he ever manages to find her and wake her up. Luna, just because she can. Hell, my own *mother* might decide to get pissed on behalf of the husband she never told me about. Or August might. And the last thing this household needs right now is someone making a valid claim of offense against us."

Quentin put a hand over his face. Dean, who had grown up in the Undersea, looked confused.

"If someone gets offended at you, can't you just fight and then apologize?" he asked.

"That's not how it works here," I said. "Marcia would have told you if you were ever at risk of doing something that would allow somebody to actually claim offense against you, but because most of the fae on the land aren't big on frontal assaults—"

"Present company excepted," said May, while Quentin hid a laugh in his hand.

I glared at both of them. "—we have to settle things in a different way. If someone insults you enough that you can claim offense, you can basically ask them for anything within their power to give. Seven years of servitude, or their mother's favorite necklace, or the head of their favorite hunting dog. Anything other than murder is on the table."

Dean looked horrified, as well he should. It was a pretty horrific concept. "That's barbaric!" he said.

"You're not wrong," I said. "That's one of the reasons it never occurred to me that there was any way my wedding invitations could put me in that position. But with Simon in the wind and some of his people still around, it's a valid concern."

"And *that's* why my parents interrupted your date?"

"Yup. They assumed, quite rightly, that I wouldn't have considered my relationship to Simon when Tybalt and I were making our plans. Tybalt *had* considered it, and wasn't telling me, so I'd be able to use ignorance as a defense. Now Patrick and Dianda know that I know, I need to do something about it."

Quentin's smile died, replaced by a look of quiet horror. "You're going looking for Simon," he said.

"Got it in one."

"But he's—you can't—this is a bad idea!"

"Yes, he is, yes, I can, yes, it is," I said. "Get your coat, if you've got one. We're heading for Shadowed Hills." I could tell him about Karen's dream later. I didn't need to make this more confusing than it already was.

"Not the Luidaeg?"

He sounded honestly puzzled, which was enough to make me pause and look at him. The Luidaeg is many things—my aunt, the sea witch, a close family friend—but when I was his age, only one of them mattered. Monster. Most of Faerie considers her the sort of thing you use to threaten children into good behavior. "Do your chores or the Luidaeg will come and carry you away." "Listen to your mother or the Luidaeg will turn your heart to wood inside your chest and you'll never love anyone ever again." None of those threats are true, of course. The Luidaeg can be cruel, but only to people who deserve it, and never, *never* to children.

She used to say she didn't like kids, because it was part of how she coped with losing her own. The Roane were killed because of Eira, and the Luidaeg spent centuries watching others wear the flayed skins of her babies, until I was able to help her make things at least partially right. Not entirely. Nothing would ever give her sons and daughters and grandchildren back to her. But there were Roane in the world again, and she could no longer say she didn't like kids without her geasa rising up and stopping the words in her throat. It was something.

Most Daoine Sidhe would have wet themselves before willingly going to the Luidaeg, or would have done it only because there was something they wanted so much they were willing to pay anything, risk anything for the chance to have it. Quentin was disappointed *not* to be going to her.

"I broke you," I muttered, before saying more loudly, "No, not the Luidaeg. I don't want her to feel like she has to offer me something, and I'm not willing to give her what Simon did. This is not a chain letter I have any interest in signing. I need him home, alive, and himself, which she might prevent. So we're going to Shadowed Hills, to talk to Luna."

Quentin's look of confusion deepened, now tempered by disbelief. "Why would you want to do *that*?" he demanded.

"Luna can open the Rose Roads, and once they're open, Spike can navigate them." I pulled the key from my pocket, holding it up so he could see the braided strands of metal that formed its head. "Before, we used this to make the Rose Roads take us to where Eira was. I need to go there again."

Quentin put a hand over his face. Even May was gaping at me. She hadn't heard this part of the plan. "Okay," he said. "As your squire, your friend, and your future King, I have to ask, *why* are we trying to go to the place where Eira is sleeping? She's the worst. Like, there are a lot of awful people running around, and I think most of them want you dead, but Eira is the actual worst of a bad lot. And she's my Firstborn, so I'm allowed to say that."

"And I should have thought of this earlier, but why aren't we going to Portland and asking Ceres if *she* can open the Rose Roads for us, since she doesn't, y'know, hate you?" asked May. "She's Blodynbryd, too, remember? She should have access. It would get us on the same Road."

"I'm not sure how good the Rose Roads are at traversing actual distance, as opposed to moving through unoccupied spaces and emptiness," I said. "Ceres might be easier to work with than Luna, but she could also open us a road we can't survive."

"I would," said May.

"True, but we don't know what happens to you if all the air runs out, or if you're stabbed by too many poisoned thorns, or all sorts of other options. The only thing we know for sure about the Rose Roads is that this key," I waved the key, "can be used to get from them to where the Luidaeg left Eira, and that they're connected to the Blodynbryd. But roses are Titania's thing as much as anything, so maybe they're booby-trapped to hell and back, and we'll only find out by getting started. Besides, we can't go to Portland without Arden's permission, and having her contact Siwan to confirm that we're allowed to go to another Kingdom and that we're not planning to overthrow the monarchy while we're there would be way more complicated." Also, there was the small but ever-present concern that this might be the time that Siwan said no.

Having a reputation for king-breaking is sometimes more of a problem than I would have thought it could be.

"Come on." I gestured for Quentin to follow me as I turned back toward the stairs.

"I don't like this," he said, before pausing to kiss Dean on the cheek. "I'll call you after we all get through this alive, okay?"

"Stop tempting fate," said Dean, pushing him away. "You know I worry."

"I know you worry too much," said Quentin. He apparently didn't have a coat, since he didn't grab anything before running after me. His cheeks were flushed, and he was grinning. I gave him a curious look.

"Yes?"

"It's nice to have something to do, is all," he said. "Things have been sort of slow recently."

"You realize you're saying you'd prefer mortal danger to having time to go out with your boyfriend," I said, disbelievingly.

Quentin shrugged. "It sounds weird when you say it like that."

"It sounds weird no matter how you say it! What are you going to do when you have to go back to Toronto and become High King? Start the Hunger Games?"

"Maybe," said Quentin. "I'll have to do *something*."

He sounded really unhappy about the idea. I paused, looking at him more seriously.

"Yeah, you'll have to be a good and considerate King who actually governs us in a reasonable fashion and puts an end to the systemic abuse of changelings and fae with animal attributes," I said.

"I know," he said, almost sullenly.

"Come on. Let's go risk our lives." I put my hand on his shoulder, and with May and Spike at our heels, we made our way up the stairs and out of the knowe.

SIX

THERE WAS A REASONABLE amount of traffic on the streets. The Bay Area is almost never completely quiet. We have too many humans living here for that to happen. Even the ones who work in the glass towers of downtown like to go out at night. The ones who can't get those jobs work the midnight shift at Safeway or 7-11 or mop floors for their so-called betters.

But then, I'm a former grocery store clerk. Maybe I have opinions about social mobility and the nonsense that is class.

We were near enough the Bay Bridge that, traffic notwithstanding, it wasn't long before we were on our way across the water to Pleasant Hill, a comfortable bedroom community occupied by people who wanted good schools and big backyards and didn't mind a little drive as a trade-off. It was about a forty-five–minute drive under normal circumstances. Thanks to my don't-look-here spell allowing me to disregard some speed limits, we made it in just over half an hour, despite the traffic. That was the good part.

The bad part was that my stomach sank and my knees went weak when I pulled into the parking lot of Paso Nogal Park. Technically, the place had been closed since sundown, but it wasn't fear of the law that put the creeping sense of dread into my veins. It was being here.

Shadowed Hills. My second home. My childhood refuge. Only now I was completely unsure of my welcome. What would be waiting for me when the door of the knowe opened?

There was only one way to find out. I took a deep breath. May put a hand on my shoulder and squeezed. I shot her a grateful look. Together, the three of us—and Spike—began trudging up the long dirt path that would take us deeper into the mortal side of the park.

Getting into most knowes requires completing some sort of trial. Maybe it's an obstacle course, or climbing the tallest tree in the world, or resisting the whispering terror of a field full of enchanted grass. When Sylvester established the entrance to Shadowed Hills, he wanted to be sure no mortals would wander into his entry hall by mistake, and he set up one of the more complicated patterns I'd encountered.

We climbed the highest hill in the park, winding up on a summit from which we could see most of the city, then crawled on our hands and knees under a cluster of spiky hawthorn bushes that hasn't been cut back since the first time I visited the knowe. After so many years of unchecked growth, they should have dominated the landscape, but somehow, they still occupied roughly the same amount of space they always had. Magic is funny that way. Getting back to our feet, we all ran six times counterclockwise around a tall oak tree. It was like watching the world's weirdest aerobics class in progress, and I hated every second of it.

For someone who dislikes exercise as much as I do, you'd think I would have found myself a nice desk job instead of going into the hero business, but no.

When we were done, I glanced at Quentin and May. Both gestured for me to go on. I turned to a large old stump and rapped my knuckles against the wood, producing a hollow booming sound that carried much too far and echoed much too long.

There was a burnt-out oak tree nearby, victim of a lightning strike sometime in the deep past. It was still struggling to put out new leaves, having refused to die even when all the odds said it should have. I had a lot of affection for that tree. I stepped back, waiting for the echoes of my knock to fade away.

Slowly and then all at once, the outline of a door appeared in the seamed bark and char of the oak. In what felt like the blink of an eye, something impossible had happened. And then the impossible swung open, revealing a dark-haired man in the blue-and-yellow livery of Shadowed Hills standing in a corona of buttery lamplight.

He blinked at the sight of us, hand dropping away from the door-knob before he asked, in a faintly baffled tone, "October . . . ?"

"Hey, Etienne," I said, and took a step toward the door. "Can we come in?"

"I . . ." He paused. "I honestly don't know the answer. You haven't been banned from the knowe, so far as I'm aware." He was being polite there; as Sylvester's seneschal, Etienne would *absolutely* know if I'd been formally banished, "but I know you were encouraged to stay away."

"I've missed you, too," I said dryly.

His face softened, and he stepped over the threshold into the mortal world, grimacing a little at the moment of transition. It doesn't hit purebloods as hard as it hits changelings, but it *does* hit them. "October," he said. "Do you think it doesn't ache, knowing you can't come home? Chelsea speaks of the warmth and comfort of your house as if she were talking about the halls of Caer Sidi. I'm jealous of my own daughter, that she gets to keep your company while I must keep my distance. Our hearths are colder for your absence."

It's not just Tybalt: all the older purebloods have a tendency to become uncomfortably flowery when they get emotional. Hearing it from Etienne, normally the most rule-abiding and straitlaced of Sylvester's knights, was still surprisingly moving. "You're an ass," I said, and stepped forward to meet him.

He closed his arms around me, the cedar smoke and lime scent of his magic enveloping me, and I breathed in deeply, enjoying the familiarity of the scent, if not the moment itself. Etienne was never a hugger before he was able to bring his human lover, Bridget Ames, home with him to Shadowed Hills and take her for his wife. Having Bridget, and more, Chelsea, around had done wonders to relax him when it came to things like showing affection to the people he cared about. I had only been a little surprised when I realized that list included me.

He let me go, stepping back again, and said, "Of course, you realize I can't let you in."

He might be more relaxed about hugging, but he certainly wasn't more relaxed about rules. I blinked at him.

"Why the hell not?"

"His Grace asked—"

"That I stay away for a little while, I know. I was there. It's been a year, Etienne. In case you forgot, I'm a changeling, I'm mortal, I pay attention to the passage of time. A *year* is long enough to qualify as 'a little while.' Anything longer than a year would be a 'a long while,' and that's not what he said." I crossed my arms and glowered. "He also *asked* me to stay away. He didn't order. He didn't command. He certainly didn't bind. I am a knight of Shadowed Hills, and I am exactly as free to walk through that door as you are."

"More, maybe," said May, in a pleasant tone. "Because Quentin and I won't try to stop her, and she's armed, which is two things she currently has over you."

Quentin didn't say anything. He just stepped forward and glared at Etienne.

Etienne held his position and his posture for a long beat before he sagged and sighed. Quentin seemed to have been the last straw for him. While I'm Quentin's knight, there are things I'm not equipped to teach him, and he'd been traveling to Shadowed Hills twice a week for lessons in swordsmanship, etiquette, and the intricacies of Daoine Sidhe magic for almost as long as he'd been living with me. Having one of his students clearly prepared to move against him while he was telling another that she was no longer welcome in her home had to hurt.

He stepped to the side. "You have my apologies. When I said I could not let Sir Daye in, I was unaware of the minutiae of the situation."

I took pity. Etienne's greatest flaw has always been his rigid obedience to the rules. It doesn't make him a bad person. It doesn't even make him a bad friend. It just makes him someone who needs an excuse to misbehave. It's hard for him to go against orders, even under the best of circumstances, and this was not that.

"It's cool," I said, and stepped inside, Spike at my heels. It rattled happily as we crossed the threshold into the knowe, and three more rose goblins popped out from behind the bookshelves, rattling their own thorns in answer. I felt a pang of something close to shame. By staying away, I had kept Spike away as well, and this was where its family lived.

It hadn't been my intention, or my choice. I looked over my shoulder at Etienne and the others.

"Well?" I asked. "Are you coming?"

They came. All three of them, Quentin in the lead and Etienne bringing up the rear. He closed the door behind himself, and it melted away, leaving a smooth expanse of wall behind.

"His Grace and the Duchess Luna are in the Moon Garden," he said, voice back to perfect formal precision.

I nodded. "That's the one past the main library, right?"

Luna has always been a gardener by both choice and calling. It's one of many things that started making more sense when I found out she was a Blodynbryd, and not a Kitsune as she'd led us all to believe. Her mother is Acacia, Mother of Trees, and she's a sort of Dryad in her own right, tied to the rosebushes growing on the land she's rooted herself to, rather than an oak or an elm. For her, gardening is a song, something that lets her call the living world into focus. Plants thrive under her hands, and she finds peace in the action. Even when she was swaddled in a stolen skin, she'd found peace in it.

Hopefully, the fact that she was in one of her gardens would improve her mood and keep her from getting too pissed when she saw me. I waited for Etienne to nod in the affirmative, and then took off down the hall, following the half-familiar curvature of the knowe, which rearranged itself on a regular basis. Quentin and May paced me, keeping up with ease. This had been home for both of them, in their own ways. I wasn't the only one who'd been in a form of exile.

We passed the large, ornately carved doorframe to the banquet hall, a room that had only been used for Beltane Balls in my lifetime, and started down a narrower hallway with wooden walls and a scuffed maple floor. Halfway down it, I paused, frowning.

"I don't think this is the way to the library," I said.

"At last she gets it," said May.

I blinked at her. "Why didn't you—?"

"The knowe is taking us somewhere," she said. "Every turn you've made has been the right one, and normally I would expect the library to be somewhere around here. It doesn't move much. But instead we're someplace I don't know, and that tells me the knowe is deciding how this is going to go."

I glanced at Quentin. He shook his head.

"The servants' markings say we're moving toward the library," he said. They were small flowers carved into the wainscoting and the decorative flourishes on the walls, all but invisible to the untrained eye, intended to make sure the small army of maids, courtiers, and servers who kept the knowe operational would always wind up where they needed to be instead of wandering in endless, bewildered circles. "I have no idea where we are."

Well. Wasn't that fun. I looked up at the ceiling. "We're sort of in a hurry here," I said.

There was no response. There never is, when I'm addressing the knowes.

I sighed heavily. "May as well see where it wants us to go," I said, and resumed walking down the hall. May and Quentin followed, and for a while, the only sound was the scuff of our feet against the floor.

There was a soft chiming, like a crystal bell being rung, and a door literally appeared in the wall ahead of us. As befit the sound of its arrival, it was made of cut crystals set into a silver weave, seemingly too loose and open to hold them in place, so they appeared to hang suspended on nothing but air. When I looked closer, I could see the finest of silver wires connecting each of them to the lattice, keeping them in place.

"Do you know this door?" I asked.

Quentin shook his head. After a pause, so did May.

"I think someone I was once knew it," she said, in an uncertain tone. "I mean, part of me feels like it's familiar. But there's no memory associated with the feeling. Just this sort of itch of recognition."

"So anything could be behind it," I concluded. "Awesome. Well, this is where the knowe wants us, so we might as well go inside." I reached out, running my fingers along the surface of the crystals as I searched for anything resembling a doorknob. There wasn't one, but one of the crystals nicked my index finger, bringing a bright, quick bead of blood to the surface. "Ow!" I yelped, yanking my hand away.

Quentin stared at me in obvious disbelief. "You get stabbed like it's the hot new thing, and *that's* what makes you show some self-preservation?"

"I wasn't expecting it!"

"Are you usually expecting to get *stabbed*?"

"When we're out in public, yes." My finger was already healed. I lowered my hand and stared as the drop of blood that had been left on the crystal was absorbed into its glistening surface, leaving a faint pink sheen behind.

Slowly at first, and then with increasing speed, that sheen spread to the crystals around it, and then to the crystals around them, until every crystal in the improbable door was tinted a faint, unmistakable shade of pink. I blinked. "Well, that's new."

"You're redecorating with blood now?" May shrugged. "I guess that's a natural next step for you."

"Ha, ha." The crystals shivered, emitting another of those soft chiming sounds, before the door swung slowly inward, revealing a room overrun with roses. I blinked again. "Whoa."

"Whoa is right." Quentin stepped forward, sticking his head through the open door. "Toby, you need to come see this."

"Quentin!" I grabbed him by the collar, hauling him away from the opening. He made a bewildered squawking sound. I released him and glared. "Dude, you're with two functionally unkillable women. *Why* would you stick your head through a mysterious, blood-drinking door when we're right here to do it for you?"

"I guess I didn't think," he said sheepishly.

"That's one more thing he learned from watching you," said May airily, before she stepped through the open door and into the green room on the other side. "All right, I'm going to be the third one to throw a 'whoa' in here. Toby, come on."

"Coming." I shot Quentin one last quelling look and followed my Fetch through the open door.

My first impression, that the room on the other side was full of roses, was more correct than I could have imagined. We were in what was essentially an overgrown greenhouse, the original flowerbeds and walkways completely overtaken by tangled vines and loops of thorns. Roses the size of dinner plates hung heavy on their stems, seeming to almost nod as we passed them, done in by the weight of their own splendor. There were no lights, only the dim gleam of moonlight passing through the mostly blocked panes of glass.

And everywhere, the scent of roses.

It wasn't a cultivar I'd encountered before, but it *was* a cultivar. They lacked the deep, primal scent of wild roses. This wasn't one of Maeve's places. I took another step forward, Quentin close behind me, and there was a chiming sound as the door swung closed.

I whirled, intending to catch it before it could shut fully. I was too slow. The door clicked back into its frame and trembled before disappearing, leaving us with no visible way out of the room.

"Oops," said Quentin.

"Very succinct." I turned back to the roses. They appeared to have grown with no intervention, wrapping their vines around whatever they desired and flowering with no regard for where people would need to walk. Despite this, there was a clear, if narrow, path through the greenery. I frowned as I considered it. Whatever this was, it seemed too easy.

"Okay," I said finally. "This probably isn't a trap. Wherever we are, it's still in Shadowed Hills. If we have to break a window to get out of here, that's what we'll do." The fields around the knowe were still familiar, even if it had been a long time since I'd been a feral child running wild through them in the company of my friends. The grounds have never changed as often as the interior did, and I'd be able to find my way.

Carefully, I began working my way along the narrow path, doing my best to dodge the thorns. There were so many of them, though, that it was inevitable that a branch would scrape across the back of my hand, leaving a series of shallow scratches behind. I winced and sucked air through my teeth, continuing to pick my way through. I could hear May and Quentin moving behind me; hopefully, I would be the one to block all the thorns, since I would recover quickly.

The branch that had grazed me withdrew of its own accord, twisting up on itself into a fernlike spiral. The branches around it began to do the same, a ripple of sudden withdrawal that more than doubled the width of the path. I rubbed the back of my hand, smearing the blood remaining there, and watched the roses move.

"Roses don't normally do this, right?" asked May. "I'm not mis-remembering the way plants behave?"

"Roses don't normally move unless there's a good wind blowing," I said.

"Cool. Good to know. We're all going to be eaten by weird magic flowers."

"Let's face it," said Quentin. "This isn't much of a surprise."

I didn't have an answer to that. I just snorted, and watched the roses pull further and further away, until we could see the shapes of the overgrown planter beds, and the light had brightened considerably as they unblocked the windows, and . . .

Oh.

And the glass coffin at the center of the growth was fully revealed. It was an ornate, geometric thing, almost a miniature greenhouse, and every inch of it shone, somehow clear of either dirt or sap. In the coffin was a woman with hair the color of fox fur, dull only in comparison to the roses, which were a richer, bloodier red; she would have blazed against any other setting, but here, she was dimmed down, reduced, made less than she should have been. Her hands were folded across her chest, like a princess out of a fairy tale, and her gown was green, seeming to have been made entirely out of rose leaves, each one connected to the one beside it with a delicate silver loop.

May's eyes widened. "Is that . . . ?"

"It is." I was the only one of the three of us who'd seen her like this, features sharp and beautiful and flawless, ears as sharply pointed as Quentin's. If her eyes had been open, they would have been the color of summer honey, perfectly golden and utterly inhuman.

Of course she was beautiful. The Daoine Sidhe always are. Titania would have tolerated nothing less.

"Rayseline," said May, with all the fondness of a woman who remembered the girl in the glass being born, remembered holding her when she was a baby, remembered thinking she was going to grow up to do incredible things. Well, she'd done that. They hadn't been good things, but kidnapping my daughter, killing Oleander de Merelands, and nearly assassinating her own mother made for a pretty incredible list, all things considered.

"She's still asleep?" said Quentin, in a bewildered tone. "But Queen Windermere made the elf-shot cure available after the tribunal said it was okay to use it. I thought . . ."

"You mean you never asked?" I turned to him. "You've been coming here every week for lessons, and you never saw her, and you never asked?"

"I didn't want to upset anyone," he said. "I thought she might be having trouble adjusting. I knew you'd pulled the Blodynbryd out of her. I guess I just couldn't imagine Luna allowing her to stay asleep any longer than she had to."

I could understand his confusion. It still reminded me that Quentin was a pureblood—a famously incurious lot. They don't like to dig below the surface of things, preferring the comfort of the obvious and the known. If Raysel wasn't there, of course he'd assumed there was a reason and left it alone. It took changelings like me and oddities like May to ask the questions that keep Faerie changing. The purebloods would be happy, by and large, to let it stay the same forever. It's safer for them that way.

"No," I said, and took a step toward the coffin. "They didn't wake her up."

There was a rustle and a faint creaking noise, and then Sylvester was saying, "We couldn't risk it with Simon at large."

I whirled around, eyes wide, and beheld my liege for the first time in a year.

He was a handsome man, Daoine Sidhe like his daughter, with the same fox fur-colored hair and golden eyes. He didn't have the build of a laborer, slim and easy in his linen shirt and simple trousers, a look of profound weariness on his face. He looked at me, weariness growing tinged with sorrow as he met my eyes, and in that moment, all I could think was how sorry I was that I'd ever been the one to hurt him. It didn't matter that in many ways he'd hurt me first—that's not math that puts anything good into the world. I'm allowed to protect my heart. I'm also allowed to grieve when I don't protect the hearts of the people around me.

Sylvester looked, for a moment, like he was going to move toward me, like maybe we were on the verge of reuniting. Then he tucked his hands into his pockets and turned his face away, suddenly fascinated by one of the roses growing nearby, and the flicker of hope I hadn't even been aware was growing guttered out and died in my chest.

"If he were safely asleep, as he should be, we'd have woken her by now," he said, tone dull, almost lifeless. "You promised to speak at her trial, or did you forget?"

"I promised to speak at her trial, and the Luidaeg has agreed not to demand she be held accountable for the Selkie woman she murdered," I said. "On account of how she was under Oleander's influence at the time."

"Oleander . . . yes. She's still the problem, even now that she's gone to the night-haunts. With Simon out there doing as he pleases, he could appear and demand satisfaction for his lover's death by my daughter's hands. Raysel's life could be forfeit to pay for killing that *monster*." He turned back toward me, and his eyes were suddenly candle-bright with rage, less golden than lambent. I swallowed the urge to step away.

My humanity is thin and faded these days, but part of me remembers what it is to be terrified of the gentry, to know that my place is so far below the least of the purebloods that looking at them can make it difficult to breathe. For Sylvester to be so angry that his magic was leaking into his physical form was viscerally terrifying in a way I had trouble articulating. I fought back the fear and stood my ground.

"I don't think he could, actually," I said, in as level a tone as I could manage. "He traded his way home for August's, so she could go back to her mother. For a moment, for his daughter, he was a hero, and I'm sorry you didn't get to see him like that. But losing his way home means he can't recognize anyone who matters to him. He wouldn't know you if you were standing in front of him." At least, that was how it had worked for August, and I had to hope it was how it would work for Simon. He'd still recognized me, after all. He'd just forgotten how much work he'd done to make amends and thought that it was his job to destroy me. There was a decent possibility he didn't even remember Oleander was dead. This spell—if I could even call it that, it was a magical working so far above a simple spell that it might as well have been a sun compared to a candle—was a brutal one.

"Would you take the risk if it were your child?" he demanded. "Would you do anything you thought might even have a chance of endangering Gillian's life?"

It was suddenly a lot easier to stand up to his anger without flinching. "If we're bringing Gillian into this, now's when I remind you that *your* daughter kidnapped and nearly killed mine," I said coolly. "I had to rip Faerie from my own child's veins to save her life—and that didn't *save* it, did it? Because it made her mortal, and what's mortal dies. Rayseline condemned my child to death when she stole her to get back at you, and I never held that against you. I never said 'oh, your family isn't worth taking risks for anymore because they got my family hurt.' I know you were a hero, Sylvester. I'm a hero now, too. When did you forget what that means?"

I glared at him until he turned his face away again, looking down at his feet rather than facing the implacable force of my anger.

"I'm sorry," he said, voice soft. "But my family . . . I've lost so much these last few years. My wife is changed beyond recognition. I fear she no longer knows what it means to love me. My daughter sleeps in a glass casket, and I can't wake her because my brother chose a monster over his own flesh and blood."

"I think the first monster he chose was my mother," I said, matching his tone. "I don't have any illusions about my own family. I'm sorry you keep losing your illusions about yours. But, Sylvester, I need help, and it's not my fault Rayseline was broken. All I've ever done is try to help her put herself back together."

He turned his attention toward the glass coffin. "I don't even recognize her anymore," he said. "She looks so much like . . ." His voice tapered off.

I didn't need to hear the name. The calendar I'm a part of began, as far as I know, with Sylvester's sister, September. Her half-Tylwyth Teg daughter, January, is a friend of mine, but September was dead long before I was born. There weren't any other red-headed Daoine Sidhe women lying around to be reflected in the reshaped bones of Raysel's face.

"She looks like her father," I said. "But she's still Rayseline Torquill, daughter of Sylvester and Luna, even if her blood isn't mixed anymore, and she's still going to have all her problems and all her sorrows when she wakes up. You're her father. It's on you to help her adjust to what her life looks like now. I'll do my best to make sure she gets to have that life, that she isn't sentenced back to sleep or worse, but honestly, that's going to be an afternoon, and I have the ear of the High King. He'll probably listen to me."

Behind me, Quentin snorted softly. I ignored him. I wasn't making any promises his father would be compelled to keep, and if I wanted Sylvester's help, this was what had to happen.

"October . . ." Sylvester rubbed his face with one broad hand. I remembered when those hands used to braid my hair, or boost me up onto his shoulders, back in the days when I'd been young enough for that not to seem strange, when I'd been his surrogate daughter, and not the near-stranger I'd become.

Oak and ash, I missed him. I missed him like I missed the rest of the family I'd once believed would be mine forever, back when

I'd thought my mother loved and wanted me, that Cliff and I would stay together, that Gillian would grow up safe and cradled in the circle of my arms. I missed him like I missed the innocence I hadn't appreciated until it was gone. I kept my hands by my sides and stayed where I was, not allowing myself to move toward him. He hadn't earned that from me yet.

Sometimes family means being willing to be the one who buries the hatchet and takes the first step. Sometimes family means they've already buried the hatchet, in your back.

"Oberon's departure was fresh in the memory of those who'd known him when I was born," said Sylvester, voice soft and dull. "My parents truly believed he would return any day, that they would see him come again. I was raised believing he'd merely stepped away, that he was still watching over us from some remove, out of sight but never out of mind."

I blinked. That didn't seem relevant. I glanced over my shoulder to May, who shook her head, a baffled expression on her face. At least she didn't get it either.

I returned my attention to Sylvester. "Okay . . ."

He looked at me, almost sternly. "Five hundred years, October. You can't fathom how long a time that is to wait for something."

"I know I'm not as old as you are," I said. "That doesn't make my heart less breakable."

"Our Firstborn told the Daoine Sidhe it was our duty to spread across Faerie, to carry the sword and the crown and protect the worlds Titania had granted into our care," he said slowly. "Almost five hundred years I waited for a child of my own. I had all but given up hope when Luna told me she was expecting. Rayseline was the culmination of centuries of dreaming."

"She still is," I said sharply. "She's still your daughter, she'll still love you when she wakes up. She needs help, she needs support, but she's not lost to you just because she's different now."

"She was perfect," said Sylvester.

I'd never wanted to slap my own liege as badly as I did in that moment. "If she was perfect before, she's perfect now," I said. "She did bad things, and she made some bad choices, but that doesn't change who she is, and she is your daughter. No matter what her blood says or what face she wears, she'll always be your daughter. She's waiting for you to give her permission to wake up and come back to the world. A lot of the things that were hurting her aren't here anymore. No more Oleander. No more impossible biology making it hard for her to think."

Even in Faerie, where the laws of nature sometimes seem less suspended than expelled, some things were never meant to happen. Rayseline Torquill was one of those things. Her father, Sylvester, was a mammal. Her mother, Luna, was a plant wearing a mammal's stolen face, looped and knotted and barely staying in place. If not for the Kitsune skin Luna had taken in order to escape her father's lands, Raysel could never have been conceived. Plants and mammals aren't meant to have children together, and the stresses of Raysel's impossible dual nature had been tearing her apart.

She might have been all right if her uncle hadn't abducted her as a child, casting her into formless magical darkness for more than a decade. The isolation and sensory deprivation had broken something in her, letting the little fractures of her nature take over and become dominant. That was why her mother had asked me to offer her the Changeling's Choice—not normally something that applies to purebloods, who don't have to decide between the human and fae worlds. In Raysel's case, the choice was between her father's heritage and her mother's.

She chose Daoine Sidhe. Not sure that was the right way to go, considering the Firstborn it left her with, but it meant when she woke up, her body and mind would no longer be at war with themselves. She had a chance.

Sylvester just needed to accept the future he and his daughter could have together now, instead of mourning the version of it that he felt he'd lost.

"Why are you here?" I asked.

Sylvester flinched before looking at me and saying, "It's my knowe. I could ask you the same thing."

"I need Luna's help."

"Why?"

Telling the truth was a risk, but it was the best chance I had. "I have to find your brother before I can get married," I said. "Legally, he's my father."

To my surprise, Sylvester smiled. Then he started to laugh. He sounded genuinely, enormously entertained. I blinked, taking a step backward. My shoulder bumped against Quentin's, who shot me a baffled look. I matched it with one of my own. Whatever this was, I didn't understand it at all.

Sylvester stopped laughing and wiped his eyes with one hand. "Oh, October. October. You asked once why I didn't tell you more about your mother. This is why. I loved you too much to let you become yoked to that man the way you have."

I blinked again. "Yoked? Because pureblood law doesn't want to admit my actual father existed? I don't think my ignorance would have changed that."

"Perhaps not. But if you knew nothing of your mother's marriage, your ignorance would have prevented anyone using my brother against you."

"Maybe not. Doesn't matter. I know what I know, and I need Luna to open a Rose Road for us."

Sylvester frowned. "Why?"

"Simon's got to be looking to wake up Eira. He lost his way home, which means all he can do is go deeper into the metaphorical woods. She's his wrong direction. Always has been. If we go to where she's sleeping, I can sniff out any traces of his magic, and know whether he's been there."

"Luna opened him no roads."

"Luna isn't the only Blodynbryd, and Simon is better at blood magic than you," I said. "He knows how to borrow from blood. I've seen his handiwork. If he could bleed a single Blodynbryd, voluntarily or no, he could get access to the Rose Roads for his own purposes."

Sylvester didn't look surprised or horrified by that proclamation. He just looked tired. "I see," he said. "Luna will be here shortly, but if you wish to be allowed to speak with her, there's something you must do for me."

I frowned. "Has she been listening through the roses this whole time?" Blodynbryd are intimately connected to the roses that belong to them. It makes them vulnerable; Raysel nearly killed her mother by salting the gardens and choking out the roots of Luna's roses. It also makes them excellent, terrifying spies. If there's a rose nearby, they could be watching you.

Sylvester nodded. "She told me to come," he said. "I don't know how you found this room, but as soon as you entered it, she knew."

"We didn't find it," I said. "The knowe brought us here." Next to me, Quentin nodded his confirmation.

"Then the knowe wants this as much as I do," said Sylvester. "If you want to speak to Luna, you must first speak to Rayseline."

I stared at him. "You can't be serious."

"Oh," said the man I once trusted more than anyone else in Faerie. "But I assure you, I am."

SEVEN

"WHILE SHE SLEEPS, her blood is closed to me," he said, wading into the roses around the coffin. They retracted at his approach, thorns twisting away from his skin. The worst of it was that I couldn't say whether that was proof Luna still loved him enough to want him unharmed, or proof that she no longer wanted anything to do with him, not even as nourishment for her roses.

Roses thrive surprisingly well on blood. I guess that's why they're such a foundational part of Faerie.

"I need to know she doesn't blame us for what's happened to her," he continued, laying a hand flat against the top pane of Raysel's coffin. It shimmered, seeming to shiver like the door that had allowed us to enter this room in the first place. Then the surface of the coffin swung open, exposing her to the rest of the room.

Glass coffins may be cliché, but at least this one meant she wasn't dusty, as so many elf-shot sleepers tend to be. She looked as fresh and peaceful as someone who was just taking a nap, the very picture of pureblood health. It hurt to look at her.

"What if she does?" I asked. "Blame you, I mean. Will that mean you refuse to let us speak to Luna?"

He gave me a look of infinite pity and equally infinite sorrow. In that moment, I remembered that we had one more thing in common: neither of us had been allowed to raise our own daughters. Simon had taken them away, returning them to us as women who didn't understand us and didn't seem to want to. In my case, I was the one he'd stolen from home, while in Sylvester's case, Raysel had been the victim, but the parallel was there.

"If you tell me the truth, I'll let you talk to my wife," he said. "I've never asked you to lie for me."

You've never done a lot of things you've been doing recently, I thought, and took a step forward. "All right," I said. "But you know she'll have to bleed for me if I'm going to talk to her while she's sleeping, right? And you know I haven't really done this before."

Normal blood magic involves sampling a person's blood to get to the memories contained there. It can be difficult and traumatic for everyone involved—the blood-worker because they can't always control the memories they get, and the one who does the bleeding because the more they try not to think about something, the more likely that thing is to show up in the blood. Don't think about elephants, in other words.

What Sylvester wanted was stranger and more difficult, and honestly, not something I was sure I was capable of, although I was willing to try. When I changed the balance of someone's blood, giving them the Choice, the process manifested as a sort of dreamscape, myself and the person standing in a landscape shaped from their own blood, able to converse.

I'd never done it without blood to change before, and Rayseline had nothing left to shift. Everything she was belonged to the Daoine Sidhe now, and I couldn't give back what I'd taken from her even if I'd wanted to. What was lost was lost forever.

"You'll do your best," he said. "I believe in you."

That made one of us. I approached the coffin, gazing at Raysel's familiar, unfamiliar face, and wished there were a way I could ask for her permission before invading her privacy one more time. She deserved to be left to recover in her own way. Which was never going to happen if her parents didn't let her wake up.

I started to draw the knife belted at my hip, and then hesitated. Luna was watching through the roses. Even if she wanted this— which she clearly did—stabbing her daughter in front of her probably wasn't the best way to convince her to help me. I turned to the nearest cluster of roses. Sylvester already knew Raysel had to bleed for me. I needed Luna, through the proxy of her roses, to consent.

"I need her to bleed if I'm going to do this," I said, reaching into the coffin and lifting one pale, limp hand with my own. The sleeve of her velvet gown fell back as I pulled her arm almost straight, revealing the creamy skin of her inner elbow. "Can I borrow your thorns?"

There: make her a part of the process, even if she wasn't here to actively help me. A long rose vine, devoid of blossoms but bristling with thorns, uncurled and swung toward me, hanging, serpentine, in the air. I nodded. "I appreciate it," I said, and reached for the vine.

It twisted in my loose grasp, driving thorns into my palm and fingers. The pain made me gasp, but I didn't let go, only looked reproachfully at the same cluster of roses.

"That wasn't necessary," I said. "I'm just doing what I was asked. I'm trying to help."

The vine didn't twist again as I tugged it toward Raysel's arm. The punctures in my hand were already healing, leaving my skin sticky with blood but otherwise unmarred. I don't like a lot of the magic tricks I inherited from Mom. The rapid healing is an exception.

Careful not to cut too deeply, I pressed the vine against the skin of Raysel's wrist, pressing until the thorns broke the skin and blood welled to the surface. Behind me, Sylvester made a wordless sound of protest. I looked over my shoulder at him, one eyebrow lifted.

"Yes?" I asked. Maybe that was a little curt of me, but nothing that had happened since we'd entered this room left me feeling charitable.

"Nothing," he said. "Continue."

"I will," I said. "Normally, if I were trying to talk to someone who can't talk back, I'd be changing their blood or at least trying, and that pulls on my power. There's nothing left in Rayseline for me to change. She's going to have to do some of the heavy lifting." I didn't know how I knew that; I just did. It's not like my mother ever gave me any lessons on our particular brand of blood magic. Everything I know how to do, I've figured out through trial and error. Occasionally massive error. It's fun and not at all terrifying to figure out an entire school of magic on my own. Really.

Turning back to Raysel, I pulled the vine away from her arm and ducked my head, bringing my mouth to the breaks in her skin. Her blood was salty and sweet at once, and between one blink and the next, the room was gone, replaced by the red veil of blood memory descending over everything.

No, I thought, keeping myself forcibly separate from the memories threatening to rise up and overwhelm me. *That's not why I'm here. She gets to keep her privacy.*

I could feel my body, but distantly, like it was on the other side of a thick wall of fog. I fumbled at my hip until I found my knife, then brought it to my other hand in a quick slashing motion, laying my palm open. As was so often the case, I cut too deep, stopping when I felt the blade strike bone. There was no pain. My body was too far away, even as I raised my hand to my mouth and drank deeply of my own blood.

It mixed with Rayseline's in a cloying flood, and the world finished the process of dropping away. It took the haze with it; I blinked, and there was nothing remotely red about the shadow-struck wood in which I found myself. Not even—or maybe especially not—roses. I was surrounded by dark trees, their trunks streaked in bands of charcoal and their leaves a green so deep that it seemed virtually black. The ground was carpeted in tiny white flowers, gleaming like stars against their surroundings, but there was no other color to be found.

"Raysel?" This had to be her creation. When the hallucinations belonged to me, they usually involved apartments I no longer lived in, or homes I'd given away. I had never seen this wood before in my life. "Raysel, are you here?"

"Where else would I be?" She sounded distantly amused, like this was the stupidest question anyone had ever asked her. The branches of the nearest tree quivered with the motion of an unseen figure, and Raysel continued, "It's not like sleeping criminals have a lot of say in where they get to go."

"You're not a criminal," I said. "Could you come down here?"

"A lie and an unreasonable request in the same breath? How could I refuse?" The branches quivered again, and Raysel dropped to the ground. She looked exactly as she had the last time I'd seen her, Daoine Sidhe to the core, sharp and poised and perfect by the standards of anyone inside or outside of Faerie. There were still no roses, but her appearance brought red into the wood in the form of her hair, bright as a flame against these trees. I was starting to understand why the Daoine Sidhe so often preferred to live alone. It let them tailor their environments to best suit their often ridiculously overdramatic coloration.

"Why are you here, October?" she asked. "*How* are you here? I made my choice." A flicker of alarm worked its way into her expression. "You can't make me do it again, can you? Because that hurt like hell last time, and I'm pretty happy the way I am now."

"I can't make you do it again, I'm afraid," I said. "I don't get to keep what I take away from people. It's not like shuffling a deck of cards. Once I pulled the Blodynbryd out of you, it was gone forever."

"Ah," she said. She didn't sound disappointed. Folding her arms, she leaned against the tree. "So why are you here? I thought we were done annoying each other until it was time for me to wake up."

"That's why I'm here," I said. "Your father hasn't pressed to let them wake you up because he's worried about what's going to happen when you stand trial."

A flicker of alarm passed over her face. "I killed two people. I deserve whatever happens to me."

"The Luidaeg doesn't intend to demand satisfaction in the matter of the Selkie woman's death, since her skin was returned to the Clans, and I don't think anyone is going to stand up for Oleander." The woman had been a monster. A true monster, not the sham people have tried so hard to make of the Luidaeg. Countless deaths could be laid directly at her feet, quite possibly including King Gilad Windermere and his wife.

The Law is supposed to apply to everyone, but if no one is willing to stand up for the dead, it doesn't. The perfect murder isn't one where no one knows. It's one where no one *cares*.

"Why would the Luidaeg be willing to stand aside for me? I haven't made any bargains with her."

"No, but I have."

Raysel stared at me, her thin veneer of cockiness dropping away. "I . . . but I've been awful to you. Why would you intercede on my behalf?"

I shrugged. "Because we're more than the substance of our scars, and I loved you before you hurt me. Because I know you've been lashing out, and people who are in pain aren't always careful about where they throw their punches. Because you loved me, too, before the world made you feel like you had to hate me."

Raysel blinked, face crumpling like a piece of paper. "I'm sorry," she said miserably. "I don't know why I felt like I had to do the things I did. They all made sense while I was doing them, but the longer I spend asleep, the less sense they make."

"Your blood was at war with itself," I said. "That has to have made it hard to think rationally about things." More and more, I was coming to suspect that all the stories about changeling madness I'd been fed as a child were actually about mixed-blood fae like Raysel. People whose blood could be traced back to some combination of either Maeve or Titania and Oberon seemed to be fine. People who were descended from Maeve *and* Titania could wind up having problems.

The bad blood between our Queens was apparently literal enough to be hereditary.

"I still did them, though," she continued doggedly. "I don't think I should get to just walk away from that."

"If it'll make you feel better, after I speak on your behalf at the trial, I'll claim offense against you and make you spend a year serving my household," I said.

It was intended as a joke. To my immense surprise, Raysel's eyes widened and she sagged, relief flooding her face. "Oh, *would* you?" she asked.

I blinked. "Um."

"I don't want to be here with my parents, not when they have all these expectations of me and who I'm supposed to be, and I don't know how to fulfill them. But I don't want to be alone, either. I don't ever want to be alone again." She wrapped her arms more tightly around herself, shivering. "Alone is where the cold comes from."

"If that's really what you want," I said.

"It is." She paused, frowning. "What's happening to your hair?"

I reeled back, reaching up to touch my head. It felt normal. Then I slid my hand down to the point of my ear, which was getting sharper by the second. I winced. "Damn." I dropped my hand. "I normally get to this space when I'm changing someone else's blood. I guess this time I'm changing my own. I need to get out of here before I'm not even partially human anymore. Are you all right with your parents waking you up so you can stand trial and move on with your life?"

"I am." Raysel nodded. "I appreciate you asking. No one ever asks what I want. And I'm sorry you had to hurt yourself for me."

"I'll be fine," I said, although I wasn't so sure. Now that I was paying attention, I could feel the fizzing burn of my blood shifting in my veins. It was slow, like a moth chewing its way through a piece of silk, but it was happening faster than I liked. "Until next time."

Problem: I wasn't actually sure how to break the connection. Well, Raysel had given us a wood, with accurate recreations of our actual bodies, which meant—yes. I felt my hip and found my knife there. Drawing it quickly, I jammed it into my forearm, not taking the time to be careful. This space wasn't real, and I needed to get out of it as soon as I could.

There was no pain, but there was blood, immediate and bright as rubies in the dimness of the forest. I pulled the knife loose and clamped my mouth down over the wound, drinking deeply of the idea of my own magic as I closed my eyes. I almost immediately began to feel dizzy and felt a pulse of dully aggravated pain shoot through my temples—the beginnings of magic-burn, a sensation that's so unfamiliar these days as to be vaguely shocking.

I was still bent double, mouth on my arm, although there was no blood and not even the healing remnants of a wound. I opened my eyes and straightened. Another wave of dizziness swept over me, strong enough this time that I fell backward, narrowly missing the nearest clump of roses as I landed on my butt in the dirt. A few thorns pierced my jeans, adding injury to insult.

Quentin rushed to help me to my feet. "Toby! Are you all right?" A pause. "What did you do to your hair?"

"I'm fine. How bad is it?" Reaching inward, I could feel what remained of my mortality cowering at the bottom of my blood, like a rabbit afraid of the hounds. Of course, it wasn't really doing that—biology doesn't work that way. Magic and science sometimes take very different snapshots of the same situations.

I was still a little bit human. Not enough. Maybe a quarter; probably substantially less. Tybalt wouldn't be upset by that, but I was. This hadn't been my intention. And even the thought of trying to shift myself back right now made my head spin and ache worse. This wasn't the time.

May moved to put her hand on my other shoulder as Quentin let go of me. I leaned against her, scanning the room until I found Sylvester. He was in the same place; I was the one who'd moved. He stared at me like he was seeing a ghost. I guess watching my hair bleach itself in real time had been unsettling for him.

Raysel was motionless in her coffin. She couldn't heal like I did, and the scratches on her arm were still gently bleeding. The scent of it hung sticky in the air, stronger to my specially attuned nose than the scent of the roses. I could taste the new makeup of her magic in the scent; it was still built on a base of hot wax, but the mustard flower was gone, replaced by crushed blackthorn fruit. Interesting. I still don't fully understand what determines magical scents, but I know they're partially a factor of heritage. She must have gotten the mustard from her mother, and now it was gone.

There would be time to think about that later. Right now, I had a quest to finish, and a stepfather to find. "She's fine with you waking her up," I said, voice low and a little rougher than I intended. "She knows she'll have to stand trial, but she's feeling better, and she's ready."

Sylvester blinked. "October, your *hair . . .*"

"Why does everyone keep saying that?" I knew why they kept saying it. My mother looks like she's been bleached. Everything about her has been drained of as much of its color as possible, leaving her a watercolor sketch of a woman who looks about as substantial as the morning mist. Every time my blood shifts away from humanity and toward the fae, I lose a little more of the coloration I inherited from my father.

"Anyway." I shoved my knife into its sheath and folded my arms, glaring at the man who was my liege and had once been the person I trusted most in all the world. "Can I talk to Luna now? Because I'm not going in to talk to Rayseline again. I don't have enough humanity left to pay for another visit." That might or might not be true. In the moment, it felt entirely sincere.

"I . . . yes." Sylvester bowed his head as he turned to the nearest cluster of flowers. "Dear, would you come to the state room, please? October needs to speak with you."

The flowers rustled before turning away from him, exactly like a sullen teen refusing to look at a parent who'd displeased them. Silence hung in the room, almost as heavy as the scent of Raysel's magic and the perfume wafting from the roses. I leaned against May, letting her steady, silent presence lend me the strength I didn't presently have on my own. She'd be with me until the end. That was what it meant to have a Fetch.

To have a sister, too.

The roses shivered again before the vines began moving, curling and expanding to form a tunnel of sorts, like the sort fancy gardens like to make with carefully constructed trellises. There were no trellises here, just the roses holding themselves upright through sheer force of Luna's magical will.

There was a momentary stillness, and Luna came walking down the tunnel.

She was beautiful in the way only the fae can be beautiful, like a natural disaster walking as a woman, and she was terrible in the same way, tall and willowy, with hair that hung past her knees in a riot of curls, pale pink at the crown of her head and darkening as it descended, until it was red-black at the tips. Her eyes were pollen-yellow, and her skin was white as bone or ivory, with no color to soften it. Luna Torquill might be one of the only people in Faerie who's actually paler than my mother.

She wasn't always like that. She was all soft browns and grays when I was younger, a warm and loving Kitsune shadow haunting the halls of her husband's knowe. Changing the blood really does change everything, in Faerie.

She walked to her husband's side and stopped, turning her dispassionate gaze on me. I fought the urge to flinch. No one can make you feel small and judged like the people who loved you as a child.

"Why are you here?" she demanded. "We have only one sleeper left for you to wake, and she isn't yours to run away with on another of your mad quests."

So don't tell Luna about my plan to claim offense against Rayseline, check. "I'm here on another of my mad quests," I said. "I need you to open a Rose Road for me."

Luna looked momentarily nonplussed before she forced her expression of dispassionate disapproval back into her face. Neutrality was apparently easier for her. Well, it wasn't easier for me, and it made me want to scream that we were better than this, that I'd done enough, risked enough, lost enough for the sake of her family that she owed me anger if she didn't owe me anything else. "Why in Oberon's name would I be willing to do that for you?" she asked.

"Because I have to find Simon if I want to get married, and he's probably looking for his liege, and the last time I saw her, she was elf-shot and asleep at the end of a Rose Road." I didn't want to say Eira's name in the presence of the roses. They might not be hers, but she controlled too many roses for me to feel safe bringing her up here. Even more, I didn't want to tell her about Karen. I wanted Luna as far away from the members of my surrogate family as possible. "I don't know how he could have reached her there, or if he has, but I'm trying to avoid going to the Luidaeg for this one, and that means starting in the places I know he wants to go. Since he can't go to Mom's tower." Privately, I doubted he could come to Shadowed Hills, either. He and Sylvester might have drifted apart, but they had loved each other dearly once, and Simon had helped to construct the anchors binding the knowe to the delicate membrane between the Summerlands and the mortal world. This place had been his home.

And right now, home was precisely what he didn't get to have.

Luna's nostrils flared as she took a deep breath and turned to Sylvester. "It's unfair of you to allow her to ask this of me," she said, voice mild. "You should never have let her back into our home."

"Technically, it was Etienne who let us in, and he did that because nothing I've done has been bad enough for my *liege* to ban me from the demesne where I'm sworn to serve," I said. "I was told it would be better if I kept my distance. I wasn't banished from the Duchy. I'd have to cross a lot more lines for that to become appropriate."

From the burning anger in Luna's eyes when she turned back to me, she didn't think I needed to cross any more lines. I had already crossed them all as far as she was concerned, and I had no business being here.

"Perhaps my husband didn't let you in, but he let you stay," she said, voice measured. "That seems like quite enough offense to me."

That word just kept coming up today. I took a deep breath, holding it for a moment before I let it slowly out. "Please, Luna," I said. "Please. I always did my best to do whatever you needed or wanted me to do. When you got sick, I would have done anything to save you. I went into Blind Michael's lands to keep you safe. I shifted Raysel's blood because you asked me to. I just need a road. I just need a way to get to the sleeper, and then I'll leave you alone."

She frowned, and for a moment, I was sure she was going to refuse me. Then she held out her hand.

"I know you don't want an ordinary Rose Road, because none of the places they can reach are the place you need," she said. "That means you brought the key."

Trying not to show my gratitude too openly and risk changing her mind, I dug into my pocket and produced the braided metal key that had once belonged to Evening Winterrose, before she was supposedly murdered and my life changed forever. "I did."

"Give it to me."

I took three steps forward and dropped it into her palm. As always, I felt a slight pang of loss at the act of giving it to someone else. It wasn't like my knife, something that mattered to me and was always close to hand, but it was something I'd had longer than almost anything else at this point, and it represented a time in my life that was over. Things had been simpler then.

In a way, it represented the transition between things being simple and things becoming very, very complicated. And when I looked at it that way, my attachment made no sense at all. I should want the thing as far away from me as possible because the last thing I needed was more complication.

Luna turned the key over in her hand before holding it up to the light as if she'd never seen it before. "I do wonder who made this," she said. "I know where you obtained it, but my aunt was never fond of working metal or making her own jewelry. Mother could have done it once, but she didn't; this isn't her handiwork."

As the daughter of two Firstborn, Luna shares the same sort of queasy, overly familiar relationship with them that I do. Her mother is a child of Titania, however, whereas most of my acknowledged family comes from Maeve and Oberon. It's a very different sort of relationship.

Her father was a son of Maeve, and an actual monster, unlike the stories Titania's children spread about the Luidaeg and her other siblings. Blind Michael alone was enough to justify many of their lies about the children of Maeve. He preyed on children.

I killed him. I sleep better at night knowing he's dead, and never coming back, and even knowing that, I can't stand the flicker of candlelight. He took that away from me, possibly forever.

"Someone may come to take this back from you someday," said Luna, almost dismissively. "When that happens, I want you far from here." She turned the key over one more time before she shoved it into the air, grimacing slightly.

It slid smoothly into a keyhole I couldn't see, that probably hadn't existed at all until Luna needed it, vanishing to a point halfway up its shaft. Luna raised her eyes to mine, and I recoiled involuntarily from the loathing I saw there.

"Whenever you touch this family, we lose something," she said.

"Sometimes things that can't be recovered. I can't be the one to banish you, and my husband refuses to take that step on his own behalf, even as I tell him it would benefit us all."

Sylvester winced and looked away. So he was still defending me, at least a little. That was good. I hadn't been counting on it.

"I don't want you coming back here until it's time for you to speak in Rayseline's defense," she continued. "I don't want you—any of you—anywhere near my family."

I blinked. "Quentin has to come here for his training," I said. "The High King insists he be properly trained to serve his people one day, and there are lessons I can't teach him."

Luna shrugged. "He should have thought of that before he agreed to damage his future prospects by being squired to you."

The urge to defend both my squire and myself, to point out all the errors and lies in what she said, was strong. I tamped it down, grinding my teeth and holding my tongue. Not easy.

"I'm quite sure Queen Windermere will be happy to take over the remainder of my training," said Quentin, in what I thought of as his "crown prince voice"—calm, measured, and polite. He was reminding Luna without reminding her that he represented the trust of his parents, and once he removed himself from their custodianship, they would lose that trust. Possibly forever.

I wasn't sure alienating the future High King of the Westlands to score points against me was a good move, politically speaking, but in that moment, Luna didn't seem to care. She grasped the key again, this time twisting it sharply to the left. There was an audible click, which seemed odd only because there were no visible locks. Luna took her hand away.

"Do you agree?" she asked.

"I can only speak for myself, but yes, I agree," I said. "Unless my liege summons me, I won't come back until you wake Raysel and it's time for me to speak at her trial."

"I agree," said May, and the judgmental regret in her voice was deep enough to drown in.

"I agree," said Quentin.

"Good. Then I'm finally rid of you." Luna twisted the key further. There was a second click, softer than the first, and she opened a door none of us could see, revealing a long tunnel lined with roses. She pulled the key out of the air and held it out to me. "Now go."

"Promise me we can come back."

She frowned, key still held out. "I just banished you, and you agreed."

"Not to Shadowed Hills, necessarily, but from the Rose Road. Swear on the root and the branch that this road will lead us home again."

She sighed, frown fading. "Fine. I swear, this is a road from here to someplace else, and home again, although it will not return you here."

"Good enough," I said, and took the key.

Sylvester, who hadn't said a word in my defense while his wife was effectively exiling me, turned his face away and didn't watch us walk into the opening in the air.

I guess as far as he was concerned, I was already gone.

EIGHT

THE DOOR NONE OF US could see slammed shut as soon as we were through, leaving us standing stranded in the tunnel of roses. I jumped but didn't turn toward the sound. Quentin started to. May grabbed the sides of his face, locking his head in place. He blinked at her, obviously confused.

"You can't look back when you're on the Rose Road," she said. "If you do, you'll be dropped off it, and you'll wind up wherever the road is running right now. We don't know where that is, and these roads are old enough to bypass some of Oberon's closed doors. Plus, I don't know how we'd get you back *on* the Rose Road. Luna's unlikely to open it for us again."

"You know, for someone who tried to put all his descendants under house arrest on his way out the door, he sure did leave a lot of loopholes," said Quentin peevishly. "Am I allowed to look around?"

"Yes," I said. "You just can't look back, even if you drop something. You can't—Spike!" The rose goblin had never come to join us in the greenhouse. I grimaced. "We left Spike behind. I hope Luna doesn't prune it or anything."

"She made the rose goblins, she's not going to hurt one of them," said May, who sounded about as confident of that as I felt.

"No, but she might clip back any new growth she doesn't like," I said. I sighed. "Maybe it can catch up with us. The first time I used a Rose Road, Spike led me to the Luidaeg's place. We don't know how much freedom of movement they have in here."

"That's true," said May. "Let's go."

We started walking.

The roses forming the walls were from a hundred or more different cultivars, and their blended perfume was a dizzying mixture that made my already aching head hurt even more. I rubbed my temple with one hand as we walked, causing May to look at me with concern.

"It still hurts?" she asked.

"It always hurts when I change my own blood, and I'm barely human anymore," I said. "I guess this is my human side giving me one last headache as a good-bye present."

May frowned. "I know you don't want to stop being a changeling . . ." she said, trailing awkwardly off.

"Even though it would make everything easier for everyone," I finished. "I know. Tybalt brought it up while we were at dinner. He's not going to try to force me to do anything, but he worries about me dying on him, even though I'm so fae at this point that it would take literal centuries for me to get old, and nothing else is going to kill me."

"I'm pretty sure you *can* be killed," said May. "Call it a feeling from someone who used to be your death omen. I think you can die and stay dead. It's just not going to be easy."

I shot her an amused look, despite the pain. "Gosh, you're so optimistic, I should bring you on *all* my ridiculous quests. It's easier to do the impossible when I have someone around to remind me that it could kill me."

"Do you actually know where we're going, or did we just let a woman who currently hates us all put us on a road to nowhere without a map?" asked Quentin. "Not that I'm questioning your judgment—it's a little late for that—but I'd like to know if we're going to wander the rest of eternity through a flower shop from hell."

"I'm pretty sure starvation is one of the ways Toby *can* die, so I'll be the only one of us wandering forever," said May blithely.

Quentin gave her a horrified look. I snorted and was preparing to answer when something rattled ahead of us, loud as a maraca being shaken by an over-enthusiastic preschooler. I angled sharply toward the sound, and relaxed as I saw a small, roughly cat-shaped creature push through the wall of roses.

"Spike! There you are, my good goblin! I was afraid we'd left you in Shadowed Hills, but no, you followed us here, because you're such a genius, aren't you?" Spike shook itself the rest of the way free, chirped, and trotted toward me, spines rattling with every step. The rules about never turning back were clearly more flexible for the rose goblins. I knelt, letting it climb into my arms. It chirped again. "Hey, buddy," I said, and scratched it under its thorny chin. Spike half-closed its eyes, as content as a cat.

May shot me an amused look as I straightened. "You're such a pushover," she said.

"Only for family, and that includes Spike." I looked at the goblin in my arms. "Do you know where we are, buddy? We're trying to find Simon. That means we need to go to the place Maeve unlocked for her daughter. The place where the bad woman is asleep. Can you help?"

Spike chirped, louder this time, an obvious affirmative, and leapt out of my arms. It trotted a few feet ahead of us, waving its tail in invitation. It didn't look back. It knew the rules of this place well enough not to look back for us, even if those rules were a little malleable where it was concerned.

"Come on," I said, and hurried after it, gesturing for May and Quentin to follow. Not a second too soon: it transitioned from trotting to a flat-out run, racing along the thorny ground. I didn't hesitate, but ran after it, the roses around us blurring into an undifferentiated wall of red, white, and pink, broken occasionally by streaks of yellow or orange. Spike didn't vary its pace, just kept on racing.

The smell of roses somehow grew even stronger. I would have considered that an impossibility, since we were already surrounded by the things, but the harder we ran, the more cloying the scent became, until I couldn't breathe through my nose without gagging.

Suddenly, and without warning, there was a gap in the wall ahead of us, a black slash among the colorful flowers, opening onto apparent nothingness. Spike chirped, still running hard, and leapt through the gap, into the darkness.

Hesitation wasn't going to help us, and I had the genuine feeling that whatever this was, it was a limited-time offer. I fumbled behind me until I found May's hand and gripped it fast. Then I leapt after Spike into the darkness, and fell, both of us plummeting into nothingness.

Someone screamed. It might have been me. May was laughing,

sounding astonished and delighted at the same time. I guess knowing you're genuinely impossible to kill makes falling an unknowable distance toward an equally unknowable landing a lot less terrifying. I wasn't too terribly worried about hitting the ground—I've survived deadly falls before—but Quentin isn't as resilient. I could hear him screaming, and he wasn't far away.

"Quentin!" I shouted, letting go of May and feeling around helplessly in the black. "Quentin, try to find my hand!"

"It's dark!" he yelled back, sounding more than a little freaked out. It made sense; we'd been falling for a long time, and purebloods aren't used to being unable to see. Their night vision is so good that anything short of a closed cave is usually navigable for them.

"Follow my voice!" I kept feeling around, until my fingers brushed against something soft. I grabbed it, hooking the fingers of both hands into the fabric of Quentin's shirt and yanking him toward me. He responded by wrapping his arms around me. I did the same with him, trying to shield his body with my own as much as I could. He clung tightly, clearly aware of what I was doing.

It would be traumatic for him if we hit the ground and I splashed all over him, but not as traumatic as dying would be.

There was a soft crashing sound below us. I didn't have time to react to it before we hit what felt like the crown of a mature willow tree, broad and soft and cushioning. It was so much less violent than I'd expected that I relaxed, allowing my grip on Quentin to slacken.

Which is when we fell out of the tree.

I tightened my hold immediately. We fell the rest of the way to the ground—less than fifteen feet, all told—Quentin landing solidly in the middle of my chest and knocking the breath out of me. Also breaking at least one of my ribs, based on the snapping sound and the stabbing pain that lanced through my left lung. I wheezed, tasting blood, and pushed him away.

"I'm sorry!" squawked Quentin, rolling away and stopping himself before he could get too far. Everything around us was still pitch-black, and it would be far too easy for us to lose each other. "Are you hurt?"

Of course I was hurt. I just took a teenage Daoine Sidhe to the sternum. I breathed as deeply as I could, swallowing blood and spit, and tried to focus on something other than the pain. It wasn't easy, since there was nothing to look at except for endless darkness, but the pain was already fading, whisked away by my body's ludicrous gift for putting itself back together. I could feel my broken rib bending back into its original position, giving my lung room to heal. Not the most comfortable sensation ever. I swallowed again, catching my breath, and managed to croak, "I'm fine. Are *you* hurt?"

Because that was the real question. May didn't heal as quickly as I did, but she could walk off almost anything, thanks to her nigh-indestructible status. I'd be back to fighting strength in a few more seconds. If Quentin had a broken leg, we'd be carrying him.

"No. I landed on you."

Thank Oberon for small favors. I wiped my eyes, more out of habit than anything else, and pushed myself into a seated position, squinting into the blackness. Nothing. Oh, this was going to be fun. "I can't believe you followed us into that hole."

"I can't believe you *jumped*." There was a weariness in his tone that told me clear as the missing daylight that he was lying. Of course, he believed I would jump. There was nothing else I could have done, and everything we'd been through together supported that.

"Yeah, you can."

He sighed. "Yes, I can."

There was a rattling sound somewhere nearby, more subdued than normal, followed by a tiny chirp.

"Hey, Spike," I said. "I know it's dark, buddy. It's okay. Sounds like this isn't where you meant to be, huh? Just follow the sound of my voice, and we'll take care of you."

The rattle came again, closer this time, and something spiny rubbed against my leg, moving with the grain of the thorns, so as not to stab me. I only know one rose goblin who's that careful with people.

"Hey, bud," I said, and ran a hand along its back. It was trembling. "Okay, we need to find some light, and we need to get out of wherever this is. Hopefully, we haven't lost the Rose Road completely with this detour."

"My phone doesn't work." Quentin sounded miserable, and a little scared. "I have a flashlight app, but the screen won't even turn on. I had a full battery when we got to Shadowed Hills. There's no reason for my phone not to work."

No reason, apart from "we were in a dark pit somewhere unknowably deep inside Faerie, having fallen from an ancient road that cut through boundaries set by Oberon himself." April's good, and her upgrades to our personal technology have been amazing, but she's still only a Dryad. She's not playing on the same field as the Firstborn, or worse yet, the Three, and I had asked Spike to follow a trail originally opened by Maeve in order for us to make it this far. We were in a hell of a lot deeper than our consumer electronics were intended to go.

"Breathe," I said. "Just breathe. Okay. We're looking for the place where that woman is sleeping." Purebloods put a lot of stock in names, and sometimes even saying the name of a powerful enough pureblood can attract their attention. Eira was elf-shot and helpless, but she'd been able to reach out through her dreams to harass Karen. I didn't know how close we were to her now, and I didn't want to find out by breaking some magical rule and having her decide to possess one of us.

I also didn't want to find out that Karen was having dreams about me solely because of the threat Eira posed to her family. If I was the only thing standing between the Daoine Sidhe Firstborn and the Browns, this was not going to go well.

"Yeah," said Quentin.

"Well, we're also looking for the places Simon has been, and hopefully for Simon himself. We know that when he kidnapped Luna and Rayseline, he placed them in a formless void of utter darkness. A bubble of space he'd created and suspended between the worlds. And we know he must have been able to access it *somehow*, and he's a magic-borrower. He could have used their blood to open a Rose Road." His void had to have been anchored somewhere. This seemed like as good a place as any.

"But this isn't formless," said Quentin, sounding horrified. He was doubtless remembering that Luna and Raysel had been trapped there for fourteen years, despite all the tricks they'd had at their disposal to try making an escape.

"No. But it's dark. And maybe Raysel was speaking hyperbolically when she said it was formless—there doesn't seem to be much around here, and it's not really safe to go feeling around for more.

Which reminds me." I sat up straighter, taking a deep breath, and was pleased to feel both lungs expand to their usual limits. Take that, blunt force trauma. "Yo, *May*! We want to get the hell out of here! Where's my Fetch at?"

There was no echo from my shout, which told me more about our surroundings. Wherever we were, it wasn't the bottom of a gulch or gully. See? We were learning things even as we sat on our asses and hoped the dark wasn't full of hungry monsters!

The pause was longer than I liked before May rasped weakly, "Up in the tree. I, um. I landed badly."

That didn't sound good. I pushed myself to my feet, academically relieved when I didn't bash my head on anything. "Keep talking. I'll follow the sound of your voice."

"Are you sure that's," a pause to cough, "a good idea?" I really didn't like the bubbling undertone to her words. I had the sinking suspicion that we were about to test just how far her indestructability went, and neither of us was going to be thrilled with the results.

"Nope," I said, with forced cheerfulness, and held my hands in front of me as I began inching forward into the darkness.

I didn't have to go far before something even more helpful than her voice reached me: the smell of blood. It was hot and thick, but not enough to become overwhelming—there was still blood inside her body, it wasn't all out here with me. The phantom scents of cotton candy and ashes were wrapped around it, ghosts of the magic May carried in her blood.

If she was bleeding magic, she was hurt even worse than I'd been afraid she was.

"Toby?" Quentin sounded worried.

"Shh," I replied, and kept walking forward, letting the smell of the blood guide me. The ground was fairly level; I didn't trip or shove my foot into an unexpected hole. That was good, except for the part where it meant we still had no landmarks apart from the tree that had broken our fall.

The fingers of my left hand hit wood. I immediately grabbed hold, feeling around until I was certain it was a tree, smooth, with a fragile, papery bark that dissolved under my fingertips, turning into motes of dust too small for me to catch as they fell away. May was very close now. I could smell it.

Even so: "May? Where are you?"

"Right here," she replied. Her voice was on roughly the level of mine. She might be in the tree, but she wasn't that high off the ground. That was a relief. It would be easier to get her down if I didn't have to climb in the dark.

I kept inching forward, feeling in front of me with both hands, and stopped when I hit the soft, yielding flesh of May's hip. The fabric of her jeans was drenched with blood. It squelched between my fingers like unpleasantly warm jelly, but I couldn't feel a wound. That wasn't great.

From the angle of her body, it felt like she was hanging draped over something, but I couldn't feel anything for her to be draped *on*. It was a terrible mystery that I didn't like at all. I ran my hands higher and froze when they hit wood. As in, the side of the huge, jagged branch that was sticking out of my sister's stomach.

"May," I said, fighting to keep my voice level and not alarming, "are you *impaled* right now?"

"I think so," she said, with a weak laugh. "I can't move much, but it feels like that branch went right through me. I can feel my toes, so I guess it missed my spine. That's good, right? That it missed my spine?"

"Yes, since we don't know whether your nerves would regenerate from that sort of trauma, that's a very good thing. Hold still."

"I wasn't planning on doing anything else right now," said May dryly.

I kept feeling around the branch, trying to establish the diameter of the wound. It was at least a foot around, occupying most of the space that should have been her abdomen. Not great. Even worse, I didn't know how we were going to get it out of her. I had a single silver knife, and even though the blade had been magically hardened to allow me to slice through most things short of metal or stone, it didn't have a serrated edge; if I tried to saw through this branch, we'd be here long after Quentin had died of hunger. May didn't have any weapons.

That left . . . "Quentin! Do you have your short sword with you?"

"You came to get me while I was on a date. Do you normally bring weapons on your dates?"

"I bring weapons everywhere. Tybalt wouldn't know what to do with me if I didn't."

Quentin made a soft scoffing noise that I could only interpret as "adults are weird." "No, I don't have my short sword with me. Or any other kind of sword. I am sword-free. Why? What's going on?" His tone turned suspicious on the last question, thus proving that he was a smart kid.

"Nothing you need to worry about," I shot back. "May, I need you to keep breathing while I take care of things, all right? There's nothing for you to worry about, either."

"I have a branch sticking out of where I'm pretty sure my liver is supposed to be," she said. "This is really more your kind of thing, and you didn't do this before I was created, so I don't have any memory of how to handle this kind of bullshit."

"A branch sticking out of her *where*?" demanded Quentin.

I swallowed a sigh. "I'm handling it! Just stay where you are and let me work, okay?"

"Okay," said Quentin, sounding uncertain.

I reached further up, finding May's shoulder, and gave her what I hoped was a reassuring pat. "It's going to be fine. I promise you, it's going to be fine."

"I don't think you get to make promises right now," she said.

"Like that's ever stopped me."

All my magic centers on blood. Well, there was plenty of blood around, and I had my knife if I needed some of it to be mine for whatever I was going to achieve. There was no way this little pocket of nothingness happened naturally—or even what passes for naturally in Faerie, where the rules are sometimes more flexible than they would be in the human world. I could tell even without exerting myself that we were standing in something created.

What I couldn't tell just yet was whether it was the bubble Simon had created to contain Luna and Raysel or something else. I wasn't sure that part mattered. If this was his handiwork, it would mean Spike had opened the door for a reason, I supposed. But it was so hard to say.

One of the other gifts of the Dóchas Sidhe is breaking things. I don't do it nearly as often as my reputation implies and it's not like I've had any real training, since that would require my mother to acknowledge that I understand my own magic well enough to use it, but I can do it. Give me a spell I don't like, and I can probably pick it apart, given sufficient time.

The tree was a part of the black void around us, which, if it had been magically created as I suspected, meant it was part of a large, complicated spell. When Simon had described making something like this, he'd called it forcing magic into the membrane between worlds. If I unraveled too much and popped the bubble, we could wind up exposed and unprotected in that membrane.

Given how hostile the roads that travel through the membrane can be, I was pretty sure we didn't want to be standing in it by ourselves. I was going to have to be more careful than I'd ever been before. More careful than came naturally if I was being honest. I drew my knife.

The whisper-soft sound of it leaving the sheath was enough to make May tense under my other hand and demand, "What are you going to do?"

"I'm going to help," I said, taking my hand off her shoulder and bringing it around to the edge of my blade. Carefully, carefully, I drew the knife along the tip of my index finger, splitting the skin in a single sharp line of pain. It was already dark. I closed my eyes anyway, sticking my finger into my mouth. This was something that didn't require vision and would go easier if I wasn't being confused by the signals I was—or wasn't—getting from my eyes.

Everyone has a distinct scent to their magic, something they're born with, and that matures and changes with them as they get older. Sometimes it can transform entirely, as with Raysel after I changed her blood, or with Simon as he'd shrugged off Evening's influence. His magic had shifted back to its corrupted state as soon as the Luidaeg had taken his way home. But what I didn't realize until fairly recently is that magic also has an appearance.

It makes sense—I have to see something if I want to take it apart in the most efficient way I can—but it was still a shock the first time I *saw* a spell. I held onto that memory as blood filled my mouth and the coppery taste of it settled on my molars. I needed to see this one.

Like a ripple spreading from a stone dropped into a still pond, the unseen space around me began lighting up with gray-and-orange lines, twisted and knotted together like the most ambitious macramé project anyone had ever undertaken. Orange and gray. I breathed in through my nose, looking for the scent of the spell. Smoke and rotten oranges. I was right. This was Simon's handiwork, and if it wasn't where he'd been keeping Luna and Rayseline, it was a trial run for the same spell.

Good. I was at least familiar with his magic. I turned my head, eyes still closed, until the spell-strands spreading out in front of me included the jagged, broken-off shape of a massive tree limb. May must have hit the willow precisely wrong when she fell, snapping it off in the impact and then tumbling to land on top of it before she could hit the ground.

Its strands were connected to the landscape around us in places but were closer to standing on their own than many of the others. This was a decorative feature, not a part of the foundation. That was good. It was a start. As gingerly as I could, I reached out and hooked my fingers into the surface tangle of the spell.

It was malleable enough that I could work my way inside. I kept breathing, kept reaching, even as the scent of smoke and rotten oranges began wafting through the air. Bit by bit, I yanked the threads out of the branch holding my Fetch in place, unmaking the magic that comprised it.

I couldn't see her with my eyes closed, since she wasn't a spell, and so it was a bit of a surprise when there was a thump and a yelp. I opened my eyes. The lines winked out, leaving me back in absolute darkness. "May? May, are you all right?"

"I'm right here," she said, from ground-level. "You sort of took my chair away." There was a pained laugh in her voice. She was still trying to see the bright side.

And I was still trying to see *her.* I blinked and realized I could make out a faint outline through the darkness, which was impossible; I hadn't been able to see my own hand in front of my face only seconds before. It was like being in a cave so deep that your brain started playing tricks.

Only this wasn't a trick. I blinked again, and she became even clearer. I turned and looked over my shoulder; Quentin was about eight feet behind me. No details yet, but I could see the outline of his body clearly enough to know where he was.

"Is it just me, or is it getting lighter in here?" I asked, doing my best to keep my voice from shaking.

"It's getting lighter," said Quentin. "I can see you. What did you do?"

"Okay," I said. "That's maybe not such a good thing. I broke part of the spell making this place in order to get May free, but if I broke too much of it, it might all fall apart, and we could be left floating in the space between the mortal world and the Summerlands."

"Oh," said Quentin, with dawning horror. "Oh, I don't like the sound of that. I don't like the sound of that at *all*."

"Neither do I, so let's hope that's not what I just did." I turned back to May, who hadn't moved since she hit the ground.

Now that I could see her, I was glad I hadn't been able to see her before. Her abdomen was a ruin, a hole punched through skin and muscle alike and most of her organs either shredded or missing. Her eyes were closed, but her chest rose and fell in shallow jerks, even though she should by all rights have been dead at this point. *I* would have been dead by this point. Still healing, sure, but absolutely dead.

"May, hey." I knelt next to her, reaching down to smooth her blood-matted hair away from her face. "Honey, I need you to wake up for me now. Things are getting sort of complicated, and we need to leave."

Now that the lights were coming up, I could see more and more of our surroundings, and Raysel's description of the place as formless void was beginning to make sense. The only landmark I could see was the willow tree, which we had landed on through pure dumb luck.

Despite the damage it had done to May, I was grateful for the willow. Quentin could have died if we'd hit the ground without something to break our fall. Even as the thought formed, the willow shimmered, dancing in soap bubble rainbows, and popped just as abruptly, vanishing from the landscape like it had never been there. I blinked.

Quentin stepped up behind me, Spike cradled in his arms. "Did you do that?" he asked, a note of strained terror in his voice.

"I did not, no," I said, as calmly as I could.

"So the spell is continuing to unravel?"

"I don't think so, actually. I think that was a part of the spell." Luna and Raysel had survived in here for *years* without seeing another soul—not even Simon. But they were both ordinary fae, and they could be killed. Something must have kept them alive. "Hold on. I want to check something."

I closed my eyes and bit the inside of my cheek hard enough to draw blood, only wincing a little from the jagged grind of molars against flesh. Then I swallowed, letting the blood light up the space behind my eyes where my magic lived. My head throbbed again, still angry from the earlier shift in my humanity. I did my best to set the pain aside. If May could stay conscious and talking with a branch sticking out of her gut, I could handle a headache.

The spell blossomed back into view, a web of gray-and-orange lines that somehow tasted of rotten oranges. The place where I'd unraveled the branch was a scar in the otherwise relatively even weave, but none of the strands looked torn, and nothing seemed to be unraveling; I'd turned the lights on, but I hadn't broken reality. I didn't think. We'd find out soon enough if we didn't get moving.

This was all surface level. I sank deeper into the spell, treating it like a blood memory, something to be ridden, studied, and learned from. Below the surface, the lines grew tighter, more closely interwoven; if the branch had been down here, it would have been impossible to remove it without shattering the spell itself. That was useful to know—or to assume, anyway. I really had no idea what I was doing.

That's never stopped me before. I bit the inside of my cheek again and used the fresh burst of blood to sink even deeper into the spell. And there, cradled inside the nest of snarls and lines and twisted threads, I found the thing I'd been looking for. It was delicate even when compared to everything around it; I couldn't have touched it without breaking it. So I didn't.

I kept my distance as I studied the sphere, which looked like blown glass or sugar when compared to the threads around it. It had an orange sheen to it, but it smelled faintly of mulled cider and sweet smoke. Simon's uncorrupted magic, the way it had been before Evening granted him power and twisted him to her own ends.

I took a breath and let myself rise up out of the spell. "The bubble is designed to keep the people inside it alive as long as it possibly can," I said. "May, I'm assuming it left the branch you broke in place because pulling it out of a normal person would have killed them. But if we stayed here long enough, it would give us food, water, whatever we needed to survive. The idea is to drive us to despair and suffering, not to starvation. So we got a tree to keep us from splitting our skulls on impact with the ground."

"That's . . ." Quentin paused. "I can't decide whether that's really evil or really sweet."

"Kid, I'm marrying a literal cat. He thinks playing with your food before you kill it is a totally normal thing to do. I think you stab it until it stops moving, you don't prolong its suffering. Maybe don't make me your moral compass."

"Too late," he said simply. "You're my knight."

I rubbed my face with one hand. "Okay, look, my head already hurts. Please do me a favor and don't make it worse."

Quentin beamed.

Now that I was reasonably sure the bubble was stable, even if I'd managed to turn on the lights, I returned my attention to May. "Are you awake, or did you pass out from the shock of not having a liver anymore?"

May cracked open an eye. "Am I not allowed to pass out from shock?"

"You're allowed, but then I'll have to carry you, and you know something's going to try to kill me and I'm going to drop you on your head. Did you want to add a broken neck to all those missing organs?"

"I did not," said May, and pushed herself laboriously into a sitting position, grunting with effort. When she was done, she looked down at the ruin of her stomach, grimaced, and asked, "Do you have any duct tape?"

"Not with me. I wasn't planning to let the Luidaeg do my hair today." The bubble had continued to grow lighter around us, until it was lit almost as well as a downtown 7-11 at three o'clock in the morning. The light had a similar artificial quality, although at least it wasn't flickering like some fluorescents. Look as I might, there were no doors or openings, not even above my eye level.

There was also no ground to speak of. Now that the tree was gone, there was nothing. We had found Raysel's featureless void. If the dark came back, we'd be able to experience exactly what she had for almost fourteen years of her life.

It was enough to make me sick to my stomach. We needed to get out of here. "Right." I turned to pet Spike. "Hey, buddy. I know you can't open a Rose Road on your own, but Luna opened this one using the key I took from Goldengreen, and Maeve may have been paying attention. Can you take us *back* to the Rose Road we were on before?"

Spike rattled its thorns uncertainly.

"Look, I'm asking a lot of you. I get that. But I can't open doors to anywhere, and if I collapse this place to escape it, we could wind up someplace much worse. So it's in everyone's best interests for you to at least try. Can you try for me, buddy? Is that something you can do?"

Spike stood up in Quentin's arms, looking more feline than ever in the moment before it leapt down and trotted away from us. It wasn't heading for the wall or for the horizon; neither of those things existed. It was moving toward *something*. The three of us stayed where we were, Quentin and I on our feet, May on the invisible ground, poking gingerly at the edges of her wounded stomach with one finger.

She's a Fetch and I'm Dóchas Sidhe. We're sisters in every way that counts, but blood doesn't make that list. She has neither my talent with blood magic nor my healing, although she still heals faster than someone who isn't indestructible. It would probably take her months to regrow her missing organs. She *would* regrow them, which put her well ahead of most people.

Spike stopped and looked over its shoulder, chirping an invitation. "Guess the prohibition against looking back doesn't apply here," I said, and turned to offer May my hands. "Come on. The rose goblin says it's time to go."

"I'm not sure I can walk," she said, but pushed off against the ground before reaching for me, clinging to my forearms for leverage as she levered herself to her feet. The motion caused another sheet of blood to fall from her wounds, mostly clotted but dislodged by gravity. Something red and meaty fell out along with it, hitting the ground at our feet with a soft plop. We both looked at it. Quentin spoke first.

"Ew," he said.

"Agreed," said May. She took an experimental step, slow and unsteady. Her legs held her, and she breathed a sigh of relief. "I'm not sure how this is working, and I'm not going to question it too deeply," she said. "As long as I can stand on my own, I'm going to be okay."

"As long as we don't have to run," I said. "We'll get you bandaged up as soon as we have the opportunity." I don't carry much in the way of first aid supplies. With the way I heal, I'd never have time to use them. Not that it would have made much of a difference if I'd been carrying an emergency kit; given the size of her wounds, she could have used all the gauze in an emergency *room* and still gone looking for more.

She leaned heavily on my arm as we moved toward Spike, Quentin following anxiously along behind us, ready to catch her if she fell.

"I'm hurt, not fragile," she snapped, and promptly winced, adding, "I'm sorry. That wasn't fair. You're not the one who hurt me."

"No, Toby's the one who dragged you into a hole in the fabric of the universe," he muttered. When I shot him a sharp look, he shrugged, and said, "It's the truth!"

"Way to have my back, squire," I said.

Spike rattled its thorns impatiently at us. We kept walking, May's blood unpleasantly warm against my hands. Was this how my friends usually felt about me? If so, I had some apologizing to do, because I didn't like it. Not at all.

When we finally reached the place where Spike waited, it rattled its thorns for a final time before leaping into the empty air and disappearing. There was no hole or visible opening; the rose goblin was simply *gone*, winking out of view like it had never been there at all.

"Well, if I tore the spell enough to turn the lights on, it's not so hard to believe that I could also have activated the emergency exit," I said. "Simon must have gotten in and out at least once, and that means he'd need a door to do it."

Still bracing May against my side, I took a big step forward, into the exact spot where Spike had jumped. The white empty space immediately disappeared, like we'd crossed the threshold of some unseen room, and we were back on the Rose Road, surrounded by walls of thorns and flowers, the scent of roses in full bloom spreading everywhere.

This wasn't where we'd left the Road; the roses here were darker, deeper in color, the red trending toward black, and the scent of them was older and wilder, like something that had never seen the inside of a garden. I tried to turn and call to Quentin that it was safe and found myself confronted by an unbroken wall of thorns. He'd have to follow on his own if he was going to follow at all.

Spike trotted a few feet down the Road, then sat and began grooming one of its forepaws, as smug as any cat has ever been since the beginning of the relationship between humans and domesticated felines. Maybe since before that. It's difficult to say.

There was no sound or rip in the air or anything else to herald Quentin's appearance. He was just suddenly staggering out of the air and into the rose-scented warmth of the Rose Road, a startled expression on his face. As I've taught him, intentionally or no, he immediately turned it into anger, rounding on me.

"You *left* me!" he shouted. "You were there and then you weren't there and—and I didn't know where you were, and you *left* me!"

"I left you and you followed," I said. "That was all you had to do. Right now, you have as much information about the situation as we do."

"What *is* the situation?" asked May. She sagged a little but didn't sit down. I guess a butt full of thorns wouldn't have improved her situation any.

"We keep going," I said. "But now we know we're on the right track."

At least I hoped that was what we knew. All I was sure of was that we had to keep going. We were in deep enough that the only way out was through.

NINE

WE WALKED FOR WHAT felt like forever, mostly in silence, except for the occasional yelp or muttered swear when someone discovered an unexpected thorn with a part of their anatomy. May had almost stopped bleeding by this point, thanks to her blood either running out or clotting so much it couldn't escape anymore. I wasn't sure she had enough blood left to allow her heart to beat. It didn't seem to be slowing her down any. She was unsteady, leaning on me or Quentin when she felt like she was going to fall over, but she was otherwise walking just fine. It was weird as hell, and that's coming from me.

The roses continued to darken as we walked, until they were no longer red trending toward black, but were simply black, obsidian roses dancing with captive rainbows, charcoal roses with smoldering hearts, raven-feathered roses whose petals were fringed around the edges. These weren't roses that could ever have grown on mortal soil. They were more akin to the roses Luna cultivated in her walled gardens.

The thought made me pause and move closer to the wall. Quentin looked at me curiously, but kept his hands on May's arm, keeping her from falling over, and didn't ask what I was doing.

"Hi," I said brightly. "Maeve, right? I'm a friend of your daughter's. Antigone, I mean. The eldest. A *good* friend. I helped her bring back the Roane. She's not sad all the time anymore."

Keeping my expression bright and guileless, I reached out and closed my left hand around the stem of the nearest charcoal rose.

It was as hot as its burning flower implied. The thorns scorched my palm even as they pierced it, and it was all I could do not to shriek and jerk away.

Still, I held on. I've gotten to be pretty good at enduring pain. "You may be wondering why we're here," I said. "To be honest, given how fetishistic your sister's eldest daughter is about roses, I'm sort of wondering why *this* is the road where the Luidaeg called on you, but hey, I'm not one of the Three. I'm not even one of the Firstborn. So what do I know?"

Quentin and May stopped walking. Quentin looked at me, face gone pale as milk. It was dangerously close to looking back, and I had to resist the urge to snap at him.

"I know these are your roses, and I know if you're still around, you listen to your daughter, and that means there's a chance you'll listen to *me*. I know you want your sister's eldest daughter to stay asleep as badly as I do, and I know the man I'm trying to find is very invested in waking her up. I know you're the Winter Queen, I know you're supposed to be the cold one, but I think . . . I think we got that wrong at some point. I think when we started turning our history into stories, we forgot who the real monsters were, and we started painting them in places where they'd never been. I don't know this for sure, but I listen to the way your daughter talks about you, and I think . . . I think you're kind. I think you care about what happens to Faerie, and what happens to your kids. I don't know where you are and I don't know why you don't come back to us, but I'm asking you now, can you help? Can you get us where we need to be? Please?"

The stem in my hand grew even hotter, until I could no longer hold onto it. I let go and stepped away, the punctures in my hand already scabbing over. Quentin caught me before I could back into May, and I flashed him a quick, grateful look before returning my attention to the wall of roses.

They were moving.

Like the roses in Luna's greenhouse garden, they were twisting away from us, vines rising up and twining together until they had formed a sort of archway, leading into yet another black hole.

"The last time we jumped in one of those, my Fetch wound up with most of her guts missing," I said politely.

"Hi," said May.

"Is there any way we could get some stairs?" Even for me, asking specifics of a missing Faerie Queen was pushing my luck. I summoned up my most winning smile, the one that reliably made Tybalt go very still and ask what I wanted *this* time. It made my face hurt.

It's not possible for roses to look amused, but these ones came remarkably close. A vine snaked through the air toward me, curling at the last second and stroking my cheek with surprising gentleness, the thorns somehow avoiding my skin. I kept smiling. Let my face hurt. We were sort of in the presence of my step-grandmother, who had been absent from Faerie for more than five hundred years, and the last thing I wanted to do was make her think I was ungrateful.

More vines uncurled and snaked into the darkness, basket-weaving together to form a latticed staircase that would have to be navigated carefully, but *could* be navigated, without any further falling. The vine pulled away from my face, its motion already slowing.

"Wait!" I shouted impulsively. May and Quentin both turned to look at me. I swallowed hard, staying precisely where I was, and focused on the roses. "I just wanted to say, before you go . . . I know you didn't have to help us. I don't know why you're staying away, but I know you didn't have to help us, and we really, really appreciate it."

The vine flicked in my direction, a small, sharp motion, and finished its withdrawal. I shivered, then started toward the opening.

"Are you sure we should go down there?" asked Quentin. He was learning to rush in, and to risk himself for the sake of the quest, but he was still more cautious than I'd ever been. It wasn't a trait I was particularly working to beat out of him. He'd make a better High King with at least a small sense of self-preservation.

"Positive," I said. "The Queen of Faerie opened a door for us. It would be rude not to use it. Big rude. Worse than insulting the Luidaeg rude—and possibly also insulting to the Luidaeg, when she hears about it, since we'll have wasted her mother's time. And also, not, because I'd lay pretty good odds that either Simon or the woman he's been looking for are down there, and I really don't want to see her. Today, or ever again. Sometimes what we want doesn't matter."

"But aren't we doing all this because you want to get married?" asked May, a note of amusement in her voice.

"You're pretty free with the backtalk for someone who's literally gutless right now," I said, approaching the opening.

"Sometimes guts are in the soul," she replied piously.

I almost turned to look at her, but it would have meant looking back and breaking the rules of the Rose Road. With the way we'd been running back and forth and chasing Spike, it was something of a miracle that we hadn't already been kicked off the road for looking back. Instead, I snorted and kept walking, trusting Quentin to guide her onto the stairs.

And they *were* stairs, made of woven rose briars, the thorns tucked down and under, so that when I stepped onto the first tread, nothing jabbed into my foot. It was solid enough to hold my weight without protest. "You're safe to follow," I called, and took another tentative step downward, into the gloom.

It wasn't darkness, exactly, especially not when compared to the infinite dark inside Simon's reality bubble. It was more like a natural, heavy gloaming, when the sun was down and the moon was hidden behind the clouds. I could see better than I expected, something which caused me to blink several times before attributing it to my recently shifted blood. Fae have excellent night vision when compared to humans, which makes sense, given that they're nocturnal by nature. The more fae I've become, the harder it's gotten for me to get out of bed in the morning. That's my story and I'm sticking to it.

At least my head had almost stopped hurting as my body recovered from what I'd involuntarily done to it. It was nice to know that I wasn't going to be punishing myself forever, although I sort of dreaded what was going to rise around me the next time I actually needed to call on my own magic, instead of using the edges of someone else's. When I was a kid, teetering on thin-blooded thanks to what my mother had done to me, it had smelled of fresh cut grass and cleanly polished copper, and that was still the scent I thought of as my own.

The more I trended toward fully fae, the bloodier that copper became. My spells were going to be blood and grass before much longer, and I wasn't sure how I felt about that. Uncomfortable, mostly. Very, very uncomfortable.

The stairs wound downward in a gentle curl, like the twining of a fern frond, surrounded by walls of roses. Still black—some of the light came from the glowing centers of the ones with charcoal petals—and still lovely. Their perfume hung heavy in the air, which was the other problem. My mother's magic is blood and roses. If I had to cast anything here, it would smell like my mother was coming, and that was the last thing we needed.

Quentin and May stepped onto the tread next to me, May's arm slung around Quentin's shoulders so that he could support her. They both looked at me. "Down?" asked Quentin.

"That seems like the best option we've got," I said. "Also, the Luidaeg's mom made this path for us. It would be unthinkably rude not to use it."

He grimaced. "Could you stop saying that?"

"Why? It's true."

"Maybe. Maybe it's not. Either way, it makes me really uncomfortable to think Maeve is still out there—close enough to hear when you call for help—and not coming home. She's supposed to come home."

"I don't know," said May. "Her sister raised her kids to kill as many of Maeve's descendants as possible, her husband refused to rein Titania in even as she was advocating for mass murder, and she wound up pulled into some unknown void or something when Toby's grandmother broke her last Ride. If I were her, I might not want to be any closer to Faerie right now either."

"Let's not remind the nice Faerie Queen who I'm descended from when we're standing on her magical staircase and she might still be listening okay?" I started descending a little faster. "I don't want to take another big fall today."

"At least this time we'd be able to see where we were going to land before we hit the ground," said Quentin, with forced brightness. "That's something, right?"

"I think May lacks structural integrity as it is. We'd wind up carrying her home in two pieces, and I don't know how we'd stick them back together. It's weird enough to be walking around with her while she doesn't have a middle."

"You think that's weird, try not having a middle," said May.

Quentin looked alarmed. "Don't say that to Toby! She might actually try it."

"I wouldn't be able to try it for long." Spike went trotting past us, descending the stairs with a rattle of thorns. "I'd heal too quickly."

"Yeah, yeah, brag about how fast you can grow a liver."

We continued gently teasing each other about May's injuries

and my tendency toward self-destruction as we followed Spike down the stairs. A thick fog began to gather, making it difficult to see more than a few feet in front of ourselves. Still, we kept on going, until I stepped down onto the next tread and realized I was standing on solid ground.

"Guys, I think we found the bottom," I said, and turned to help May and Quentin off the stairs. Wherever we were, we weren't on the Rose Roads anymore.

As soon as we were all clear of the stairway, it pulled away from the ground, rolling itself up like the world's most elaborate rope ladder. It took the smell of roses with it, somehow removing it entirely from the air, until all I could smell was the hot, humid vitality of the primal, fog-draped forest surrounding us.

The fog was thick and white and cool, at odds with the heat of the air around us. It felt like I was standing in someone's description of Florida. Trees appeared through the fog as sketched charcoal lines, dark against the whiteness. Thinner, looping lines told me where the briars were. Nothing visibly moved out there in the gray, and that was a good thing. I'd only been here once before, and then I'd had the Luidaeg to protect me from this place's natural dangers.

Quentin moved closer to me, seeking comfort in the presence of something he knew would stand between him and even a rumor of danger. "Where are we?" he asked, voice barely above a whisper.

"You know how Blind Michael had his skerry?" I asked.

Quentin nodded silently.

"Well, this is like that, only it doesn't belong to Blind Michael. It belongs to your Firstborn."

There was a long pause before he said, in a deeply unhappy tone, *"What."*

Well, that wasn't the reaction I'd expected. I turned to face him. "What's the problem? You knew we were on our way to find Simon, and that might mean finding her. We need to know she's still asleep."

"Yes, but . . . if my Firstborn made this place, she should have made it perfect for the Daoine Sidhe, and this is *not* perfect! This is like something out of one of Chelsea's creepy horror movies, and I don't like it!" He sounded personally offended, like Eira's terrible taste in environments existed purely to spite him.

I couldn't resist. I reached over and ruffled his hair with one hand, something that was a lot easier back when he was shorter than me. "Kiddo, if you think that woman has ever done anything in her life to benefit someone who wasn't herself, I haven't been training you well enough. She's the worst."

"No, your mom's the worst."

"Fair point. Can we agree that they share the title, and get moving?"

"Please," said May. She was leaning against one of the charcoal-sketch trees, a hand pressed to the gaping hole in her belly. "I'm getting tired, and while this isn't going to kill me, I should probably be in a bed by now. Holding very still, while someone spoon-feeds me pear sorbet and potato soup. So if we could get this over with before any more of my organs decide to fall out of the gaping cavity that was my abdominal wall, that would be peachy-keen."

"Right." I closed my eyes, tilted my head back, and sniffed the air.

There wasn't much wind, and I was willing to bet that this deep into Faerie, in a shard realm that was only accessible via one of the old roads and with a helping hand from a missing Queen, there wasn't an ordinary day-night cycle either. That meant magic that would have long since dissolved in the mortal world might still be hanging around for me to find.

All I could smell was the green, mossy loam of a healthy forest. No roses, and no magic apart from the faint scent of cotton candy and ashes that surrounded May as her body fought to keep itself together. I adjusted my stance, bracing my feet to balance myself better, and took a deeper breath, inhaling through my nose until my lungs ached.

And there, on the absolute edge of what I could detect, was the faintest scent of snow.

I let the breath I'd been holding out and pointed in the direction the scent had come from. "She's that way. If she's awake, she's not slinging magic around yet. Let's go."

Quentin hesitated. "Won't she be able to take me over if she *is* awake? Daoine Sidhe can't argue with her."

"If she tries to tell you what to do, I'll punch her in the throat," I said solemnly. "You're my squire. I'm not going to share."

"Trust Toby to punch the unstoppable force of chaos," said May. "You know she'll do it."

"Yeah," said Quentin uncomfortably, and started walking again.

I couldn't blame him for his discomfort. I'd completely forgotten Eira's impact on her descendants in my hurry to reach Simon. It's like that for most of the Firstborn. Amphitrite, the First among the Merrow, triggers either violence or unconsciousness in her descendants. The Selkies always trusted the Luidaeg, no matter how ridiculous the lies she was telling them should have seemed. I don't know what Mom inspires in her descendants—she mostly makes me want to slam doors in her face these days, and while I desperately wanted to please her when I was a child, there's nothing unusual about children wanting to please their parents. That's practically what it means to be a child.

Still, if Eira tried to mess with him, I'd find a way to stop her. She was powerful and awful, sure, but she wasn't omnipotent. Firstborn can be defeated. They can even be destroyed. I've done it before. If this one wanted to test that, I'd be happy to oblige.

The fog didn't thin as we worked our way deeper into the forest, assuming "deeper" was the right word when we'd started in the middle of the place. We could be moving toward the forest's edge. I didn't think we were. The possibility still existed, and we kept moving, dodging the tangled heaps of briars, trying not to run into trees. The farther we walked, the more frequently May had to stop and brace herself against a tree, breathing turning increasingly ragged. I moved toward her, putting a hand on her shoulder.

"Do you need to wait here?" I asked. "Because we can handle the next part without you if we have to."

"You don't know that," she said, panting. "You don't know what the next part *is.* You've gone haring off without a real plan before, and it never ends as bloodlessly as you think it's going to. No. I'm your Fetch. I'm coming with you."

"You're not my Fetch anymore," I corrected. "You're my sister. Sisters are invited, but they're not required."

A small smile twitched at the corners of her mouth. "All sisters?"

"Well, maybe not *all* sisters," I said. "I think August would be something of a liability right now. And that's compared to you, the gutless wonder."

"I still have my metaphorical guts," she protested, swiping at me as she pushed herself away from the tree. I laughed and started walking again. May shuffled along beside me. Guess the tendency to keep pushing myself forward even when there was no point predates my developing the ability to heal from mortal wounds, since she and I split before there was any inkling that I would eventually be able to do that.

I paused occasionally to sniff the air, tasting it for traces of snow, and found plenty. The smell of roses began to mingle with it, weakly at first, but growing steadily stronger. I frowned.

"What is it?" asked Quentin.

"Roses," I said.

"I don't smell any roses."

"No, it's not that. It's . . . everyone's magic has a distinct smell."

"I know," said Quentin.

He did, too: blood magic is what makes that scent easy to pick out and decode. It took me an embarrassingly long time to figure out that not everyone can tell who cast a spell by the way it smells, and that the stronger someone's talent for blood magic is, the more information they'll be able to get from a single sniff. I'd always been told that I was ordinary trending toward weak. Anything I could do couldn't possibly be special.

Or if it was special, my mother was a filthy liar. That had seemed like the impossible answer when I was a kid, so of course it had turned out to be the true one. As a Daoine Sidhe, Quentin could smell magic almost as well as I could, but he didn't have the built-in database of scents that would allow him to recognize even things he'd never encountered before and couldn't possibly know. I rubbed at my face with one hand.

"Everyone's magic has a distinct smell, and it's at least partially influenced by who their parents were," I said. "I wish I'd met Simon and Sylvester's parents, because between the two of them they have two kinds of flower, one fruit, and one elemental scent. It doesn't make sense. Most of the Daoine Sidhe I've known have had something floral about their magic. Simon doesn't. He never did. Do you follow?"

"Like my magic smells like steel and heather," said Quentin. "My mom's smells like fresh-cooled steel and dried hay, and my dad's smells like heather—there's a lot of different kinds of heather—and celandine poppies. So Mom doesn't have a flower, but I got the metal from her."

"Right." Maida Sollys had been born a changeling, with only one fae parent. I was willing to bet that her human parent was somehow where the metal had entered her magic, which was why Quentin could inherit the scent of something that could do him serious harm. "Well, the magic of the woman we're walking towards smells like roses."

"Right," said Quentin, puzzled.

"And so does my mother's. And Acacia's children literally bond to roses so tightly that they can be killed by hurting those roses."

"But they're all descended from Titania, so maybe they got the roses from her," said Quentin. "The Luidaeg's magic doesn't smell like roses."

"Mom isn't a daughter of Titania," I said. "She's all Oberon's. And Amphitrite's magic doesn't smell like roses. But Maeve's does."

"This is fascinating, but could the magical theory class wait until I'm not leaking?" asked May. "I ask because I feel like we could potentially hurry this the fuck up."

"Language," I said, in my primmest tone. "I'm asking important questions about the nature of Faerie here, and we're still walking."

"We swear on the rose and the thorn when something's really important," said Quentin. "Maybe we do that because both Queens had roses in their magic . . . ?"

"It would explain a lot," I said thoughtfully. "But Mom isn't descended from either of the Queens. She's descended from Oberon and a human woman." Janet's name was another one I didn't want to invoke when we were this far off the beaten path. It seemed like a good way to get hurt.

The mingled scents of snow and roses were getting stronger, managing to coexist without becoming contradictory. I rubbed my nose, trying to dull the scent. It didn't help. If anything, it made things worse.

Then we stepped through a break in the trees, and there she was. Eira Rosynhwyr. Evening Winterrose. No matter what we called her, she was beautiful, and she was deadly.

And she was asleep.

She was stretched atop a bier of brambles, their vines looped and tangled together until they were as snarled as a ball of yarn, impossible to pick or pull apart. Their thorns were longer and sharper than any I'd ever seen, some as long as my index finger. All of them pointed outward, away from her, protecting her from any threats that presented themselves. Not that I was sure anything in this mist-shrouded realm was capable of threatening her. Nothing but us, anyway.

She was beautiful as always, with skin as white as snow, hair as black as the roses that led us here, and lips as red as the blood magic she'd passed to her descendants. Some people believe mortal fairy tales were inspired by actual encounters with the fae, and if they're right, we can blame all those endless Snow White re-imaginings on Evening, who started the whole messy monochrome myth. She was wearing a crushed velvet gown only a few shades darker than her lips, with red roses in her hair. She hadn't been wearing that the last time we'd been here. She hadn't been stretched out on a bier, either. I was willing to believe the briars could have arranged themselves that way to make her comfortable, but I didn't believe they were capable of changing her clothes.

"I know you're there," I said, raising my voice as I turned in a slow circle. "You can come out now."

"Why, October, I thought you'd never ask," said Simon, stepping out from behind a nearby tree.

He was holding a short recurve bow in his hands, an arrow already notched and pointed, not toward me or May, but directly at the center of Quentin's chest.

Well, shit.

TEN

SUPERFICIALLY, SIMON TORQUILL LOOKS exactly like his twin brother, Sylvester. Once you take the time to really look at them, they don't look anything alike at all.

Simon carried himself more stiffly, like he remembered and cared about the etiquette lessons Sylvester had abandoned decades ago. His shirt was frayed at the cuffs and collar, and his trousers fit too loosely. He'd clearly lost weight since the last time he'd been able to see a tailor, but as he had a belt, I knew we weren't going to be saved by a well-timed pratfall. There was no softness in his expression. He looked at us like we were vermin, worthy of notice only in that he had to notice us in order to destroy us.

That was wrong. Everything about this was wrong. Sylvester rejecting me was wrong; Simon forgetting how much work he'd done to begin making amends with me was wrong. It was wrong, and I hated it.

"If you'd do me the immense favor of stepping away from my lady, I might see fit to do you the immense favor of not putting an arrow through the brat," he said. "I mixed the elf-shot myself, and the ingredients available in this forest are more potent than the ones to be found in the Summerlands. I'm not entirely sure what they would do to someone of average magical strength. It might be a two-hundred–year slumber, instead of the normal one. Or it might be instant death. Won't it be fun to find out?"

"Whoa, whoa, let's not be hasty here," I said, putting up my hands and backing away from Evening's bier as quickly as I dared.

May did the same, more slowly, due to her injuries. "We're not here to mess with your lady. We're here because we were looking for you, and this is where the Rose Road led us when we asked it to take us to you."

"I can't find Oleander," he said, a brief, pensive look crossing his face. "I went to the apartment I bought for her, but she wasn't there. There was no sign that she'd been there for years. It doesn't make any sense. She always tells me before she goes on a long journey. She says it's to make sure I don't forget her."

"Oleander de Merelands?" asked Quentin. "But she—" He caught the pleading look on my face and the way I was subtly but frantically shaking my head as I tried to signal him to silence. "Um," he said.

Simon narrowed his eyes. "Do you know where she is?" he asked.

May coughed into her hand. The sound was dry and somewhat alarming. "She's with my family now," she said.

Simon swung around to aim his bow at her. "Ah, yes, the little Fetch. Still following our dear October like a lost puppy, I see. Haven't you figured out yet that she doesn't know how to stay dead?"

"If she did, I wouldn't be here," said May. "I thought you wanted her to survive. Isn't that why you pushed her into the water instead of leaving her to choke to death on the air?"

For the barest of seconds, Simon looked confused. Then smug assurance crowded out the expression as the Luidaeg's spell asserted itself, leaving him as malicious as before. "I wanted her to suffer. Turning her into an animal rather than a tree was the best way I could think of to guarantee she'd have time to understand and agonize over what had happened. Changelings are scarce better than beasts to begin with. It was a small enough change to make."

May narrowed her eyes. "That's revisionist history if I've ever heard it. I was there, remember? I remember everything about that day, and you didn't look at us like you wanted us dead. It was scary. It hurt. But you helped us into the water. You saved October's life. I wouldn't be here if she'd died that day, so you saved mine, too. You're a good man, Simon Torquill. Your so-called 'lady' is a monster, like all the Firstborn. You're better than this. Be better than this."

"Shut your mouth," said Simon. He pulled back the string on his bow. Not enough to fire, but enough to make it clear that he was primed to do so. "You have no right to say such things about my lady. She is the heart of my regard."

"What about Mom?" I blurted. Simon swung his attention—and his arrow—around to me. May sagged as the threat of another elf-shot slumber was removed, then tensed as she realized I'd put myself into the line of fire. I had so little human blood left that ordinary elf-shot probably wouldn't kill me, but what Simon had brewed wasn't ordinary elf-shot.

He'd learned to make the stuff at the knee of Eira Rosynhwyr, the woman who'd ensured it would be fatal to anything mortal, and he'd brewed it from ingredients harvested from her land. Not only was it likely to be stronger than normal, but there was no telling how it would interact with my remaining humanity.

"What about your mother?" he asked, a sneer in his voice.

"Mom. You know, Amandine the Liar? Your *wife*."

"Your jests are not amusing ones," he said. "I never married. Amandine chose another. And if I *had* married the woman, one such as you could never call her 'mother,' for no wife of mine would ever have had cause to seek a mortal man's bed and company."

That was interesting. When the Luidaeg had taken August's home away, she'd known who her mother and father *were*. That was part of what had made it a punishment—she was allowed to know she wanted to go home, wanted to go back to her parents, but she couldn't find them, or recognize them when she did. The same spell, applied to Simon, seemed to have stolen most of his memory of who he'd been.

But how could he justify selling himself to Evening if it hadn't been in an effort to find his daughter? It didn't make any sense. "If you never married Amandine and your own daughter never existed, why do you work for *her*?" I gestured toward Evening. "How did she possibly talk you into selling your soul when she didn't have that to hold over you?"

Again, that momentary flash of confusion. The Luidaeg is incredibly powerful, but the spell she'd used to rob August of her way home had been tailored to her, and when the Luidaeg had moved it over to Simon, it had been forced to find a new way to do what it was designed to do. It was struggling. His expression hardened.

"My relationship with my lady is none of your concern," he said. "Only the fact that you have yet to let your filthy mouth pollute her name keeps me from shooting you."

"Okay, cool, we're back to threatening me, but I think you don't *want* to, or you'd have done it already, so let's change directions—why are you here? *How* are you here? We had to petition Maeve to open a path."

"My lady trusts me so profoundly that she granted me a gift of her blood many years ago," he said. "I accessed a Rose Road using blood taken from my shame of a sister-in-law, and once there, it was a simple thing to call a door to lead me to my lady." His face lit up with brief smugness, then fell. "But it seems I mistook how attached this place was to keeping what it claims, and I've been unable to find a way out. Imagine my surprise when I heard your voices through the fog. Really, you should learn to be more subtle."

"I think Toby's allergic to subtle," said Quentin. "It makes her break out in hives or something. There's not another good explanation for why she is the way she is."

"Quiet, you," I said. "We're in mortal danger right now. This isn't the time to be mean to me."

"We're pretty much always in mortal danger. When is the time to be mean to you?"

"How about next Tuesday?"

Simon, who had been glancing back and forth between us through this whole exchange, scowled and pulled his bowstring back a little further. "Both of you, *be quiet*," he snarled. "You're not taking me seriously. I hate it when people don't take me seriously. My lady takes me seriously. She would silence you forever if she were awake."

"Wait a hundred years," I suggested. "You have the time. In the meanwhile, I'd appreciate it if you'd take a trip with us. Not a long one. But it will help clear some things up for you."

Simon blinked. "What?"

"I just need to take you to see the Luidaeg, so we can discuss a tiny little insignificant spell you're currently laboring under. Once that's cleared up, you can come right back here and sit by your lady's side until she wakes up and lays waste to Faerie in Titania's name. Won't that be nice? Just put down the bow and come with us."

Simon narrowed his eyes. "Is *that* why you've come seeking me?

To convince me I should leave my lady undefended? I won't be tricked by my brother's dog, however much he might believe I can be."

"Oh, oak and fucking ash, Simon, will you get *over* yourself?" I snapped. "Sylvester didn't send me. He's barely speaking to me right now, and that's mostly because of you, so if you could cut me a little slack, I'd appreciate it. I know you're a bastard, and right now that's all you can even conceive of being, but you were a good person once, and I hope he's still in there. The man who saved Patrick Lorden's pixies wouldn't shoot me just for talking back."

"Patrick . . . ?" Simon hesitated before doing something I would have considered inconceivable.

He lowered his bow.

"How do you know that name?" he asked.

I blinked. "He and his wife are friends of mine. And my squire is courting his son." I wasn't sure Simon had had enough recent interaction with the human world to have picked up on the concept of "dating," and I didn't want to confuse the matter when we were finally getting through to him. "Dean's a good kid. A lot like his dad, thankfully, since I'm not sure San Francisco is set up for a land-dwelling version of Dianda."

"You're lying," said Simon, sounding more than a little lost. "Patrick Lorden has stopped his dancing."

"What?" asked Quentin, sounding baffled.

"What?" echoed May.

"No, he isn't," I said, a horrible picture starting to form. Simon had been absent, presumably mourning Oleander, when Patrick and Dianda had come to the land courts for the first time in my lifetime. It was Rayseline who'd kidnapped Dean, Peter, and Gillian. Simon hadn't been involved. Evening *had* been, but why would she have felt the need to tell one of her toys what another of them had been tasked to do? Especially after Simon had failed to kill me, his estranged wife's daughter, how could he be trusted to know that the children of his former friend were in danger?

Simon was titled but not landed, and he hadn't been a part of the political structure of the Mists for at least a hundred years, if he'd ever been one before. Evening had been controlling where he went and what he did since August's disappearance, and there had never been any indication that she'd sent him to the Undersea.

How much had he lost in the earthquake? How much had he

allowed her to take away? And how much more had the Luidaeg taken when she took his home out of his chest, leaving his heart an empty hall? He'd known Patrick was alive when we'd walked together through my mother's lands. But Patrick was part of his home, and it would have been far too easy to excise him from memory.

"I swear, Patrick's alive," I said. "If you'll come with me, you can see him for yourself." He owed me, after the stunt he'd pulled at dinner. A little quality time with his former bestie was really the least that he could do.

"You would take me to him?" he asked dubiously. "Me, who is your enemy?"

"I know you're my enemy right now, Simon, but I assure you, I've never been your enemy. Not before today, and not now." I quirked a shadow of a smile. "This is a one-sided rivalry, and I'm not planning to start playing along."

He adjusted the aim of his arrow, keeping it trained firmly on me. That was better than aiming it at Quentin.

"Dude, if you shoot me, no one's going to take you to Patrick," I said. "May and Quentin certainly aren't going to do it. I'm telling you, Patrick and Dianda are alive. They're in Saltmist. They have two sons, and they're happy. Patrick misses you. I think your lady told you a few fibs to make sure your loyalty would remain focused on her and her alone."

His obsession with finding August would have been a useful tool for her to use. His isolation from Amandine would have been a lever. But his attachment to Patrick, a genuinely nice person who wouldn't have approved of the things Simon was being manipulated into doing, would never have been anything but a barrier to complete control.

"Keep my lady from your lips," said Simon, but his aim was wavering. He wanted to know what I was offering to show him. He wanted it more badly than I had ever seen him want anything.

Slowly, I raised my hands, palms up, in the traditional gesture of surrender. "So come with us," I said. "Let me take you to him." And if we happened to make a little pit stop at the Luidaeg's first, well, that was only to be expected, really. It didn't make me his enemy.

"I don't think so," said Simon. "I have a better idea." He relaxed his grip on the bowstring, allowing it to return to neutral without firing the arrow, and dipped his hand into his pocket, pulling out half a dozen rose thorns and scattering them on the ground between us.

I tensed immediately. It's never a good thing when the magic-users start throwing random bits of natural debris around. "What are you—"

That was all I had time to say before thick rose vines erupted from the ground, growing rapidly until they were several inches in diameter. They whipped out and wrapped themselves around the three of us, pinning my arms to my sides without breaking my skin. May and Quentin were similarly cocooned, and I didn't smell blood. Thankfully. Simon was being careful.

He smiled a little as he walked toward me. "I'm sorry," he said. "I couldn't trust you not to attack me, or to tell me truly what I need to know. Words deceive. Only one thing tells the complete and honest truth."

I fought the urge to struggle against the vines. I couldn't break free, and hurting myself wasn't going to make this any easier. "I pinky promise that none of us was planning to attack you!" I protested. "My squire's unarmed, and my Fetch is currently hard at work growing herself a new liver. How's the regeneration going, May?"

"Slow but steady," she said, sounding utterly unconcerned about our current predicament. The break to argue with Simon seemed to have done her some material good; her color was better, and while I couldn't be positive, what I could see of the hole in her abdomen through the vines looked like it had gotten smaller. "Don't worry about me. I don't have the strength to rush you, and I'm not the stabby one. That's October's job."

"I'm not worried about any of you now that you're properly secured," said Simon as he lowered his bow and walked toward me. His steps were slow and deliberate, and it would have been easy to read them as arrogant, but as I watched, I saw them for something else:

Simon was afraid. He was afraid that if he left us with the freedom to move, we'd attack him. He was afraid we were setting him up for some sort of ambush, and it hurt my heart to watch him. He was like this because he'd cared more about saving his daughter than anything else in the world. When things got bad, he'd been unwilling to give up on family.

I didn't know when it had happened, and I didn't entirely understand *how* it had happened, but somewhere along the way, he'd become the Torquill brother I felt safer trusting. That didn't mean I was actually going to do it, especially not when he had me wrapped in rose vines and held immobile, but unlike Sylvester, he had never betrayed me without good reason, and that made all the difference in the world. As Simon approached, I tensed, but forced myself not to start fighting against the vines. If I cut myself on the thorns, I'd heal almost immediately. That was the good part.

Since he didn't believe I was my mother's daughter, the speed with which I healed might convince him I was lying about everything, and that I was actually a Toby-shaped thing trying to trick him.

Given that I had always been reasonably sure he was one of the people responsible for sending a Doppelganger to my doorstep shortly after my escape from the pond, the idea had a certain beautiful irony to it. Not enough to force my hand, but enough to make me smile a little. Everything was silent as he made his way toward me. Even Quentin and May were biting their tongues for once, while Spike huddled against my vine-wrapped ankles.

The rose goblin had an excellent sense for when I was in danger. If this had been Simon trying to trick me, Spike would have been rattling wildly. The fact that he wasn't made me relax still further, until Simon was right in front of me, superficially cocky expression doing nothing to blunt the fear in his eyes.

"Only one thing tells me the truth," he said again, and made a complex gesture with his hand. The vines around me immediately constricted, thorns piercing my skin.

Only my skin. Neither May nor Quentin made a sound. Interesting. He was trying to do as little harm as possible.

It was hard to give him much credit for that under the circumstances. I winced as the thorns ripped into me, ripping holes in my tank top and bringing blood bubbling to the surface of my skin almost everywhere. I coughed, forcing myself not to struggle, and met his eyes as I said, "You don't have long. I heal fast. Drink. See what you need to see, believe me, and let me take you home."

That last word made him wince, as if on some level he knew and understood what he had allowed the Luidaeg to do to him. But he reached into the briars around me with his free hand and grasped my wrist, pulling it through a gap in the thorns and closing his lips around my thumb.

There was a brief jolt of magic in the air, smoke and rotten oranges and a hint of spice, like the mulled cider and sweet smoke scent that was his by right was trying to reassert itself. It was quickly washed away by the scent of blood, and a narrow ribbon of my own cut grass and copper. It did at least still smell somewhat like metal, and not entirely like a slaughterhouse. That was enough to let me relax a little.

Not completely. He was drinking my blood and with it my memories, and there's no way to control what a blood-worker sees when they ride the blood—at least not any way I know of; Eira has demonstrated the skill to edit her blood memories in a way I would have sworn was impossible. For all I know, I could do that also, if someone trained me. But I know that thinking too hard about the things you don't want someone to see can cause them to rise to the surface and become the focus of the memory. So I didn't think about all the complicated reasons I had for reaching out to Simon, or how horrified I was by this assault, or how much I hated Evening. I thought about Patrick instead. Frustrating, glorious Patrick, and his disastrous danger of a wife.

If someone had told me a couple of years ago that a mermaid and a man who thought marrying a mermaid was a good idea would be two of my most trusted allies, I would have laughed in their face. But however mad I was at them, the Lordens were good people. Confusing, sure, and subject to a set of laws that was just different enough from the laws I had to follow that we didn't always align, but good.

I thought about Dean and Peter, and about the pixies in the swamp between my mother's tower and the Luidaeg's back door. I thought about Poppy—and maybe that was my mistake. Poppy was a member of the pixie colony Simon protected on Patrick's behalf when Patrick married Dianda and moved under the sea. She isn't anymore, because she gave up her pixiehood for Simon's sake, to save him. She's Aes Sidhe now, one of only two that I know of in the entire world.

Simon pulled my thumb out of his mouth, blood crusting around his lips, and stared at me, honey-colored eyes gone wide and disbelieving. "Poppy?" he breathed. "You let her hurt herself to save me?"

"She seems happy," I said. "The Luidaeg is teaching her things. I don't know exactly what things, because I'm not the Luidaeg's apprentice, but Poppy's safe and taken care of, and figuring out how to move in the world of larger fae."

Simon shook his head. "You should have stopped her."

I blinked. "Yeah, no, I needed you awake, and she's a big girl. Bigger now than she was then, sure, but either way, she had the right to make her own choices. Wait—does this mean you remember?"

"Remember, no; none of what I saw in your blood is a memory to me, and I don't feel them as memories," he said, before reaching up to wipe his mouth self-consciously with one hand. "But it was a memory to you, and as I know of no method through which you could manipulate your own memory, either you speak truly, or you are the most cunning trap that has ever been set to capture me. If the latter proves true, I would like to know, for my own sake and for the sake of my lady, who has the skill to do such things with blood."

"So you'll come with us, and not threaten to elf-shoot anyone?" I asked, trying to mask my eagerness. We had a cure for elf-shot, but given the strength of what he'd supposedly brewed, I didn't want to test it.

"I suppose I must, if I want to know the truth of the matter," said Simon. He stepped back, expression turning wistful. "Even if your memories lie, I believe you're speaking truly when you tell me Patrick is . . . when you say the man I knew survived the earthquake. Your memory could have been modified and gilded like the proverbial lily. No one could have made a vision of him intimate enough to fool me. Of all the people in this world, I would always know him."

I wanted to ask what else he'd seen, if he knew now what we were and what we had been to one another, if he could see my mother in my face. I didn't. Getting him to come with us was miracle enough for right now, and I didn't want to push us too close to bringing him home.

He snapped his fingers. The vines uncoiled from around all three of us and pulled back into the ground, leaving us free to stand on our own feet. My wounds were already healed. My shirt was still ruined.

"You have my word that this is not some sort of trick to leave your lady unguarded, and since right now, you have my blood," I gestured toward the red streaks on the back of his hand, "you know I'm not lying to you."

"I do," he said. "And I had hoped you wouldn't notice that."

"I've learned to pay really close attention to where my blood is going. Self-preservation," I said. I looked down at my feet. "Spike, can you get us out of here?"

The rose goblin rattled assent and trotted deeper into the forest, presumably to a place where the Rose Road would open. Simon watched it go.

"That is one of Luna's goblins, is it not?" he asked.

"No, it's mine," I said. "But it was hers, before I named it. I didn't realize when I did that rose goblins took names as a claim of ownership." The longer I spent with Spike, the less comfortable that made me. It was intelligent enough to understand me when I spoke to it, making it at least as smart as a mortal dog, and it had access to some reasonably impressive magic tricks. Was it really right for it to be *owned*, by anyone?

But it had chosen me of its own free will, and I had little doubt that if it wanted to go back to Shadowed Hills on a permanent basis, it would. I was just where it wanted to be right now.

Sometimes being where you want to be is the most important thing of all.

May pushed away from her tree, and Quentin fell into step behind me as Simon and I started to walk, following the rose goblin into the gloom, leaving the slumbering form of Eira Rosynhwyr behind.

ELEVEN

CONVENIENTLY ENOUGH, Spike's door back onto the Rose Roads had been tucked away in a grove overrun by roses, their flowers blooming broad and bright and perfuming the air with a scent almost identical to Evening's magic. Simon had paused to pluck one of them and tuck it into the pocket of his shirt, a wistful look on his face. He was still her creature. He might be willing to come with us and hear what we had to say, but he was hers, because he didn't remember how to be anything else, and we couldn't afford to forget that.

The new stretch of Road was carpeted in white-and-yellow roses, their petals ranging from pale cream to a shocking sunset orange so bright it probably glowed in the dark. Their perfume was brighter and fresher than the roses along the last stretch had been, and while it was still cloying, it was oddly easier for me to breathe.

"Did you really ride Dianda down a hill?" asked Simon abruptly. When I nodded, he chuckled, and said, "I would have liked to have seen that. Your memory of the moment is of necessity less impressive than actually watching you ride a shrieking mermaid into the Bay."

"She didn't enjoy it very much, no," I said, trying to keep my tone neutral. He'd taken my blood by force, and I had no way of knowing what all he'd seen in my memory. I needed to be cautious with him. He was still under the Luidaeg's spell, and I didn't fully know what *that* had done, either. He hadn't just lost his way home:

he was still losing it, over and over, forever. If he started to truly believe that I was leading him to safety, he could forget everything that had happened in an instant, turning on us without remorse.

"It had probably been decades since anyone had thought to take such liberties with her," said Simon. "A Duchess of the Undersea is not someone to toy with, especially not one who's been able to hold onto her domain for a full century. That long without being deposed will have shaped the already-fearsome woman I knew into a force to be reckoned with. Anyone with sense would dread her wrath."

"I certainly do," I said, unable to keep the statement from coming out fondly. I was still sort of pissed at her, but Dianda was a menace by any reasonable standard. She was remarkably restrained for an Undersea noble, at least according to everyone I knew who had much to do with the Undersea, and I attributed her good behavior to the influence of her husband, who probably wouldn't have been comfortable with her going around assaulting people all the time, whether it was culturally appropriate or not. They both made concessions when they got married. He moved to the bottom of the sea, where the environment wanted him dead, she stopped punching people quite as much.

"Wise." Simon turned to gaze at the roses as we walked. "Some of what I saw in your blood was . . . confusing. Difficult to believe."

"But it was blood memory, which means it's true."

"Indeed. Blood memory can't be altered, unless it's by someone as powerful as my lady. And you are nowhere near her league." He turned to look behind us, firing an arrow before I had a chance to react. There was a soft sound of impact, followed by the much louder sound of someone crashing to the ground. Quentin yelled in wordless dismay, telling me who Simon's target had been.

I grabbed my knife and had it almost out of the sheath before Simon shoved me away, sending me staggering into the nearest wall of roses. I didn't fall through into the void beyond the Rose Road, which was a good thing. I did get stabbed by several hundred tiny thorns, drawing more blood than seemed possible for a garden verge, which was the opposite of a good thing.

"Simon! What the hell are you doing?" I tried to lunge for him. The thorns snagged in my skin and my clothing—and my hair—refused to let go. The vines had yet to wrap around my arms, but they were still intentionally restraining me.

"What must be done," snarled Simon, grabbing Quentin and yanking my squire back, until he rested against the other man's chest. Quentin had gotten substantially taller over the past few years. He was still shorter than Simon himself, and when Simon produced a second arrow, resting its point against Quentin's cheek, Quentin froze, eyes going wide and cheeks going pale. He strained both against the arm that was locked across his neck, and to pull his face away from the arrow.

"Don't move too much, *Prince Sollys*," said Simon. "You wouldn't want to cut yourself. And as for you, *October*, when you let Amandine modify the memory in your blood, you should have been more careful. She left in some things you probably didn't want me to see. She inserted others you should have known I would never believe. Married to your mother? Foul enough, but to claim I was the one who cast my lady into slumber . . ." He shook his head. "Blasphemy. Vile slander. I could *never*."

Oh, oak and ash. He'd seen himself being the one to elf-shoot Evening. Of course that would seem unbelievable right now. He was too deep in her thrall.

"Simon, please," I said. "Let my squire go. We can still salvage this."

"Let the Crown Prince of the Westlands *go*? When I know there's a cure for elf-shot? When my lady could wake tomorrow, tonight, and not in a century's time? I think not. This child will be the coin that buys me everything I've ever wanted. I'll have my lady and my place back, and she'll help me locate Oleander."

"You know it's not going to happen like that," I said, still struggling against the thorns. They were definitely working their way deeper, fighting to keep me in place. I kept my eyes on Simon. The rose in his pocket had blood on its thorns now, and I was willing to bet it was mine. He'd saved it for the moment when he needed me out of the way. "You said it yourself, we have a cure. If all you can threaten him with is elf-shot, Queen Windermere's army will take you down and wake him after the fact."

"Ah, but that's ordinary elf-shot. As we've already discussed, mine is more powerfully brewed. There's no guarantee your 'cure' would work, or that the target would survive."

"Toby, he shot May," said Quentin miserably.

"I know," I said. "Just hold still. Don't give him an excuse to shoot you." May couldn't be killed. Even Simon's extra-special terror-blend elf-shot wouldn't be enough to take her away from me. I thought. I hoped. Honestly, it was difficult to say. As was so often the case, we were in uncharted waters.

Simon looked at me and smiled. It seemed like a sincere expression, close enough to the man I'd been getting to know that for half a heartbeat, I could almost let myself believe in it. I sagged, ceasing my fight against the thorns.

"The people who sent you to find me did you no favors," he said, voice almost kind. "They should have built you a better set of false memories. Something with no lies too big for me to swallow. But I'm grateful to you all the same. Patrick is alive. I believe that much—no one could have modeled the man so well without proof—and I might never have known that without you." He began walking backward toward the other wall of roses, pulling Quentin with him.

I resumed my struggles, drawing more blood as the thorns worked their way deeper into my flesh. Try as I might, I couldn't break free.

"Simon!" I yelled. "If you do this, I'll hunt you to the ends of the earth! Don't think for a second that I won't!"

He smiled again, and once again, the expression verged on kindness. He was so much the man I'd come to find that it hurt, because he wasn't that man at all. Not right here, and not right now. Right here and right now, he was someone else altogether, and I didn't want to hold this against him after we brought him home, but I knew I was going to.

I knew it as he pulled Quentin up against the roses, and as the roses unfurled, the vines unlinking, the flowers spreading until they had created an opening wide enough for a man to walk through, dragging a half-frozen teenager with him, and I was alone.

The thorns were digging in too deep, and the pain was making it hard to focus. I closed my eyes, inhaling the scent of my own blood, and followed it to the root of the spell Simon had cast on the roses. It was simple sympathetic magic, tying their thorns to the rose he was carrying, and since that rose was somewhere else now, it was even simpler for me to snap the threads binding them together. The strange tension went out of the vines holding me, and I was able to pull myself free, only losing a little more blood in the process.

I spun on my heel and ran for the spot where May had fallen.

She was crumpled in a heap on the leaf-strewn floor of the Rose Road, an arrow sticking out of her shoulder. The bastard. The predictable, enchanted bastard.

With normal people, leaving the arrow in place would have been the right thing to do. May wasn't normal people. May was a Fetch, and more, May was *my* Fetch, meaning the rules for her were different. I gathered her into my arms, lifting her off the ground, and snapped the arrow's shaft off about six inches from her body, gouging my palm in the process. My blood made the remaining arrow slippery and hard to hold as I grasped it, adding splinters to my current list of complaints, and shoved as hard as I could. May didn't react, not even to twitch or gasp. She was under that deep.

The arrowhead emerged from her back. I kept pushing, careful not to let it touch my skin, until enough of the shaft had passed through her body for me to grab it and pull the entire arrow free.

She bled. That was a good sign—it probably meant the elf-shot hadn't killed her after all, since corpses don't bleed—and also a bad thing, since I had no medical supplies. Lowering her to the ground, I grabbed my knife and used it to hack off the bottom of her already-shredded shirt, which had been so horribly damaged by the tree branch that it was destined for the rag bag no matter what I did to it now. It only took a few seconds to come up with a functional cloth bandage.

Of course, it was already soaked with blood, but at least that blood was dry. I wrapped it around her shoulder, packing the wound. The hole in her stomach was almost closed, skin stretched taut and new across an abdomen slightly too concave to contain all the organs it was supposed to hold. Maybe this was a good time for her to take a little nap. It would give her body time to recover from the hell it had been put through since we left.

May would be unconscious until I could get her to Walther, the only alchemist I knew who stood a chance of brewing a version of the elf-shot counteragent strong enough to contend with elf-shot brewed in the presence of Eira Rosynhwyr. I refused to let myself think of her being asleep any longer than that. I no longer had a model for any version of my life that didn't have May in it, the sister I'd never gone looking for, the one I'd never realized I was going to need.

My heart was beating too fast, but my eyes were dry as I gathered her in my arms and stood. She was the same height I was; cradled against my chest like this, she felt much smaller. She had always been my responsibility. I was the reason she existed, in more ways than one.

"Spike, get us out of here," I said wearily. The rose goblin chirped and took off at a run. I followed more slowly, trusting it to wait when it reached whatever exit was going to take us home. We wouldn't be able to access the Rose Roads again without a Blodyn-bryd's help, but I could go to Portland and ask Ceres if I had to. Not that it mattered. Simon wasn't at the other end of the Rose Road anymore. He was loose in the world, ready to wreak havoc on behalf of his sleeping lady, and he had my squire.

More, and maybe more immediately pressing, he knew Patrick Lorden was alive, and there was a chance that in his desperate fumbling for connection, for anything that would make him feel like home was an achievable goal, he'd go looking for his old friend. I needed to warn Patrick and Dianda. This whole fool's errand was their fault, but that didn't mean they deserved to be menaced by a frantic Daoine Sidhe who'd already demonstrated that he wasn't above abduction and assault.

"I really messed this one up, huh, May?" I asked my sleeping Fetch. As expected, she didn't reply, just hung peacefully in my arms. Most of the time, it wasn't upsetting to look at her and see my own face—I'd had plenty of time to come to terms with the fact that she looked like the woman I used to be. Now, with her fully relaxed into slumber and a smear of blood down one cheek, it was unnervingly like I was carrying my own past self toward an unknown future.

But that's what we're all doing every day, isn't it? We carry ourselves forward through time, with no possible way of knowing what's on the other end. We have to keep going, because standing still isn't an option. It never has been. That's where people like my mother and Eira get it wrong: they think if they stomp their feet and hold their breath, they can keep the world from changing. And it doesn't work that way. It never has.

Spike had stopped just up ahead, waiting for me to catch up. It looked at me and rattled its thorns, giving an inquisitive chirp. I hesitated.

"We don't want to go back to Shadowed Hills if we can help it, not with me exiled and everything. I guess we can figure out a way to pick up the car later. Can you put us out in Berkeley? Is that possible?"

Spike looked at me witheringly, like I was a fool for asking, and rattled its thorns again.

"Oh, right, the Berkeley Rose Gardens," I said. I would have slapped my forehead if my arms hadn't been full of May. "All right, put us out there, and I'll carry May to campus."

And hopefully I could cast a decent illusion with May in my arms, and we wouldn't get busted by the local police for being the victims of a clearly violent assault. I don't have the best relationship with the Bay Area police departments—pretty much any of them. Not only am I a private investigator, which means our paths have occasionally crossed in ways that made me look less than squeaky-clean to their trained eyes, but I'm an unsolved disappearance who has never been able to quite account for her fourteen missing years.

Oh, and then there's the little matter of my various arrests for disorderly conduct, and the fact that one of the SFPD's officers vanished without a trace while he was following me around the Bay Area, something he shouldn't have been doing, since *I* hadn't been doing anything wrong. I'd been trying to find Chelsea Ames, who had been teleporting uncontrollably due to her powers being greater than her capacity to control them.

But Officer Thornton hadn't been able to leave well enough alone, and he'd decided I had something to do with Chelsea's disappearance. He'd continued to follow me until his actions had brought him into the crosshairs of Duchess Treasa Riordan, who had been trying to use Chelsea to her own ends. As a consequence, he'd spent more than a year lost in Annwn, one of the deeper, supposedly sealed lands of Faerie.

Human minds aren't designed to handle the stresses of deep Faerie. Human bodies didn't evolve to thrive there. Much as the mortal world slowly damages the fae, between dawn ripping down our magic and iron shredding our bodies and souls, deep Faerie harms humans. I still don't know how he managed to survive for as long as he did.

I'd stumbled over him when I went back to Annwn looking for August, and I'd brought him back to San Francisco. I hadn't been able to give him back his life. He was still a missing person as far as the police were concerned, and any family he had was still mourning him, convinced he'd been swallowed by a world that isn't always friendly toward law enforcement. Which, while technically true, didn't extend to "and now he's in a magically-induced coma in the Luidaeg's spare bedroom, and we have no idea when he's going to wake up, if ever." So if my illusions didn't hold, we were more likely to wind up in a police station than an emergency room.

Not that the emergency room wouldn't be bad enough. May might be healing more slowly than I would have, but she was healing so much faster than any human, as well as missing several essential internal organs. The doctors would have no idea how she was still alive, or why her ears were pointed, or . . .

No. Avoiding the police was our only good option. Spike paused in front of another patch of wall, which twisted and writhed apart into a familiar-looking opening. I took a deep breath, gathering my magic in a bloody haze. It came swift and easy, so thick I could virtually taste it. It tasted more like blood than ever before, coating my tongue and back teeth, and nearly making me gag. I swallowed and closed my eyes, grabbing the rising magic with mental hands, and spinning it around the pair of us like a veil of cotton candy, thin and tenuous and surprisingly sticky.

Making us look human would have been more work than making us disappear entirely, and so I went with what felt like the easier option, draping us in the delicate folds of a hide-and-seek spell before I stepped through the opening.

The world performed a sickening duck and roll, sending my stomach and my equilibrium spinning. I held tight to May, refusing to allow myself to either drop her or fall over.

Eventually, the world calmed down, and my stomach calmed with it. I lifted my head, risking a deep breath of cool night air, and looked around at our new surroundings.

There was no question of whether we'd returned to the mortal world: the streetlights a few yards away from and above me were a clear illustration of where we were, and if that wasn't enough, telephone wires hung above them, heavy and black, blocking out swaths of sky. They wouldn't have seemed so jarring if we hadn't just been wandering around in Faerie, where that sort of thing has yet to take hold.

We were in the rose gardens, as I'd requested, a sort of rustic amphitheater formed of rose beds and twisting pathways, all winding their way down toward a swath of green lawn. Spike's door had let us out about halfway down one of the paths, which meant I would have to carry May all the way back up to street level. I adjusted my grip on her, glanced one more time at the rosebushes all around us, and started walking.

These roses were almost reassuring, because healthy and vibrant as they were, they were roses I *understood*. They had been planted in mortal soil by human hands, and some of them weren't perfect. There were holes in their leaves where the aphids had been at them, and there were bruised edges on their petals. These were roses that would inevitably lose those petals and fade away, returning to the soil.

Sometimes people assume I have a death wish, and in a way, I think they're right: one of the first things I learned in Faerie was that to be a changeling is to be mortal. We burn bright because we don't have a lot of time when compared to the elegant immortals around us. Changelings are mortal, and mortals die. So part of me grew up knowing I didn't have forever, and that part is still with me now, motivating me, driving me forward. It's an essential part of who I am, and on some level, I'm afraid that if I give it up, I won't be October anymore.

I couldn't see May, but I could feel her, heavy in my arms, her hair tacky with half-dried blood. Everything we'd been able to research or deduce about Fetches told me she'd be fine, once she'd had time to recover from her injuries; she wasn't going to die, because that wasn't possible. She might be the only truly immortal being in all of Faerie. And still, I was terrified for her, almost as much as I was for Quentin. The thought that she might somehow slip away made me feel like my skeleton had been replaced with a block of ice, and I knew it couldn't happen.

Was this how Tybalt felt every time he saw me covered with my own blood and trying to yank someone else's armory out of my intestines? If so, it was sort of a miracle that he hadn't held me down and shouted until I agreed to remove my own humanity a long time ago.

Carrying May to the top of the rose garden pathway was as difficult as I'd expected it to be: I didn't drop her, and I only had to stop to rest and reposition her twice before I reached the fence that kept people from wandering into the rose garden when it was closed. Like, say, after dark. I freed one hand to shake the gate and check for weaknesses, then pulled away with a hiss of pain.

Wrought iron. Of course it was wrought iron. The stuff isn't even attractive—it's like the bold type equivalent of a chain-link fence, all bulky and aggressive and unnecessarily prone to rust— but something deep in humanity's genetic makeup remembers that the fae are out there, roaming the night, and that sometimes when we get bored, whole villages can disappear. So they deny we ever existed out loud, and they quietly ornament their homes and gardens with as much iron as they can yank out of the hills. They're still working at keeping us out.

Well, right now, they were doing a much better job of keeping us *in*. I took a step back, trying to see a way out of this. There wasn't an obvious one. The fence ran all the way around the rose garden, the gates were locked, and even if they hadn't been, they were made entirely of iron. I needed a way out of here. I'm pretty good at picking locks—it's a skill I spent a lot of time developing when I was one of Devin's stable of private street rats—but that wasn't going to help if I couldn't touch the bars without burning myself.

Gingerly, I carried May back down to an oak tree that had been planted among the roses on the first tier. It probably wasn't much longer for the garden, having grown and thrived until it cast a wide shadow visibly stunting the rosebushes around it. This wasn't the Berkeley oak tree garden, and its success was going to be what inevitably condemned it to the ax. I settled May in the grass at the base of the tree, careful not to peel her out of the hide-and-seek spell I'd cast. Of the two of us, she was currently the bloodier, and the much less equipped to cope if we attracted the wrong kind of attention.

The spell I'd spun was strong, but not subtle. It refused to split into two pieces. In the end, I peeled it off myself and settled the whole thing over May, letting her disappear from the world. I combed my fingers through my hair as I straightened, pulling it over my ears. From what I could feel of my face, I still looked enough like myself that anyone human who saw me wouldn't jump straight to "call Tolkien, one of his elves got loose," not when "pretty person thinks the laws don't apply to her" was a much shorter leap.

It's funny that I still have trouble thinking of myself as pretty when I look so much like Mom these days. But Mom is beautiful according to any standard you want to use—delicate, refined, built on a scale humanity has never had access to—and if I look like her, I must at least qualify as pretty.

It was an act of will to turn my back on May, especially since I knew that if anything capable of detecting her presence came along, I wouldn't know she was gone until I came back and found my spell not covering anything at all. The fae versions of invisibility all have their issues.

I began making my way deeper into the rose garden, looking for dancing lights where there shouldn't have been any. It took longer than I'd expected, probably because of that wrought iron fence. Eventually, however, I saw specks of light, like a Christmas tree gone feral, buzzing and dancing through the air around a large lavender bush. I angled myself in that direction, relaxing when I confirmed that I'd found one of the local pixie flocks.

"Hi," I said, before I got too close. The pixies froze, some in the act of picking flowers, others hovering in midair. "I'm October Daye, and I need your help."

The pixies remained frozen for a few endless seconds, long enough that I began to worry they would attack me when they finally unfroze. I took a step backward, raising my hands in a defensive position. "Sorry to bother you, I'll find another way to—"

Wings chiming in joyous cacophony, they flung themselves at me and swirled around me in a bright spiral of glittering lights, every color of the rainbow dancing past my eyes. I tensed until I realized they weren't attacking, only rejoicing in the movement and the moment and the wind that lifted them up and the gravity that bore them down. They began to settle on my head and shoulders, wings still chiming, and while I didn't recognize any of them—not the way I recognized the pixies who belonged to Poppy's original flock— they seemed pleased to see me.

That was a nice change.

"Hi, so, my Fetch and I are trying to get to campus," I said. "But it's after dark and the fence is locked, so we can't get out of here. I can't touch the lock long enough to pick it without burning my fingers. Do you have any ideas? I know this is an imposition, but I need your help."

The pixies listened solemnly, tiny faces grave, before they turned to each other and began to argue in their squeaky, high-pitched voices. I couldn't understand a word they were saying. The size difference between us was too great.

The size difference. I stood up straighter, inspiration lighting up my eyes. I probably looked like I was having a stroke, when really I was having an epiphany. "I hate to ask this of you, and I'll owe you, like, an entire Thanksgiving dinner prepared specifically for your flock if it's something you can do, but you're small enough to fit between the bars, and the flock that lives in the swamp beyond my mother's tower used their magic to make me and my traveling companions pixie-sized once, when we stumbled into their territory uninvited. I know it's a big request to make, but if I go get my Fetch, do you think you could make us both temporarily small enough to exit?"

A series of loud, excited chimes followed my request as the pixies conferred among themselves, before a female pixie glowing the bright cherry-red of store-brand NyQuil launched herself off my shoulder and came to hang directly in front of my face, expression grave. She nodded, then raised her hands, palms outward. I took a quick step backward.

"Wait!" The pixie lowered her hands, and ringed a perplexed chime. I smiled unsteadily. "I need to get my Fetch," I said. "I left her by the big oak, and it would take too long for me to walk to her if I were your size."

The pixie chimed an inquisitive note. I started walking back the way I'd come, gesturing for the flock to follow. "Do you know Shade?" I asked. "She's the local Queen of Cats. I bet she can help me find a safe place to lay out a whole Thanksgiving dinner for your flock, without attracting the attention of the mortal authorities."

The pixie chimed again, flying a lazy circle around my head as I walked. I took that as an affirmative. With our current communication barriers in place, it wasn't like I could do much of anything else.

"She isn't a close friend or anything, but she knows who I am, and she knows I have ties to San Francisco's Court of Cats; I think she'd be willing to help me out, if it's for the sake of her local pixies." I had reached the tree where May was sleeping. I reached down and felt around until my fingers hit something they tried to insist was a tree root, despite the fact that it was soft and yielding and tacky with blood. The spell I'd used to hide her was doing its best to keep her hidden, even from me.

That's the thing about magic. We can spin it, shape it, and put it into the world, but once it's there, it's going to do what it was made to do, not what we later decide we wanted. The spells are shaped by intention on the part of the caster. They aren't changed just because we realized we were wrong.

I hooked my fingers into the air and hissed a quick line from one of Shakespeare's sonnets, focusing on how much I wanted the magic to unravel and return to its unshaped form, and let me have May back. There was a pause while the smell of cut grass and bloody copper rose around me, and I almost thought it was going to refuse. Then the spell burst like a soap bubble, taking the magic with it as it wafted back into the world around us, and May was revealed.

As one, the pixies recoiled, their wings ringing a clarion chorus of alarm. I straightened, raising my hands.

"Hey, hey, it's all right! She's alive, she's just been elf-shot. And, you know, wounded."

Looking at May, it wasn't hard to understand why the pixies reacted that way. She looked even worse now than she had before, partially because I'd had a few minutes away from the severity of her injuries. The hole in her stomach was gone, but her clothing and hair were drenched in blood, not all of which had dried. She looked like the result of a one-woman assault on an entire army, and it wasn't clear whether she'd come out on the winning side.

The pixies rang again, more cautiously this time, and the ones nearest to me were watching me uncertainly, like they expected me to reveal myself as a serial killer at any moment. I bent and scooped May's body awkwardly into my arms, hefting the functionally dead weight of her as I straightened back up. Her arms dangled like the victim in a monster movie. I braced myself, fighting to keep us both upright, and breathed in through my nose.

"There's a neat little lass and her name is Mary Mac, make no mistake she's the girl I'm gonna track," I recited, as slowly and sonorously as I could. "Lots of other fellas try to get her on the back, but I'm thinking that they'll have to get up early . . ."

Magic rose, consolidated, and collapsed around me, crashing with such force that it was almost dizzying. My head gave another throb of pain, almost as an afterthought. The magic-burn from shifting my blood too quickly was still with me, but the problem now was that I didn't know how hard to pull when I wanted to cast a simple spell.

It didn't matter in the moment. The magic drifted over both of us, leaving me still holding May in my arms, but leaving her entirely changed. The blood and tattered clothing were gone, as was the limp, boneless sweep of her body, replaced by a girl roughly Gillian's age, her head propped against my shoulder, sleeping.

I'd still have a problem if the police wanted to pick us up for her apparent public drunkenness, or if they wanted me to wake her up for some reason, but Berkeley is a college town. Students get blackout drunk sometimes, and then their friends have to carry them back to their dorms. This was cause and cover story all in one illusion.

I turned my attention back to the pixies. "All right. We should be able to make it to campus now, if I can just get her out of here." I walked toward the fence as I spoke, trying to get this over with faster. We'd wasted enough time already, and the urgency of the situation was starting to weigh on me.

Simon had Quentin. Patrick might be in danger. All of us might be in danger, if Simon was able to remember enough about what was *actually* happening to find someone who'd have access to the elf-shot cure. This felt like a monster of my own creation, even though I knew that much of the blame for our current predicament could be laid firmly at the feet of the Firstborn, who needed to stop prowling around and trying to manipulate us all the damn time.

Knowing something is true doesn't make it feel true. If it did, we'd spend a lot less time pointing fingers at each other.

The pixies looped and swirled around me, wings chiming. I offered them a smile, hoping it would look as sincere as I needed it to. "All right," I said. "I'm ready."

The pixies swooped closer and closer, leaving glittering trails of pixie-sweat in the air behind them, and the ringing of their wings got louder until it sounded less like chimes than it did like the tolling of massive alarm bells, and I kept walking, but I didn't seem to be making any progress, for all that the fence was so close that it seemed to have more than doubled in size, and I—

Oh.

The pixies began landing all around me, and some of them were taller than I was, their bodies glowing bright in the dim Berkeley evening. Many of them were armed, tiny knives and bows that I hadn't been able to see well enough to notice before. I clutched May to my chest and tried to keep smiling.

I had asked for this, after all.

But no one ever accused me of being a genius.

TWELVE

THE NYQUIL-COLORED PIXIE who'd been sitting on my shoulder before gestured toward the fence as she stepped forward. "Our magic can only sustain you at this size for so long," she said. She had a surprisingly pleasant speaking voice, low alto and sweet. It had sounded like the chittering of a chipmunk or some other small mammal when we'd been different sizes.

We miss so much of the world around us. No matter how much attention we think we're paying. We miss so, so much.

"I appreciate this more than I can say," I said, and started toward the fence again. The distance that had only seemed so reasonable before seemed like the length of a football field now. No matter. I could carry May a lot farther than that if that was what I needed to do.

"My flock hasn't had much interaction with you, but we've heard about you," said the pixie, pacing me. "The changeling who thinks our lives are worth saving. You're a story we're happy to repeat. Although some of the things the other flocks say are ridiculous enough to be unbelievable."

"Well, that makes sense. My life can be pretty unbelievable sometimes." I didn't like the looks of one of the pixies who was walking with us, a hulking male with candy-pink wings and the expression of a professional wrestler getting ready to turn heel in order to win the match.

"The Swampland flock says one of their number left them to go with you, and never returned," said the NyQuil pixie. "They say she traded her home and harbor for the service of the sea witch and walks among the bigger people now."

Oh, swell. We were going to rehash this. Just what I always wanted. "Poppy felt she owed a debt to Simon Torquill for saving her flock when she was a child," I said. "So when the magic her flock used to knock us out made him sick, she sold her own magic to the Luidaeg for a cure. She's Aes Sidhe now, and Simon is . . ." I trailed off. How to explain what Simon was, without causing the pixies to rescind their willingness to help? "Simon is fine," I concluded.

The pixie blinked. "So they tell truly?" she asked, tone disbelieving.

"I can't say whether they tell truly about everything, since I don't know everything they've been saying, but the broad strokes are probably true," I said. "Most of the pixies I've known have been essentially honest." It's probably easier to be honest when no one understands what you're saying. Not much benefit to falsehood. But maybe lying was just one of those habits the pixies never picked up.

The pixie gave me a thoughtful look. "You're not as I expected you'd be."

"I hope that's a good thing."

"Everyone says you're a hero. A kingbreaker. Heroes are supposed to demand, not ask. And certainly not offer to pay for what they need."

"Speaking of which, while I can understand you, are there any specific sides you want with your turkey dinner? I'll make sure you get the standards, but I can't predict anything I don't know about."

"Can we have real cranberry sauce?" asked a pale blue pixie. "The kind you make yourself, not the kind that comes out of a can."

"You can, although it won't be the kind I make myself, because I don't know how to make cranberry sauce," I said. We had reached the looming wall of the fence. The lowest bar was slightly below my waist. I'd have to climb over it. "But I can promise homemade cranberry sauce as a part of your payment, absolutely."

I stopped, looking at the fence, and adjusted my grasp on May. The NyQuil-colored pixie followed my gaze, smirked, and snapped her fingers. "Zinnia, get her over the fence," she commanded.

Most of Faerie follows a strict set of rules where names are concerned, doing our absolute best never to name anyone after anyone else, save by inference; I'm October in part because I'm technically a Torquill, and Simon and Sylvester's sister had been a woman named September. Also because my mother's first daughter was August, and I'd been born as part of a foolish attempt to patch the hole August's absence had torn in the world. Pixies don't follow those rules. Their lives are too short, on average; even when you're a glowing, flying, magic-using person the size of a Skipper doll, you're still the size of a Skipper doll, and the world is filled with terrible dangers, many of which can be traced back to fae my usual size. So they name their children after things the same color as their wings, keeping their rosters simple, and they never retire a name. They'd run out.

The scowling pink pixie scowled even more before flinging himself into the air, swooping over, and grabbing me under the armpits, not pausing to ask if I was ready. I squawked, startled by the speed of his movements, but I didn't lose my grip on May, not even as he carried us over the iron crossbar of the fence and set me—none too gently—on my feet at the edge of the sidewalk.

"You may have convinced Rose that you're our friend, but bigs aren't for trusting, never," he said, spinning me to face him. "You'd best not be around here again in a hand of days, asking for more, or it's going to end bad for you. Understand?"

Pixie idiom can be hard to follow—their grasp of grammar is fluid at best—but I've spent enough time around Poppy to have a pretty decent idea of what's being said, usually. "Understand," I said. "I assume Rose is the red pixie who helped convince the rest of you to make us small? Please let her know I appreciate it, and I'll arrange delivery of your promised dinner as soon as I can talk to Shade. Now, if you can just re-big us, we'll get out of your hair, and you can have your evening back."

The pixie—Zinnia—scowled again before leaping into the air and returning to where Rose and the others waited. Rose smiled and clapped her hands, and I abruptly couldn't make out the expression on her face anymore. It was too small, and she was too far away, a diminutive figure standing in the scrubby grass on the other side of the fence.

I glanced around me as I straightened, checking to make sure no one had seen my amazing *Alice in Wonderland* impression. Pixies are protected from mortal eyes by their innate wild magic, which is less controlled than the magic of larger fae, but is older, and keeps them safely hidden. Fae like me or May lost that ability a long time ago. We can be seen.

Fortunately, this time, there was no one else on the sidewalk, and if any of the people living in the nearby houses had security cameras pointed at the street, they would doubtless attribute my sudden appearance to a glitch in their software. Humans are predictable that way. At least we looked like we belonged to their number. I adjusted my grasp on May once again and began plodding toward campus.

Berkeley is not a city built on level ground. Little hills and uneven sidewalks dominate even the most over-priced and gentrified of areas. I had barely gone two blocks before my arms started to ache in earnest, making the rest of my journey feel insurmountable. I took a deep breath, focusing on how worried I was about Quentin, and resumed pressing forward.

By the time the familiar outline of campus loomed ahead of me, my arms felt like they were going to drop off, and there was a deep, throbbing pain in my lower back that spoke to strained muscles and severe overexertion. My body was patching itself back together as quickly as it could, but the injury was ongoing, and would be until I found a place where I could set my sister down. That place was hopefully somewhere up ahead.

Maybe it wasn't fair of me to assume Walther would be at work—he must have had a life outside of being my alchemist on call, and I sort of thought he might have something going on with my honorary niece, Cassandra, who definitely wore shorter shorts and tighter shirts when she knew he was going to be around—but to be fair, in my experience, he was almost always in his office when there wasn't some terrible disaster happening. Also to be fair, the terrible disaster was usually either my fault or happening to me.

Thoughts of terrible disasters past distracted me enough to make it onto campus without tripping over my own feet or allowing May to tumble from my increasingly numb arms, and once I was actually on campus, it was easier to tell myself I only had to take ten more steps and I'd be to the next landmark. Ten more steps and I'd be to the parking garage. Ten more steps and I'd be to the stairs that led to Walther's building. Ten more steps and I'd be at the door. Come on, October. You're not injured enough to be unable to take ten more steps.

Just ten more steps.

By the time I reached the door to the chemistry building, I couldn't feel my arms, my hands were having trouble keeping a proper grip on May's body, and my back was screaming so loudly that it was a miracle no one could hear it. The door suddenly seemed like an insurmountable obstacle. If I put May down, I was never going to be able to pick her up again.

No one else was in sight. Unless there's a football game happening, or a concert at the Bear's Lair, or one of those weird live-action games where people run around pretending to be vampires, the Berkeley campus tends to be fairly deserted at night. I took a deep breath before bending forward, ignoring the screaming in my back as much as I could, and putting May gently down. I propped her against the wall so that it would look like she was sleeping, possibly drunk, but not in any trouble at all, if anyone happened to see her.

Fortunately, the spell making us look human was anchored to us individually, not shared the way the hide-and-seek spell had been. I straightened, brushing my hair away from my apparently rounded ear, and waited for the pain in my back to subside enough that my hands would stop shaking. Muscle pain always takes longer to fade than stab wounds or broken bones, probably because whatever factors control my body's healing don't see it as life-threatening the way they do active bleeding or a snapped femur. If Tybalt and I ever have kids, I'm going to sit them down and teach them every single thing I've managed to piece together about my whacked-out magic. They won't have to learn the way I have, through trial and error and agonies.

As the pain slipped away drop by terrible drop, I straightened further, wiping my hands on my jeans, and tested the door. Locked, of course. The campus was closed, and anyone with a legitimate reason to be in the building would have a key.

Or, in my case, a set of lockpicks. I produced them from the inside pocket of my jacket and got to work. If there were security cameras pointed at this door, we'd have a problem, but that was something for future-Toby to deal with. Present-Toby needed to get inside and see her alchemist, and she didn't care if that created issues for an hour from now. Worrying about the future has never been my strong suit.

The security at UC Berkeley has improved since I was a teenager running around campus and trying to avoid anyone who might ask what I was doing there, but it's still pretty primitive, thanks to the budget allotted by the state for facilities upgrades, which hasn't been increased since before I went into the pond. In less than three minutes, I heard the distinctive click of a lock yielding to the inevitable, and when I tried the door again, it swung open easily. One problem down.

I looked morosely at May as I tucked the lockpicks back into my pocket. So many problems yet to come. My back wasn't howling anymore, but it still ached, telling me that my body wasn't finished dealing with the soft tissue damage, no matter how much I needed it to be. Still, I couldn't leave her out here; illusion making her seem human or not, someone would eventually notice the unconscious woman on the chemistry building steps, and then things would get a lot more complicated.

Moving slowly in anticipation of pain to come, I knelt and scooped her into my arms. Even with my body rebuilding itself as quickly as it knew how, this was getting harder every time. Soon enough, I wouldn't be able to do it anymore without at least an hour to rest.

"Oof, May, we need to talk about how many layers you wear," I said. She couldn't hear me, but it helped me remind myself that she was still my Fetch, my sister, and an integral part of my life.

She dangled in my arms, limp and seemingly lifeless, only the shallow rise and fall of her chest confirming that she was still breathing. I sighed and gathered her closer to me, staggering through the open door and into the darkened hall.

Most campus buildings are either built to be as straightforward and linear as possible, or to challenge students with the Labyrinth of Crete before they can attend the office hours of their favorite professors. Fortunately, the buildings more likely to catch fire or be evacuated due to chemical spills tend to follow the first model. The hallway was long and straight, lined with closed doors leading to empty classrooms. My footsteps echoed dully as I plodded along, heading for the only door with a narrow band of light slipping out from the crack along the frame. Almost there. Ten more feet, and then another ten, and I'd be finished with this part of my problems.

There would be new problems ready and eager to show their faces in no time, and this wasn't the only problem darkening my door, but taking care of it would be a start. It would be a start, and all I had to do was travel ten more feet.

Walther's door was closed when I reached it, and I couldn't bear the thought of putting May down and trying to pick her up one more time. I heal like it's a competition, but all the healing in the world can't keep me from getting tired. I leaned forward until my forehead touched the wood, then used my head to knock three times, not terribly hard. Cracking my skull on top of everything else didn't seem like the smartest idea I'd ever had.

Someone inside the office startled, knocking something over. It smashed when it hit the ground, and a squawk of distinctly feminine dismay followed, along with Walther's voice shouting, "Just a moment!" I straightened, swallowing the powerful urge to smirk. Yes, everything was awful, and I needed to get my squire back, but the rest of the world was as confusing and complicated as it had ever been. Something about remembering that my problems don't actually stop the world can be remarkably comforting.

Seconds ticked by, and the door was wrenched open, revealing Walther Davies, hair mussed, glasses askew, and human disguise firmly in place, making him look like an average, if attractive, college professor in his mid-thirties. It wasn't enough to dull the unnaturally piercing blue of his eyes, which shone through any illusion not designed to render him actually invisible, thanks to his Tylwyth Teg heritage, but it was enough to let him pass for mortal.

He blinked those too-blue eyes in surprise, looking first at me and then at May, before he mustered up the presence of mind to ask, in a querulous tone, "T-Toby? Is that you?"

"It is," I replied, and he relaxed slightly. I guess he'd been asking which of the two people was me and was relieved to know I was the conscious one. That made a certain amount of sense. Unconsciousness is so frequently my fault. "Can we come in?"

"Um . . ." He hesitated long enough to confirm my conviction that he wasn't alone in his office. Finally, he said, "Sure. Cass and I weren't doing anything important."

There was a sound of protest from behind him, but his body blocked the source from view. He managed a strained smile, still hanging off the door with one hand. "So what's going on?"

"Long story," I said, and pushed past him into the office, where my niece was sitting in his desk chair, a sullen expression on her face as she finished doing up the buttons on her shirt. "Hi, Cassie."

"Hey, Aunt Birdie," she said, and squinted at the body in my arms before she asked, "Who hurt Aunt May?"

Cassandra is the eldest daughter of my oldest friend, Stacy Brown, and her husband Mitch. Like many changelings, the pair of them have proven to be substantially more fertile than your average pureblood: they have five children, an unthinkable number when compared to a couple like Sylvester and Luna, who tried to have a child for literal centuries before Raysel came along. Like all her siblings, Cassie's hair started blonde at the crown of her head and darkened along its length, finally turning black for the last few inches. Coupled with the lynx-like tufts at the tips of her ears, it gave her a vaguely feline air that I found ironically amusing, given how much time I spent with Cait Sidhe.

Like Walther, her eyes were blue. Unlike Walther, they were an ordinary, middle-of-the-road shade that wouldn't have seemed out of place in a human face. They were also fixed on May, studying her with a surprising degree of intensity. I blinked, carrying May to the desk and using my elbows to nudge aside a half-empty pizza box before laying her down among the papers and office supplies.

"How did you know it was May?" I asked.

Behind me, Walther closed the office door and walked over to join us.

"The air around her, it's all," Cassie made a frantic gesture with one hand, like she was trying to mime a hailstorm. She stopped after a few seconds, a frustrated expression on her face. "It's agitated."

"Can you see the illusion I cast on her?" Mitch and Stacy have never shown much in the way of magical talents, but it's not that unusual for mixed-blood changelings to display strengths their parents never did, and thanks to Mitch's contribution, Cassie was more fae than her mother. Like Karen, Cassandra could see the future, although she did it by reading the movement of air, not through dreams.

"No." Cassie shook her head. "She looks human. I just know it's May because of the way the air is moving."

"Okay, well, this is fascinating, and I should ask you more

questions about it later, but right now, I need to move." I wove my hands together, pulling the illusions away from myself and May and shaking them off my fingers like cobwebs.

Both Walther and Cassandra gasped when May was revealed. Cass clapped a hand over her mouth, looking revolted. Walther's reaction wasn't as dramatic. He just moved to straighten May's legs and tuck a folder of newspaper clippings under her head as a make-shift pillow.

"What happened?" he asked, voice soft.

"We went looking for Simon, because I can't get married unless I invite him to the wedding, or there's a chance he'll claim insult against my house and try to use that to wake up his patroness," I said. "Karen had a dream and saw me succeeding if I went with only May and Quentin, so we did that. Well, we found the place where he kept Luna and Rayseline, when they were missing. We fell into it, and May got a little bit impaled. She's mostly recovered from that at this point, but that explains most of the blood."

Walther nodded, eyes still on May. "It does. Toby, I don't know if you understand how much blood normal people have, but there's no way she should still be alive, not if her injuries were as severe as this amount of blood loss indicates."

"I do understand how much blood normal people have, since I used to be one, and I nearly bled to death at least once before my body got with the program and started making more as quickly as it does now, and May's a Fetch. She can't die unless the person she's here to be a death omen for dies first."

I could feel both of them looking at me, trying to figure out how serious I was being. Let them wonder. Waking May up was more important.

"We got out of the bubble Simon created, and we managed to track down the man himself," I said. "He was in the sub-realm where his mistress is sleeping. He knows about the elf-shot cure, although he hasn't been able to get his hands on a sample of it, or he would already have tried to wake her. Instead, he grabbed Quentin and elf-shot May so he could make his escape."

Walther visibly relaxed. "Oh, this is elf-shot, not shock? I can fix elf-shot—"

"I don't think it's going to be that easy," I said. When Walther raised his head to blink at me, I said tightly, "This is elf-shot brewed from ingredients grown in the presence of a sleeping Evening Winterrose. It's a lot stronger than anything we've had to deal with here, where everything's a little washed out and further away from Faerie."

"I can take some blood samples, compare them to what I have, and start working from there," said Walther. "You look antsy. Do you need to go somewhere?"

"He has *Quentin*," I said. "He took my squire and he leapt through a hole in the world, and there's no telling what he's going to do in his attempt to ransom Quentin for his mistress' life." It was safe to say Eira's alias here—"Evening Winterrose" was three perfectly ordinary words strung together, there was nothing about it to attract her attention, much less mystically wake her up—but I didn't want to get back into the habit. Caution was still important.

That might be the first time in my life that I'd even thought that sentence, much less meant it. Maturity comes for us all. I flipped open the pizza box I'd shoved aside to put May down.

"Are you done with this?"

"Our date is well and truly ruined now, thanks to the blood-drenched sleeping woman in the middle of the room, so go for it," said Cassandra.

I ignored her sarcasm. "That's really nice of you," I said, and gathered three slices from what remained in the box, stacking them on top of each other. "My car's back in Pleasant Hill, I haven't seen Spike since I got to Berkeley, and I don't want to call Tybalt and tell him everything went to shit as soon as he let me have five minutes to myself. Can I borrow your phone? The Rose Roads drained my battery."

Walther looked at me blankly before slowly nodding and producing a cellphone from the pocket of his jeans. It was larger than mine, with a slippery black screen that came alive when he pressed his thumbprint to the bottom of it.

"Who are you calling?" he asked, offering it over.

"Who do you think?" Summoning the keypad was easy enough. Once that was done, I tapped the keys necessary to spell out the opening line of "Mary Had a Little Lamb," pressed the pound sign, and raised the phone to my ear.

There was a distant ringing sound, like a bell tolling underwater, in submerged canyons no human eyes have ever seen. Its echoes reverberated as if from a million miles away, and I kept the phone where it was, refusing to be dissuaded. The bell stopped ringing, replaced by the sound of glass shattering against rocks, thrown up like so much chaff by a wave like the hand of an angry god. I barely breathed.

There was a click, and then the Luidaeg said, "You haven't called for a while. What's going on?"

"Simon kidnapped Quentin and is planning to use him as leverage to get the elf-shot cure in order to wake your sister up," I said, going for "tell the truth as openly as you can and hope it doesn't get you killed" as a solution to my current predicament.

The Luidaeg inhaled sharply enough that it sounded like chastisement before saying, flatly, "What the hell are you talking about?"

"Simon kidnapped—"

"No, I got that part. What I want to know is why you were in a position where he could do that. Did you go looking for him?"

I said nothing.

"You *did*," she said, accurately interpreting my silence as an answer. "October. Why didn't you call me first?"

"Because Karen saw me succeeding if I went with just May and Quentin, and there were enough prices I didn't want to risk you naming that I thought it was better to do this on my own."

There was a long pause before she said, in a softer voice, "I'm sorry you have to think of me that way."

"Luidaeg, I—"

"I didn't say you were *wrong* to think of me that way, just that I'm sorry you have to. Be glad your sister, spoiled brat that she is, doesn't have the power to curse you for her own amusement. Once a family starts slinging curses and geasa around like party favors, it's all over but the screaming. So Simon has Quentin. Is he going to hurt the kid?"

I hesitated before saying, "I don't think so. He seems to think he can use Quentin as leverage to get the elf-shot cure for his mistress."

The Luidaeg sighed. She knew who I meant as well as anyone could have, and why I was avoiding saying the woman's name as much as possible. "And how did he decide Quentin was leverage?"

"I told him Patrick Lorden was alive. He bled me to confirm it."

She made an indignant noise.

"I didn't think he'd assault me! When you took his sense of

home, you took any chance that he'd remember Patrick hadn't died in the earthquake. He didn't want to believe me, so he took my blood to prove it, and he knew I didn't have the strength to edit my blood memories. He . . . saw things. Things he maybe shouldn't have seen."

The Luidaeg groaned. "So you gave the failure what he wanted most in the world—you gave him proof his friend was still out there to find—and you gave him the identity of our prince in hiding at the same time. Good show, October. Sometimes I wonder how you haven't gotten us *all* killed just yet."

Her words stung all the more because I knew they were true. The Luidaeg can't lie. She can be sarcastic, and she can omit things to force people to fill in the blanks themselves, but she can't tell an outright untruth. It can make conversations a little fraught sometimes, especially since I know that when she says something casually cruel, she means it.

I paused before saying, in a small voice, "Uncool. I'm just trying to fix things."

"What, exactly, were you trying to fix by haring off after Simon Torquill without sufficient backup or, I'm guessing, a solid plan for how you were going to deal with him if you found him? I said I needed you to find him. He still doesn't get his way home back until the terms of August's debt are fulfilled, which means someone *finds my father.*"

I was reminded again that part of why I'd taken off the way I had was to prevent the Luidaeg from ordering me to find her father. No one, hero or not, wants to be ordered to find the missing King of Faerie. I figure someone that infinitely powerful only goes missing because he wants to, and considering what I've seen of his kids, I couldn't blame him. I probably would have done the same thing in his place.

Pinching the bridge of my nose, I said, as patiently as I could manage, "I know that. I also know my debts to you are currently balanced, which means you can't order me to go looking for Oberon, and I have no intention of going back into debt until after my wedding. Tybalt has been waiting for long enough. He's starting to think I've got cold feet."

"Don't you?" She sounded genuinely interested, and the shock of her question was enough to make me pause again. This was a conversation defined by awkward silences, made even more awkward by the fact that Walther and Cassandra were listening in as intently as they could while pretending not to eavesdrop on my private business. Having friends is awesome and great and never complicated at all. Honest.

"Of course not," I sputtered. "I want to marry Tybalt. But Patrick Lorden came to see me, and he made sure I knew Tybalt and I couldn't get married without inviting Simon to the wedding, or we'd give him an opening to claim offense against my household. And Karen had a dream where she saw us on the Rose Roads." Saying it all aloud, in such simple terms, made me feel a little foolish for haring off the way I had. It had seemed like the right thing to do at the time, and May had agreed at least enough to come with me—but May and I shared enough of the same memories that sometimes, we were fundamentally the same person, and that person could be wrong.

Had this whole thing been a huge mistake? Had I put the people I loved in danger for no good reason, and a lot of really, really bad ones? No. The threat of Simon Torquill, a man who believed manners were best when they were weaponized, turning pureblood etiquette against me and using it to push Eira's agenda in the wake of my marriage, was all too real. If listening to Patrick and Karen had been a silly decision on my part, it was because I was surrounded by people who lived and died according to silly decisions. I was just following the crowd.

"Toby, remember, Devin talked to me, because he considered me to be in his debt."

"Weren't you?" According to Devin, he'd prevented the Luidaeg from being burned to death by an angry mob. He'd been a liar and a thief and a cheat for as long as I'd known him, but he'd never been stupid enough to lie about the sea witch. That's the sort of choice that gets you killed.

Of course, so was getting into a fight with Eira Rosynhwyr, and he'd done that, too. It was difficult to say whether one of those things had been responsible for putting the gun in the hands of the young changeling who'd shot him, or if that had been on Devin himself. His habit of playing games with the desperate, emotionally fragile children he surrounded himself with might have worked if he'd truly been the Peter Pan figure he'd pretended to be, but reality is never as easy as an archetype.

The Luidaeg snorted. "Please. I'm Firstborn, remember? He stopped me from being burnt at the stake. Literal stake, literal fire. Burning won't kill one of the Firstborn. It'll make us uncomfortable as all hell for a while—regrowing your skin isn't fun, and I don't recommend you try it any time soon—and we won't be pretty until our bodies finish putting themselves back together, but it won't kill us. Not without some very specific ritual steps, and those of us who are still around have gone to great lengths to make sure those rituals aren't remembered."

I didn't even know the necessary steps for killing one of the Firstborn with fire. Iron and silver, I could do, but then, I've always had an affinity for stabbing things. Even things I probably shouldn't be close enough to stab. "Huh," I said.

"He *did* intervene, and I don't know if you've forgotten this or what, but I was really lonely for a long time." Her voice took on a peevish note toward the end of the sentence; that wasn't something she'd wanted to say. Being under a geas that forces you to tell the truth is even less fun than it sounds. "As long as he believed I was in his debt, he was careful about what he asked me, because he didn't want to accidentally square up our accounts. I think he thought I'd kill him the second he did." The peevishness faded, replaced by amusement. "So he didn't ask me to do anything I didn't want to do, and I got someone to talk to. I would have been furious at you for letting him get himself killed if you hadn't started coming to see me right afterward. You're better company than he ever was, and I like you more. But he told me how easy it was to convince you not to marry your mortal man, even when you'd believed you loved him with all your heart. You should have fought like a wildcat, demanded your freedom, and reminded him he didn't own you anymore. And instead, you just gave in. Why do you think that was?"

"I . . . we're getting away from the point. Which is that Simon knows who Quentin is and why he's important, and he's planning to use him to get his hands on the elf-shot cure. We can't let him wake Evening up!"

"Which is why you went to find him in the first place, so he couldn't use claiming offense as a lever to force you to help him wake her," said the Luidaeg. "I know. I understand."

"You do?"

"I do. I'm going to torment you for days when this is all cleared up, because Tybalt isn't the only one who's noticed your reluctance to let that boy marry you. But I understand. You thought you were protecting your family—you *were* protecting your family—and there's not much that matters more to you than that. Get over here, and we'll figure out what to do next."

"Yeah, about that . . ." I glanced at Walther, who was bent over May with a scalpel in his hand, trying desperately to pretend he wasn't paying attention to anything I was saying. "I'm in Berkeley. At Walther's office. I'm actually using his phone. And my car is back in Pleasant Hill, and I lost Spike somewhere along the way, and I don't want to call Tybalt, since I made him stay home while we went looking for Simon, and he's going to be pissed off that I lost Quentin and let May get elf-shot . . ."

"Can't Walther fly you here?"

"No, he's working on May. The elf-shot Simon used was brewed from plants grown in the sub-realm where your sister's sleeping."

"How did you even *get* there?"

"I asked your mother for help."

There was a clatter as Cassandra dropped the dish she'd been holding for Walther and turned to stare at me. She knew as well as anyone who the Luidaeg's mother was. I waved for her to stay quiet, trying my best to focus on the phone.

In a low, dangerous voice, the Luidaeg said, "You asked my mother?"

"Yes."

"And did she answer you?"

"I think she did. The roses on the Rose Road changed. They got darker and older-looking, and the next opening we found led to exactly where we needed to be. And I smelled something familiar, roses, like the last time you asked her to help us."

"Oh, you smelled roses on the Rose Road? You should be very proud of yourself." Her tone was sarcastic. Her words were, of necessity, sincere.

"I am. But Walther's going to be busy for a while, and I need May awake before I have to tell Jazz she's been elf-shot. I can take BART into the city if you want, but I'd rather not; it would take such a long time."

She sighed heavily. "Hang up."

"What?"

"Hang up. I'll send someone to get you as soon as I can." Her end of the line went dead, and I lowered the phone, staring at it blankly.

Well. Oak and ash, but this was getting complicated.

THIRTEEN

"TOBY, YOU WANT TO TELL us what you meant by 'Simon knows who Quentin is'?" asked Walther, still bent over May. "I ask purely out of curiosity and intellectual interest, and not because I'm afraid you've led a homicidal, mass-murdering monster to my door."

"We don't actually know that Simon killed anyone in Evening's name," I protested. "We know Oleander did, and we know he was sheltering her, but that doesn't mean he held the knife." It was a pale distinction, and I felt bad even uttering it. It still mattered.

If Simon committed a single murder himself, he could be held responsible under Oberon's Law, if anyone could prove he did it—something that's rendered functionally inevitable by blood magic, since only the Firstborn can change what blood remembers. I wasn't happy with the man, but he'd been starting to atone when the Luidaeg's spell had undone all of his progress. I didn't want him to die before I could really get to know him as himself, and not as Evening's puppet.

"Well, he may have committed one entirely on his own," said Walther grimly. I shifted my attention to him, blinking. He looked back at me, stone-faced and serious. "I've never seen elf-shot this strong, and it's interfering with May's ability to breathe. It's a miracle she isn't dead already."

"We don't think she *can* die," I said. "Fetches are indestructible until their targets die, and then they fade away on the spot. Now that we're not tethered to each other the way we were in the beginning, the thing that kills her can't happen."

"I bet she can still suffer brain damage if she's deprived of oxygen for long enough."

I wasn't actually sure of that, but it wasn't something I wanted to gamble with. "Can you make the counteragent?"

"It would be easier if I had an uncontaminated sample of the original elf-shot, but I can do it using what I already have as a base." Walther removed his glasses, setting them to one side as he allowed his human disguise to dissolve into a thin mist and the scent of ice and yarrow. His eyes somehow managed to get even bluer without the illusion to blunt them.

Cassandra sighed. "Date night's over, huh?"

"Date night's over," he confirmed.

"So you're officially dating now?" I asked. "Cass, did you tell your parents?"

She raised an eyebrow. "Did you tell your mother before you started hooking up with the local King of Cats? I'm eighteen. I don't live at home anymore. I don't have to tell them what I'm doing unless I'm planning to drop out of school—and even then, technically, I don't *have* to tell them, I just know it's going to get back to them, and I'd rather control the way they find out something that life-changing. Yeah, we're going out. Officially, or as officially as we can when he's faculty and I'm a student."

"She's not in any of my classes; I have no power over her or influence over her grades," said Walther hurriedly, like he was reassuring me about a whole series of infractions I hadn't even gotten around to imagining yet.

I shook my head. "I don't actually care. It's just weird to think of Cass as old enough to date—and you're like, more than a century old. Isn't she a little on the young side for you?"

"The War of Silences was barely a hundred years ago," he protested. "I was a child when it happened—I would never have been able to escape the Kingdom if I'd been recognized as an adult member of the royal family. The age difference between you and Tybalt is much more extreme."

That was something I hadn't considered in my initial response to the idea of Cassandra dating. I blinked again, then shrugged.

"You're right. It's none of my business, and as long as you're both happy, that's all that matters."

"That, and not telling my mom," said Cassandra.

"Why does that matter so much to you?" asked Walther.

"She's always been weird about the idea of any of us dating," she said. "She saw me holding hands with a Hob changeling I went to high school with once, and she lost it. Like, complete maternal meltdown. Way out of proportion with a little completely innocent hand-holding. I never dated after that. Technically, I'd never dated before that."

I blinked. This was new information, but then, I'd missed most of Cassie's adolescence and childhood, thanks to Simon and Evening. "Never?"

"Never." She shook her head. "Karen and Anthony are old enough to be thinking about it, but they're afraid to even admit when they might have a crush on someone, because Mom gets all weird at them. Were her parents weird about her dating?"

"No, her parents were dead." Stacy had lived with her fae grandparents when we were kids. I never met them, because they didn't like changelings, and didn't want Stacy bringing her filthy friends home with her, and at some point in the intervening years, they had left, moving to a kingdom that didn't harbor reminders of their lost child and unwanted granddaughter.

Something about that story didn't add up. I'd never really stopped to think about it before this, but it had never been my business. If Stacy's grandparents wanted to wall themselves off from the only family they had left, that was their call. But Stacy was thin-blooded. For her to be as weak as she was, her fae parent must have been a changeling. How could two people who hated changelings so much that they refused to meet their grandchild's friends have raised a changeling child?

"Did she date?" pressed Cassie.

"As much as any of us did, I guess. There were a few Hobs in the kitchen who liked to get handsy, and she'd get handsy right back at them, like it was some sort of game." They hadn't lasted long. Melly and Ormond didn't tolerate disrespect from the staff, and the first time one of those boys had made a cheeky comment in Melly's hearing, they'd been off to find another household to serve under. "This is really weird, Cass. I don't know why she'd be like that. Unless your father—"

"He used to ask me why I didn't go to any of the school dances," said Cassandra. "I think he was disappointed that he never got to intimidate any boys on my behalf."

"I am not volunteering to be intimidated," said Walther. "Toby's bad enough without adding your father to the mix."

Cassandra pouted at him briefly. "But you're my boyfriend," she said. "If anyone's going to get intimidated, it should be you."

"And your father is a foot taller than I am and could twist my head off like a bottlecap if he decided it was necessary," said Walther. "By the time I was your age, my sister and I had both gone walking out with a variety of suitors, with the full supervision and understanding of our parents, who wanted to see us happy." His face fell. "They never had the chance."

Cassandra walked over to stand beside him, sliding an arm around his waist and resting her cheek against his upper arm. It was an intimate gesture, and it spoke more than anything else to how close they'd grown. I turned my face away, giving them what privacy I could while waiting for my ride to San Francisco. Walther's early life hadn't been easy. Born into the royal family of the Kingdom of Silences, he'd been old enough before the war to have started his studies in alchemy and etiquette, and to have a fairly decent sense of who he wanted to be when he grew up. On some level, the war had been of personal benefit to him, because it had made that person possible. If not for the Mists invading his family's kingdom, overthrowing their nobility, and installing their own puppet king on the throne, he would have been expected to stay where he was and be the perfect princess he'd been intended to be. The war had freed him.

That didn't mean it had been a good thing. His kingdom, his people, and his family had all suffered under the yoke of King Rhys and the nameless pretender Queen who'd been holding Arden's throne through the whole thing. Yes, he'd been freed to live his own life, and not the life his parents would have mapped out for him, but it had cost more than anyone should have been willing to pay.

Walther shrugged off his momentary melancholy, turning to kiss Cassandra on the forehead before he said, "I can keep May stable while I work on the cure. A sample of the elf-shot Simon used would make this go a lot faster, if you can find it."

"Check," I said. "I'll try to bring you the entire Torquill, if I can."

"Not if he's wearing his evil pants, all right? I just got tenure; I don't want to have to change schools because this one has been overgrown by enchanted roses that put all the students to sleep."

"I don't think he has that kind of power. Not with his patroness out of commission." The thought of him successfully waking Evening was too much for me to contemplate. It couldn't be allowed to happen. No matter what else came out of this, she had to stay gone.

Walther shrugged. "I don't know anymore. I'm just an alchemist. I'm here to mix potions, bandage wounds, and try not to die."

"You're so much more than just an alchemist," I objected, laughing a little.

The laughter died in my throat when a perfect circle of glittering light opened in the air. It smelled like redwood bark and blackberry flowers, and I relaxed almost as quickly as I had tensed. Arden Windermere, Queen in the Mists, stepped through the circle half a breath later, wearing the blue jeans and Borderlands Books sweatshirt that served as her usual "I am not currently on-duty" attire.

Clothing aside, she looked the way I'd always assumed a Queen would look when I was a little girl: she was beautiful, with hair so deep a red that it became almost black, like the hearts of those charcoal roses, missing only the slumbering fire to make the comparison complete. Her eyes were mismatched, one glacial blue and one silver bright as mercury, and her ears were sharply pointed, because she hadn't bothered to don a human disguise before opening a portal between two known, safe locations. She looked at me and frowned.

"So you're the reason I'm playing taxi service tonight?" Arden shook her head. "Why are you all bloody this time?"

"I'm not," I protested. "At least not compared to normal, and none of it's mine. And you're playing taxi service because . . . actually, I don't know why you're playing taxi service. I assumed the Luidaeg would call Etienne and ask him to come get me." When I said it out loud like that, I didn't know why *I* hadn't called Etienne. I'd reached the point of asking the Luidaeg for help, and after that, I'd just trusted her to take care of things.

Maybe that wasn't the best habit to be in, but it was mine, and I was holding onto it.

Arden shifted her attention to Cassandra. "I know you're off-duty until morning, but can you pick up paper towels on your way home? Nette 'accidentally' left them off the shopping list again, and I'm tired of not being able to clean up my own spills."

"Will do," said Cassandra, nodding. She was in service to Arden's Court as chatelaine, meaning she was responsible for the smooth running of the household. It's a position rarely filled outside of large holdings, and Arden's Court barely qualified yet—she'd only taken her father's throne a little over two years ago, and she was taking her time building a household she could trust. Eventually, Cass would be in charge of dozens of servants and courtiers. For the moment, she was handling a skeleton crew, large enough to keep the knowe running and to welcome visiting dignitaries, but not too much more.

It was probably her position under Arden that had freed her to begin seeing Walther, if Stacy was really that opposed to her children dating. It was such an odd thing to try to reconcile with everything I knew about my old friend, but if anyone was likely to know the truth here, it was Cassandra. Parenthood makes us into different people. There were times when all I wanted to do with my own daughter was find a room with no doors or windows that I could lock her inside, to keep her safe from the rest of the world, forever. It ached, how much I loved her, and how little she wanted to do with me.

"Who's Nette?" I asked.

"New housekeeper," said Arden. "She's a Hob, and very good at her job, but she feels like purebloods shouldn't depend on human fripperies, and that as a queen, I'm above wiping up my own spill when I knock over a wineglass. Are you ready to go? I was in the middle of doing absolutely nothing when the Luidaeg called and told me to put pants on. I don't get to do absolutely nothing nearly as often as I used to. I'd like to get back to it."

"I'm ready," I said, and stepped close enough for her to link her arm through mine. She tugged me with her as she stepped back through the circle, and Walther's office was gone, replaced by the familiar confines of the Luidaeg's living room.

Arden wasn't a member of the Luidaeg's inner circle, even if she was apparently sufficiently indebted to the sea witch that the Luidaeg felt comfortable using her as a taxi service. Consequently, the illusions that kept the apartment from looking as nice as it actually was were all back in place. It wasn't lying if the Luidaeg never referenced it aloud.

The air smelled like a marsh at low tide, thick and salty and tinted with decay, until I had to take shallow breaths through my mouth to stop myself from gagging. Illusion or no, the smell was strong enough to make me lose my lunch, and I needed it to stay inside me, since I had no idea when I was going to eat again. Patches of luridly colored mold ate away at the carpet, furnishings, and wallpaper, and maritime trash was strewn in random piles around the floor, sometimes half-submerged in shallow puddles that had collected below the leaks in the roof. A cockroach the length of my palm skittered from a crack in the baseboard up to squirm into the gap between window and wall.

The Luidaeg was nowhere to be seen. But she must have lowered her wards in order for Arden to open a portal inside the apartment. Arden herself was looking around, nose wrinkled, making faint gagging sounds in the back of her throat.

"I'm gonna go," she said. "All I was asked to do was get you here, and I did that, so my debts are discharged for tonight. You'll tell me what this was all about when you're finished, right?" It wasn't a request. Arden isn't my liege, but she takes her duties as Queen in the Mists very seriously, and she likes to know what's going on inside her kingdom.

"Of course," I said, and she was gone, stepping back through another circle in the air, this one providing a glimpse of a plushly appointed suite that looked very different from either the Luidaeg's apartment or Walther's office.

The portal closed. Something rustled behind me. I turned to see the Luidaeg stepping out of the kitchen, drying her hands on a white rag. "It's a little much, huh?" she said, almost apologetically. "Sorry about that. I hadn't been counting on company tonight, and so I threw it up in a hurry when I realized Arden would be coming here. I'll take it down." She snapped her fingers, and all the illusions in the room fell away.

Including my own. A ribbon of cut grass and copper mixed with the oceanic scent of the Luidaeg's magic, dispelled as easily as if it had been one of her own spells. More easily, probably, since her magic was an order of magnitude stronger than my own.

Without the illusions making it look decrepit, the apartment was quite nice, and would have looked perfectly normal occupied by a mortal family or a changeling like myself. The couch against the wall had been reupholstered recently, and the only signs of poor housekeeping were a few small holes in the fabric of the Luidaeg's favorite overstuffed armchair. There were no cockroaches. Since I'd seen her eat them before, that always confused me a little; either there were real roaches that she somehow hid when her illusions were down, or the Luidaeg liked to snack on illusions. Either way, it was considerably easier to breathe with the stench gone.

The Luidaeg herself didn't change. As far as I've been able to determine, she never uses illusions to conceal her face; shapeshifting is enough to let her make any alterations she feels the situation demands. She looked like a girl in her late teens, skin pocked with old acne scars and dusted with freckles, dark, curly hair gathered in twin pigtails and tied off with electrical tape. She was wearing a pair of denim overalls, and no shirt or shoes. She looked perfectly normal. That was the most frightening thing about her.

I sagged at the sight of her, which had long since become comforting. "I need to find Simon before he hurts Quentin," I said.

"We already know he hasn't contacted the Queen," said the Luidaeg. I blinked. She smirked. "What, you think I called Queenie for fun? There were plenty of people who could have given you a ride without involving Kitty. Calling her meant confirming Simon hadn't gone to Muir Woods without starting a panic."

"She could have decided not to tell you," I said.

The Luidaeg snorted. "Not so much. She has to come when I call—choices are for people who don't need to ask me for favors—but she would have argued more, or sounded more upset, if I'd been pulling her away from something important. Simon has yet to make his grand appearance."

"That's good," I said. "That means there's a chance we can catch him before he drags anyone else into this. Unless he jumped straight to looking for Patrick . . ." I trailed off. "Goldengreen. He would have seen that in my memories, too. He could be on his way to the knowe, and Dean won't know he's coming."

"Before you work yourself up again, I need you to take a moment, take a breath, and tell me exactly what happened." The Luidaeg folded her arms. "I know you're worried. I know you have damn good reason to be worried. I also know that I'm better at helping you when I understand what you're asking me to do. Start at the beginning and tell me what happened."

I opened my mouth to yell at her about wasting my time, caught myself, and shut it with a snap. The Luidaeg likes me. I'm probably her favorite living niece. She's also said, repeatedly, that she's going to kill me one day, and the Luidaeg can't lie. Her patience isn't infinite. Pushing my luck could bring "one day" into the present a lot faster than anyone liked.

"Tybalt decided we needed to have a proper date for once," I began, and explained what had happened at Cat in the Rafters, going back to add more detail when prompted, although the Luidaeg stopped blessedly short of asking what we'd actually eaten for dinner. I think I might have screamed.

When I reached the part about Patrick and Dianda approaching our table, she leaned forward, suddenly intent. "And they said they could fix the situation? They said they could make sure Simon was better after this?"

"Not in so many words," I said, casting my mind back to the conversation. It had been a lot of blood loss and panic ago, and the details were already getting fuzzier than I liked. "Dianda said she'd hoped he was going to leave Mom, and Patrick said I had to invite him to the wedding or risk him claiming insult against me, which Tybalt seemed to think was a genuine enough concern that he agreed to let me go." He hadn't been happy about it, but if he'd really wanted to stop me from leaving without him, he could have done it. No question. Having an immortal boyfriend who can walk through the shadows to find me wherever I go would be upsetting and unsettling, if I didn't like it so much.

"Hmm," said the Luidaeg thoughtfully. "I think they may have found a solution."

"What's that?"

"I don't want to say until I know for sure. Guessing is too close to lying sometimes." She shook her head, beginning to pace in the living room in front of me. "So they interrupted your date and you decided to go haring off without any real support, is that correct?"

"No," I said. "Karen called before dinner and told me about her dream, that I'd succeed if I took May and Quentin with me, so that's what I did. You know, my indestructible sister and my squire, whose job it is to go with me when I do things like this. I didn't want to come to you, because Karen had already told me I wouldn't, and I was worried you'd say that if I wanted help finding Simon, I'd have to agree to kill him for you."

The Luidaeg scowled. "You should have thought better of me and worse of her. She's still in training; she can still be wrong. If you'd considered that, we might have been able to avoid some of this mess."

"Maybe," I said. "I don't know one way or the other. So we started out by going to Shadowed Hills, and asking Luna to open us a Rose Road, so that we could get back to where your sister is sleeping."

"Is that when you decided to trade in half your humanity for a nice dinette set?"

I flushed, resisting the urge to tug my hair down over my ears. "Is it that obvious?"

"To everyone? Probably not. But I know you pretty well, and your ears are sharper than they've ever been. Your eyes are whiter around the edges. Your cat's going to notice, too, so if you don't want him to say anything, better put yourself back to the way you were before."

I hadn't even stopped to ask myself whether I could do that. I flexed my fingers, feeling the magic move under the surface of my skin. It would be easy enough; it was a small adjustment on the face of things, more a minor tweak than anything else.

Tybalt had asked so earnestly when I was going to give up my humanity, not because he wanted to change who I was, but because he didn't want me to leave him. It was hard not to respect that. He loved me. I loved him. Couldn't I love him enough to be immortal for his sake? Difficult as I was to kill the way I was, I was pretty sure old age was the one exception to my current invulnerability. I still had a way to leave everyone I loved.

"No," I said, slowly lowering my hands. "I don't think I'm going to do that."

"Ah." The Luidaeg smiled like I had just passed some particularly difficult test in an unexpectedly clever way. "Why did you do this?"

"Sylvester said he'd only let me talk to Luna if I'd talk to

Rayseline first, about whether or not she was ready for them to wake her up," I said. "Every other time I've been able to speak to someone who's asleep or enchanted, it's been because I was changing their blood. There's nothing left in her to change. I guess my magic needed something to grab onto, and it grabbed onto itself."

"That's not a great habit to get into. You're going to run out of humanity sooner or later, and you never know when being able to make yourself more resistant to iron or immune to certain types of spells might be an advantage," she said.

I blinked at her. The idea of humanity as an active advantage had never occurred to me. "Trust me, it's not something I was planning to do on a regular basis. Shifting my blood is painful, and I'm not very good at it, which makes it hard to do things with any sort of precision. And it's not like anyone can teach me how to do better."

"I know Amy won't, but your sister might be able to," said the Luidaeg, as casually as if that wasn't the most ludicrous thing in the world. August and I weren't friends. We were only sisters on a technicality. She certainly wasn't going to teach me how to better control the magic we'd inherited from our mother. The Luidaeg looked at my expression and shook her head. "I know you hate her. Believe me, I have a lot of experience with hating sisters. I don't expect you to be her friend. But she may be the only other person in the world right now who understands how to use the tools you've been given, and that understanding is powerful. It could help you. At some point, one of you is going to need to swallow your pride and figure out how to get through this. So you went to Shadowed Hills, and you burned out half of your remaining humanity in order to talk to Rayseline. What did she say?"

I blinked, almost startled by the sudden shift back to the original topic. "Um. She's willing to wake up, if I'm willing to testify for her. I think they're finally going to give her the cure. Luna came in. She opened a Rose Road for us, and she banished me from Shadowed Hills. I'm not welcome in my own liege's halls until she changes her mind, and I don't think she's going to. From there, we followed Spike into the roses. He found an opening, and we went through it, and we fell, all the way to the ground in a pitch-black little bubble-realm. The one where Simon had kept Luna and Raysel. He'd anchored it to the Rose Roads."

"The failure was always good at borrowing and bending magic, when he had access to the blood that held it, and he had Luna," said the Luidaeg grimly. "Go on."

"I broke the realm enough that we were able to get out of it, and then I . . . I called on your mother, and she answered. Luidaeg, Maeve answered *me*." I stared at her in brief and burning awe. Now that I wasn't actually in the moment, the importance of it was settling across my shoulders like a heavy shawl, weighing me down. "She was listening, and she helped us."

"Mom always listened to travelers. She said her sister wouldn't do it, and her husband could only hear the ones who belonged to him, so it fell on her," said the Luidaeg. "No one ever said the Three were dead—or, sorry, no one who would know what the hell they were talking about ever said they were dead. I'm sure someone, somewhere, said it at least once."

I frowned. "If you're sure, how is that not lying?"

"I walked it back before it could hurt me, and I didn't intend to lie when it came out of my mouth, and I'm not the topic right now—you are, and where Simon may have taken Quentin. I want that kid back as badly as you do. I don't have so many friends that I can afford to act like any of them are expendable."

Her words hit home, and I winced. This was taking too much time. It didn't matter if every piece of it had been absolutely essential, time was the one thing we couldn't beg, barter, or buy more of, and every minute we wasted trying to decide what to do was another minute that Simon had to do whatever he wanted, unchallenged and unopposed. I swallowed, mouth suddenly dry, and said, "We were back on the Rose Roads, thanks to Spike, and we kept walking until I realized the roses didn't look or smell the same anymore. That was when I called on your mother, and she answered me, and we found our way into the shard realm where your sister is sleeping. It was still a forest, like it had been before, and still too warm to be comfortable, but everything was shrouded in this weird thick mist that wasn't there when I went with you."

"She's always done that when she slept," said the Luidaeg. "She's not the only one of us, either. You know how the King is the land in the Summerlands? Well, it's worse for a Firstborn in their own realm. When Cailleach Skerry was mine to call my own, it would flood and surrender itself to the sea every time I slept. After my children died, the waters failed to recede, and it was lost. I wonder if it's going to come back now that the Roane are home again. As long as the mist remains thick and unchanging, my sister is safely unconscious."

"I'm surprised it wasn't cold. She's a winter-thing, isn't she?"

The Luidaeg hesitated, and then said, "That's a very human way of looking at the seasons. Remember that Titania was the Summer Queen. She's a creature of feast and harvest, growth and plenty . . . and decay and destruction. The summer isn't only about good things. Humans just think of it that way because they fear the cold. Roses don't bloom as well in winter. Apples don't ripen. My sister was always a summer creature."

"Well, then she's living up to her origins. She's asleep, and Simon was there when we arrived. I know neither Luna nor Ceres would have voluntarily opened him a Rose Road, so he must still have some of Luna's blood to work with. He had a bow and arrow and elf-shot he'd brewed himself from the herbs and simples growing near the bier. He said it was powerful stuff. Walther's confirmed it. May was already injured, and I didn't want Quentin getting hurt, so we tried to talk to him like rational people."

"That's where you made your biggest mistake," said the Luidaeg. "Simon's way home has always been an external one. He's a kind man, and he can be a good man when the situation allows for it, but he's never been a generous man. His essential selfishness shines through unless he cares. Without knowing who you are to him, he won't care about you."

"Luidaeg, he didn't even remember being married to Mom," I said. "Everyone says they were together for literally centuries. How could one spell make him forget that much of his life?"

"Not forget," said the Luidaeg. "Revise. It remade his memory to give him the life he would have had if he'd never found his way home in the first place. He'd always been at risk of losing it. His relationship with his brother was never as strong as it was with his sister; Sylvester cared more, in those days, about being seen as a pureblood scion on a noble line, and claimed Glynis Torquill as his mother, forcing Simon to do the same. Simon never fully forgave him."

I frowned. "Why not?"

"Because Celaeno Torquill was the woman who carried the boys beneath her heart for nine long months, and it was her body that bore them, and her hands that held them to her breast. Sylvester couldn't forgive her for the crime of being mortal, and Simon couldn't forgive his brother for the sin of refusing to be known as changeling-born."

"I . . . wait." I knew surnames had come from the human world, not out of Faerie; even this many centuries removed from our King and Queens, there hadn't been so many of us that we needed to track our family lineages that carefully. Quentin was a Sollys because his mother had been born a changeling. I had just assumed the Torquills had a mortal ancestor further back along their family tree, someone long forgotten, their mortality purged by a hope chest in the days when such things were more common, and less likely to be dismissed as little more than legend.

The Luidaeg nodded. "The Torquill brothers were born as changeling as you were. Their parents took the mortality out of them while they were too young to remember, and Amy's first great act of blood magic was noticing its absence while they all played in the garden, and no one who was there could ever say whether she'd understood what she was asking, or what she might be capable of doing. That was when we realized she would have to be hidden. If Faerie knew a living hope chest walked among us . . ."

Sometimes it was hard to learn new things about my mother. They always left me wishing she'd been a better person, because she'd been through so much when she was younger that made me wish I could go to her now, and hold her, and tell her she had value beyond what she could do for other people. Unfortunately, the damage ran too deep, and there were no reassurances I could offer that she'd be able to hear.

I stood and stared at the Luidaeg in silent shock as she continued, "Your mother's love was never good for him, but it was the best thing he'd ever found for himself, and he anchored himself by it for so long that as long as he remembered her, he could never be entirely lost. Almost, yes, but not all the way. So the spell took that from him, and with it, took August, and anything else he might hold onto."

"Your magic can be cruel, Luidaeg," I said, not quite admonishing, not quite forgiving. "He wasn't attacking us, and I thought maybe if I could convince him he was doing this for Patrick—he still remembered Patrick—he'd be able to come back here with me, and give me permission to get married, and then go back to waiting for his patroness to wake up until the heavens fell down."

"An exciting plan," said the Luidaeg. "How were you planning to convince him?"

"He thought Patrick was dead." I still wasn't sure he'd known Patrick wasn't before the Luidaeg cast her spell. It was precisely the kind of casual cruelty both Evening and the false queen thrived on. "I promised him that Patrick wasn't, and thought that might be enough. It wasn't. He wrapped me in rose briars and stole a taste of my blood to convince himself that I was telling the truth. But he saw himself stabbing your sister with the elf-shot arrow, and decided we'd been able to manipulate my blood memories somehow."

"Is that all?"

"He also saw Quentin's true identity, which is why he seized him. He said he was going to use Quentin as a bargaining chip to get access to the elf-shot cure." My phone, tucked in the pocket of my jacket and with my battery recharged, remained stubbornly silent. Arden would have called me if Simon had reappeared with my squire in tow . . . wouldn't she have?

I was starting to second-guess absolutely everything I thought I knew. This night had been dizzying and convoluted, and it wasn't over yet. "He'll also have seen you helping to wake Dianda at the conclave," said the Luidaeg. "He knows Patrick is alive, and that the Undersea has access to the cure."

"Meaning?" I asked.

"Meaning he'll have gone for both his goals at the same time. He was always a man who valued efficiency. Poppy!" She cupped her hands around her mouth as she shouted, amplifying the sound. Even that couldn't account for how loud she suddenly was. She didn't have the physical stature to yell that loudly.

There was a distant clatter, too deep into the apartment to make sense with the apparent floor plan, and then a much more ordinary voice yelled back, "Doing the things as you told me wanted to be doing, aren't I? Should I be all for giving up now?"

"I have her sifting lentils out of fireplace ashes, for practice," confessed the Luidaeg, before she yelled, "Stop for the moment, and come out here. I need to talk to you."

I somehow managed to resist the urge to put my hand over my

face. "Luidaeg, we don't have *time* for this," I said. "You already made me explain everything, and that wasn't fast. We need to be getting to Goldengreen before Simon shows up there and does something to Dean."

"Oh, Simon's already there," she said, waving my concerns away.

"*What?*" Attempting to throttle the sea witch wouldn't end well for me. In that moment, I was still deeply tempted. I stared at her instead, opening and closing my mouth without another sound.

"Stop making that face, you look like a koi," she said. "Patrick's son holds Goldengreen, which used to belong to my sister, may she never tread those halls again. Simon's going to see that as an affront to his lady's honor *and* a way to get to his lost friend, all at the same time. Simon's at Goldengreen. And since he was there when most of the wards were set, he's inside by now. Haring off half-cocked isn't going to make it easier for us to win this. It's just going to make things worse. Like you did when you decided to go looking for the failure on your own."

"I wasn't—"

"Your Fetch, who only has your memories up to the point of her creation, when, might I note, you weren't a hero yet, and didn't know your ass from an answer, and your half-trained squire, don't count. They're friends and companions. They're not backup, and if your kitty-cat wasn't so worried about you calling off the engagement if he so much as sneezes, there's no way he would have agreed to you walking away with just the pair of them for protection. It doesn't work. So we do things my way."

I glared at her and was still glaring as Poppy came bounding down the hallway, ash on her hands and smudged on her cheeks. She looked like an orange-haired Daoine Sidhe, apart from her wings, which were long and thin and patterned in a dozen shades of sunrise orange, like the world's biggest and most ridiculous piece of wearable stained glass. She was wearing jeans and a loose tunic that had clearly seen better days, and she beamed at the sight of me.

"October!" she exclaimed. "I knew we had company, and suspected as it might be you, what with the good officer stirring in his sleep—he likes you better than he likes much of anyone else, because when you come to see us, he almost wakes up, and he doesn't do that when you're gone. But I had ashes to tend."

"How's it coming?" asked the Luidaeg.

Poppy held out her hands, opening them to show sooty palms full of lentils. The Luidaeg nodded.

"Good," she said. "You can get back to work. October and I are going to Goldengreen."

"Am I for coming?"

"No," said the Luidaeg. "I want you to stay here. If anyone tries to get in before I come back, seal the door. No matter who they are. No one in and no one out, do you understand?"

Poppy hesitated, worrying the corner of her mouth between her teeth before nodding solemnly.

"Good," said the Luidaeg. She gestured for me to follow as she turned to walk away from her apprentice. "You, come on. We're taking a shortcut."

"If you have all these shortcuts, why did you need to send Arden to pick me up?" I asked, following her across the living room.

"I wanted to. Sometimes she needs to remember who she belongs to, and this seemed like a good way for both of us to get what we want." She stopped at the only door on this side of the room, yanking it open to reveal a closet cluttered with cleaning supplies and stained towels. She scowled. "Wrong door." She slammed it and pulled it open again, this time revealing a stretch of beach beneath a Summerlands sky. The stars were so close and clear that it felt like I could reach up and touch them.

"Out we go," she said, planting a hand in the small of my back and shoving me through. The world spun uncomfortably, but I didn't lose my balance or what little remained of my lunch. Whether this was a door she used with reasonable frequency or I was just that much more fae, I couldn't tell. Either way, the sand was soft beneath my feet, and I stumbled before getting my balance back and turning to glare at her.

"Not cool," I said.

"Sort of cool," she replied, and stepped out the door after me. Her clothing changed as she crossed over, going from overalls to a long blue gown that appeared to have been sliced out of the night sky itself, even down to the little flecks of silver glistening on the skirt and bodice. She pulled the door closed behind herself.

It was set into a crumbling stone wall that looked like something out of a Scottish castle. I had never seen it before, and I like to think I know most of the landmarks in and around the fae side of

San Francisco. I lifted an eyebrow. She glanced over her shoulder at the wall, then waved her hand. The door disappeared. She looked back at me.

"Better?"

"Not really." I waved a hand vaguely at the wall, which hadn't disappeared. "I've never seen that before, and I thought I knew all the local Summerlands beaches."

"Ah. This one's isn't local. This one's mine."

California doesn't allow private ownership of actual beaches. The Summerlands overlay California, but they're not subject to mortal laws. The Luidaeg began walking, her dress frothing around her ankles like kicked-up water. It was a beautiful effect and would have been lovelier if it hadn't been so unsettling. It was getting harder to ignore how much it looked like she'd stolen a strip out of the sky.

Fae, especially the more powerful purebloods, love forcing random pieces of nature to behave like couture. Gowns made of living butterflies, or feathers, or strips torn out of the wind, aren't uncommon. But convincing the sky to stay that dark and wrap itself around her so tightly, without turning clear or wisping away, was a display of casual power more blatant than she normally bothered with. She was the Luidaeg, the sea witch, immortal and unstoppable.

And if she was showing off, even to this degree, she was afraid. I didn't like that. Anything that worries the Luidaeg is something lesser fae should stay far, far away from. I hurried to pace her. The ocean beside us was perfectly calm, a flat sheet of black glass stretching all the way to the unseen line of the horizon. The conflicting light from the half-dozen moons overhead glittered and danced across its surface, painting it with rainbows, beautiful and cold.

"Do you think he's going to wake her up?" I asked.

She glanced at me, and her eyes were glass-green, devoid of the darkness that sometimes lingered there. "I think he's going to get a nasty surprise if he does, since he's the reason she's asleep, and *she* has no prohibitions against killing her mother's descendants. Or my mother's descendants. She can murder with impunity because who's left to stop her? Only me, and I'm bound too tightly to raise a hand in anyone's defense."

Something we'd learned all too well when Evening had literally

killed her, leaving her body discarded on the floor of her apartment. I had arrived before the night-haunts, and it says something about my life that my first response had been to bring her
back from the dead. It says something else about my life that it
hadn't been the first time I'd done something like that—although
it had been the first, and so far only, time with one of the Firstborn, and it had exhausted me in ways I hadn't had the words for.
One of the first things she'd said upon waking up was that she
hadn't been dead for long enough: her geas still bound her. Meaning if Simon *did* wake Evening, the Luidaeg wouldn't be able to
fight her.

Meaning also that she couldn't help me against Simon himself.
The only way she could hurt a child of Titania was if they know-
ingly and willingly entered into a bargain with her. Once that was
done, the rules changed, at least for the duration of their exchange.
So while removing Simon's way home had absolutely hurt him—
and was still hurting him according to any reasonable means of
measure—it hadn't violated her geas.

My mother is a nightmare and my sister isn't much better, but
whenever I have to think too hard about the family politics among
the Luidaeg and her siblings, I'm very, very glad my family is the
way it is. Sure, it would be better to have a mother who didn't lie
to me and kidnap my fiancé when she wanted things, and a sister
who didn't think I was vermin for being part-human, but given the
choice between them and Evening, I'm happy to stick with what I
have.

The beach continued in a straight line for what seemed like forever, silvery sand glistening in the moonlight. Ahead of us, I saw
what looked like a palace made of delicately interwoven seashells
rising out of the surf and towering over the cliff that provided it
with partial support. The shape of it wasn't familiar from this
angle, but its planes and faces gleamed with pearlescent light, pale
pink and impossibly iridescent. I had never seen it before. I knew
it all the same.

"Goldengreen?" I asked, glancing to the Luidaeg for confirmation.

She nodded. "My sister wanted her privacy, so she drove its
foundations deep into a place I had already gone to great lengths
to hide. From everyone but *her*, of course, since there's no true

privacy between sisters." The loathing in her voice was palpable. "Technically, Goldengreen is built on my own claimed, unceded land."

"You never told me that."

"It never came up."

Her simple dismissal stung. I'd been the custodian of Goldengreen for long enough that I should have known if I was risking offending the Luidaeg by performing my duties. "Is there any way to move it, now that it doesn't belong to her anymore?"

"Not without destroying and rebuilding the knowe, and I never got the impression you wanted to do that." We were getting closer, the walls of Goldengreen rising above our heads. As was often the case in the Summerlands, the distance we were walking and the distance we'd actually traveled didn't quite add up. No one really knows how big the Summerlands are, but while locations on that side of reality will roughly correspond with locations in the human world, they're not quite built on the same scale.

"No," I said quietly. "No, I don't want to do that. I wouldn't want to do that, even if Goldengreen still belonged to me. It's not the knowe's fault that it was built by a bad person." None of us can be blamed for who our parents were. And if the knowe was truly as alive as I had always believed them to be, Evening was its mother. Talk about fruit of the poisoned tree.

Instead of heading for the cliff or a previously unknown exterior staircase, as I had expected, the Luidaeg led me around the wall of the knowe, to the place where the cliff wall extended out over the water and formed a gentle slope. "This is the part you're not going to like," she said.

"As opposed to all these other parts that I've absolutely adored?"

"If we don't want to climb half a mile of cliff face—and we don't, these walls weren't designed to provide easy handholds, and falling is just going to slow us down even more—then we need to go in through the cove."

Her meaning hit me like a hammer. I took an involuntary step backward, eyes going wide. "What? No! There has to be another way in!"

"Not one that will get us there with any speed, and I thought you wanted to save the kid." She raised one hand, studying her fingernails. "You planning to tell me I'm wrong?"

"That's not fair."

"Who the fuck told you Faerie was fair? You should deck them the first time you have the opportunity because they didn't do you any favors with that one." She lowered her hand. "That mean you're good to go for a little swim with me?"

I hate water. I've managed to get past most of my issues—I let people in now, I try not to charge into danger without consideration for the people around me who care and would be hurt if I went and got myself killed—but I still hate water. Even the thought of submerging myself can bring back full-body flashbacks to the moment when my gills opened and my lungs stopped working and the land rejected me for what felt like it was going to be the rest of my life. I don't remember much of the fourteen years I spent swimming in the Japanese Tea Gardens. Fish don't have the best sense of time. I remember enough to know that there's a reason I wake up sometimes in a cold sweat, with a heart that's beating too fast to let me go back to sleep, and why I can't take baths anymore. The water is death.

And the sea witch was looking at me with barely disguised impatience, waiting for me to get over myself. I swallowed hard and asked, "Do I have to turn into anything?"

"I know you think I can do whatever I want, but those potions I mix up aren't just for show; the accessories matter when I'm doing big magic and want it to last more than a few minutes. All I could turn you into without proper preparation is something simple, and I don't think either of us wants that."

A fish. She was saying she could turn me into a fish without access to her tools, and she was right: there wasn't much in the world that I wanted less than I wanted that. Quentin being hurt badly enough that we couldn't save him made the list. I closed my eyes, trying to focus on my breathing, and keep myself from losing control of my nerves. "All right, then," I said. "Do it."

There was a pause. When she spoke again, there was a hitch in her voice. "October . . . Toby . . . you do understand what you're asking me to do, don't you? It's a small enough thing that we don't have to make a bargain for me to do it, but it's still going to be—"

"We have to get under that wall, and I can't swim well enough to make it," I said, cutting her off, not opening my eyes. "Whatever you're going to do, do it now. Before I come back to my senses." I paused before adding, in a very small voice, "Please."

"If you insist," said the Luidaeg. She clapped her hands, and the smell of the sea, which had already been all around us, rose and grew until it was overwhelming. Until I was choking on it.

Until I couldn't breathe.

FOURTEEN

"**Y**OU AREN'T THE TRAITOR'S GRANDCHILD; that baby died in your grandmother's womb, an unexpected victim of a night that had been coming from the beginning but should still never have happened." The Luidaeg's voice was low and earnest; the voice of a woman who was taking advantage of some sort of loophole in the world to say things she otherwise couldn't. I kept my eyes closed, tensed against the transformation I knew was coming. "No human child could survive being exposed to that much transformation magic, and while your grandmother wasn't the one changed, her lover the traitor was, and the baby was too close to the spells my mother was using in her own defense. I don't think she meant to kill the bairn. She was never cruel to children. But she was fighting for her own life, and it was a mortal babe, and they were so common and died so often in those days, and so I don't think she ever paused to ask herself what she was doing."

She stepped closer, the fabric of her dress rustling against the sand, and cold fingertips caressed my cheek. "Your grandmother's body never changed, save in the ways a mortal woman's body is meant to change, and Mother took more than half of those away from her when she stopped the clock and bound her to immortality, but she was singed by the flames of her lover's transformations. Her blood remembered. Your blood remembers. It is the weakness of your line, October Daye, daughter of Amandine the Liar. You will always be easy to change, because your blood still sings with my mother's work, even at this distance, and it always will. Don't be too angry. Every line has a weakness. At least yours is balanced by your strengths."

She touched my cheek again, I knew she did, but it felt like she was reaching down this time, which made no sense. I couldn't be getting smaller. I could still breathe. After the initial shock of the rising scent of the sea, I had gotten my breath back. If I was getting smaller, I wouldn't be able to breathe, would I?

"Transformations last longer with the children of Amandine's line, because your bodies yield to them so easily. It makes you a pleasure to change. I can show the full strength of my art. Or could—if you weren't so easily upset." She sounded almost amused.

I opened my eyes, and she was far, far above me, towering like a titan. But I could still breathe. The air hadn't left me. I tried to protest, and all that came out of my throat was a guttural squeak that bore no real resemblance to speech. What the hell had she done to me?

I looked down at myself. I didn't have to look far. My body was a tubular stretch of brown fur, ending in short, clawed hind legs. I was naked, except for, again, the fur, and spending time around Cait Sidhe has taught me that no one with a decent pelt is ever really naked. I looked back up at the Luidaeg and squeaked again, furious and confused.

She stooped down to scoop me into her arms, carrying me toward the water line. I didn't fight. I was too busy glaring at her.

"You thought I was going to turn you into a fish, and I'd be mad at you for that if you were in your right mind," she said. "I would never do that to you if there were any other choice in the matter. That kind of cruelty is my sister's domain. But sea otters have been native to the Pacific coast since long before the fae sailed here in our tall-masted ships, and the body you're wearing knows these waters better than you can imagine. Go to the wall, and down, until you find the opening in the wards Dean carved out for the Merrow of Saltmist. They'll let you in as well. They know you."

I wrinkled my nose, feeling my whiskers crinkle—not a sensation I was used to—and tried to roll over in her arms. My body still wasn't sure what shape it was, and it didn't want to do what I told it. Those didn't seem like the ideal circumstances for a dip in the ocean.

Not that I was going to have a choice. The Luidaeg bent forward and tipped me into the water. It wasn't as cold as it had seemed

from the shore, or maybe my fur was insulating me more than I
expected, because it felt like being dropped into a pond, something shallow enough to be completely warmed by the sun. I rolled
onto my back, the air pockets in my fur letting me float without
effort.

She smiled down at me. "You're adorable, and much less mouthy
this way," she said. "Now go on, swim. Save your squire. I'll be
right behind you."

I cocked my head, waiting to see what she was going to turn
herself into. Nothing as adorable as an otter, that was almost guaranteed, and indeed, as I watched, she folded inward on herself
before blossoming outward like a flower, flesh turning corrugated
and rough, arms going boneless. Her skin flushed vivid orange,
then darkened to a deep, bruised gray, as the massive black octopus she had become swirled through the water next to me.

It was impossible to say whether Disney had gotten something
right, or whether she was making fun of them for being so far off
the mark, and it didn't matter either way, because she was diving,
vanishing in an instant and leaving me alone. I squeaked in surprised alarm and dove after her—or tried to, anyway. The same air
pockets that had been allowing me to float without effort kept me
functionally stranded at the surface, refusing to let me duck more
than a few inches below the water.

I would have had better luck diving as a human. The thought
was frustrating enough that I spun in the water, effectively centri-
fuging the air out of my pelt. This time, when I tried to dive, it
worked, better than I could have imagined. I sliced through the
water like a knife through flesh, scything smoothly and unerringly
downward.

The Luidaeg was there, about ten feet below the surface, floating motionless with all her limbs extended. Each of them ended in
a hooked claw, like the talon of some great raptor, and her suckers
flexed hungrily, eager for prey. I steered clear of her reach, not
wanting to tempt whatever instincts her new body came with. The
mind matters more, absolutely, but every shape I've ever worn has
had its own opinions about what I should do.

The wall loomed ahead of me, smooth and gray and faintly
pearlescent. I swam close enough that my tail brushed the stone—
another strange sensation—before diving deeper, looking for the
opening that had to be there. Patrick and Dianda used it, and Di

wasn't small, especially not in her natural form, where the muscu-
lature of her tail would necessitate a reasonably sized hole.

Deeper and deeper I dove, until I started to wonder if the hole
even existed. I didn't feel any discomfort; while I hadn't intentionally held my breath when I went under, this body knew what to do,
and it was happily doing it. The Luidaeg flashed by me, deeper
dark against the increasingly shadowed water, and then she was
gone. I angled my body in her direction and was rewarded with a
vast circular opening in the wall. It was probably no bigger than
a manhole, but in my current reduced state, it felt broader than a
highway. I tucked my body down and shot through it, moving faster
than anyone bipedal could have even attempted. Otters are much
more aerodynamic than people.

Why wasn't everyone an otter, all the time? Patrick would probably have had an easier time dealing with the transition to the
Undersea if he'd been an otter. Just float around looking cute, eat
the occasional raw fish, and swim like it's your job. The water here
felt shallower than the water on the other side of the wall, and I
shot toward the surface, breaking through into the light of the
cove-side receiving room. I scrubbed the sides of my face with
both paws, wiping the clinging water off my whiskers. It was getting harder to focus on what we were here to do. Otters are mammals. They have more room in their brains for complicated thoughts
than fish do. They're still not people. I'm not a natural shape-
shifter; my magic wasn't protecting my thoughts from fading into
the thoughts of the animal I had become.

That was enough to make me roll in the water, making an alarmed
chittering sound. I wasn't going to be able to save Quentin if I didn't
have thumbs. Thumbs seemed like a fairly key component to getting
things done.

The water next to me churned, before the head of a large gray-
purple octopus broke the surface, alien eyes fixed on me. The Luidaeg reached out and wrapped two tentacles around my body,
stopping my panicked roll. They were tense and muscular, like
being restrained by two boneless snakes, and something about
them set off a deep-set instinct that wasn't normally mine. In the
face of increasing panic, I did the only thing that came naturally.

I bit her.

What flooded my mouth didn't taste like blood, exactly, or not
blood as I normally understood it; it tasted too strongly of salt and

copper, like it had been boiled down to the essentials of what blood could become. The octopus heaved in what I would probably have seen as a sigh had she been in her usual shape, and began swimming toward the beach with her six free arms, still holding me tight, even as I bit into her rubbery flesh again and again. Neither memories nor magic sparked in the thick substance filling my mouth; if this was her blood, one or both of us was too changed for me to read it.

The thought that a simple transformation could be enough to lock me away from my magic made me panic more and bite harder, until the Luidaeg's grasp loosened and I slipped out of her arms, swimming as fast as I could toward the only thing that looked remotely like safety: the long, creamy crescent of the cove shore, which gleamed in the pearly light emanating from everywhere and nowhere around us. If I could get to land, the octopus that was trying to attack me would be unlikely or unable to follow, and I could go back into the water farther down the shore, well away from the mighty predator.

So I swam until my paws brushed the shore, then ran up onto dry land with an odd, rollicking gait that felt almost like I was jumping every time I tried to take a step. When I was well clear of the water, I turned and chittered triumphantly at it, giving that octopus a piece of my mind.

It wasn't there. I stopped, blinking, and sat back to scrub at my whiskers again. I had defeated it, clearly, driving it back down to the depths where it belonged.

I barely noticed the water starting to churn. It extended upward into a tall column, and popped like a bubble atop a frothing wave, leaving a woman standing on the surface of the water. She was dark-haired and oddly dry, wearing something long and flowing that merged into the water beneath her feet. She walked toward me, held up by the tide, and I backed away, chittering in as warning a manner as I could manage. No, human. No, this is my beach. No, you are not welcome here.

Then she was stepping onto the sand, looming over me, an odd expression on her face. I hissed before chittering louder, showing her the sharpness of my teeth. She had already encountered the sharpness of something else's teeth; her forearm was punctured and torn, as if something had tried to gnaw it off of her body. The injury didn't seem to be bothering her, or making her any more cautious or clever, because she reached for me with that hand as she bent forward, ignoring my increasingly frantic threat display. She was between me and the water, and I wasn't fast enough on land to evade a human that wished to do me harm.

She grabbed the scuff of my neck, seizing the loose skin that hung there in a tight grip, and I twisted around, sinking my teeth into her wrist.

Blood filled my mouth, and a red haze dropped over my vision, taking the world away.

It always comes down to the sea. Creatures of the land like to think dryness is the natural state of living things, but that's arrogance and nothing more; the sea came first and the sea will come last and everything in the middle is only a story sung by children who have achieved temporary mastery of the air.

I have spun this stretch of shore with my own two hands, and it will not take the place of Cailleach Skerry, but it is close enough, for I am alone in the world now, and need offer no comfort to my children. The wind blows hard here and the sea clashes wild, and I will never love again, for my heart has gone to ice and ashes. Nothing more can matter in the face of all that has been lost. It is a terrible thing, to be a mother with no children. It is a terrible thing, to be alone.

But what is this? My wind dies down, and my waves turn placid, and something stretches toward the sky, spun like a spider's web of pearl and bone. It is beautiful. I hate it.

My sister. She pollutes even this, which should have been mine and mine alone, and she will not stop until she sees me utterly destroyed—

The red mist broke just enough for me to unclamp my teeth from around her wrist. I dangled, limp and dazed, chittering softly, as she raised me to the level of my face.

"I'm sorry," she said. "I forget sometimes, how quickly instinct overwhelms you. It's part of being so easy to change. But we got through the door, and that's what matters." She blew on my face. Her breath was strangely sweet, like the wind blowing across a field of fresh seagrass.

Everything shifted, getting smaller and bigger at the same time as my field of vision expanded. My feet brushed the sand. The Luidaeg left her hand on the back of my neck, more cupping it than grasping it, and looked me solemnly in the eye.

"Are you all right?"

"I'm fi—oh, fuck, I *bit* you!" Everything I'd done after my thoughts started getting fuzzy was still with me, even the parts that no longer seemed to make any sense now that my mind was my own again. "I'm sorry, I didn't mean to, I—"

"Don't lie to me," she said, sounding amused. "You absolutely meant to. I was big and frightening and a potential predator, and you reacted accordingly. Never get mad at a dog for biting, or for a changeling you've transformed into a sea-dwelling weasel for reacting with aggression when cornered. You meant to do it, but it wasn't your fault. New instincts are powerful things. What did you see?" She took her hand away.

"I think . . ." I reached up and rubbed the back of my neck where her fingers had been. "I think I saw Goldengreen being built. She really did just crash in here without permission and try to take away what you were making for yourself."

"That's my sister for you. Do you have your land legs back yet?" I nodded. "I do."

"Then let's go. The beach is empty. That doesn't mean the rest of the knowe will be."

With the Luidaeg leading the way, we crossed the sand to the long staircase that spiraled upward into the knowe, compensating for the distance between beach and cliff. We climbed the stairs as quickly and quietly as we could, the Luidaeg in her gown of night moving with absolute silence, me grimacing every time my shoes scuffed against the treads.

The door at the top of the stairs was locked. I paused, blinking at it blankly, before leaning close and murmuring, "You know me. I held you once, although I gave you up. I have no right to command you now—I know that. Still, I think your master is in danger. Please, let us pass."

There was a click as the door unlocked itself. I smiled and caressed the doorknob. "You are a very good knowe," I said. I wasn't sure whether the prohibitions against saying "thank you" applied to buildings, and I didn't want to find out the hard way. Offending the knowe when we were trying to move through it uninvited didn't seem like the best of plans.

The Luidaeg was looking at me oddly when I straightened. "You know, if you can sweet-talk locks into opening for you, I don't understand why you decided to become a detective instead of a thief," she said.

"Devin would have preferred the latter, and I did my share of stealing. I prefer working for a living." I eased the door open. It had never creaked before, but it's hard to say with knowes whether something that's true today will be true tomorrow.

And, indeed, the door opened on a hallway I'd never seen before, long and featureless, with no furnishings, and gently curving walls that gleamed in the same pink mother-of-pearl shade as the ones outside. The door swung closed behind us and disappeared. I glared at the spot where it had been.

"Oh, come *on*," I snapped. "That's just dirty pool. How are we supposed to get out of here if you take all the doors away?"

The knowe didn't respond. I shifted my attention back to the Luidaeg.

"Do you recognize this hall?" I asked.

"I think this is one of the ones my sister built herself, rather than waiting for the knowe to develop them in its own time," said the Luidaeg. "If I'm right about that, there are only a few places it can lead. Come on."

She started walking, the speed of her steps betraying her urgency. I followed in her wake, hurrying a little to keep up. She was a few inches shorter than me, and her stride shouldn't have been long enough to rush me the way she was, but somehow she ate distance more quickly than should have been possible.

The hallway curved, and she shifted trajectories to accommodate, the Luidaeg walking faster all the time, until the hall abruptly ended in a door. It looked like it had been carved from a single large piece of oyster shell, polished and placed perfectly to bar our way. The Luidaeg nodded, looking satisfied. "This was one of the first pieces she placed."

"How do you know that?" It was hard not to picture Evening smugly walking her sister through the halls, showing her each fixture and structure, proving without needing to say a word that she had claimed this space, it was hers now, and she was never going to leave or return it.

"There used to be these giant bivalves off the coast. They were here when I made the beach, and I figured either they'd happened on their own, or one of my siblings had lost track of them, and either way, I didn't care, so I let them stay as long as they weren't bothering me. Well, my sister wasn't as live and let live about weird slimy things that lived in the water. She dredged them all up, killed them, and used their shells in construction. For this door to be made from their shells, it must have gone up early. There were never very many of them." Her face fell as she reached out and traced her fingers along the surface of the door. "We're as bad as the humans are, in some ways. Give us a world, and we'll barely stop to take a breath before we start devouring it."

The door shivered at her touch, creaking slightly open. The Luidaeg nodded and pushed it the rest of the way. I hesitated before following her.

"Is there any chance she had some sort of ward set that would banish you to the old parts of the knowe if you ever came here?"

"Not that I'm aware of," she said. "She would never have considered me enough of a danger to warrant banishment, and the times I did have cause to walk in Goldengreen, nothing of the sort occurred. She was never afraid of me after I was bound not to do her any harm. Smart enough to make no bargains, yes, but never afraid. She wouldn't have set any attempts to banish me."

"No," said Marcia, stepping around the corner of the hall on the other side of the door. "That was me."

FIFTEEN

"OH, REALLY," SAID THE LUIDAEG. Anyone who didn't know her as well as I did might have missed the sudden tension in her neck and shoulders, illustrating just how unhappy she was about having someone join us without warning. "And when did you gain the ability to command Goldengreen's defenses?"

"I'm Dean's seneschal," said Marcia. "If I'm the ranking member of the household staff present in the knowe, it tends to listen to my requests. It's easier than fighting with me." Her voice was dull, almost dead; she sounded exhausted. More than that, she sounded defeated.

I stepped forward, hesitating when I got a better look at her. She was wearing a simple yellow sundress, with a rip at the neckline and suspicious brown stains that could have been chocolate milk or could have been something else along the base of her skirt. More alarmingly, her lip was split, and there was a smear of what I couldn't possibly pretend was anything but blood on her left cheek. The smell of it permeated the air around her. She looked at me with eyes as dull and empty as her voice.

"I'm the only one here," she said.

"Marcia, what happened?"

She worried her lip briefly between her teeth, wincing when she hit the split, and said, "The staff was serving dinner in the main room when he showed up. Just walked right in, through a door no one realized was there, like he owned the place. Like he was *allowed*." A note of confused offense crept into her voice. "He walked in like he thought none of us would stop him, and I suppose none of us did, because he did it."

"He who?"

"The man with the red hair," she said, looking at me solemnly. In case that wasn't enough, she added, "And the yellow eyes. But he wasn't Sylvester Torquill. He just stole his face and used it to go where he wasn't meant to go. He had Quentin with him, and an arrow, pressed against the side of Quentin's neck, and when Dean demanded he let go and step away, he did . . . things." She shuddered, voice going high and sweet and childish on the last word, like she was trying to put some distance between herself and the memory. "He said he was looking for Duke Lorden. Dean told me to get away. So I ran, and I asked the knowe if anyone came from the beach, to please send them here, where he wouldn't think to look for them. No one comes here. We're too far away from everything useful."

I moved closer, putting an arm around her shoulders. She nestled against me, blinking wide blue eyes up through the tangled fringe of her hair. As always, they were ringed in a thick corona of fairy ointment, a simple cream blended for her by one of the local alchemists—sometimes that meant Walther, sometimes that meant one of San Francisco's many changelings just trying to get by—so she could see Faerie. I've never unsnarled Marcia's exact heritage, but she's thin-blooded, no more than a quarter fae, and without the fairy ointment, she wouldn't be able to see the doors to the knowe, much less pass through them.

"Marcia, where's the man with the red hair now?" I asked.

"He left," she said, eyes still wide. "When he couldn't find me, he left. He took Quentin with him. That's why you're here, isn't it? You're looking for Quentin?"

"I am," I said, stomach sinking. Simon had been here, done something terrible to leave Marcia with blood on her dress and glassy shock in her eyes, and left again, taking Quentin with him. "Can you take us to Dean?"

"No," she said. "I don't think I can do that. I don't think anyone can do that anymore."

My stomach sank further. "Can you take us to the last place where you saw him?"

Marcia considered for a moment before nodding solemnly and

pulling away from me. "I can do that," she said, and started walking down the hall, not waiting to see if we were following.

I glanced back at the Luidaeg, who looked at me with confusion and shook her head, clearly not sure exactly what was happening. Together, we followed Marcia down the hall and down a short flight of wooden stairs into a small room at the very back of the kitchen. It wasn't a pantry, more an antechamber disguised as a pantry, and once we left it, we were in the kitchen proper, surrounded by the smell of baking bread and simmering broths. The stove was still on, burners heating the pots above them. Magic means not worrying about burning the house down if you step away for five minutes. Just one of the many wonderful services it offers.

Marcia stopped in the middle of the kitchen, eyes going to the rafters, anxiety written clearly in the thin line of her mouth. I followed her gaze, and paled when I realized what she was looking at—or wasn't looking at, more importantly. There were no candy-colored bodies fanning their wings in the gloom, and no dog-sized spiders sneaking up behind them.

Goldengreen sat empty between Evening's supposed death and my taking the knowe over. It hadn't been as well-sealed as Arden's knowe in Muir Woods, which had been locked by the Luidaeg herself, and things had been able to creep in around the edges. Nothing big—we hadn't been forced to evict a dragon or anything of the sort—but big enough to be a nuisance. Normally, Goldengreen had a thriving population of pixies, as well as a large colony of bogeys, shapeshifting spiders that liked to make people uncomfortable. I had always acknowledged them as the true owners of the knowe, and while Dean hadn't chosen to do the same, he'd never tried to evict them, choosing instead to establish a stable, if occasionally frustrating, peace.

They were always here. Even when Marcia was away from the knowe, her kitchen was alive with small bodies, stealing bits of bread, adding unexpected seasonings to the stew, and generally making a polite nuisance of themselves. I had never seen the rafters empty before.

"They rose to defend the knowe," she said dreamily. "This is their home and they love it, and they love being accepted as a part of the household when so many would have had them evicted for the crime of being small and simple, so they rose to defend what they love when they felt it was in danger. And now we're the only ones left."

The hole in the bottom of my stomach felt like it was opening wider and wider. Soon it would be a gaping chasm, and May and I would match again. "Take us to where you last saw Dean," I said, in a very small voice.

Marcia nodded, and the three of us left the kitchen together.

The smell of smoke and rotten oranges completely filled the hall, thick enough that I gagged as soon as I inhaled. Simon had not only been here, he had been flinging spells around with wild abandon. It was probably too much to hope for him to have exhausted himself in the process, although it was likely. There were traces of other magical signatures blending into his, but none were strong enough to imply that anyone had been able to successfully fight back. We kept walking.

When Goldengreen had belonged to Evening, it had been centered around the receiving room where she had kept her throne— as if anyone expected a Countess to sit a proper throne, like she thought she belonged among the upper echelons of the nobility. Etiquette didn't demand that level of formality from anyone below the ducal level, but Evening had always been one to strive for extra credit when it meant she'd have the opportunity to look down her nose at someone. As one of the Firstborn, she'd probably considered it her due. After I'd taken over Goldengreen and moved in the survivors of my friend Lily's unaligned Court, we had abandoned that receiving room, moving the knowe's social center and heart to the courtyard.

If there had been a specific goal in mind when the Goldengreen courtyard was designed, no one has ever been able to tell me what it was. It's set up almost like a smaller version of the rose gardens in Berkeley, large and circular, with walls arranged in six shallow concentric tiers, terminating at a floor-level central promenade, which is no more than sixty feet across. Tiny, for something with that design. Massive, by the standards of an indoor room. Goldengreen doesn't have a ballroom, and I've often wondered if that was because the courtyard made it irrelevant.

The tiers had each been fitted with their own garden beds, and planted with a wide variety of plants, ranging from herb gardens and flowerbeds to vegetables, grasses, and trees whose root networks could survive the limited space. The top, and largest, tier was dominated by a copse of willow trees that Lily's former hand-maids had transplanted from her knowe before it finished the pro-cess of sealing itself after her death. Even knowes can mourn.

Goldengreen was going to be in mourning soon if we didn't do something about it. We stepped out of the hallway, into the courtyard, and the Luidaeg made a sound barely shy of a gasp, a strangled inhalation that sounded entirely alien coming from her. The air was even thicker with the cloying smell of Simon's magic, forcing me to breathe through my nose to stop it coating my tongue and the back of my throat. Debris littered the floor, weapons, cook-ing implements, and other, less martial artifacts—books and eye-glasses and tumblers, all the things people would have been carrying in their hands when they were unexpectedly interrupted by Simon Torquill and his captive.

There was no blood. There were no bodies. But the lowest tier of the gardens, usually reserved for Marcia's kitchen herbs and easier-to-grow vegetables, like zucchini and tomatoes, was sud-denly clogged with trees. Oak and ash and hawthorn and yew, all the sacred woods of Faerie were growing there, where I knew for a fact they hadn't been on my last visit.

I could see screaming faces pressing against the bark, distorted by the grain of the wood, but recognizable all the same. Nothing else about them was recognizable. Looking at the trees, I couldn't say which one was Dean, or who any of the others might have been.

The soil around them was dense with red-capped toadstools and even larger mushrooms with purple-and-yellow caps. The toad-stools glowed faintly, in a variety of colors that didn't match the red of their caps. I turned back to the Luidaeg, pressing a hand to the base of my throat as both a signal of distress and an attempt to keep myself from vomiting.

"Did Simon really do *all* this?" I whispered.

Marcia, meanwhile, had drifted over to stand in front of the largest of the new oaks, her hands clasped in front of herself like a very small child and her eyes filling with tears. "He told me to run," she whispered. "He saw what was happening, he saw he wouldn't be able to stop it, and he told me to run. So I ran. Maybe if I'd stayed, this wouldn't have . . . maybe I could have . . ."

"Hey," said the Luidaeg. "No. Don't do that to yourself. My own mother couldn't have stopped this. The magic that shaped this was Simon's, but the power beneath it belonged to my sister. She should never have given it to him."

"Because he's using it irresponsibly?" I asked.

"Because it's destroying him! You think I don't just hand out bottles of my blood because I'm being greedy? Sweet daddy's ass, Toby, you've had to use my blood. You know how strong it was, and that was under controlled circumstances, when I spilled it to save your life. He's flinging her powers around like there won't be any consequences. Taste the spell. You'll see for yourself."

I frowned before taking a shallow breath, this time trying to taste Simon's magic, rather than shutting it out. There was the smoke, and the flavor of rotting oranges, and the absolute absence of anything approaching mulled cider, which would have told me Simon was coming back into himself . . .

And there, under all the rest of it, was a hint of snow, of cold, of the winter's incipient descent. For all the Luidaeg's protests that Evening was a summer creature, her magic had always held the scent of snow and roses, like she was the purest part of winter given physical form and malicious intent. Now that I was looking for it, it was everywhere. It was freezing the rest of his magic, encasing it from the inside out. What would happen when it took over completely? What happens when Simon Torquill's magic grows red with roses?

It's a question I doubt anyone has needed to ask in a long, long time, not since the Firstborn were common and Faerie was learning to cope with the size of their powers. I've known more Firstborn than anyone needed to, really, but I've never used their blood the way Simon was using Evening's. He was using powers that had never been his to channel, that his body wasn't equipped to handle, and people were going to be hurt. Very, very badly.

I stared at the Luidaeg. "We have to find him."

"I know."

"We have to stop him."

"I know."

"He'll be trying to get to Saltmist next, since he can't find Shadowed Hills and he's forgotten the tower is even relevant to him and ugh, Luidaeg, next time you need to ruin someone's entire life in exchange for a candle, can you do it by turning them to stone or something like that? So they don't go around making things harder on the rest of us?"

"I'll do what the magic allows," she said stiffly. The Luidaeg set her own prices, yes, but sometimes they were too strange and too specific to have been her own idea. Taking August's way home when she really wanted my sister to find Oberon wasn't just steep, it was cruel, in a way the Luidaeg usually wasn't. Not for the first time, it occurred to me that I didn't fully understand the geas she'd been forced to live under.

"Speaking of what the magic allows, this is Simon's spell, though spun from my sister's strength," she said, turning her attention to the nearest tree. She reached out and ran the tip of her finger along a seam in the bark, expression turning contemplative. "The world isn't meant to bear this sort of strength, not the way it used to. We've left this pain behind."

"Can I help?" I tried to see the spell the way I'd seen the one Simon used to weave his shard realm, the way he'd woven the spell that had almost turned Jazz into a fish in my kitchen the first time he'd approached me after the pond. I got a brief, wavering glimpse of what looked like macramé, only to lose sight of it as soon as it appeared, wisping away into the air. A bolt of pain lanced through my head. I winced.

The Luidaeg turned to me, and her expression was barely shy of outright sympathy. "Hurts, doesn't it? You're not supposed to behold our workings so directly. The ways of the Firstborn are subtle and dreadful, and sometimes even our own parents couldn't contain us, although they were far more equipped for the attempt than you could ever be. No, this isn't something you can unmake. I can try, although my sister's involvement means it may or may not work."

"And if it doesn't—"

"Either you or Marcia is going to wind up becoming the new custodian of Goldengreen. Which means probably you, since I doubt even Arden could be convinced to put a thin-blooded changeling in charge of a county."

I stared at her, mouth going dry. Finally, I swallowed and asked, "Are you really saying Dean and the others could be *lost*?"

"Look at this room." The Luidaeg waved her hands. "No windows. No skylight. The plants are sustained by the knowe's magic, but dawn will never find them here, and without dawn to weaken the transformation, if I can't tear it down, you'd need to wake my sister and convince her to do it for you. I know you like to wake up sleepers and ask them to do you favors, but I think this one would be a little bit beyond even you."

"Believe me, she's the last person in the world I want to see wake up." I shook my head. "I need to get out of here. I need to find and stop Simon. You're going to stay here and break the spell?"

"If I can."

"Then there's just one more thing I need for you to do."

"What's that?" she asked, warily.

Good for her. A little wariness was justified, under the circumstances. I took a deep breath, refusing to allow myself to look away.

"I need you to tell me how to give Simon my way home," I said.

SIXTEEN

DANNY MET ME in front of the museum, seated in his car with the window down and a worried look on his face. "What's going on?" he asked, not bothering to say hello. "Why'd you call sounding so upset?"

"We need to go to the Norton house right now." I ran around the car and flung myself into the passenger seat, managing not to recoil from the smell of Barghest that rushed out when I opened the door. "Fast as you can. Break some laws."

"Cops won't see me," Danny promised, tapping the bundle of herbs hanging from his rearview mirror with one massive gray hand. I blinked. Until that moment, I hadn't realized he wasn't wearing any illusions to make him seem human. He smirked, catching the look on my face. "Upgraded the aversion charms," he said. "Clover thought I was takin' too many risks when I took the kids out for their nightly drive."

Clover was his mechanic, a Gremlin woman I'd never met, but whose work came highly recommended, mostly by Danny himself. The "kids" were his pet Barghests. "What kind of risks?" I asked, as he hit the gas and threw the car into a tight, tire-squealing turn. Humans tended to either overlook the Barghests completely or see them as some weird new breed of designer dog. Like the pixies, they had their own simple magic that hid them from mortal eyes when necessary.

"Sometimes they get outta the car and I have to crank the windows down, and they don't like the makeup," he said, waving a hand vaguely in front of his face. Just in case I'd missed what he meant, he added, "You're not wearing any. S'a nice change, seeing your face the way it's supposed to be. I don't like the way you change it, but unlike the Barghests, I don't bite." He laughed uproariously, stopping only when he saw that I wasn't smiling. "Tobes? What is it? Kitty-boy get himself hurt again?"

"Not so far as I know, although I guess that's something I should add to the list of things I'm worried about," I said. Danny was mashing the pedal all the way to the floor, sending us careening along the road at a speed that seemed likely to end with at least one corpse, and probably a lot of insurance companies getting involved. Since he wasn't going to get pulled over no matter what he did, and had been driving professionally for years, I wasn't as worried about it as I maybe should have been.

The drive between Goldengreen and Half Moon Bay, where the Norton house is located, normally takes about forty-five minutes. Simon had at least that much of a head start, and unlike many purebloods, knew how to drive. He could easily have stolen a car and made it most, if not all the way, there already.

But he didn't necessarily know that most of the Nortons had been permanently bonded with their skins, giving up their place as Selkies in exchange for becoming a much rarer and more permanent part of Faerie. The Roane were back, and even if he'd seen them in the memories echoed by my blood, he was still walking into a situation he didn't fully understand.

I touched my pocket, where I had tucked the stub of a hastily shaped candle pulled together from things the Luidaeg had scavenged in Marcia's kitchen. Walking into situations we don't fully understand is virtually the family business, after all.

"Simon's back," I said tightly. "He's kidnapped Quentin. He went to Goldengreen, and when he didn't find what he was looking for there, he turned everyone in the knowe into trees and left, we presume for the Norton house, because he's trying to reach Saltmist. He's armed, he's dangerous, and I'm going to stop him. Any more questions?"

"Yeah, where's Tybalt? I don't normally see you rushing into danger without the cat standing by to make sure you get *out* of danger on the other end."

It was a fair question, and no matter how fast he drove, he couldn't entirely eliminate the distance we had to travel. I sighed. "I told him to stay home before I knew how dangerous this was going to be, and I haven't quite worked myself around to calling and telling him I was wrong." Or that May was injured and elf-shot and maybe not waking up, or that I'd lost Quentin, or that I was about to do something *monumentally* stupid for the sake of potentially saving Simon.

Simon Torquill. The man I'd once considered to be my greatest enemy. The man I was now willingly risking everything I had for the opportunity to save. Faerie isn't fair, and the world doesn't make sense.

"You sound scared."

"I am."

"If this is somethin' that scares you . . . I know it's not my place to pry, Tobes, but maybe this would be a good time for you to go ahead and make that phone call." Danny shot across a four-way intersection against the light and barely ahead of a truck that could have crushed us without so much as breaking a headlight. "If not for your sake, or for his sake, for my sake. You really think your cat won't gut me like a fish if he finds out I let you do something that scared you without involving him? Think about me if you can't think about yourself. Think about my kids. Who's going to feed them if your boyfriend kills me for the crime of helping you kill yourself?"

"If I call him, he'll come, Danny." My phone was a heavy weight in my pocket, impossible to ignore. Sometimes I miss the days where people were out of touch if they weren't at home, where we'd have to go hunting for a payphone to reach out. It's a human way of thinking. No matter how fae I become, I figure I'll always have a few of those. "I don't want him here. Not for what I'm about to do."

Danny slanted an alarmed glance across the car at me, keeping most of his attention on the road. "I didn't mean it about helping you kill yourself. You know that, right? If that's what you're planning, I'm out. I'm happy to be your personal chauffeur—I smile every time you think to call me, even when you're screaming, or covered in blood, or a fucking fish—but I'm not going to sit by while you do something that can't be taken back."

Oh, no. What I was planning could absolutely be taken back, either by passing around a curse like some sort of evil hot potato, or by finding Oberon and bringing him home to the children he'd chosen to abandon. No big deal. But either way, there were more people who cared enough about me to try than Simon had, and I would be better off than he was.

I thought. Probably. At least Evening and I had never been close enough for me to make waking her up my new life's mission—even when I'd considered her an ally, I wouldn't have gone that far. Again, probably.

"I'm not planning to do anything that can't be taken back, but I'm planning to do something that could save a lot of people, Quentin among them," I said. "It's worth it. I've made up my mind. I can do this." And if I forgot I was supposed to be planning a wedding, maybe people would stop nagging me about when it was actually going to happen. That would be a nice change.

That's me, looking for the upside of everything, even the things that have no upsides.

"I worry about you, October," said Danny, passing two cars that were going too slow, at only fifteen miles over the speed limit, for his current tastes. "Sacrificing yourself isn't the only answer to every problem you come across. It would be nice for the rest of us if you realized that someday. I don't want to have to bury you."

"I don't want to be buried," I assured him. "I'm doing the best I can. I want to get married. I want to see Quentin grow up, and what kind of king Raj is going to be. I want to meet my own kids. Me and Tybalt . . . we're going to have incredible children. And all those things mean I need to stay alive long enough to get there." They were ridiculous dreams for someone like me to have. I was never going to get a happy ending. Heroes never do. Just look at Sylvester; he found the woman of his dreams, married her, settled down, had a daughter, and lost it all because of all the secrets that he and the people around him had been keeping for years.

Camelot never endures. No matter how shining the castle on the hill seems, it's still capable of falling. Falling is what every shining city seems designed and destined to do.

Danny gave me another worried look before returning his attention to the road. I hated the thought that we might be driving into another aftermath, but Etienne hadn't answered the phone when I tried to call him, and the Luidaeg and I agreed that this wasn't a favor to ask of Arden. She had a kingdom to care for. As her pet hero, protecting it was my job. Playing taxi for me all over the Bay Area wasn't hers.

As for calling Tybalt . . . that would only hurt us both, and I wasn't entirely sure he'd be willing to take me where I needed to go once he realized what I was planning. Faced with a choice between my safety and the safety of the Mists, I couldn't promise he wouldn't choose me. He loved me, and he wasn't a hero.

The road ran by outside the window, lights blending and blurring together until they were nothing but a sparkling stream. To Danny's credit, while he was clearly unhappy about what he saw as driving me to my doom, he didn't slow down or veer off our chosen course, and in less than twenty-five minutes, we were pulling off the freeway into Half Moon Bay.

We had to slow down once we reached the residential streets, if only because they were narrower and twistier, winding past homes and businesses. The sidewalks were mostly deserted this late at night, although some people were out walking their dogs. One of them stepped obliviously in front of us, unable to see our enchanted car. Danny swore, hauling the wheel to the side and hitting the brakes at the same time, sending us into a stomach-wrenching spin. I grabbed the handle above the door, hanging on for dear life, suddenly grateful that I hadn't eaten anything since Walther's pizza.

The screech of the brakes split the night like the crack of thunder, Danny grimacing as he pulled the wheel, the car shuddering to a stop against the far curb. Miraculously, we'd managed to avoid hitting anything, including the woman and her dog. She was looking around in confusion, probably trying to figure out where that noise had come from. Her dog, on the other hand, was looking directly at us, front paws braced in a defensive stance. He was ready to challenge the car for the sake of his mistress, which would have been more impressive if he hadn't been a Corgi.

I've never seen a Corgi fight a car and come out the victor, but this one was clearly ready to try. The woman leaned down and patted his head, trying to calm him. He cast her a look full of heartbreaking adoration, and she said something I couldn't hear through the closed windows or over the sound of Danny's labored, stress-laced breathing. The woman laughed and continued across the street, dog by her side.

A kelpie stepped out of the shadows of an alley right where she'd been standing. Like the dog, it looked directly at us. Unlike the dog, it knew what it was looking at. We locked eyes across the road, and it began to trot daintily forward, probably assuming we were in more distress than we were.

"Danny, you need to drive," I said. The woman was in no danger—kelpies will stalk humans, but they almost never attack them, and I've never heard of one attacking a human with a dog; they're cowardly creatures at heart, and they don't want to go up against anything that might fight back. A kelpie vs. a Corgi wouldn't end well for the dog, but the kelpie wasn't going to push the issue if it thought there was easier prey around.

For all that they have big appetites and the teeth to match, kelpies usually content themselves with fish and garbage scavenged from human dumpsters. I'd say they were no better than seagulls, if that wouldn't be such a massive insult to seagulls.

"I almost hit her," Danny moaned, hands shaking where they gripped the wheel. "She never woulda seen us coming. How could she?"

"Danny . . ." The kelpie was getting closer, head down and ears up, scenting the wind for signs we were as helpless as we appeared. Rolling down the windows to release the smell of Barghest might have dissuaded it, but even a kelpie could tell the small predators weren't in the car. I didn't want to start gambling on the problem-solving capacity of kelpies. "How much actual steel is left in this car?"

"Huh? None. I had it stripped and replaced with spelled wood years ago. It's perfectly safe. How have you been drivin' with me this long, and you don't know that?"

"Then you *need to drive*, because there is a *kelpie* coming *toward the car*," I snapped.

Danny sat up, hands still clutching the wheel, and turned in the direction I was facing. "Huh," he said. "Wouldya look at that. I'd figure the Selkies would do a better job of keepin' the kelpies off their front porch, but I guess they don't mind murderous water horses as much as the rest of us. That lady and her dog clear? We're not going to be handing them over to the kelpie if we leave?"

"She's gone," I said. "Come on, drive."

"Tobes, I'm made of stone, and every time I ask you to be more careful, you take great joy in reminding me that you're basically indestructible. What's that kelpie gonna do, break its teeth on us?"

"I'm indestructible, but pain hurts." No one likes kelpies. They're dangerous predators, invisible to humans, which makes them even worse. But they only come out at night, when the streets are close enough to empty that there's not a lot of damage they can do, and killing them for following their natures has never seemed entirely fair. Plus, every time there's been a major cull, the kelpies that inevitably escape react by going on a murderous rampage through the surrounding cities. Fewer humans die when we just leave them alone.

But oh, it stung sometimes. It stung even now, as Danny restarted the car and began driving, much more slowly and cautiously, down the street. There was a rattle in the engine that hadn't been there before. Danny grimaced as the kelpie dwindled in his rearview mirror.

"Clover's gonna yell," he said. "She always yells when I do somethin' stupid to the car."

"Not hitting a woman and her dog wasn't stupid," I said. "If anything, it was smart, since a hit-and-run with no vehicle would have attracted attention."

Danny brightened. "You really think so?"

"Yeah." We were passing out of the city limits, onto the even more twisty, winding residential streets that led to the beachfront homes. Those houses came in one of two varieties: either so nice that no one outside of tech millionaires and celebrities could afford them, or old, somewhat rundown, and in the same family for generations. About a mile outside of town, we came to the curling driveway leading to one of the latter houses.

It was massive, almost large enough to compete with some smaller knowes, and had the distinct appearance of having been built up over the course of several decades, with each new architect ignoring whatever blueprints the former might have left behind. Porches and cupolas sprouted almost at random, and windows bristled on every possible surface.

But the shutters were all painted the same cheery shade of blue, and the white paint covering the house itself was fresh and new. The roof was freshly shingled, and none of the many porches sagged. About half the windows were lit up from inside, although there was no porch light. The fae wouldn't need one. A variety of cars were parked out front, filling what would otherwise have been the yard and clogging the drive. I waved for Danny to stop the car, rolling down my window and sniffing the air as I listened for the sound of screams.

Instead, I heard someone playing the violin, distant and sweet and drifting through the night air like some sort of promise. I smelled saltwater and seagrass and all the freshest parts of the ocean. And clam chowder, coming from the open kitchen window. I didn't smell smoke or oranges.

Maybe we'd been wrong. Maybe this wasn't Simon's destination after all.

"Stay here," I said, unfastening my belt. "I'll be back as soon as I can."

"What, you're gonna make the strong guy made of living rock sit in the car 'cause you think it's too dangerous?" Danny demanded.

No sense in lying. "Yes," I said.

Danny scowled at me. "I hate you sometimes."

"I hate me sometimes, too," I said, and opened the car door, sliding out into the cool night air. I didn't look back as I started toward the house.

The smell of smoke and rotten oranges had yet to put in an appearance by the time I reached the porch and rang the doorbell. Someone shouted inside; someone else shouted back. There was a brief scuffle before Diva, daughter of the former Selkie clan leader, opened the door. Her hair was disheveled, hanging mostly over her strikingly green eyes and also—more importantly—hiding the points of her ears. She blinked at the sight of me, in all my own uncovered glory, and shoved her hair back with one hand.

"It's Toby!" she yelled over her shoulder. "Told you no one human would be ringing the bell after midnight!" Laughter and some good-natured grumbling answered her pronouncement. She lunged over the threshold and caught me in a tight hug.

"Oof," I said, and patted her back with one hand.

I like Diva. She's about Gillian's age, but unlike my daughter, she grew up within Faerie, aware her parents weren't human and that that meant she wasn't either, not entirely. Because her mother had been a Selkie when Diva was born, she'd technically been a changeling until we'd sat down together after the Duchy of Ships, to have me shift her Roane heritage into dominance. Now, she's as fae as they come, and has a much better grasp of what it means to be Roane than most of her cousins, who didn't have the advantage of being halfway there before the Duchy.

Diva let go, stepping back and beaming. "I told Mom you'd be coming by," she said, voice bright, betraying no sign she thought anything was wrong. "She said you had better things to do with your time, but I said that boy was your squire, and there was no way you wouldn't come to pick him up."

My blood ran cold. "That boy?" I asked carefully. It said something about how tense I was that I didn't even point out that she and Quentin were practically the same age—calling him "that boy" made about as much sense as me talking about Danny that way. "Is he here?"

Diva nodded vigorously. "He's in the kitchen," she said. "Having chowder with Elsa and Nathan and where are you going? Don't you want to talk to me?" I'd pushed past her as soon as the word "kitchen" left her lips, barreling across the front room—packed with Roane, many of them holding musical instruments, none of them wearing human disguises—toward the kitchen door.

I hit it with my shoulder, one hand going to the knife at my hip while I was still moving. The three people sitting around the kitchen table looked up from their chowder, blinking in varying degrees of confused surprise. Two of them were Roane, familiar in the vague way that all Roane are familiar to me now, whether or not we've been introduced. My magic went into the rebirthing of them. They're not my descendants, with the exception of Gillian, but my blood knows them all the same, and sings to their presence.

The third was Quentin.

He was wearing a fresh shirt, one without any blood on it, but he looked unharmed—and untroubled, as he dismissed me with a glance and went back to eating his chowder, reaching for the bread bowl at the center of the table and extracting a yeast roll to start dipping in the broth. I stepped fully into the kitchen, letting the door swing shut behind me.

"Quentin," I said, in as loud and carrying a voice as I could manage without shouting, "what the *fuck*?"

The two Roane pushed their chairs back and got to their feet, looking at me with obvious alarm. "Is something wrong?" asked one, a girl with hair the color of sun-bleached driftwood and eyes even greener than Diva's.

"Yeah, my squire's sitting here eating soup when I've been running all over the Bay Area looking for him." I knew from talking to Marcia that he'd been at Goldengreen; how could he be this calm when Dean had been transformed into a tree?

Easy: magic. Sometimes that's the only answer anyone's going to offer you. I took a deep breath, forcing myself to calm down, and walked toward him.

"Was there a man with him when he got here?" I asked. "A red-haired man with yellow eyes, and a big-ass bow?"

"Yes," said the other Roane. He looked a little older than Quentin, dark-haired and dark-skinned, and as baffled as his counterpart. "He went down to the shore, but he said Quentin was hungry, and he was right."

"He's had six bowls of chowder so far," said the girl, glancing at Quentin, who was back to eating like he was afraid his food was going to be taken away. Which wasn't an unreasonable concern, under the circumstances. "Is something wrong?"

"Yes," I said curtly. "Quentin, I want you to leave the bowl behind and stand up."

His only response was to pull the bowl closer to himself and start shoveling chowder into his mouth even faster than before, like a starving dog who knew with absolute certainty that once this food went away he was never going to get more, ever, for as long as he lived. I scowled and moved toward the table, sniffing the air.

There, under the smell of chowder and fresh-baked rolls, was a ribbon of smoke. It was subtle; if I hadn't been looking for it, I would have missed it, and Simon would have gotten away with this.

"He's under a compulsion," I said, for the benefit of the two Roane who'd been keeping an eye on him, however unintentionally. "Is Liz home?"

"She's upstairs, um," said Elsa.

"Drinking," said Nathan, more baldly.

Elsa smacked him in the arm. "We're not supposed to tell outsiders that," she snapped.

"This is October. She's beloved of the sea witch," he said. "She can't be an outsider anywhere in the presence of the ocean. It doesn't work that way."

I sort of wanted to ask him how it *did* work, if I had been somehow adopted by the sea because I spent too much time around the Luidaeg. Was there a membership card or something that I was supposed to flash? But for the moment, Quentin was more important.

"Can you please go tell her I'm here?" I asked, fighting to keep my voice both level and pleasant. The two of them looked unsure. I ground my teeth together, forcing a smile. "Please? I haven't seen her in a while."

Casting uneasy glances at Quentin all the while, the two teenage Roane stood and left the kitchen, leaving me alone with my squire. I didn't have time to do this subtly, not with Simon down at the shore and working on a way to get himself to Saltmist. I drew the knife from my belt, eyes on Quentin the whole time to be sure that he wasn't about to bolt or throw his chowder at me or something equally stupid.

He didn't move. When Simon had enchanted him, he'd done so with no functional knowledge of what a Dóchas Sidhe was capable of. He'd forgotten August entirely, and he didn't remember being my ally or almost-friend, so why would he know the tricks of my bloodline? This spell had been constructed under the assumption that it would be taken down in the normal manner, assuming it was taken down at all.

I ran the edge of the knife along the pad of my thumb, splitting the skin, and waited to start bleeding before sticking my thumb in my mouth, sucking greedily. I wanted as much blood as possible, but I wanted to avoid cutting myself a second time if I could manage it. The smell of copper and cut grass began gathering around me. Quentin didn't look alarmed; far from it. Quentin didn't look like he necessarily realized I was still there. All his attention was focused on his chowder.

It seemed odd for Simon to have hit him with such a strong compulsion and given it such a narrow focus, instead of building something more useful and complex. Then again, if Simon was still using Evening's blood to boost and modify his magic, he might not have meant to hit Quentin that hard. Controlling strength borrowed from a Firstborn isn't exactly easy, and the few times I'd done it, I'd been working with the blood of a Firstborn who actively wished me no ill will. I couldn't say the same of Evening.

The wound in my thumb had already healed. I pulled it out of my mouth and swallowed, taking another step toward Quentin as I raised my hand and hooked my fingers, like I was preparing to jerk away a net. In a way, that was exactly what I was doing.

The kitchen door slammed open as Elsa and Nathan returned, now with a clearly inebriated Elizabeth Ryan in tow. Diva's mother was a tall, blonde-haired woman whose face had already started to youthen, courtesy of her transformation from part-time fae to actual pureblood. Unlike most Selkies with children of her own, Liz hadn't needed to give her skin away if she wanted her child to be immortal. Diva got Faerie from her father's side of the family.

Hopefully, she'd inherited more than that from him, and would dodge her mother's alcoholism. Liz was holding a tumbler of amber liquid in one hand, a baffled look on her face that only deepened when she saw me.

"October," she said. "You're really—they said, but I thought—I didn't think you'd come here so soon. Show your face here so soon. What're you doing here?"

Sometimes I envy people whose metabolisms are slow enough to let them drink. Other times I wonder if I looked that ridiculous back when alcohol was an option for me, and I'm privately grateful for my limited options. This was one of the second times. "You have my squire," I said, swallowing my mouthful of blood and trying to hold fast to the magic I had raised in the kitchen. "I wanted him back, and that meant I had to go where he'd been taken."

"Oh." Liz blinked, bewildered. "Well, what's your squire doing here? He doesn't live . . . he's not . . . he shouldn't be here."

"I didn't ask you to go *get* her," I said, glaring at the two young Roane who flanked her. "I asked you to tell her I was here. Not the same thing."

"You said you hadn't seen her in a while," said Nathan. "That made it sound like you wanted her to come. We were trying to help."

I resisted the urge to put my hand over my face. "Good job, kids," I said. "All right, Liz, Quentin is under a compulsion spell, and I don't have a lot of time before the man who cast it causes some pretty serious problems between us and the Undersea. Can you take your teenagers and give us a moment's privacy so I can take the spell down?"

"No." Liz crossed her arms, nearly spilling her drink in the process. "I can't do that. I'm not leaving you alone to hurt this boy."

Elizabeth Ryan has never particularly cared for me. First, I was the changeling of no particular status or bloodline who was trying to have a relationship with one of her Selkies—my old boyfriend, Connor O'Dell. Then, after we'd been safely dissuaded from getting involved and Connor had been married off to Rayseline Torquill, I had been the semi-disgraced knight responsible for the loss of a Selkie skin when it was caught, along with myself and Quentin, in an exploding car in Tamed Lightning. As if that wasn't enough, I had been dating Connor again after his marriage ended, and I was with him when he died. Elizabeth Ryan had plenty of reasons to dislike me.

And that was all before she had become de facto guardian of my teenage daughter, a formerly mortal girl who had abruptly hop-scotched over dozens of patiently waiting Selkie kinfolk to find herself draped in one of their lost skins, granted admission to the waters by none other than the Luidaeg herself—Elizabeth's former lover. And *then* I'd accompanied the Luidaeg to the Duchy of Ships to help her call in the bargain that originally created the Selkies.

It was no wonder that I wasn't Elizabeth's favorite person. It was something of a miracle that she didn't have standing orders for me to be shot on sight.

"Fine," I snapped, and drew my knife again. "Just don't get in the way. I need my squire back."

Quentin was still eating his chowder, not appearing to notice any of the drama unfolding around him. It was a well-crafted compulsion, if a bit more brute force than I tended to prefer. I could almost admire it, and probably would have, if it hadn't been cast on my squire.

The two Roane teens flinched, looking worried, as I ran the blade of the knife across the ball of my thumb again. I winced at the pain. The original wound was healed, but it sometimes feels like my body remembers and resents it when I cut myself in the same place more than once in a short period of time. Blood welled to the surface of the skin, and once again I stuck my thumb in my mouth, calling my magic back out of the air.

A bolt of pain shot through my temples. The strain I'd placed on my magic when I'd involuntarily changed the balance of my own blood was still there, ready and eager to make things difficult for me. I swallowed anyway, trying to coax more blood out of the already-healing wound. It didn't want to come, and I didn't want to cut myself a third time, so I abandoned the attempt, pulling my thumb out of my mouth and taking a long step toward Quentin.

The air around me was practically crackling with my magic. It was hard to say whether Liz and the teens could smell it—the capabilities of the Roane are still a little unclear to me, and the Luidaeg hasn't exactly been forthcoming about the strengths and weaknesses of her reborn descendants—but I knew Quentin should have been able to. And yet he ignored the swelling static in the air in favor of reaching for another roll, still eating like he thought he was never going to have another opportunity.

I stopped a foot or so away, close enough that I could have reached out and touched him if I'd wanted to, and allowed my eyes to unfocus until a sickly web of gray-and-orange lines appeared around him. They were more tightly woven than the spell in the shard realm had been, maybe because the spell was smaller and simpler and didn't need to stand up to as much strain, or maybe all spells had the same number of strands and I just hadn't looked at enough of them to know what I was seeing. I hated using Quentin as a test subject. I didn't see any other option.

Reaching out, I hooked my fingers through the top layer of the web and yanked it apart as hard as I could, wrenching and ripping until the strands began to fray and snap, releasing the smell of smoke and rotten oranges into the air. I gagged but refused to let go. I was only going to get one shot at this; I might be able to attempt tackling the spell again, despite my growing headache, but Quentin might know what I was doing, and I couldn't imagine the spell wouldn't at least attempt to protect itself from me if it was aware that it was being broken.

It's safest when working with magic to assume that everything is at least a little bit alive. I kept yanking and ripping, until a new sound appeared—one that would normally have been unwelcome, but which was, under the circumstances, proof that I was doing something right.

Quentin started screaming.

The spell wasn't visibly harming him, not transforming him or wrenching out chunks of his magic. It was just fighting back, trying to work its hooks more deeply into the tender parts of his psyche. I continued pulling, hard and unmerciful, until it came apart under my hands. Quentin stopped screaming and stared at me, cheeks pale, eyes wide and glossy and filled with unshed tears. He glanced at the bowl in front of him and his pallor turned greenish as he shoved it away and lurched to his feet.

I couldn't see any fragments of the spell left in the air around him, but that didn't necessarily mean anything. I allowed my eyes to focus properly again. "Hey, kiddo," I said cautiously. "How are you feeling?"

Quentin responded by sprinting past me to the kitchen sink, where he was loudly and vigorously sick. I turned to watch him go, raising an eyebrow. "Guess you had a little too much chowder, huh?"

Liz belatedly seemed to realize my squire was throwing up on her household dishes. "Hey!" she objected. "Use the toilet like a normal person!"

"I think it was either the sink or the kitchen floor," I said. "He made the right choice."

Liz frowned. "He's doing those dishes."

"No, he's not," I corrected. "As soon as he's done throwing up, we're leaving."

For a moment, I thought she was going to argue and force me to play the Luidaeg card. The fact that I was here on semi-official business for the sea witch had to count for something, even if I'd been the one to get her involved. Fortunately, I didn't have to say anything. Liz's shoulders sagged, and she took a swig from her tumbler—probably a larger one than was a good idea with what looked and smelled like reasonably decent whiskey.

"Fine," she said sullenly. "Just get him out of my house before he vomits on a couch." She turned and strode out of the kitchen, shoulders back and head high, like she thought she was somehow making a dramatic exit.

I guess enough alcohol can turn anything dramatic. Quentin was still throwing up. I walked over to him, rubbing his back with one hand.

"Hey, buddy," I said. "I'm sorry you got grabbed. Are you okay?"

"He said he'd be back for me, and that until he came, I should sit quietly and have something to eat," he said, turning to look reproachfully at me. "He said I didn't need to worry about a thing until he came back for me. I knew I knew you. I knew you were important, but I couldn't worry about that. I needed to eat, and I needed to wait, and I needed not to think about anything that could possibly be upsetting."

"That sounds like a very carefully considered compulsion," I said. "Did you notice anything strange about it?"

"You mean apart from the fact that it was heavier than it should have been?" He clutched his stomach, still green around the edges. "I think I would have kept eating until I literally burst, because I couldn't stop. Normally, compulsion spells can't make you hurt yourself unless that's all they're designed to do. They certainly can't make you do it as a *side effect*." The loathing in his voice was thick as heavy cream. He wasn't going to be forgiving Simon for a while, if he ever did.

"He's using Evening's magic to supercharge his own." Her name should be safe enough here, this close to the ocean, where Maeve's magic overwhelmed Titania's. "It's going to hurt him soon, if it hasn't already. But we can't count on him running out of her blood, not when he had so long to collect it. Did he say anything about where he was going?"

"Just that he wouldn't need me as a bargaining chip." Quentin paled further, eyes getting even wider. "Dean," he gasped. "He . . . he hurt . . . we went to Goldengreen before he brought me here, and he hurt Dean. And all the others. I don't think . . . I don't think anyone's alive in Goldengreen."

I'd been halfway hoping he wouldn't remember that until we were done dealing with Simon himself. "They're not dead, Quentin," I said. "He turned them into trees and toadstools, but those are living things, and the Luidaeg is working on bringing them back right now."

"Really?" he asked, voice small and hurt and hopeful. It was painful to hear.

"Really-really," I said. "She'd be here if she didn't need to wake them up. And he didn't get everyone. Marcia got away."

Quentin frowned. "No, she didn't," he said. "I saw her in the courtyard. I wanted to scream, but I couldn't do anything but watch what he was doing to them. I wanted to kill him. I still want to kill him." He blinked, expression guileless. "Please may I kill him?"

"I'd really prefer you didn't kill him until he knows who he is and where he's supposed to be going. Remember that he's doing all this while under the influence of the Luidaeg's spell."

"Which he took on himself voluntarily."

"Only to save his daughter," I said. "If this is anyone's fault, it's hers. She's the one who decided she knew better than anyone else, and that she could be the one to bring Oberon back. Simon didn't do this to himself because he wanted power. He just wanted to bring August home. Now come on."

"Where are we going?" asked Quentin, still clutching his stomach.

"To do the same for him," I said grimly, and led him out the kitchen door, into the cool air of the coastal night.

SEVENTEEN

MOST UNDERSEA DEMESNES ARE huge by land standards, consisting of miles upon miles of sea floor and coast. Half Moon Bay was as adjacent to Saltmist as San Francisco, and thanks to the presence of the Roane—formerly the presence of the Selkies—the paths between the two were better worn here.

We made our way along the beach, heading for the rocky tower rising in the distance, a natural result of time and erosion. There are wonders in this world that have nothing to do with Faerie. Natural archways created by ceaselessly rushing water created doorways into the center of the rock formation, and we walked through the largest of them, into a moon-washed chamber with salt-stained walls. The surf ran out halfway across the "room," creating a line of darker, heavily moistened sand.

And there, at the edge of where the ocean met the shore, was Simon Torquill, bow still in his hands. He was facing the water, eyes locked on the reflection of the moon on the waves, looking like he was on the verge of tears. It was odd to see him that way. It was odd to see him in any way that wasn't cool and conniving and somehow three steps ahead of the rest of us.

"What did you think was going to happen?" I asked, once we were close enough that I didn't have to yell to be heard above the waves. Simon whipped around, starting to raise his bow, then sagged and let it fall back to his side. He looked at me like a man defeated. I shrugged. "Did you think the seas were going to open at your approach?"

"I thought I'd steal a skin from one of the Selkies, and let it carry me down to Saltmist," he said, voice dull. "Once there, I could breach the doors and find Patrick. If they're holding him captive down there, I can get him out. That boy, in Goldengreen . . . he looked so much like my Patrick, and nothing like him at all . . ."

I'd never thought Dean looked that much like his father, but it was possible Simon had seen something I couldn't. "Patrick's no one's captive. Dianda isn't in the habit of kidnapping her own husband."

"Then why did he leave me for so long?" Simon glared at me, anguish in his voice and eyes. He barely seemed to realize Quentin was there. That was probably a good thing; Quentin clearly wanted to hurt him for what he'd done to Dean, and if he made another move toward my squire, I would help. I wouldn't need to invite Simon to my wedding if he was dead. Sometimes the easiest solution to a problem is also the best one.

"He didn't leave you," I said. "He fell in love, and when the earthquake happened, both of you got distracted. He had to help Dianda rebuild Saltmist. You were looking for your daughter. I know you can't remember her right now, because she's part of your way home, but please try to believe me when I tell you she's real. Her name is August. She loves you very much." That was as close as I could come to praising my sister, who was every inch our mother's child.

Simon frowned, shaking his head hard. "No. I could never—I would never—you're telling me I have a child and I've somehow *forgotten* her? Is that how little you think of me?"

"I think you've been the monster under my bed for more than a decade," I said. "I think you terrify me. I think you made a lot of really bad choices, and it doesn't matter if you made them for what you thought were good reasons, because why you do a thing doesn't matter nearly as much as what you do. And I think that no matter how powerful you are, magically, you're not too powerful for the Luidaeg to enchant. You put a compulsion spell on my squire. She put a slightly more elaborate spell on you. It's the same thing."

"I don't know how to fix this," he said, sounding utterly miserable. "I've never encountered anything I didn't know how to fix before. This is . . . terrible."

He raised the bow again, in a single smooth motion, pulling back the string and aiming his already-notched arrow directly at the center of Quentin's chest. My squire made a small, strangled sound of dismay. I fought the urge to jump between them. I was the one with the potential to fix this. If I got myself elf-shot, I couldn't do that.

It was the right decision. But leaving Quentin to take the risk of what would happen if Simon's hand slipped was more painful than anything else I'd done since this whole mess began.

"Simon, if you hurt him, I will kill you, and Oberon's Law be damned," I snapped. The Law was full of loopholes anyway. If Simon shot Quentin with elf-shot so powerful that it overwhelmed his system and he died in his sleep, he wouldn't be considered guilty of Quentin's murder. There were always ways to argue around the consequences of your actions in Faerie, if you could make yourself stop caring about who got hurt in the process. And if Simon hurt Quentin again, I was going to be way, way past the point of caring.

Simon blinked, a look of brief consternation on his face. "You really mean that," he said.

"I don't understand why you're so surprised. You were with Oleander de Merelands for years, and I don't think anyone will ever be able to accurately verify her kill count."

Simon shook his head. "She never killed as many people as she was given credit for. I think Faerie just wanted another monster, and she was the best candidate we could find."

"She killed King Gilad, and she killed the mother of his children, and she killed Lily," I said. "That's at least three corpses I can place at her feet, and she already had a reputation as a killer when she killed Gilad and his lover."

Simon shook his head again, harder this time. "I never said she was a good person. Just that she wasn't as much of a monster as they accused her of—uh-uh, boy." He shifted the angle of his bow, keeping the arrow trained on Quentin. "You don't move. I'd rather not die today, so I'm holding my fire. You'll excuse me if I don't trust you to do the same."

"I won't excuse you for *anything*," spat Quentin. "You hurt Dean. You say you're looking for Patrick because you care about him, but you hurt his son, and he won't ever forgive you for that. I won't forgive you for that either. I love him, and you hurt him, and you made me stand there and watch. I hate you."

Simon frowned and switched his gaze back to me, clearly trying to dismiss Quentin as unimportant—and just as clearly failing. "Patrick will come home. He always comes home."

"Patrick is happy in Saltmist. He's not going to come here just because you decided to stand on the beach and chuck rocks at his roof. And you're lucky you didn't find and steal a Selkie skin. Not only would the Luidaeg have hunted you to the ends of the earth for interfering with her plans for them, you wouldn't have been Daoine Sidhe anymore. A Selkie transformation is permanent." Rayseline had dodged that change only because she had never actually used the skin she'd stolen, choosing instead to wear it as a simple disguise. She might never know how close she'd come to becoming the Luidaeg's charge instead of Titania's.

"I don't remember *any* of this," snapped Simon. "You've been lying to me since we met."

"I've never lied to you at all," I said. "It's your patroness who lied to you, and who's still lying to you, because you're in her service and you shouldn't be. She never meant you well. All she ever did was help you get lost."

To my surprise, Simon sighed. "I know that," he said, in a soft voice. "You think I don't know that?"

I blinked. "Um, yes. I thought you didn't know that. If you know she's lying to you, why are you breaking things to try and wake her up?"

"Because I have nothing else. I can't find Oleander, my parents are dead, Sylvester rejected me when he found his Luna, Patrick— Patrick let me think he was dead. I'm alone in the world except for my lady, and if she wants to lie to me, then let her lie. At least I know I'm useful to her. At least I know she's not going to leave me."

The thought of Evening Winterrose as the last dependable person in Simon's life ached. I took a step forward. "It doesn't have to be that way. Let me take you back to the Luidaeg. She can help you find your way home."

"Does that require someone to find Oberon?" asked Quentin.

"If that's what has to happen, that's what has to happen," I said, keeping my eyes on Simon. "Come on, Simon. Let me bring you back to your family. They miss you." August did, anyway. I couldn't be so confident about Mom. Mom rarely seemed to miss anyone, and she'd left Simon when he'd demonstrated that he cared more about August than he did about her.

My family sort of sucks sometimes.

Simon looked, for a moment, like he was considering my request. Then he raised his bow again, aiming squarely for the center of my chest. "No," he said. "I don't think so."

Things began to happen very quickly after that. Quentin lunged forward, shouting. Danny's own shout echoed a second later, the massive man running down the beach with a wide, ground-eating stride. For a second, it looked like he was going to reach us on time, like this was all going to have a very different ending.

Then Simon let the arrow go.

It flew swift and true and faster than any of us could move. I looked numbly down at the arrow protruding from the left side of my chest. It had missed the heart, although it was probably embedded in my lung. Well, that wouldn't be the first time. Not by a long shot. I started to reach up and pull it out, but midway through the gesture, my arms stopped obeying me.

I was unconscious before I hit the beach. I never even felt myself fall.

EIGHTEEN

I OPENED MY EYES on a world wreathed in fog, the sort of thick, gray, all-consuming fog that hasn't been common in the Bay Area since I was a little girl. I sat up, pleased to find I still had arms I could use to lever myself, and a body that could do the sitting, then pushed myself to my feet. So far, so good. Everything seemed to be working normally.

There was a faint ache in the left side of my chest, like there was something lodged there that didn't belong, but I tried not to dwell on it. If Quentin and Danny wanted to leave the arrow where it was until they could get me to someone who could help, that was their choice. I didn't have many choices left to me right now.

I felt surprisingly good, for someone who'd just been flung into a chemically induced dream state by an asshole with a bow and arrow. That could probably be partially attributed to how little humanity I had left. Elf-shot puts purebloods to sleep. It kills humans and changelings. I was still human enough that it would kill me eventually, if it didn't start shutting down my body's autonomic functions before it had the chance to poison me. Really, life in Faerie is an endless string of delights.

But I was almost a pureblood now. I had so little humanity for the elf-shot to attack that I might as well have had none at all. I held tightly to that thought as I stepped forward into the fog, trying to make out literally anything that could tell me where I was.

When I wind up in these weird dreamscapes, there's usually a reason for it. And yeah, the reason is frequently either "you're dying" or "you're attempting some act of blood magic that isn't just beyond you, it's literally impossible, and yet you've decided you can do it anyway," but those are still reasons. Since I'd just been elf-shot, I was willing to bet "dying" was the answer here.

I took another step into the mist that swirled and eddied around me like a flag. The smell of roses drifted through the chill, and I recoiled, trying to move away from it. Not fast enough; not well enough. My shoulder bumped into something solid that couldn't possibly have been behind me, and I turned, glacially slow, to gaze upon the face of the woman I was increasingly convinced had been my enemy since long before I existed.

Eira was back in her Evening Winterrose guise, beautiful, yes, but no more so than any other member of the Daoine Sidhe. Her long black hair was unbound and filled with glittering oil slick rainbows that shifted and danced despite the absence of any clear light. Her skin was so pale that it would have looked completely white if not for the mist surrounding her, and her eyes were a deep, frozen blue, like jewels dredged up from the bottom of the sea. She was beautiful and she was terrible and just looking at her made it harder for me to breathe, like she was stealing all the air from the rest of the world.

She was draped in a dress that appeared to have been crafted from layers of mist, tied over her shoulders in careless ribbons that shifted and faded away at the ends. I will never fully understand what it is about the Firstborn and wearing the weather. Although I guess if I had that kind of power, I'd show off, too.

"Well, well," she purred. "Amy's little castoff. I'm not allowed to kill you myself, but it seems I'll have the opportunity after all. I'm inside you now."

"Since you weren't invited, that's a massive violation," I said. "I'd go be in someone else if I were you."

She laughed, sounding as giddy and delighted as she ever had, back when she'd been pretending to be my friend. "Still the same little October, I see. The most impatient month of the year."

My knife was still at my belt. It would take nothing to slide it into her belly and spill her arrogant Firstborn guts on the mist-draped ground. It also wouldn't do me any good. As a Firstborn, she couldn't die unless her killer used silver *and* iron. I lost the ability to carry iron without hurting myself a long time ago. My fingers still itched to make the attempt.

"You're supposed to be asleep, remember? You invented elf-shot. The least you could do is let it do its job."

"Oh, *now* you respect my work? You, who did everything in your power to do away with it? I don't believe you get a say in how it's used now."

"I don't think you're supposed to be having a say in anything, since you're currently asleep in a couloir at the end of the Rose Road, where no one's ever going to find you or set you free again."

"Of course they will. In a hundred years I'll wake up, if nothing else changes, and I have the Torquill boy." She waved a hand dismissively. "He'll keep fighting for me forever, thanks to you and my briny sister. You know, she treats you as poorly as I ever did, the way she keeps sending you off on her errands with no concern for whether you can survive whatever you find. I don't understand why you like her so much better than you do me."

If not for how dark her hair was, she could have been swallowed entirely by the mist around her. She was almost the spitting image of my mother, which made me wonder why it had taken me so long to realize they were sisters. Well, half-sisters. They shared a father, but their mothers couldn't have been more different if they'd been trying.

"The Luidaeg has never lied to me," I spat. "Unlike you."

"Ah, but she would, if she was able. She would tell you all the same pretty, self-serving lies you hated so much from me, because we're Firstborn. We're better than you. You've never done anything to earn the truth from either one of us—she gives it to you because she doesn't have a choice, not after my mother cursed her."

"Why did she do that?"

Evening shrugged, the edges of her dress blending into the mist. "She thought she had reason. Someone must have told her Maeve's daughter was spreading lies about her, and about me, and about all her other children. Someone must have said there was a danger. And that someone must have gotten exactly what they wanted, because when we're honest with you, our fragile little descendants, you realize too quickly that we're not the same. We're so far above you that you'll never be our equals, even if you try forever, and so there's no sense in trying."

I had always known the Luidaeg's honesty was a punishment. I'd never considered that it might have been a punishment intended to make us more afraid of our own Firstborn. Something had to have changed to take them from being beloved parents and family members and turn them into gods and monsters. Something had to have caused us to pull away. Was one curse on one woman that something? I stared at her.

"You can't be serious," I said. "How long have you been working to betray Faerie?"

"Oh, a long, long time," she said. "Longer than your tiny mind is capable of comprehending. I work on a scale you can't understand even in your fantasies."

"Uh-huh." I studied my fingernails. "Sure you do. But you know, here's the thing: I know you can still lie."

Evening blinked. "What does that have to do with anything?"

"If you had so much time, why would your dogsbody be working so hard to wake you up? Why would you even care about being put to sleep for a century? That's no time at all to someone who works on a scale I can't comprehend." I lowered my hand and smiled at her. "I think you're full of shit. I think you're working on a much tighter timeline than you want me to believe. And I think you're *desperate* to wake up before we manage to dismantle any more of your plans. When you faked your death to try and take me out you had, what, two kingdoms in your thrall? That's not counting the nobles who owed you their positions, or Goldengreen, or Simon, oak and ash, *Simon*. That man only ever wanted to bring his daughter home, and you used that wanting like a knife you could slide between his ribs over and over again until he bled out on your floor. You had everything, and now you have what? A rose bier in a place none of your faithful can reach? One last servant, who's killing himself trying to control your magic long enough to wake you? Simon's about used up."

"He was always weak," she said dismissively. "Son of a human woman playing at being good enough to be a member of my bloodline, panting after my tainted baby sister like she meant something. My blood was always going to be the death of him, regardless of what drove him to start abusing it, because only purity can handle purity."

It was my turn to blink at her. "Wow. I really hope this is some sort of messed-up hallucination, and you're not really talking to me right now."

"Oh? Why is that?"

"Because the Evening Winterrose I knew was arrogant and smug and thought too much of herself, but she was never this kind of bigot. Although I guess, with everything I've learned about the Daoine Sidhe since I stopped calling myself one, none of this should be a surprise. You are your mother's daughter."

"My mother's *favorite* daughter," she corrected. "You've met two of us now. Can you honestly believe Acacia would ever be as well-beloved as I was?"

The count was actually three: I had also met Amphitrite, the Merrow Firstborn, during our trip to the Duchy of Ships. Three daughters of Titania, one aligned to each of the three major schools of magic. It was interesting, and somewhat telling, that the only one of them I'd spend any time with socially was the most water-aligned of the three. Water is traditionally Maeve's domain, but the lines aren't hard and fast.

"I'm not sure I'd brag about being Titania's favorite," I said. "It seems like an honor with very few selling points."

Evening scowled, red, red lips pursing in a moue of displeasure. "I'll thank you to keep my mother's name out of your mouth."

"I'll thank you to stop messing with my friends and family members because you think being Firstborn makes you better than us." The pain in my chest was getting worse, radiating from the place where the arrow had pierced me in the waking world. I grimaced and touched the spot, trying to massage the pain away. It didn't help. Evening's scowl melted into a smile, as smug as the cat with a mouthful of canary.

"Oh, does it burn?" she asked. "That'll be the poison doing its work. My little dogsbody, as you call him, has a nimble mind but no imagination. It's been easy enough to influence him since all he knows how to do is bleed the world around him for his own benefit."

"He's been using more and more of your blood because you wanted him to, hasn't he?" Evening didn't answer. She also didn't deny it or look away. That was something of a relief since the wave of rage that washed over me made it easier to ignore the pain. "It's the blood. The more he uses, the more you can tell him what to do. Even elf-shot, you're still pulling the strings."

"The humans have a fairy tale about me, did you know that?" She smiled again, more magnanimously. It was probably easy to be magnanimous, now that she thought she was winning. "They say I ate a poisoned apple and spent a century asleep in a coffin made of glass, until I was brought back to the land of the living by the mercy of true love's kiss. I didn't love the man. He just happened to lay his shameful little fetish at my perfect feet as the effects of the poison left my system, and so I woke up and allowed him to be useful."

"I'd heard rumors," I said warily. The connection between Eira Rosynhwyr and Snow White was more than just skin-deep. The people of the mortal world had seen a beautiful woman with skin as white as snow walking through the forest, untroubled by the frost, and they had explained her to themselves, spinning a story to suit the facts they had and replace the ones that they were missing. That's mortal magic. They patch the holes in the world with words, and sometimes those words can hold long after the truth has worn away.

"I'm strongest when I'm sleeping," she said, still with that smug little smile on her lips. The desire to slap it off was stronger than I wanted to admit. "Out of all my siblings, even Amy, I'm the one who understands the blood we were gifted by our parents the best. I can see what it intends, not just what it is. And I can order it to conceal the things I don't want to share. Simon has been in communion with me since he was foolish enough to take my sister's bargain and remember what it means to be mine. Every time he's let me past his lips, he's been listening to me as he will never listen to anyone else. I told him how to brew the elf-shot from what he could find growing in my lands. I told him which roses to gather, which streams to attend upon, and how to patch the empty places with my blood. Sleep is my gift."

I stared at her. "Your blood is in the elf-shot he's using."

"I've been trying to tell you that." She took a step toward me, the fabric of her dress fading and almost drifting away with the motion. "I'm inside you now, little blood-worker girl, and no matter how strong you think you've become, you're never going to be as powerful as I am. I was the first of our kind. Without me, you'd have had no one to learn from."

"You're wrong," I said, and refused to step backward. She didn't get to intimidate me. Not here, not now. Not ever again. "Oberon would have been there even if you'd never been born."

"And where is he now? My precious father, who loved his children so dearly that he left us the second he had the opportunity to do so? I suppose you'd know something about absent fathers, though, wouldn't you? Born of Amandine's line. Tam Lin couldn't wait to run. Not once Maeve's Ride was broken by your grandmother." She paused, smirking.

Clearly, she thought she'd just dropped a bombshell, something that would stun and disorient me. That seems to be the real reason purebloods are so obsessed with keeping secrets: they treat them like weapons, assembling their armories one blade and bludgeon at a time, only to deploy them when they can do the most damage. Too bad for Evening that I already knew who my grandparents were, and who they weren't. Janet had been pregnant when she'd gone to break the Ride, and the strain of the magic she'd been barraged with had been enough to make her lose the baby. It would have been mortal if it had lived, and like all mortal things, it would have been long since gone. The Ride was centuries ago, after all.

"Your father and my mother's father are the same man," I said patiently. "If he was absent for her, he was absent for you as well, and I don't see how it has anything to do with me. Oberon vanished after the Ride was broken."

"You mean Oberon *left*. Maeve was taken, my mother was banished, and Oberon left us to fend for ourselves, after chasing us out of our rooms and locking the doors to trap us here like naughty children. He laid down what bindings he thought were essential to keep us from killing each other in his absence, and then he was gone, and we had no one left to protect us. We were children, and our parents abandoned us."

"Children" seemed like a funny way to describe a group of immortal, ageless fae, many of whom had children and grandchildren of their own by the time Oberon left—and some of whom had already, like the Luidaeg, buried those descendants. But for Evening, who had always possessed Titania's protection and what passed for her approval, it must have been a shocking, almost unendurable change. It didn't make me feel bad for her, even though that was clearly what she'd been trying for. It did make me feel like I might be able to understand her just a little bit better.

"I don't know why Oberon left, or why Titania was banished; I'm not entirely sure why Maeve disappeared, because you all hint at it and talk around it, instead of saying anything simply. I know it had something to do with the breaking of her Ride." I shrugged. "If you want to explain, it's not like I have anywhere else to be right now."

The pain in my chest was getting worse and worse, making it increasingly difficult to concentrate. I didn't like that. I tried to turn my awareness inward, to make sure I wasn't involuntarily changing the balance of my blood again, but my magic refused to respond. It wasn't there to listen to me. I lifted my hands and stared at them, wide-eyed.

Evening laughed, the sound of ice breaking at the edges of a frozen lake, sharp and beautiful and terrible, all at once. "You're in my domain now, traitor's child. You have no power that I do not choose to grant you."

"That's real nice of you, Ms. Winterrose," I said, lowering my hands and glaring at her. "It's because your blood is currently inside me, right? Well, it isn't in my veins, and unless you have a way to stop me healing, it won't be there for long."

"Oh, October, October, don't you understand how dreams work?" Her smile was sweeter, and smugger, than it had ever been before. She took another step toward me. "You can dream for *years* in a single night—not even a night. Most dreams last only minutes when they're measured outside the sleeper. Out there in the waking world, you haven't even hit the ground yet. I have all the time with you I could possibly need. By the time I allow this dream to end, you'll be mine as sure as Simon is, and your only wish will be to fulfill my deepest and cruelest desires. As soon as he shot you, you belonged to me. There was no other outcome left."

I raised an eyebrow. "That's it? That's your grand and glorious plan? To get me elf-shot so you can use the presence of your blood inside my body to manipulate me? Don't you ever come up with anything new? At least last time, you managed to get me to swallow it myself. This is sort of cheating, don't you think?"

"Mock me all you like, child, you'll have time enough to regret it. No roses here for you to pull, no herbs to gather; I could tell you 'lady, let alone,' but it would make no difference, not when your transgressions are so dire."

I blinked, taking a step backward. "Wait—say that again."

Evening looked confused. "Mock me all you like; you'll have time enough to regret it?"

"No, not that part—the part about leaving things alone. Where have I heard that before?"

"It's what the man who would have been your ancestor, had your grandmother not bewitched my father with her mortal charms, said when he found her stealing roses from his good green wood."

The ballad—of course. It was a line from the ballad of Tam Lin, the song Amandine used to sing me when I really *was* a child, the song that commemorated the devastation my family had accidentally unleashed on Faerie. "She had not picked a rose, a rose, a rose but barely one," I said slowly. "When up there came the young Tam Lin, said 'lady, let alone.'" But where had I heard that recently?

Evening stepped toward me again, expression growing impatient. "No more foolishness. It's time for your education to begin."

The pain in my chest was growing intense enough to make everything else seem irrelevant. It was like someone had scooped out my lung and replaced it with a burning ember, scorching my ribs and charring the flesh around it. I gasped and clutched my chest, dropping to my knees in the soft, unseen sand of the beach. Above me, I heard Evening's disdainful laughter.

"Really, October? Feigning a heart attack to avoid the inevitable? You may as well surrender now, for nothing is going to change what's coming."

My heartbeat was perfectly normal. I raised my head. "This isn't a heart attack," I spat.

"Well, what is it, then?"

I smiled. "Salvation," I said, and opened my eyes.

My eyelashes were frozen together. I felt some of them shatter when I pulled them apart. The cold struck me a moment later, ice caking my face and hair. I couldn't move, but I could freeze. That was normal enough. Danny must have called for Tybalt before he'd come running, and then my glorious, reckless fiancé had carried me along the shadow roads, as he always did when he needed to save me from the consequences of my own actions.

I allowed my eyes to drift closed again, not quite comprehending the blurry shapes and lights of whatever I'd been looking at. It seemed less important than lying quietly and starting to thaw. I wasn't sure I'd ever been so cold.

Cold or no, the feeling was coming back to my fingers, and I could tell that someone was clutching my hand so tightly that it would probably ache, once I was capable of comprehending pain.

"—her up," said Tybalt, voice quick and urgent. "You need to wake her up. She can't sleep for a century. I can't endure a century without her. I've endured too many already."

"She's awake," said Walther. He sounded utterly exhausted, which made sense; he'd already been fighting to wake May and must not have been expecting to have me dumped on his plate as well. I made a mental note that we owed the man some good strong coffee, and maybe a trip to the massage parlor of his choice. He was going to need to relax after this night.

"Why didn't you tell me?" demanded Tybalt.

"She *just* woke up," said Walther. That was all he had time to say before Tybalt was gripping the sides of my face, lifting my head off whatever I'd been lain out on. I tried to open my eyes again. They refused to accommodate me.

"She's awake, but she's not likely to be responsive for a while," said a third voice—the Luidaeg. I officially had no idea where we were. Evening must have been lying about how long I'd been asleep. That was no real surprise. Tybalt was fast. He wasn't *that* fast. "My darling sister put her blood into that elf-shot mixture, or more accurately, convinced the failure to do it for her. Toby's not a descendant of Titania. The stuff will be eating at her until she manages to expel it."

"Can we help at all?" Walther again. Good old Walther. How does anyone function without an alchemist on call? I guess they have to make much more of an effort not to get poisoned, which seems like a lot of work.

"You're already helping," said the Luidaeg. "But your countercharm doesn't purge the body; it just breaks the connection between the ingredients. There's no way to purge blood from her system without some really nasty side effects. Like exsanguination."

"I should never have allowed her to go off without me, whatever the little dream-walker said she saw," said Tybalt, slowly taking his hands away from my face. He didn't move away; I could still feel his presence, warm and close and comforting. "She always gets herself into trouble when I'm not around."

"Be fair to yourself, kitty-cat," said the Luidaeg. "She gets into trouble when you *are* around. She gets into trouble like my father is paying her for it."

Her father. Something about Oberon . . . my conversation with Evening wasn't fading like an ordinary dream, maybe because it hadn't been a dream at all. It had been all too real, and I had come all too close to being trapped there. But something Evening had said about Oberon was nagging at me.

I opened my eyes again. This time, the room around me came more immediately into focus; I was looking at the ceiling of the Luidaeg's apartment, not at Walther's office. How many people had Tybalt transported?

"Welcome back," said the Luidaeg. "I'd say I'd been worried, but I can't lie. Your kitty is another story. Maybe reassure him."

Tybalt's face appeared in my limited field of vision, as his hands returned to the sides of my face. "October?" he asked. "Are you all right?"

Well, I couldn't speak or shake my head, so clearly, I was not all right. I blinked, and promptly regretted it, as my eyes didn't want to open again once they were closed. This was getting tedious.

Opening my eyes took the kind of effort I normally associated with hard labor, but I was determined, and Tybalt was holding me, and in the end, I achieved it. He looked me in the eye and laughed, an oddly choked sound that teetered on the edge of becoming a sob. I wanted to comfort him, and the fact that I couldn't was one more thing I was never going to forgive Evening for. That woman had a laundry list of offenses to answer to, and while many of them weren't crimes by either human or fae standards, I was going to hold her to them as if they were.

The thought was comforting enough to make me feel a little warmer, although that could just have been the ice in my hair continuing to melt. This time when I blinked, my eyes opened again easily. That wasn't enough for Tybalt; he gave me a concerned look before turning to look at someone I couldn't see, hands still cupping my face.

"She's not moving. Luidaeg, why isn't she moving?"

"The little alchemist—"

"Walther," Walther interjected, mildly as if he weren't interrupting the sea witch.

"—was able to counteract my sister's new elf-shot blend, barely, but it had time to do plenty of damage, and October is still piecing herself back together. Yes, this is unusually slow for her, but I don't think it's a problem: she's had my sister's blood inside her body a lot longer than would be good for *anybody*, much less one of my father's children with nothing of Titania in her to fight back. We can be sure she's all right once she starts talking."

Talking. The idea was appealing and incredibly daunting at the same time, like a mountain too insurmountable to consider climbing. I took a deep breath and tried to force a sound out from between my lips, succeeding only in making a squeak so soft it was barely audible even to my own ears. No; there wasn't going to be any talking for a while yet.

I wanted to know who else was here. Danny had called Tybalt, and there was no way they'd left Quentin on the beach while they carried me back to the Luidaeg. But where was Simon? Was Cassandra here? Were we almost finished with this day's work, or was it just beginning?

I tried again. This time, I made a louder sound, one that was audible outside my own head. Tybalt's head snapped around, pupils narrowing to slits as he stared at me. "October?"

I took the deepest breath my lungs allowed and finally managed to whisper, "Quentin . . . ?"

"He's here," said Tybalt, stroking my cheek with one hand. "He was with you on the beach when I reached you. That boy should have been Cait Sidhe, he has the heart of a lion. He had the knife from your belt in his hand and was squaring off against a sorcerer with bow and arrow. He is, perhaps, a little too accustomed to your invincibility, and forgets he isn't actually your son. He can bleed almost as well as you can."

I blinked again, managing to force the slightest sliver of a smile. Tybalt laughed in earnest this time, beaming down on me.

"Once you can sit up, you can see him. I'm afraid he's been banished to the couch for the crime of hovering."

"Getting *real tired* of having people cast compulsion spells on me," snapped Quentin, irritation and exhaustion painting his Canadian accent in broader strokes than usual. "I need to pee, and I can't get up!"

"Should've listened the third time I told you to sit your butt down or I'd make you," said the Luidaeg, sounding almost jovial. "Most kids your age listen when the sea witch tells them to do something."

Quentin made a rude scoffing sound. I really did break that boy.

My muscles were still in near-rebellion, refusing to obey when I told them I wanted to move. At least there was no pain, and blinking was getting steadily easier. I made a frustrated noise. Tybalt straightened, giving me an almost unobstructed view of the ceiling. I could still see his shoulder and the side of his head, which kept the "motionless and can't see anyone" tension from kicking back in.

"How much longer?" he asked.

"Poppy is upstairs with Officer Thornton, and she's promised to bring a strengthening potion with her when she returns," said the Luidaeg. "I'm sure your alchemist could brew something almost as good, if you don't want to wait."

Walther sighed gustily but didn't argue. It wasn't just that the Luidaeg can't lie, meaning she wouldn't have been able to say that if she didn't *really* think her strengthening potions were better. Which, again, sea witch. If anyone had had the time to really refine what they were doing, it was her.

"I'm here! Here's me!" As always, Poppy made announcing her own arrival sound like something of vast and unspeakable import. "Brought what you asked for, yes I did, but the man's restless as anything. He doesn't want to stay asleep or abed. You'll need to be seeing to him, because I've reached the limits of what I can do."

Poppy suddenly appeared in my field of vision, looming over me in all her orange glory. She had an uncorked bottle in one hand and beamed like this was an ordinary situation. "Want you up and about, we do, so it's time to help with that," she said, and slid her free hand behind my head, lifting it away from whatever I was lying on until she could press the bottle to my lips. "Drink careful."

The liquid tasted like bubblegum, blueberries, and tequila—not the best combination ever, but not the worst I'd ever come across. She trickled it past my lips slowly enough that I could swallow without choking, which was good, because she seemed determined not to stop until I'd swallowed it all. I did my best. After the first few mouthfuls, she took her hand away, and I was delighted to discover I could hold my head up without assistance. For that, I would drink all the weird bullshit she wanted.

She kept pouring, stepping backward as she did, forcing me to follow her if I didn't want the liquid to dribble down my front. Tybalt gasped. I ignored him and kept swallowing until Poppy pulled the bottle away and smiled radiantly, and I realized I was sitting upright, unsupported.

"Better, isn't that?" she asked.

I looked around, still a little dazed and dizzy, and the rest of the Luidaeg's living room became clear. There was Quentin on one end of the couch, with Simon on the other. Neither of them was standing, although Quentin looked like he wanted to. Simon looked like he'd been hit in the head with a plank and was lolling limply. If not for the fact that I knew it wasn't her way of doing things, I would have suspected the Luidaeg of hitting him with elf-shot.

Danny was looming off to one side, looking profoundly uncomfortable, with the Luidaeg standing nearby, back in her "ordinary, harmless human teenager" guise, down to the electrical tape in her hair. She smiled at me, and that was the last thing I saw before Tybalt swept down and grabbed me in a fierce embrace, burying his face in my shoulder.

This time, when I tried to move my arms, they obeyed, and I wrapped my arms around him, stroking his back with one hand.

"Hey," I said. "Hey, I'm okay."

"Elf-shot, May still sleeping, Quentin kidnapped, half of Gold-engreen enchanted, and you'd call that 'okay'? My love, we need to buy you a dictionary." His voice was slightly muffled by the fact that he was speaking into my shoulder, but he at least sounded amused enough that I probably wasn't in any real trouble.

At least not with him. If Walther didn't wake May up soon, Jazz might be a different story. I twisted around to plant a kiss on the side of his head, and said, "We found Simon."

"Which is most of the problem, as far as I'm concerned."

"Don't worry; I have a bigger problem for you to deal with." I pulled away. He let me go reluctantly, and I turned to the Luidaeg. "I need two favors, and I am willing to pay for them if you feel it necessary."

She raised an eyebrow. "Are you, now? I've never met anyone so eager to fall into my debt. What can I do for you, October, daughter of Amandine, returned once again from beyond the borders of death? The night-haunts must curse your name every time you deny them, and dream of the day their bellies will be full."

"I need you to wake Simon up, and I need you to unlock Officer Thornton's room," I said.

Her second eyebrow climbed to join the first. "Such small requests to risk your soul upon. I assume you have what you consider a good reason?"

"I do," I said. "To be clear, August traded her way home for your father's return, and Simon took her debt upon himself. If he found your father and brought him back, would his way home be fully restored, no conditions, no strings?"

"That's the deal as struck, yes," said the Luidaeg, still looking at me quizzically. "It's a simple enough thing, on the face of it. Find one man in a vast universe largely made up of spaces he can reach, and no one else even knows for certain still exist, and convince him to come back to his eldest daughter who misses him very much. If Simon can find and recover my father, his debt is paid."

"What if someone else did it?"

"Then Simon's debt becomes unpayable, and he is lost." The confusion faded from her face. "October, what is it you think you've done?"

"We'll find out in a moment, won't we?" I slid off the Formica table where I'd been stretched out like a corpse, walking toward Simon. My knees were still weak and a little wobbly, but that was fine; that made it easier to hide my nerves. If I was wrong . . .

I wasn't wrong. It all made sense. Things in Faerie never start making sense until the moment they're ready to unravel, and then they all fall into place at once, like the mystery has gotten tired of holding its breath and just wants to be finished. I walked toward Simon as if I were in a dream, only realizing when I was halfway there that I was unarmed; the knife that was normally at my belt was absent.

I turned to face Quentin. "I need my knife back."

He looked at me mulishly, jaw jutting out at an angle entirely unbefitting someone who was going to be asked to rule a continent someday. "You could have *died*," he said. "You left me alone with Simon. If I hadn't taken the knife, he was going to shoot me, too."

"And if you think a knife was going to stop him from letting go of a bowstring, we need to call Etienne and arrange for more lessons," I said. "Knife, please. Luidaeg? Can Quentin get up now?"

"Give the lady back her pokey toy, kid," said the Luidaeg. "I want to see what she's about to do."

"I don't," said Tybalt.

He was right. He didn't. If there had been a way to make him leave, I would have taken it, for distressing as this was going to be for the rest of us, I had no doubt it was going to be twice as bad for him. I didn't turn. If I saw his face, I would probably lose my nerve. Instead, I stayed exactly where I was, hand outstretched, waiting as Quentin sullenly stood, stomped across the room, and slapped the hilt of my knife back into my palm.

"I appreciate it," I said. Something Tybalt had said finally clicked home, and I blinked. "Half of Goldengreen enchanted?"

"I had time to restore most of the larger occupants of the knowe to their customary forms before I got called away by the rolling emergency that is your ongoing existence," said the Luidaeg dryly. "When this adventure is over, I'll get back to work, and restore the rest of them. I'm sure someone will get around to paying me eventually, since the alternative is a pissy, ill-treated sea witch hanging around making nasty comments about people who don't pay their bills."

"Right." That explained why Quentin looked sullen, not hysterical. If Dean was bipedal again, half of his problems were solved. Good thing for both of us that I was about to produce some new ones. I turned back to Simon. The Luidaeg snapped her fingers. He opened his eyes, stiffening when he saw his surroundings, and started to slide a hand over the cushion next to him in the time-honored "searching for a weapon" gesture.

I held up my knife, wiggling it at him. "Maybe chill," I said. "We're not going to hurt you."

"I might," said Tybalt.

"We can start a club," said Quentin.

The Luidaeg didn't say anything. She didn't have to. The woman could radiate quiet malice like it was her job. Simon paled.

"Stop being terrifying, everyone, I know what I'm doing." I approached the couch, kneeling in front of Simon as I pulled the candle stub out of my pocket. "You may not remember this, but you made a bargain with the sea witch," I said. "You gave her your way home in exchange for your daughter's freedom, a daughter you immediately forgot, because if you knew she was there to find, you could never be truly lost. You promised Antigone of Albany, daughter of Oberon and Maeve, born when the tide was a toy and the sea was a wonderland, that you would find her father and bring him back to her. Do you remember?"

Wordless and wide-eyed, Simon shook his head. He couldn't seem to decide whether he should be looking at me or at my knife, which was an understandable dilemma. I have trouble figuring out whether to focus on the warrior or the weapon when someone's that close to me with something that can do me harm. At the end of the day, though, a knife's just a knife; what matters is the hand that holds it.

"N-no," he said, finally seeming to realize I was going to wait until he gave me an answer. "I'm sorry, but I don't remember any of this."

"You will," I said, and placed the candle on the floor in front of me as I raised the knife, placing the point of it against my chest, right in front of my heart. A quick, hard thrust would be enough to drive it home. "Simon Torquill, by fae law, you are, and have always been, my father, whether we've accepted it or not. I spent most of my life not knowing what you were to me, and now you've forgotten what I am to you. But as your child, born of blood or no, I have the right to claim your debts as my own. Do you agree?"

"I'm sorry," he said again. "You seem to have gotten the wrong idea. I assure you, if I had a child, I would know—"

"Do you *agree* that a daughter has the right to take her father's debts?" I hissed, between my teeth. I could hear Tybalt making an angry growling noise behind me, and I had little doubt that only the presence and obvious approval of the Luidaeg was keeping him from lunging forward and disrupting what I was preparing to do.

I had a man who loved me more than he loved his own safety. Who loved me enough to stand idly by while I did the wrong thing for the right reasons. Oh, sweet Maeve, I hoped I wasn't about to take myself away from him.

"I agree," said Simon, in a puzzled tone.

"Good," I said, and slammed the knife home as the candle lit itself.

NINETEEN

THE PAIN WAS LESS extreme than I expected it to be. It washed over me like a wave breaking on the shore, disappearing as soon as it passed across my skin. There was still a knife sticking out of my chest. It just didn't hurt.

The candle burned a clear and lambent blue, the shade of swampfire, the color of magic.

Simon stared at me, horror and confusion in his eyes. Then he blinked, and while the horror didn't disappear, the confusion did, replaced by something far worse: comprehension. "October?" he said, in a puzzled voice devoid of either hostility or dislike. "What have you—what have you *done*?"

I could feel feathers in my throat, tickling and scratching me as something moved there. I coughed, trying to force them back down, and said, "I've paid for your freedom. Don't worry, I have a plan. And Patrick is waiting for you."

Now the confusion was back, leavened with a sliver of hope. "Patrick? My Patrick? I remember you saying—but that can't be true, can it? He's alive?"

"He's alive, and the reason this is happening, so yeah, I'm telling the truth." The feathers in my throat were getting harder to swallow. I bent forward, catching myself before I could fall, and vomited a live bird onto the floor next to the candle.

Unlike the bird I'd seen the Luidaeg extract from Simon, which had been lovely and swallow-tailed, designed to be admired as much as anything, my bird was a pigeon, wings of slate and breast gleaming with greens and purples. But it was beautiful all the same, even if it wasn't a valued or refined beauty. It was beautiful. And it was mine.

The Luidaeg leaned forward and picked up my bird. I felt a pang of loss, like this was something that absolutely couldn't be allowed to happen—something impossible and forbidden. I pulled the knife from my chest, intending to fight her for the bird, and she fixed me with a look that froze me where I knelt, making any further motion as good as impossible.

"You agreed to this," she said. "You *chose* this. As much as if not more than anyone else who has ever made this particular bargain with me. I just hope, for all our sakes, that you're right. We can't afford to lose another hero right now."

I might be frozen, but Simon wasn't. He lunged to his feet, moving to put himself between me and the Luidaeg. "She may have agreed to this, but I didn't! I don't! Take it back, right now! Don't do this to her! Please, Luidaeg, if there's any good left in you, please, don't do this to her. Don't hurt her for my sake."

The Luidaeg fixed him with a look like a spear, and asked, "Do you think I would if I had any choice in the matter? She's worth a hundred of you, *failure*, and I didn't want to do this. Thank your Firstborn, if you're ever unlucky enough to see her again. She can finish devouring you and tell you that you're welcome as she picks her teeth with your bones. I believe this is yours." She reached into her overalls with her free hand, pulling out a bottle. A bird was trapped inside, wings beating weakly against the glass. She popped the cork with her thumb and the bird flew free, slamming into Simon's chest and disappearing.

His gaze cleared further, and he dropped to his knees in front of me, nearly setting his trousers on fire as he gathered me clumsily into his arms. "October, October, I'm so sorry," he moaned. "I never wanted to hurt you again, I never wanted to hurt anyone, but I got so *lost*, and it was like I was someone else, someone who didn't care enough to stop himself from doing all those terrible things . . ."

"Apologize to Quentin, not me," I said, and forced a smile. "I signed up for this. He didn't. Patrick's probably going to be a little pissed at you for turning his eldest son into a tree, though."

Simon paled again. Apparently, the thought of Patrick being

angry with him was even more distressing than I'd expected it to be. Interesting.

But not for long.

"Again, I'm sorry about this, and I hope you're right," said the Luidaeg, and shoved my pigeon into the bottle. It should have been too big to fit, but somehow it just got smaller and smaller until it was inside, and she pushed the stopper home. Something snapped under my breastbone, leaving me untethered. The world got fuzzy around the edges, and I couldn't breathe.

I blinked several times, trying to clear the dizzying specks from my eyes. Someone was touching me. No one was supposed to be touching me. I pushed them away, and managed not to shriek when I saw that it was Simon Torquill, my liege's brother, a man who'd never been willing to give me anything more than a smirk or a sneer when he saw me in the halls of Shadowed Hills. Sweet Titania, was he one of those perverts who liked changelings more than he should, because we were usually younger than any pureblood girl it was acceptable to fuck?

I scrambled to my feet, spinning to see the rest of my surroundings. I was in someone's living room, shabby and lived-in, with a large, comfortable couch up against one wall and a variety of other chairs and small tables scattered invitingly around the place. There was a candle burning by my feet, and no television. Whoever lived here must not have liked fun.

It was impossible to guess which of the people around me lived here. There was another Daoine Sidhe in addition to Simon, a boy barely out of his teens, with hair in an improbably deep shade of metallic bronze. He was staring at me like I'd just sprouted another head. He must have been one of those sheltered kids who'd never seen a real changeling before, the ones whose parents wanted to keep them "pure" and uncorrupted by the human world and its byproducts. There was a Tylwyth Teg man standing in front of what looked like a really sweet chemistry set, boiling a bunch of rose petals in a beaker. Great. I'd fallen into a pureblood drug den. It wasn't the first one. But alchemists in living rooms didn't usually intend anything good for the local changelings.

A Bridge Troll stood near one wall, looking at me miserably. Maybe he knew what that alchemist intended, and why I'd been brought here. Bridge Trolls don't tend to have changeling kids of their own, on account of them being too big; they'd break any human they tried to get intimate with. Maybe that's why they're generally pretty mellow about us.

The other three people in the room didn't make things any easier to understand. There was a woman with orange hair and stained glass wings, who didn't look right to be an Ellyllon, but was too tall and not scrawny enough to be a Puca; a human teenager in overalls, who had probably been brought here for the same terrible purpose I had; and—

"You fucker!" I pointed at the Cait Sidhe man who was watching from the other side of the room, his face an impassive mask. Like the others, he wasn't wearing any illusions to make himself look human; unlike the last time I'd seen him, he wasn't manipulating his form to seem closer to Daoine Sidhe, either. His hair was striped like a tabby cat's and looked halfway to becoming fur. His eyes widened when I spoke to him. Probably startled that I dared open my mouth in his presence, the jerk.

"O-October?" he said, voice wavering a little. "What's wrong? What has she done?"

She? She who? There were two options, and while the human girl was closer to me than the woman with the orange wings, neither of them looked hostile. "Nothing's wrong, except someone's decided it would be a fun time to abduct me, and of the available options, you seem like the most likely." I kept pointing at him. "The only other person here I know is Simon, and he wouldn't snatch me off the street. Sylvester would never forgive him if he did."

Once I knew where I was, I could run for Shadowed Hills. Sylvester would protect me. Or I could go Home. Between Sylvester and Devin, I'd be safe. There was no one in this room who'd dare to go up against both a Daoine Sidhe Duke and a changeling crime lord in his own den. I'm good at pissing people off, but none of my enemies are remotely that powerful. Sometimes I'm still stunned that my allies are.

Tybalt's face fell, and for a confusing moment, he looked like he was going to cry. That didn't make any sense, but then, nothing about this day made any sense. I took a step backward, trying to put the end of the couch between me and the rest of these people. Simon grabbed my arm before I could get past him, jerking me around so he could stare into my eyes. He really did look almost exactly like his brother. Twins are creepy. Faces should be like fingerprints: one copy ever, no imitations allowed.

"October, wait." He held me tightly, not letting go. The smell of smoke and sweet cider began to rise in the air around him, surprisingly strong. He must have been preparing one damn doozy of a spell. "No one here is your enemy."

"Like hell, Uncle Creepy." I jerked my arm out of his grasp. He let go, realizing I was going to hurt myself if he didn't. I glared at him. "You're like the evil grand vizier from a Disney movie. You only show up when you *want* something, and then Sylvester has to chase you away again before you get your slimy hands all over Shadowed Hills. He," I hooked a finger toward Tybalt, who hadn't moved, "*hates* me. He always has. Any room containing the two of you isn't a room that means me well. Devin didn't train no fools. I don't give one sweet fuck about how much you want me to stay here. I'm not hanging around so you can hurt me."

"October—"

The human teenager, who must not have been all that human, to be surrounded by this many fae—fuck, was I even wearing an illusion?—and not be freaking out, held her hands out toward me in a calming gesture. I reached up to feel the point of my ear and confirm that I could currently pass for human, and nearly screamed when my fingers found something much more pointed than it should have been. The entire shape of my ear had changed. What's more, it didn't itch; I wasn't disguised. I backed deeper into the corner, trying not to hyperventilate.

"What the *fuck* did you people do to me?" I demanded.

"We loved you," said the teenager. "That's all. The rest, you did to yourself. I know better than anyone what you're fighting against right now, but if you can focus, even a little, I think that will make things easier on everyone."

There was something happening to her eyes. They were changing, going from green as a broken glass bottle to solid black from side to side, like the eyes of a shark. I raised one shaking hand and pointed at her, whispering, "Eyes like pitch and a friendly face. I know you. I *know* you. You're the sea witch, aren't you?" Greatest of Faerie's demons. Worse even than Blind Michael, who Rode the hills and stole children away in the middle of the night. She couldn't be here. I couldn't be here *with* her. This wasn't possible.

This wasn't happening. The thought was strangely appealing.

Simon had a flair for illusions. I let my hand drop to my side and turned on him, spitting, "Stop this."

He looked at me like he was innocent, hurt and confused and a little perplexed. I leaned over and planted my hands at the center of his chest, shoving him. There was blood under my fingernails. Why was there blood under my nails? I always tried to have as little contact with blood as I could manage. The stuff was disgusting, and the fact that Mom used it in her magic didn't help.

"I said *stop*!" I yelled, as he fell backward into the couch.

"Wow, this spell really tailors itself to the target," said the teenager who might be the sea witch, blinking her black eyes but looking otherwise unconcerned. "August ran into the woods like nothing had changed. You went full evil mastermind and started trying to kill us all . . ."

"I would already have apologized for that if October had been in her right mind and willing to listen," said Simon abashedly.

"Always an excuse with you," said the teenager. She snapped her fingers, and I couldn't move, not to shove Simon again, not even to back deeper into the corner. "I know you can't believe me right now, but this was your idea," she said, eyes on me. "You thought you had the answer to breaking this curse so your fucked-up branch of the family can stop passing it around like some sort of unwanted vase. Now stay here. I have to keep a promise." She turned, heading for the door.

"What promise?" demanded Tybalt. There was an inexplicable note of panic in his voice.

"I told your lady fair that I'd unlock a door," she said, and stepped into the hall, leaving me immobile and surrounded by people I either didn't know or didn't like.

"I hate it when she slings magic around like it's nothing," grumbled the younger Daoine Sidhe. He walked toward me, pausing to bend and gingerly retrieve a silver knife from the floor. It looked sharp. It also looked well-used; there were flecks of blood dried on the hilt, and streaks of something much fresher on the blade. "I'll just, um, hold this for you, for now," he said. "I promise I'll give it back when you're ready."

"You can't give it *back* when it's not *mine*," I snarled. At least I could talk. I tried to move my little finger, but even that was apparently forbidden. "I don't know who you are or what you want, but the sea witch isn't anyone to mess around with, kid. She's not your friend, and she's not going to grant your heart's desire just because you helped her hurt me."

"Ignore her," said the alchemist. "I know it's hard when someone you love starts saying things like that, but she's not herself right now. Literally." He looked over his shoulder at me. "Lily would never have spoken so highly of you if you had been like this."

"You know Lily?" I calmed a little. Lily has always had excellent taste in people. If this man was someone she knew, then he probably wasn't working with Simon, the sea witch, or King Asshole over there, who was looking at me like I'd just killed his puppy. Assuming he'd have a puppy, or that he wouldn't kill it himself.

"I *knew* Lily," he said, and turned back to his chemistry set. "She took me in when I came to the Mists. I didn't have a place, and she was willing to give me one, even though I offered her nothing but another alchemist with an irregular education. All the noble households—even your beloved Shadowed Hills—needed to know I'd be useful before they'd offer me more than the barest requirements of hospitality. But Lily loved you. Lily said you were worth more than the nobles around you. Please don't prove her wrong."

I blinked at him. He was talking about Lily in the past tense. But that didn't make any sense. Lily was in the Tea Gardens. Lily would always be in the Tea Gardens. There's virtually nothing in Faerie that can kill an Undine.

No one said anything. Silence fell, broken only by the pounding of my heart and the sound of Tybalt's inexplicably labored breathing. He was still looking at me like I represented some great, heartbreaking betrayal, and I couldn't for the life of me figure out why.

The teenager stepped back into the room. She nodded when she saw I was still in the corner where she'd left me. "Good," she said. "I was half afraid you'd remember enough to break free, and not enough to know that you didn't want to." She stepped to the side, looking expectantly back the way she'd come. "Not long now."

I had no idea what she was talking about, unless they'd brought me here to be fed to some great and terrible beast. I tensed as much as I could through the spell binding me, prepared to scream my head off if that was the only option I had.

Something moved in the hall. It seemed too small to be any-thing really dangerous, which was ridiculous. *Pixies* can be dan-gerous when there are enough of them, and they're basically the size of Barbie dolls. The orange woman clapped a hand over her mouth. "Awake, then?" she asked, in an accent I couldn't place.

The teenager nodded. "Awake, and already out of bed when I came to unlock the door. Something has him all stirred up." She glanced at me, black eyes unknowable.

I still couldn't move. A man—a human man, by all appearances, with brown hair, tawny brown skin, and brown eyes—appeared in the doorway, looking wildly around the room. He was wearing sweatpants and a white tank top, and he looked like he hadn't shaved in weeks. Not quite long enough to grow a full beard, long enough to look incredibly scruffy. His feet were bare, and they sank into the carpet as he stumbled toward me, not quite walking steadily.

The teenager snapped her fingers, and the spell holding me in place collapsed. All the tension I'd been gathering was released at once, and I fell forward, landing on my knees in the carpet. I barely missed knocking over the candle. The man kept staggering toward me. I scrambled to get back to my feet before he reached me.

I didn't quite make it. He stopped in front of me, chest heaving, and reached down with one hand to gently cup my chin, tugging as he guided me the rest of the way upright. "Jenny?" he asked, in a voice filled with wondering awe. "*My* Jenny? You came for me? You *found* me, who should have been unfindable?" His eyes flicked to my ears, and he paused.

When he spoke again, he sounded older, and sadder. "No. Not my girl. The child, perhaps. She was so sure it would be a boy, but you look just like your mother. Almandine, that was the name we settled upon. Are you my Almandine?"

The teenager laughed, a little wildly, and when she spoke, she sounded dazed, like she was watching something impossible. "I knew it. I always *knew* my father wouldn't have approved of nam-ing his newest daughter after a trout dish."

"My name is October," I said, staring at the man. "How do you know my mother? But her name isn't 'Almandine,' it's 'Amandine.'"

"Oh, Jenny, you always were fond of shortcuts," said the man. "Forbidden places, forbidden flowers—forbidden hearts. My girl never saw a rose she didn't think was ripe for plucking."

"I'm sorry," I said. "I don't know you."

"How do you not know me?" asked the man. "You were the one who brought me home."

The world shattered then, and fell down around me in prismatic, candy-colored shards, and everything was different, and everything was exactly the same.

TWENTY

OFFICER THORNTON—WHO HAD NEVER really been Officer Thornton; that man had never existed in the way humans think about existence, had never walked the world as an independent, mortal being, although he'd laughed and breathed and lived a life that was as much an illusion as the ones I sometimes wore—looked at me with patience and an infinitely kind acceptance, like he was waiting for me to catch up with his place in the story. It was suddenly hard to breathe. I pressed a hand to my chest, trying to stop my heart from beating too fast and breaking free.

The candleflame was roaring now, so tall that it crested my shoulder, still lambent blue.

From the other side of the not-so-human human man, the Luidaeg watched me warily, eyes black from side to side, the way they were when she was having trouble keeping her composure. I still wasn't sure what all the little changes in her appearance meant, but I had a fairly decent grasp of her eyes at this point.

"Feeling better?" she asked, voice low.

"I was right," I said.

She nodded, biting her lip. "You were right, and I couldn't see it. His magic has always been greater than my own."

"Makes sense," I said, and held my hand out to her. "Please?"

She understood what I was asking and produced the small glass bottle from inside her shirt. When she removed the cork, my pigeon forced its way through the opening and flew unerringly back to me, disappearing into my chest. The last traces of her spell dissolved, like cotton candy in the rain, and I returned my attention to Officer Thornton—to Oberon.

"I got you home," I said. "You were lost in Annwn, and I got you home."

His smile was like the rising sun, radiant and bright and almost too much to look at directly. "You know me now," he said. "You didn't before."

"We've been playing pass-the-curse around to make sure someone found you; it was my turn to have no idea who I was in the world or who loved me until I brought you home," I explained. I still felt a little light-headed, but it was easier if I didn't try to emotionally engage with what was happening, and if I didn't look at Tybalt.

The Luidaeg seemed to feel the same way, minus the not looking at Tybalt part. She was still standing in the same place, not approaching her father, even though she must have been aching to put her arms around him and demand that he never leave again.

"Are you really . . . ?" I asked, as delicately as I could. He had to be: the Luidaeg's magic is never wrong, and the curse that kept me from seeing my own way home even when it was right in front of me had started to lift as soon as he'd entered the room. And the Babylon candle I'd bartered from her as part of learning to give Simon my way home was a bonfire now, too bright to be anything but reacting to its purpose.

He shook his head, running a hand through his hair, an achingly familiar gesture that I remembered copying from my mother when I was too small to understand that no amount of pretending would turn me into the daughter she wanted me to be.

"Not quite," he said. "Not yet. You have to say the words if you want me to be. But you brought me home, and you came here looking for me, and so I came to you."

"What words?" I looked into his brown, perfectly human eyes, and saw no answers there. Behind him, the Luidaeg shook her head, expression helpless. She didn't know either.

But the key to his location had been in Evening's taunting reminder of what he'd said when I first pulled him out of Annwn, believing him to be a human man in need of saving. "Lady, let alone," he'd said to me, in a dirty San Francisco alleyway. Why, unless he'd looked at me and seen my grandmother, the woman who'd borne his youngest daughter, the one who'd been instrumental, however accidentally, in the loss of his wives? No one had ever claimed Oberon had been kidnapped. Everything I'd ever heard had implied he left of his own free will, taking the time to put his affairs in order before walking calmly away.

And going into hiding, it seemed. It made sense. If his daughter could make herself seem so human that magic couldn't tell what she was, why couldn't he? The Three were supposed to be as much more powerful than their children as their children were than the rest of us, which was a horrifying thought. We were standing in the Luidaeg's living room with a physical god, and I was casting around for the keys that would unlock the prison he'd placed himself in.

Simon hadn't moved since Officer Thornton stepped into the room. I wasn't even sure he was breathing. He was just staring at the man, eyes wide and jaw slack, a look of profound confusion and dismay on his face. He looked like a man who'd just lost everything, which didn't make sense, since he had his way home back, and now he was going to get to keep it. I guess meeting the father-in-law for the first time is terrible for everyone.

I shivered as I offered my hands to Officer Thornton, resisting the urge to turn and run across the room, throw myself into Tybalt's arms, and never think about any of this ever again. I was a hero. I had finally come to accept that. Being a hero didn't mean I was equipped to handle actual gods.

But someone had to. And even if the spell was broken, the Luidaeg was standing lost and silent, waiting for someone to finish the process of bringing her father back to her. He slid his hands into mine, and they felt perfectly ordinary, perfectly human, like there was nothing strange about any of this. The heat from the Babylon candle was warming our skins, and we shared the same physical space, man and grandchild, as ourselves, for the first time.

"Tam Lin" didn't quite feel like the answer. Maybe the ballad told the story of how my grandparents met, but Oberon wasn't part of the narrative as it had been written down. Still, it was what we had, and if he was looking for something specific from me, I couldn't imagine what else it would be. Maybe with a little alteration, it would work. "I forbid," I said, voice low and level, "you maidens all who wear gold in your hair to come or go by Caughterha, for Oberon is there. And none shall go by Caughterha but they leave him a pledge, either their rings or mantles green or else . . ." I tapered off.

Somehow, the idea of looking my grandfather in the eye and saying the word "maidenhead" was just a step too far for me.

Thankfully, the Luidaeg was there to pick up the slack. "Ye shall no sooner be entered into that wood, if ye go that way, he will find the manner to speak with you, and if ye speak to him, ye are lost forever. And ye shall ever find him before you, so that it shall be in manner impossible that ye can scape from him without speaking to him, for his words be so pleasant to hear that there is no mortal man that can well scape without speaking to him. And if he see that ye will not speak a word to him, then he will be sore displeased with you, and ere ye can get out of the wood he will cause rain and wind, hail and snow, and will make marvelous tempests with thunder and lightnings, so that it shall seem to you that all the world should perish, and he shall make to seem before you a great running river, black and deep." She stopped to take a breath, and added, "The Book of Huon de Bordeaux, John Bourchier."

As the Luidaeg spoke, Officer Thornton stood up straighter and straighter, and he changed. It was a subtle thing at first, a lengthening of the spine and a shedding of what seemed to be layer upon layer of weariness. Then the subtlety melted away, and with it, his humanity.

Antlers sprouted from his brow, many-pointed as an ancient stag's, brown as weathered bone. They didn't bleed. There was no velvet to soften or gentle them, but as they reached what I assumed was their full span, flowers bloomed along their points, small and white and smelling strongly of a forest's sweetness. The part of my magic responsible for recognizing and cataloging smells couldn't put a name to them. Maybe they were something that only existed when Oberon did.

His eyes remained brown but grew darker, irises spreading to devour his sclera, pupils dwindling until they were a dot of black amidst the layered brown. Predator's eyes. His ears shifted as well, growing sharply pointed before elongating, becoming as flexible and responsive as a stag's.

His body didn't change in any measurable way. I suppose it would have made a certain sense for him to have the lower body of a stag, given the rest of him, but how could Faerie have wasted so much time and energy hating anyone they viewed as bestial if their forefather had been a beast himself? I'm sure we would have found a way—the fae are nothing if not self-contradictory—but it would have required effort, and purebloods tend to also be profoundly lazy.

The bones of his face shifted under his skin, until he looked like the same man and not the same man at all, humanity replaced by something impossibly beautiful, impossibly feral, glorious and terrifying. Looking at him felt the way looking at my mother used to feel, back when I was so much closer to human. I would have collapsed if he hadn't been holding tightly to my hands, blunt claws denting the skin without breaking it.

"Lady, let alone," he said, and smiled radiantly, showing me the razor points of his incisors. Then he let me go, and I *did* fall, or began to. Simon was there to catch me, wrapping his arms around my waist and giving me something to lean against. Together, we watched in silence as the lost King of Faerie turned to face his daughter. The Babylon candle guttered out, its purpose finally fulfilled, and the room was suddenly cold.

The Luidaeg bit her lip as she stepped toward him, black tears escaping from her eyes and running down her cheeks. They left tarry streaks behind, like she was crying off her mascara, but she was actually weeping the color out of her irises, leaving them driftglass green and clearer than I'd ever seen them.

"Daddy?" she asked, in a voice that was barely bigger than a whisper. It shook on the second syllable, breaking.

"Hello, my little Annie," he said, turning to face her, and then he took her into his arms and held her against his chest while she wept into the white tank top that had carried over from his time as Officer Thornton. The fabric drank her tears, and it, too, changed, becoming a doublet of rough brown velvet over a long-sleeved poet's shirt. She couldn't possibly have cried enough to transform his sweatpants, but they grew tighter and more fitted, becoming simple brown breeches. He didn't need any ornamentation. He was Oberon, crowned in horn and flower. That was enough.

That had always been enough.

Simon made a choked sound, loosening his grasp on me. I pulled away before Oberon could look my way again and root me to the floor, flinging myself into the open space between me and the person who needed me most in all the world.

Tybalt met me when I was barely halfway across the room, pulling me into a crushingly tight embrace and surrounding me with the scent of musk and pennyroyal. He held me so close that for a moment it felt like I wasn't going to be able to breathe, and for the same moment, I didn't care. If this was how I died after everything I'd been through, that was fine by me.

By the couch, Oberon and the Luidaeg were holding each other just as tightly, being stared at by Simon on one side and Quentin on the other. Neither of them looked like they were capable of moving. Unsurprisingly, it was Danny who spoke first.

"Titania's fucking ass, is that *actually* fucking *Oberon*?" he asked, in a tone that managed to remain reverent, despite the mortal profanity.

I choked on my own laughter, pulling away from Tybalt just enough to lean back, look at Danny, and say, "I know who you are, so yes, it is."

"And don't think we're not going to discuss that, at length, later," said Tybalt, voice low and menacing. I turned back to him. His eyes were narrowed, pupils hairline slits against the green, and he was looking at me like he'd never seen me before. "There are things you do not gamble with. My heart is one of them. Your memory is another. By gambling with the second, you could have destroyed the first."

"I know." I freed a hand to touch his cheek. "Will it help at all if I say I wasn't gambling? By the time I traded my way home for Simon's, I was already sure I knew where Oberon was."

"It would help if not for the fact that you and the Luidaeg had clearly already begun the conversation, and she knew what you would want. Did you know where Oberon was then?" He could see the answer in my eyes, because he grimaced, a pained look flickering across his face, and turned away. "Of course you didn't."

"Tybalt, I—"

"Don't you have someone you need to save?" he asked, and opened his arms, and let me go.

I stumbled a few feet back, looking at him with wounded bewilderment. I knew he didn't like it when I risked myself, but this had been for us. If I didn't save Simon, we couldn't get married. I hadn't been trying to get hurt. Had I?

Sometimes that's the hardest question of all to answer, and at the moment, it wasn't the important one, because my answer didn't matter as much as Tybalt's, or as Quentin's. We still had messes to clean up. May. All the people at Goldengreen who had yet to be returned to their original forms. The question of whether or not I had screwed things up with my fiancé could wait until I had the space to breathe and give it the attention it deserved.

I took a deep breath and turned to Simon. "Can you undo the rest of the transformations you performed in Goldengreen so that the Luidaeg doesn't have to?" I asked.

He shook his head, looking sheepish. "Not without more of what enabled me to cast them," he said.

"You mean blood."

"Yes."

"You mean *Evening's* blood."

"Yes."

"But it'll kill you if you don't stop using it."

"I suppose it's a yes to that as well," he said, and shook his head again. "Addiction is a terrible thing. I can't say I'm not addicted to the power she has to offer me, or that I wouldn't be glad to have a reason to give in to the temptation one more time, but the risk of her getting her hooks into me again is too high. I finally have my way home."

He said that last word with so much longing that I stopped, really looking at him for the first time since I'd agreed to take his place under the Luidaeg's spell. He looked exhausted, wearied and worn away by what he'd been through; he was too thin, and while the fae don't age the way humans do, I would have sworn he looked years older than his brother. But he was standing up straighter than he had been before, and he wasn't cringing from every little sound in the room. He was a free man.

Free to make his own choices, and his own mistakes. I turned to Walther. "Hey, Walther," I said.

"Hey," he said. "Welcome back."

Unlike Tybalt, he didn't sound angry; if anything, he sounded almost amused, like this was part and parcel of an ordinary day.

"Where are we with waking May up?"

"Cassandra's working on her now. The elf-shot is still interfering with her breathing, and it's hard to keep her stable long enough to administer potions. Someday I'm going to figure out how to make a lot of these things injectable without also making them harmful, and then this will all be so much easier."

"If anyone can do it, it's you." It felt almost sacrilegious to be having such an ordinary question in front of Oberon, like the lost

King of Faerie appeared in the Luidaeg's living room every day, but maybe that was why we needed to have it. Oberon's return changed everything, and it changed nothing. May was still asleep. Tybalt was still angry with me. Life went on.

"I'll get back to work as soon as I get back to my office," agreed Walther. "It's going to be fine."

"I hope so." I couldn't get to Quentin without approaching Oberon and the Luidaeg, which meant it was time to bite the bullet and interrupt two of the most powerful beings in the world. No pressure. I stepped forward, knees only shaking a little, and cleared my throat.

Neither of them moved.

"Um, excuse me?" I managed. "Luidaeg?"

She didn't lift her head from her father's shoulder as she replied with a sullen, "What is it?"

"We need to restore everyone who's still transformed in Goldengreen, and Simon can't break the spell without drinking more of your sister's blood, which will make it easier for her to influence him again. We just got him back. I think Patrick will kill me if I let her mess this up."

"You just got him back? He's been running around playing at evil for what, a handful of years? I've been missing my father for *five centuries*. You can give me an hour."

"I . . . right." I had no idea what Oberon's return would mean for Faerie. I didn't think any of us did. But he was back, and that meant things were going to change. There was no way to avoid that anymore.

Everything was going to change.

TWENTY-ONE

MY CAR WAS PARKED in the alley outside. I looked at it wearily before deciding I didn't want to know how it had come to be here. None of the options I could think of were particularly appealing, save for maybe "Bridget drove it here, and then Etienne opened a portal to take them both home." My keys were in the engine, protected by the soap bubble shield of a ward that burst with the faintest scent of salt as I approached. The Luidaeg had been looking out for me, as she so often did.

"I'll take Walther back to campus," said Danny gruffly, careful to stand far enough back as to not place himself between me and Tybalt.

"I appreciate that, Danny," I said, biting my tongue before I could tack on a "thank you."

"I'll get back to work waking May," said Walther. The edges of the sky were starting to burn with the approach of dawn. He looked at them and grimaced. "So much for date night. I'm going to have to make this up to Cassie."

"I'll buy your next pizza," I said.

He smiled, lopsidedly. "Aw, you know she loves you, but she'll really appreciate someone else picking up the tab."

"Doesn't Arden pay her?"

"Sure she does, and Berkeley pays me, but wow, that girl can put away a slice. We go through a *lot* of pizza. And alchemical supplies and physics textbooks aren't cheap, either." He grimaced. "Sometimes I think Faerie adopting human ideas of currency and capitalism was a bad idea."

"Only sometimes?"

"Most of the time I *know* it was a bad idea." He stepped over and hugged me. "Welcome back. I know you had a plan, but that was terrifying, and if you ever do it again, I'm going to kick whatever your boyfriend leaves of your ass. Got it?"

"Got it." I looked past him to Danny. "Can you hang around campus until May's awake and then give her a ride home?"

"I was already planning on it," he said.

"I'll put a pot of coffee on." Danny won't let me pay him for driving, citing a favor I did for his sister almost twenty years ago as a debt that he's still trying to pay off. I don't actually remember what I did for her that was so impressive, but at this point, if anyone's in debt, it's me. Coffee was the least that I could do.

Danny smiled, expression as rough-hewn as the rest of him, and lumbered toward his car. Walther followed, shoulders stooped, exhaustion showing in every line of his body. He'd had a hard day.

I turned back to my remaining companions. Tybalt was still holding himself farther back than was his norm, unable to forgive me for the risk I'd taken. Quentin was balancing things out by standing closer than he usually would, like he was afraid I'd vanish if he took his eyes off me for a second. Simon was in the middle, weary and wary and too thin by half. I wanted to pause long enough to get the man to a warm bed and a square meal, but I was afraid we didn't have the time.

"The Luidaeg will break the spell on the rest of the people in Goldengreen once she's done welcoming her father," I said. "Dean's already back to normal, which means you shouldn't be in *too* much trouble when his parents find out."

"He's still in trouble with me," muttered Quentin.

"You ate too much chowder," said Simon. It was the first time he'd directly addressed my squire since recovering his way home. Quentin and I both blinked at him. "Even after it started making you feel sick, you kept eating it. Why?"

Quentin didn't answer. Simon frowned.

"*Why?*" he repeated.

"You put me under a compulsion spell," snapped Quentin. "I couldn't stop. Even when I knew I shouldn't eat any more, even when it made me feel bad, I couldn't stop, because you wouldn't let me!"

"And that's why I hurt all of you," said Simon. He looked from Quentin to me, to Tybalt. "I don't claim to have no responsibility in what happened. When my former patroness offered power in exchange for service, I took it because my child was missing, and I was half-mad with the fear that I'd never see her again if I waited to find a better way. Power corrupts, and it ate away at me, making worse and worse choices seem like they were reasonable ones, but the fact remains that the first decision was my own, made when my mind was clouded by nothing more than grief."

"Much as it pains me to say this, you may be wrong," said Tybalt. Simon and I both turned to him. He looked at Simon, shutting me out entirely. "You were Daoine Sidhe standing in the presence of your Firstborn. Anything she said or suggested would have seemed reasonable, whether or not you had good reason to resist her. Even that first choice may not have been yours to make."

"I want to accept that," said Simon. "I want to be blameless. I want to lay all the horrible things I did and said and allowed at someone else's feet. But to do that would be to admit I have no honor of my own, because some of those choices *were* mine. I've watched August and October fight their Firstborn for as long as they've been alive. Can I really claim a grace I would refuse to my own daughters? Either I made my choices, or Amandine has always allowed our girls to rebel. And she would never have risked August in that way."

"Mom's going to be thrilled when she hears Grandma gave her the wrong name," I said, with a sliver of satisfaction. "I just wish I could be there when she finds out."

"Regardless." Simon returned his attention to Quentin. "I made the first choice either entirely or partially on my own, as you chose to follow your knight down a road that might not have a happy ending. And then I made the choice to save my daughter from her own choices, which were not necessarily good ones, and lost any chance I had to make the right choice in the future. Once the sea witch had my way home, all routes to becoming a better man were closed to me. I am genuinely sorry to have done you harm. It was unfair of me to target you. I swear the secrets I learned from October's blood will be kept, and not used against you if I have any choice."

"What does *that* mean?" asked Quentin sullenly.

"It means I still belong in part to a woman who does not easily give her toys away, and she has few enough of them in this time that she's likely to come looking for me when she inevitably wakes." Simon turned his gaze on me, eyes suddenly wide and borderline panicked. "When they elf-shoot me, you mustn't use the blend I brewed. Her blood makes too great a portion of it, and she'll be able to find me in my dreams. She'll twist me back into her creature, and I'll do you harm. Please, please, put me to sleep with something your alchemist makes for you. You owe me nothing. I know that. But let me have the peace of knowing I'll do no further harm."

I blinked, slowly. "Simon . . ."

"I deserve little grace. Give me at least the grace of being kept from her."

Tybalt stepped forward, finally putting himself closer to me. "What you've done in the past may be unforgivable—I have no intention of forgiving you—but that doesn't mean we'll deliver you back into the arms of a monster. Such a thing would make *us* unforgivable, and we are better people than you are."

To my surprise, Simon actually smiled. "You always have been, Sir Cat. Even when you followed my sister more like a lost puppy than a prince, you were a better man than I."

I cleared my throat. "Simon, do you have any objection if Tybalt and I get married?"

He looked startled at the idea. "Why would I think I had the right to object, even if there were anything to object *to*? It's clear to anyone with eyes how much he loves you, and I've held your blood on my tongue. Your love for him flavors everything you are. If I'd tasted any doubt or absence of desire, I might answer differently, because I want you to be happy, but as it is, no, I have no objections. I just hope you'll choose something pleasant for a cake. Some of the things you remember eating and enjoying are appalling." He was clearly trying to lighten the mood.

I wrinkled my nose at him. "Okay, good. Then, on behalf of Tybalt and myself, and to avoid someone trying to claim offense on your behalf, would you please come to our wedding?"

Simon couldn't have looked more startled if I'd hauled off and slapped him. He stared at me for a long, frozen moment—long enough that I started to fear the answer I was going to receive wasn't the one I wanted. If he was invited and chose not to come, would that leave any avenues open to offense? Pureblood etiquette is awful.

"I . . . October, I don't expect you to wait a century for me to wake before you marry," he finally said.

"She's not going to wait another six months before she marries," said Tybalt, voice low and dark. "After stunts like she pulled today, she'll be fortunate if she waits six *days*."

"I don't think we can pull a wedding together in six days without leaving someone off the guest list and offending them forever," I said. "Especially not when we're supposed to get married in Toronto. Quentin's parents will never forgive us if we just go down to the courthouse." Although it was tempting.

Simon shook his head. "I would love to be in attendance. I don't think . . . I mean, you can't intend . . ."

"To keep you awake? Yeah, we sort of do." I glanced from him to Tybalt. "Everyone get in the car. We're going on a road trip."

"Shotgun," said Quentin, heading for the front seat. He paused to check the back for intruders, a habit he'd picked up from me, and Tybalt smirked as he stepped around him to claim the front. It was a familiar routine, and a comforting one. I turned toward the car.

Simon grabbed my arm before I could take a step. I gave him a quizzical look. "Yes?"

"October, what I've done—my brother will never forgive me."

"You're probably right about that. Although, honestly, I'd be a lot more worried about Luna. She's not very forgiving these days, not since she lost the skin she stole." I shook my arm free of his grip. "It's about time we stop holding the past against each other, don't you think? Oberon's back. Anyone wants to be a jerk about letting you keep your eyes open, I'll just point to the actual King of Faerie and tell them you helped me find him."

"But I didn't—"

"You kinda did. If not for Riordan deciding she was going to re-colonize Annwn, he would never have followed me through Chelsea's portal and been stranded in deep Faerie while playing at being human. If not for August having taken a Babylon candle and journeyed there, I wouldn't have gone looking for her, and wouldn't have found him. I don't know why he wasn't able to shrug off his own spell, but presumably he had a reason." One I would be very interested to learn, once we had the chance to sit down and talk this all out. There were going to be so many long, awkward conversations in my future.

Well, as long as no one was trying to stab me, I'd be fine with sitting down for a few awkward conversations. I'd pretty much had my fill of stabbing for the moment. "And while the Luidaeg has been hinting that finding her father might be on the docket, I wasn't planning to go looking for him until I absolutely had to. It was looking for you that let Evening get her hooks back into me, even if it was only for a few minutes, and she accidentally told me where to find him. So you see, without you, none of this would have happened. Now get in the car."

I slid into the driver's seat, glancing at Tybalt, who was already securely buckled and looking straight ahead like a man on the way to his own execution. "Hey," I said softly. Quentin could hear us, but it wasn't like I had that many secrets from my squire. This certainly wasn't one of them. After all, he'd been there. "Are we gonna be okay?"

Tybalt started to huff, probably intending to tell me that no, we weren't. Then he caught himself, reaching across the front seat to rest a hand on my thigh. "I don't know," he said softly. "What you did to me, what you did to yourself—it was the only way forward, and you made your choice with all the information needed to bring yourself back."

"I didn't mean to—"

"Stop." His tone was gentle. I stopped. "Had you failed to find Oberon, I might have been able to convince the Luidaeg that if Simon being married to your mother made him your father, us being engaged made me your husband, and your fate could be my own. My anger isn't because you did it. It's because you did it without explaining to me what you were doing, or why, or how you hoped to have it undone. I know you're accustomed to leaping first and looking during the fall, but I need you to tell me when you're going to jump. I need you to give me the opportunity to jump with you."

At some point during that speech, the car door had opened and closed again as Simon slid into the backseat alongside Quentin. Neither of them spoke. Both of them were smart enough to know that they wouldn't enjoy my reaction if they did.

I took a breath, put my hand over Tybalt's, and squeezed his fingers. "I'm sorry," I said. It seemed silly to be having a serious relationship conversation with the King of Faerie less than twenty feet away—or maybe twenty miles; distance is always a little negotiable when the Luidaeg is involved. That didn't mean we didn't have to have it. Life went on. In the face of heroes and villains, gods and monsters, life went on, and I didn't get to opt out of the hard parts unless I wanted to risk losing the pieces of it that really, truly mattered.

"Just don't do it again," said Tybalt, and exhaled slowly, seeming to release some tightly coiled inner tension.

"Wasn't planning on it," I said, and started the car.

As always, Tybalt's focus shifted to the road once we were moving, hands locking down on the dashboard so hard that it seemed impossible for him not to leave indentations when he finally let go. I smothered my smile. His dislike of riding in cars was well established, and the fact that he was not only willing to do it for my sake, but willing to do it in human form, where we could all talk to each other, was a statement of incredible trust and love.

Simon, who was roughly the same age, was much more relaxed in the backseat, but then, I knew for a fact that Simon used to have a car of his own. Maybe he still did. A lot of purebloods have systems in place for long-term protection of their assets, and I'd never cared enough about Simon's car or lack thereof to ask. I smirked and drove a little faster.

"*Must* you?" asked Tybalt, sounding aggravated.

"Do you want to go home and put all this behind us?"

"Yes."

"Then, unfortunately, yes, I must."

He sighed loudly and closed his eyes.

In short order, we were pulling up in front of the museum. It was early enough that the parking lot was entirely empty. "Everybody out," I said, pushing my door open with my foot.

Tybalt and Quentin tumbled out of the car, the one because he was desperate not to be confined any longer, the other because he was desperate to get inside and see his boyfriend. Simon didn't move.

"Simon?" I opened my door and peered over the seat at him. "We're here. Come on. Get out of the car."

"You can't expect me to face them after what I've done," he said. "I can't—this is cruel, to everyone. Please don't make me do this."

"This is the easiest way I know of to get a message to Saltmist, and you should probably apologize to Dean before he tells his parents what you did," I said, and closed my door before opening his and taking hold of his arm. "Come on. Get out of the car before I drag you out of the car."

"This is assault," he said mildly, unbuckling his seatbelt and allowing himself to be tugged free. "I'll have you know that this is behavior entirely unsuitable for a lady."

"Good thing I'm a knight, not a lady," I said, letting go of him and starting toward the shed that would grant us access into the knowe. Quentin and Tybalt hurried to pace me, while Simon lagged behind, which made sense, given how little he wanted to be here. Goldengreen had been his second home when it belonged to Evening. Now, he was an enemy, unwelcome in these halls, and had no reason to expect a warm reception.

And that didn't matter, because we were nearly finished, and that meant pressing forward until we reached the ending.

We passed through the shed into the knowe, which was a much easier and more pleasant transition than approaching through the Summerlands, for all that I'd learned things on the other route that I had very much needed to know. Evening had been shaping and reshaping the Mists for a long time. She must have had a reason. What was it about the place that kept attracting Firstborn?

Hell, what was it about the place that had attracted *Oberon*? Every time I tried to think too hard about his presence, it was like my mind flinched away from the concept, refusing to consider it more than absolutely necessary. Oberon. I'd found Oberon. I'd interacted with Oberon. The King of Faerie was here, in San Francisco, in his eldest daughter's living room, and it was because of me. But why had he been pretending to be a human police officer? Had he been hiding as a human for five hundred years? What possible utility could that have?

The main hall of Goldengreen was empty, the witch-lights burning pale gold in their sconces and beating back the shadows. No pixies flitted by overhead; they must have still been mushrooms in the courtyard, unable to spread their absent wings.

"I've never been a tree," I said quietly. "I was almost a tree once, but the spell was never finished. Do trees know what's happening around them?"

Tybalt reached over and took my hand, squeezing my fingers.

I shot him a grateful look. He smiled. It was, for a moment, almost pleasantly normal.

"No," said Simon. "They don't, or if they do, it's only in the slowest of vegetable manners. They're essentially asleep without dreaming, until such time as they're released back to their original shapes. Sap and silence are all."

"That's terrible," said Quentin. "Why would you do something so terrible to people?"

Simon gave him a startled but appraising look. "If you had to remove someone from your path, and your choices were killing or changing them, which would seem the kinder?"

"I don't know," said Quentin.

"Changing," said Tybalt.

"Killing," I said.

Simon smiled a little. "You see? There is no agreement. Everyone must decide on their own, when the situation arises and cannot be set aside. A man who has become a tree cannot do you harm, or flee, or anything else. So long as you don't intend to set either ax or flame to his roots, it has always seemed to be the kinder choice, at least to me."

"I don't like it," said Quentin.

"No one's asking you to," said Simon.

We were approaching the kitchen. The lights were on, spilling warm and buttery into the hall. This was Marcia's territory; she'd be inside if she wasn't out of the knowe running an errand for Dean. I motioned for the others to stay where they were, pulling my hand out of Tybalt's, and hurried forward to stick my head into the room.

As I'd expected, there was Marcia, kneading dough on one of the counters. She was back in her usual clothing, no signs of blood or trauma, and her hair had been brushed sleek. That was a good sign. I rapped my knuckles against the doorframe. "Marcia?" I called.

"Oh!" She jumped, barely managing not to drop her dough as she spun around and clutched her flour-covered hands against her chest. "October! I didn't expect to see you so soon. The Luidaeg just left."

"I know," I said. "I've been at her apartment. We had to take care of a few things. Where's Dean?"

"Down in the cove," she said. "He's understandably shaken by the events of the day, and he needed time to clear his head. If you have any business for the County, you can present it to me, and I'll do my best to help you."

"Unfortunately, my business is with Saltmist," I said. "I need Dean to call his parents, and I should probably get the rest of my party out of the hall before—"

A shrill scream from the hall penetrated the kitchen air. I grimaced.

"—someone sees them," I finished. "Dammit." I spun and ran back into the hall, Marcia close behind me.

One of Lily's former handmaidens, a delicate Silene with willow boughs braided in her cascading green hair, was pressed against the wall, knees shaking, pointing at Simon. Marcia grabbed a broom from beside the door and strode forward, pushing past me in her hurry to smack him upside the head with the bristles. He yelped, shielding his face with his arms. She hit him again. As she was pulling back for a third swing, I grabbed the broom handle, and was relieved to find that I was sufficiently stronger than her to stop her before she could continue her assault.

"Marcia, he's with me," I said, trying to wrestle the broom away from her.

She didn't let go. Well, I couldn't entirely blame her for that. As long as I was holding one end of the broom, she at least wasn't hitting Simon anymore. She snarled—literally snarled—and tried to kick him without letting go of her portion of the broom handle. Simon yelped again, ducking behind Tybalt, who looked mildly amused by the whole situation.

"Still a coward, I see," he said, shifting his body just enough to shield Simon from further assault. "What else hasn't changed, I wonder?"

"My profound dislike of pain also remains intact," said Simon stiffly. Unlike Tybalt, he sounded distinctly *un*amused.

"If we could stop hitting each other, that would be nice," I said, giving the broom another hard tug. This time, Marcia let go. I managed not to stumble. "Simon needs to apologize to Dean for what he did, and then we all need to speak with Patrick and Dianda."

"How is he *with you*?" Marcia demanded. "He—he—he attacked us all! He's a monster!"

"No," I said gently. "He's a man, and men make mistakes. The woman who thought she'd purchased his soul, she's a monster, and she's asleep. She's going to be asleep for a long, long time." Although I was going to have to talk to the Luidaeg about that. After what Evening had said about her power being strongest when she was sleeping, I wasn't sure leaving her elf-shot forever was really the safest thing for the rest of us.

But that could wait.

"I am profoundly sorry for my actions here; if I could take them back, I would," said Simon, stepping out from behind Tybalt now that Marcia was no longer armed. "I acted under the constraints of a spell which clouded my mind and left me unable to tell friend from foe. You have my apologies."

"Friend from foe and right from wrong," said Marcia. "I don't go around turning people into trees just because they're not my friends."

Simon looked, for a moment, like he wanted to remind her that she didn't have the power to do anything of the sort. Then he shook his head, expression clearing, and said, "That as well. It won't happen again. I've been freed from the consequences of my own actions and have no intention of selling my soul to anyone else. I'm quite done with masters of that sort. I have no reason to expect you to forgive me, but still, I hope that you can learn to see me as something other than your enemy."

Marcia glanced down the hall to the courtyard door. "I'm not ready for that yet," she said, in a tone which made it clear that she might never be ready. This was a betrayal that ran deep and would continue to do so for some time.

That made sense. As a former member of Lily's household, Marcia had already lost one home due to Simon, and all the "I wasn't myself at the time" in the world couldn't change or undo what had been done. No one here was going to force her to forgive him. Not even me.

"Dean's in the cove, you said?" I asked.

Marcia nodded silently.

"Then we'll go down," I said. "I'll see you when we're done."

"All right," she said, and held out her hand. I gave her back her broom, and she stepped back into the kitchen, leaving us to proceed on our own.

The normal door to the cove receiving room was present and unlocked, saving me from the need to go searching for it. That was something of a relief, as it meant the knowe at least partially approved of us going to speak with Dean. I patted the doorframe reassuringly as we passed through it, trying to signal to the knowe that we meant no harm. Tybalt gave me a tolerantly amused look.

"Someday your penchant for being kind to buildings will stop entertaining me," he said. "Not today."

"I can't keep you and Simon both around," I said. "You both talk like you think Oscar Wilde is going to come along and give you dialogue notes, and there's only so much I can take."

He laughed, and the four of us began to descend the stairs.

Architecture and distance are fluid inside knowes. It felt like the descent took less time than it had in the past, Quentin and Simon all but racing one another in their hurry to be first to the bottom. Tybalt and I followed at a more leisurely pace, fast enough not to let them out of our sight, slowly enough so as to not create a total traffic jam. It was almost pleasant.

Then we came around the curve of the stairs and Dean's private beach appeared beneath us, and two things happened at once. Quentin slung a leg over the banister and abandoned all pretense of walking down the stairs like a normal person in favor of sliding to the bottom, precariously balanced enough that if he hadn't been plummeting toward sand, I might have been worried he was about to crack his skull open, and Simon froze dead where he stood, not descending any farther.

Tybalt and I exchanged a look, nodded, and as we caught up to Simon, each of us grabbed one of his arms and lifted, hoisting him neatly off his feet as we continued our descent. He looked first to Tybalt and then to me, before protesting, "Oh, no—no, I can't. I'm terribly sorry, but I can't—this isn't appropriate, not with their son right there—"

"That's cool," I said. "You're technically my prisoner right now, thanks to you having committed all sorts of crimes."

"Nothing I did was against the Law!"

"We have access to Oberon now," I said reasonably. "We can ask him for more Laws, if you think we need them. But you've been a bad man, and if we leave you to your own devices, someone's going to elf-shoot you and stuff you in a closet just so they don't have to think about you anymore. And that means you're technically my prisoner, until I hand you off to someone else who's willing to take responsibility for your actions. Normally, I think that would be Mom, but let's be realistic; she doesn't take responsibility for her *own* actions, and I'm also sort of not speaking to her on account of how she kidnapped my fiancé to blackmail me into finding my sister. So I'm just going to carry you down the stairs to the nice man who's been worrying about you, okay?"

"I'm the fiancé, and I'm going to help her," said Tybalt.

Simon looked at me bleakly but didn't struggle, and after a few more steps, even began walking again. I was grateful for that. He wasn't the largest man I'd ever met, but it had been a long day, and my upper body strength has never been the best in the world.

Quentin tumbled off the banister as he reached the bottom of the stairs and bolted for Dean—no longer a tree—who was standing at the edge of the water. Patrick and Dianda were with him, Patrick standing, Dianda seated on the dock, her fins dangling in the shallows.

Quentin slammed into Dean, wrapping him in a hug far more enthusiastic than most of their public displays tended to be. Dean slipped his arms around Quentin in return, and for a long moment, the two boys stood there, clasping each other tightly, and no one moved, or said a word.

Then Dianda glanced toward the stairs, and froze before standing, scales falling away, her sapphire-colored shirt growing longer, until it formed a diaphanous dress that stopped just below her knees. Patrick gave her a startled look, then turned to see what she was looking at. He straightened, paling as the blood ran out of his face. Dianda fumbled for his hand. He gripped hers, holding it fast, and neither of them moved.

Dean finally let go of Quentin, the two of them pulling a little bit apart—only a little—so that Dean could see what his parents were looking at. His expression was one of dismay and displeasure, but not fear or outright loathing. I suppose growing up in the Undersea, where any sort of political conflict can be resolved with actual violence, made getting turned into a tree seem like the kinder, gentler option for someone who was invading someone else's territory.

Simon was walking on his own as we reached the bottom of the stairs. Tybalt and I kept hold of his arms, pulling us with him as we approached the Lordens. Neither Patrick nor Dianda moved, and when we were only a few feet away, we let Simon go. He looked down at his feet almost immediately, like he was afraid anything else would be seen as inappropriate. No one said a word.

Well. That wasn't going to work for me. "Simon says he'll come to the wedding, which means no one gets to claim insult against me and try to use it to ruin my life or fuck up my honeymoon," I said bluntly. "Not that we're going to *get* a honeymoon, since someone is inevitably going to try to murder or abduct or transform one of us into something unpleasant, so right now, I'll settle for damage control and being allowed to get married."

Simon didn't say anything. Neither did Patrick or Dianda, both of whom were staring at him like he was the most impossible thing ever to walk the earth.

Right. "If you don't want him, we can take him back to Mom, who doesn't know we've found him yet, but I figured since you were the ones who cared enough to make me invite him to the wedding, and he turned your eldest son into a tree earlier tonight—sorry about that, Dean, how are you feeling?—you might want to see him before she disappears him into her tower."

Simon paled as Dean looked him square in the eye, "I'm feeling much better now. I much prefer being a mammal. I've had a lot of practice, and I think I'm pretty good at it."

"That's nice," I said. "I prefer being a mammal, too. How about you, Tybalt? Are you pro-mammal?"

"I've never been anything else, so I suppose I must be," he said, sounding decidedly entertained by this entire situation. "I do like warmth."

"Then maybe you'd make a good lizard," I said, and turned my attention back to Patrick and Dianda. "Should we get him out of here?"

"*Please* don't," said Patrick, voice beginning to shake. "Please don't return him to that woman. He deserves better than to be passed from Firstborn to Firstborn like some sort of trinket."

"You know, then?" asked Simon.

"Your Amy grew less subtle after you were lost to her," said Dianda. "She started behaving more like her father's daughter all the time. At this point, I doubt there's anyone left in the Kingdom who doesn't know her for a Firstborn."

"I got the memo pretty late," I said mildly.

"Even so," said Dianda. "She hid it better once, when she cared more about being a part of fae society and less about having her own way in all things."

"It's time to be finished with Firstborn, Simon," said Patrick. "You deserve better than their poisoned fruits. You deserve your freedom. It's been absent for so long."

Simon's face fell. Not all at once; it was a slow process, like watching a sandcastle undermined by the incoming tide. It nibbled around the edges at first, until finally everything collapsed, and he began to cry, wailing, "I thought you were *dead*. I thought the earthquake took you, too, and I had to find my daughter, I had to find her before Amy went mad and left me alone, and Ei—" He caught himself before he could finish saying the name. "The woman I worked for told me she could help me bring August home if I'd only do as she said and let her take care of everything else. It sounded so simple. It sounded so *easy*. It couldn't bring you back, but you were better off without me, always had been, and my little girl was lost, and my wife was losing her way, and I agreed. I agreed to everything she said. Until I gave the Luidaeg my way home to ransom August's, my choices were my own. I did what I did because I thought that it was right, and not because anyone was holding a knife to my throat. I don't deserve anything better than I have. I don't even deserve what's already mine. I did what I did because I *wanted* to do it."

"You didn't hurt my son because you wanted to," said Dianda. "That was the Luidaeg's spell making the worst possible choices seem like the best ones—and even then, you didn't *hurt* him. We use stones and turtles in the Undersea, not trees, but the idea of getting your enemies out of the way by turning them into something slow is an old one."

"Only because I had allowed a monster to become the only thing I had left that could substitute for a home."

"You think we don't know the monster claimed you because you interceded on my behalf?" asked Patrick sharply. Simon turned to look at him. Patrick shook his head. "She never lived publicly as our Firstborn, but when Daoine Sidhe did things she didn't approve of, they would take a meeting with the Countess of Goldengreen, and the misbehavior would stop. I had my own meeting with her, remember? I came out of it convinced Dianda was beneath me, and no good son of the Daoine Sidhe could find a future beneath the waves. I would have rejected her, and destroyed my own hopes for a happy life, if not for your intercession. You helped Dianda return me to my senses, and you spoke to the Countess, and she never interfered with me again. Honestly, I'm not sure she ever spoke to me again. She had someone more faithful to serve her. Someone who already knew what it was to serve one of the First, even if we didn't know her for what she was."

"We should all have known long before we did," said Simon, sounding more subdued. "We should have seen the way she bent the world by moving through it. She lied to us, and we allowed it, because something in us knew that any protest would see us slapped down and denied. She hated King Gilad because he stood outside her control. We should have *known*."

"You knew as much as any of us could." Patrick took a cautious step toward him. "You knew about Amandine."

"Not until August's birth," said Simon. "I believed her when she told me she was Daoine Sidhe, before that. It didn't matter. I had a human mother. That put us far enough apart not to be siblings, and so we could marry without concern of impropriety."

That was the first time I'd heard a pureblood even imply that incest might be frowned on. I blinked at him, suddenly putting the lists of surnames I associated with the nobility into a new context. There was always something to learn about Faerie, even now.

"Amandine had a human mother, too," said Quentin. "We've met her. She's a weird lady."

"Five-hundred-year–old humans usually are," I said. "I guess once you get cursed by the Faerie Queen you betrayed, you get a little squirrelly."

Simon turned to frown at me, snapped out of the shell of his reunion with Patrick. "Amy's mother was a human?"

"Oh, buddy, you have a lot left to learn about the family you went and married into, although I have the feeling someone here is getting ready to fix that little problem," I said.

Simon looked startled, then turned back to Patrick. "What is she talking about?"

Patrick reached for his hands, and when Simon didn't pull away, grasped them firmly, twining their fingers together and holding Simon fast. "Dianda and I have discussed this, at length, since you and October brought August home, and you lost your own way. We want you to divorce your wife."

"What?"

"You can now," said Dianda. "August being back means both your children can declare which parent's bloodline they want to belong with. Her absence was the reason we didn't bring this up a long time ago—not that you would have listened while you were still trying to find her. Amandine doesn't treat you like she loves you. She treats you like a useful pet, and maybe that's how she knows to love, but I wouldn't tolerate it if Patrick treated me like that, and I won't stand by while someone I care about is treated like that."

"What?" said Simon again, sounding even more puzzled.

"You can divorce Mom now," I said. "August and I can both approve it. No one can stop you. Mom never tried to get you away from Evening. When you went looking for August and she knew it was hurting you, she didn't help. She never even told me about you. She cut you out of her family a long time ago. Now it's your turn. Cut her free. Cut yourself free."

"You lost your way home and she did nothing," said Tybalt. "I died today, watching October follow you into the dark. I can't imagine sitting by and allowing her to remain lost as Amandine has done with you. Love can't always save you, but love should always try to guide you home."

"I can't leave Amy," said Simon. "August would never forgive me. She must still be so confused after being lost for so long . . ."

"Amandine already left you," said Patrick. "A long time ago. You owe her nothing."

"I think your relationship with August might be improved if she didn't have to worry about whether Mommy and Daddy are going to be fighting again," I said. "And we don't know what she'll choose if given the opportunity to observe your divorce. Maybe she'll go with you. The parent who kept looking for her after the other one had given up and moved on."

"I don't have anywhere to go," said Simon. "My brother will have me elf-shot on a slab before I can finish telling him that I'm coming home to stay. I don't have a home in the human world any longer; I sold the apartment after my patroness feigned her death and left me with no need for legitimate business ties. Amy's tower is the only home available to me right now."

"That's never been true," said Patrick. "Even if you think it is, it's not the case. I would have taken you with me from the start if not for Amandine. I love you."

"*We* love you," said Dianda. She stepped forward, resting a hand on Patrick's shoulder, while Dean looked quietly horrified. "I've never forgotten how much help you were when I was courting Patrick. We could never have navigated the differences between our cultures if you hadn't been there to encourage him to try and keep me from swimming away. You had his heart before I did, and part of it has always belonged exclusively to you. I've never tried to win it away."

Simon stared at her, speechless. I had to admit, I understood the reaction. I'd known they wanted me to find Simon because he and Patrick had been friends when Patrick still lived in the Mists. I hadn't expected it to be because they were trying to get me to facilitate a threesome.

Not that I minded, exactly. It was just a bit of a surprise.

"Leave her," said Patrick, voice low and urgent. "Walk away from that woman, who has never deserved you, not even for a moment. Let your daughters declare themselves one way or another, and you walk away. Come home with us."

"You'll be safe in Saltmist," said Dianda. "We'll keep you safe, and well away from all the dangers the land has to offer you. And before Amy gets any ideas about coming for you, we'll marry you ourselves, and keep you in the deeps forever."

"I . . ." Simon stopped, and simply stared at the two of them. Patrick and Dianda smiled hopefully back, Patrick never letting go of his hands.

"Okay, gotta admit, this is a solution I never thought of," I said, leaning closer to Tybalt. Dean still looked horrified, although confusion was rapidly overwhelming his expression. Quentin just looked confused.

"It's one that is not open to us," said Tybalt firmly. "I refuse to share you, or to be shared."

"Wasn't going to ask you to," I said. "I'm still human enough to prefer the standard model of marriage. Also not a Firstborn, and not planning to let you wander off on some life-threatening quest while I hang out with another dude for a decade."

"Thank Oberon for that," said Tybalt, and kissed me.

It was a good kiss, not glancing, deep enough to distract me from the scene around us, as he gathered me into his arms and pulled me against his chest. The scent of musk and pennyroyal, once so unfamiliar, now so comforting, surrounded us, and I wondered briefly if he'd learned to love the scent of copper and grass as much. It would make sense if he had.

In far too short a time, he let me go again. I understood why— neither of us was overly fond of making a spectacle of ourselves— even as I slightly resented it. I looked back to the others and smiled.

Simon was kissing Patrick.

They were still holding hands, but they were closer together now, their bodies pressed tight, like they were trying to make up for lost time. Dianda was beside them, one hand resting on either man's shoulder, keeping their circle complete. Dean and Quentin had moved a little way down the beach, heads together, talking quietly. Dean still looked uncomfortable, but I suppose "hey, kiddo we want to open our marriage and include the man who just turned you into a tree" was a little awkward for everyone.

"This is better," I said, and it was. It really was.

TWENTY-TWO

SOMETIMES THE WORST PART of a life-changing adventure is the aftermath. I scowled at my reflection in the bathroom mirror, trying to figure out why my hairclips refused to stay level with each other. I'd done everything short of breaking out a ruler, but somehow they always wound up at least an inch out of true.

"Toby? Are you ready *yet*?" May's call was accompanied by a knock on the bathroom door. I transferred my glare to her direction. Maybe she couldn't see it, but it was nice to have something else to glower at for a few seconds.

"My hair is fighting me," I said flatly.

"I told you to call Stacy. Can I come in?"

"I didn't want to call Stacy just to make her come to my mother's divorce proceedings, and you know Cassandra doesn't want her there. Walther's supposed to be showing up to speak on Simon's behalf, and she's still trying to keep him and her mother apart." I opened the bathroom door, gesturing to my hair with my free hand. "Fix it."

"Oh, Toby, how are you so bad at this?" She shook her head and gestured to the toilet. "Sit. I fix."

"How are you so good at this? You have my memories." I closed the lid on the toilet and sat down, tilting my chin up to make it easier for her to get to my hair.

"Not only your memories, and I've been a couple of lady's maids in my time," she said, stepping over and starting to untangle the clips from my hair. They were twisted silver, meant to invoke the twisting shapes of rose canes without actually driving tiny thorns into my scalp. Blood rarely improves a formal outfit. "I know how to deal with hair way more complicated than yours. You just want it to stay out of your eyes today, right?"

"Right," I said, and gestured to the sink. "The rest of the clips are over there." The other half of the set was a series of tiny silver chains studded with polished garnet chips, like falling rose petals or drops of blood. They connected to the clips with narrow loops, adding weight to the accessories, and matched the waterfall earrings I wasn't wearing yet.

"Tybalt get you these?" she asked, picking up a brush.

"Simon."

May's own hair was teased and fluffed into something that wouldn't have seemed out of place in a John Hughes movie, spangled with flecks of rainbow glitter that both enhanced and clashed with the electric blue streaks among the dishwater brown that was her natural color. It was held in place with a stasis spell, rather than an entire can of hairspray, but the effect was the same. She smelled of cotton candy and ashes, strongly enough that I questioned whether anything she was wearing actually existed. But she was less likely to get attacked over the course of the evening than I was, so if she wanted to wear a dress that could be dissolved with one misaimed spell, that was fine.

She pulled my hair into place, roughly enough to sting but not enough to hurt, and clipped it into place with two quick, vicious twists of the clips. Then she retrieved the chains from the sink and began affixing them, humming to herself as she did. I started to relax. She shoved the earrings into my ears.

"Good thing you got these pierced before you healed like it was a competition, huh?" she asked.

"I don't like clip-ons," I confessed. "I always lost them when I was a kid and Mom would make me wear them to formal events." She hadn't allowed me to pierce my ears until I was twelve, a rare degree of parental concern from Amandine, who had frequently seemed surprised to have a child at all when she'd stumble across me playing in the garden or reading in the drawing room. I paused, suddenly wondering if that was because she'd expected me to heal the way August always had and had only relented when she finally accepted that my mortality meant I'd have time to develop the necessary scar tissue.

"I remember," said May, and picked up the necklace that went with the rest of my jewelry, fastening it around my throat. "Can I do your makeup, please, or do I need to let you screw it up first and then ask for help? Because we only have like twenty minutes before we need to leave and it's going to take me almost that long to get your eyeliner right."

I glared at her. "I'm a grownup, you know."

"I know." She picked up the eyeshadow palette I had selected, scowled at the colors it contained, and put it down again. "I'm just going to run to my bathroom and grab a few things."

"Grownups generally know how to dress themselves."

"You're the exception to so many, many rules. Be right back, *don't move.*" She blew me a kiss and ducked out of the bathroom, leaving me sitting there in my robe, abandoned and annoyed.

There was a rattle as Spike trotted into the bathroom, chirped, and rubbed against my ankles, careful to move with the grain of its thorny "fur." I still didn't know where it had gone after our time on the Rose Road, but it had been home when we'd returned there, curled up on the couch with the cats, seemingly none the worse for wear. I wasn't going to look a gift rose goblin in the mouth. I leaned forward, scratching it gingerly on the head.

"Hey, buddy," I said. It chirped again, utterly content. "You're a good little ambulatory rosebush, yes, you are. I appreciate you."

Spike sat back on its haunches and lifted a front paw, licking it daintily before running it across its muzzle.

"I appreciate you, but this isn't the biggest bathroom in the house, so go hang out somewhere else. May needs to fix my face before I head to Muir Woods."

Spike made a disappointed chirping sound, but rose and trotted back out of the bathroom, leaving me alone. I started to slump forward and put my head in my hands but stopped as I considered how annoyed May would be if I messed up my hair again.

It had been a week since Walther found the right combination of herbs, simples, and magical brute force to wake her up. His counter had required a blood donation from the Luidaeg, to chase down and burn away her sister's contribution to the mix. I was starting to think that minimizing contact with the Firstborn, or at least the shitty ones, might be the right answer after all. That was the last any of us had heard from her. She'd dropped the blood off in his office at Berkeley, leaving it on the desk without visibly appearing or opening the office doors, and left a note with it that read only, "Not now. Leave us alone. -A." Out of self-preservation, we had listened, and even I hadn't tried to call her.

Quentin had attempted to go by the apartment once, to tell her the divorce was moving forward, and hadn't even been able to find the alley, much less the door. He'd walked the block where it was supposed to be for almost an hour before coming home and informing me wearily that she didn't want to be found.

It made sense. She was in the middle of the most intense family reunion imaginable. Most people still didn't know it was going on. We had all agreed without discussion that we weren't going to tell anyone who hadn't actually been there to witness what happened about Oberon's return. It was a big secret to keep. It was a bigger secret to spill. Silence seemed like the best and only option we really had.

Tybalt was still being clingier than usual, keeping a close eye on me when we were in the same place and checking in constantly when I went out to work. It would have seemed pushy and overbearing, if not for recent events—and if he didn't calm down soon, he was going to wind up crossing that line, and he would *not* like what he found on the other side. Even I have my limits. Still, I can understand that it's unsettling for the people who love me when I nearly get myself killed, or go and completely forget who they are due to taking Firstborn curses onto myself to save an old enemy, and I can be forgiving.

It's easier to forgive when you're hoping to be forgiven. We care about each other. So we apologize, and we try, even when it's not the most convenient thing that we could do.

May bustled back into the room, a wicker basket full of cosmetics slung over one arm. "Stay," she commanded me, even though I hadn't so much as shifted positions while she was gone. She dumped the basket on the corner of the sink, grabbed my chin, and began smearing fixative around my eyes, blending it with her thumbs.

"This will keep your eyeshadow from sliding down your face as the night goes on," she said. "And it'll help to keep your eyeliner from smearing. Tybalt loves you no matter what, but if you're facing Mom tonight, you should do it looking majestic and heroic, not like someone's slapped tits onto a raccoon."

"You jerk," I said, trying to keep my head from bobbing as

I swallowed my laughter. "Nothing too heavy, okay? I like to be able to recognize my own face when I see it in the mirror."

"Don't worry. Stacy's planning *much* heavier for the wedding. Now close your eyes and relax your face."

"Yes, ma'am." It was easy enough to do as she said. I trusted her not to hurt me, and that alone was a wonderful thing. There aren't many people in this world who I can trust like that.

May worked quickly and silently, not asking for my opinion or my choices of color. She knew I didn't care enough to make good choices, or at least not choices that she would approve of enough to honor. In what felt like hours but was probably less than fifteen minutes, she dropped the mascara back into her basket and said, "You can look now."

"Permission appreciated." I stood, turning toward the bathroom mirror.

May's makeup choices for herself are often "1980s mall décor as aesthetic." She favors heavy neons, contrasting colors that worm their way right up to the edge of clashing before they back off, and glitter. So much glitter. Glitter by the gallon. For me, she had gone in virtually the opposite direction, building up a smoky eye with black eyeliner and half a dozen shades of shadow, made dramatic only by the inclusion of a deep red that mirrored my jewelry and a few highlights of arctic white that made it easier to see what little color my eyes still possessed. She had highlighted my cheekbones so as to accentuate the actual color of my skin and painted my lips in a shade of deep pomegranate. I looked lovely and mature and not remotely like my mother, which, today, was a good thing. I turned back to May, earrings brushing my cheeks. She beamed.

"See, this is why we skip the stage of you pretending you're going to do it yourself and go straight to letting me make sure you're ready for your public," she said. "Your dress is on the bed. Get it on, and we'll get out of here."

"I can dress myself."

"I know!" she said. She was still laughing as she left the bathroom.

I threw a hairbrush at her.

Someday I'll move beyond the dresses we had made for me when I was a child, but as those were expensive, specially tailored to grow up with me as I matured, and most importantly of all, largely in my closet already due to repeated raids on Mom's tower, "someday" isn't going to be particularly soon. The dress spread out across my bed was from that era, long and flowing, with a high neckline that still managed to seem revealing, thanks to the "back" of the dress consisting simply of a band of fabric about four inches across that went over the back of my neck and provided structural stability to the entire bodice. It had been made when I was about nine. I didn't remember what it had looked like before I hit puberty, but I had to hope Amandine hadn't actually commissioned a backless gown for her pre-teen daughter.

It's hard to say, one way or the other. Sometimes fae ideas about appropriateness can be pretty dramatically distinct from human norms.

It was made of gunmetal gray fabric, sleek as satin and softer than velvet, and it sealed to a point just above my hips before running out of fabric. I dropped my robe and worked the dress over my hips, pressing the fabric together with my thumb and forefinger to close it. Nothing so gauche as a zipper here; the dress knew what it was expected to do, and so it simply did it, courtesy of some pureblood seamstress who was probably centuries older than I was and would be appalled to know that a gown made decades ago was being worn in the company of a queen. The fae never get rid of anything. They still have opinions about how often a wardrobe should be refreshed.

Faerie is a construct of constant contradictions. Take them away, and what remains is a jumble that can't even hold its own shape most of the time.

I smoothed the front of the gown with the heels of my hands and returned to the bathroom to retrieve the bangle bracelets that went with the rest of my jewelry, slipping them over my hands and looking at myself in the mirror. I wasn't going to win any Summerlands beauty competitions, but no changeling ever will; we'd be competing against people who've worked for millennia to refine beauty into a weapon. I wasn't going to embarrass myself or my household, and that was what mattered. Tybalt always liked it when I took the time to dress up, saying it was a pleasure to watch the purebloods who'd ignored me when my circumstances were different stand confronted by what they were no longer allowed to have.

Personally, I thought he just enjoyed being a jerk. As with most of the dresses from Mom's place, this one lacked a slit through which to draw my knife, and so I fastened my scabbard around my waist, wearing my weapons openly. A little gauche, maybe, but it was either go gauche or skip the event, since there was no way in hell I was going to *this* party unarmed.

My shoes were by the door. I stepped into them and left the room, heading down the hall to the stairs. Quentin and Tybalt were already in the hall. They straightened at my approach, Quentin looking me over with the assessing eyes of someone for whom the pureblood court system, where appearances were more important than actualities, was second nature, Tybalt just looking. The pure appreciation in his eyes was almost enough to make me uncomfortable.

Only almost.

"No Shadow Roads unless someone is trying *really* hard to murder us," I said. "This dress doesn't have a back, and I'll freeze."

"You do realize that by saying this, you've all but guaranteed someone will attempt to murder us in a way that suits your definition of 'trying *really* hard,'" said Tybalt. "Turn around, please."

I turned around. He made a low growling sound. I smirked at him over my shoulder.

"I take it I have your approval to leave the house like this?"

"Unfortunately, yes," he said, and offered me his arm. "As your escort, I will absorb the envious looks of those who cannot touch you and keep them as my due."

"Gotcha." He and Quentin had both lived up to the night's call for formal dress in their own ways. Tybalt was wearing his customary leather pants, this time in a deep gray that matched my dress, and a dark gray poet's blouse, complete with lace at the cuffs and throat. His boots were black leather, knee-high, and much sturdier looking than my dancing slippers. It was a rakish overall look, and would probably offend my mother's sensibilities, which made it perfect. Quentin was more subdued in gray linen and wine-colored velvet, and he could have appeared in any BBC period piece without raising an eyebrow. His cuff links and belt buckle were bronze, matching his hair well enough to make its odd metallic sheen seem more intentional. Pureblood Daoine Sidhe are experts in dressing to match their hair. They sort of have to be.

"Where's Raj?" I asked.

"Already in Muir Woods," said Tybalt. "May and Jasmine have just left, courtesy of Daniel. It seemed unreasonable to cram five people into your car when we had another vehicle available to us and you wouldn't allow me to carry you there."

"If you carried me, we wouldn't have a car when we were done, and we wouldn't be able to stop for takeout on the way home, and our collection of teenage boys would be at active risk of withering away and blowing off in the first stiff wind," I said.

"I starve, I fail, I fall," said Quentin, deadpan. "If the rest of us can tolerate Toby's driving, you can put up with it for a short trip."

Tybalt hissed at him. I laughed.

"Come on, you dorks. We need to get to Arden's before someone starts a diplomatic incident."

"Is that likely?"

"We have a minimum of two Firstborn, reps from both the Mists and the Undersea, my sister, and all of Arden's court. Also potentially Sylvester and Luna. It's likely."

I started for the door. They followed.

It was a beautiful night, the air crisp and cool without trending into actual coldness. Which was a good thing, considering how much of my dress the seamstress had forgotten about. I slid behind the wheel of my car, fastened my seatbelt, and turned to watch with a certain smugness as Tybalt got into the passenger seat. He waved a hand. The scent of musk and pennyroyal swirled through the air as he wrapped a don't-look-here around the car, protecting us from prying human eyes. I smiled at him, and he smiled back, the nervousness that always accompanied rides in my car still lingering around the edges of his expression.

Which wasn't fair, honestly. I'm a very safe driver. I hardly ever get into car chases or crash on purpose anymore. I started the engine and pulled out of the driveway, clicking on the radio. Quentin hadn't been messing with my settings recently, and the soothing sounds of Toy Matinee blasted into the cab as I turned down the street and began the long, increasingly familiar drive to Muir Woods.

I know people who think anything outside of San Francisco is "the boonies" and not worth thinking about. There have been times in my life when I verged on becoming one of them and may only have been saved by the fact that my liege's knowe is anchored in a small human suburb, and my mother's tower is anchored nearby. I never had the option to shut myself away in San Francisco to the exclusion of all else, and that's proven to be a good thing, since now that Arden's back and holding her family's throne, we're back to attending formal Courts in Muir Woods at her knowe without a name.

Not all knowes have names, obviously, but most of the more modern ones do. They take their names from geographical features, like Shadowed Hills, or from rare treasures, like Goldengreen, or from the person who holds them, like Lily's knowe, or the old Queen's knowe. The knowe in Muir Woods was opened by Arden's grandparents, and while I've heard people try to refer to it as something more specific than just "Muir Woods," nothing ever seems to stick.

Maybe that's for the best. Maybe we've been narrowly guarding our own places and protectorates for too long, and we need to spend some time dealing with the fact that Arden's responsibilities neither began nor ended at her doorway. If it happened within the Mists, it was her problem, and she was allowed to involve herself. I spent a lot of time as Arden's problem.

It would still have been nice if it had been a slightly shorter drive.

The roads were clear. Tybalt relaxed enough that he no longer looked like he was getting ready to leap for the Shadow Roads if I had to hit the brakes harder than he approved of, and Quentin kept leaning forward, making rude comments about my taste in music and trying to get me to put a CD on. I finally snorted.

"You complain because you think the 80s are too 'retro,' but you want me to play a bunch of whaling songs that people have been singing exactly the same way for hundreds of years," I said. "What do you call that?"

"Traditional," he said. "Sea shanties are the heartbeat of the sailing man."

"Do you even know how to sail?"

"Of course," he said, sounding stung. "I don't get to here, because none of the coastal demesnes were looking for a foster when my parents decided it was time to send me away—or maybe Evening convinced them they weren't looking, since she wanted me in Shadowed Hills—but I sailed all the time back when I was home."

"The Duchy of Ships was even better for you than I thought, huh?"

He beamed at me in the rearview mirror, all of us silently agreeing not to discuss what Evening had or had not wanted when she'd convinced his parents to send him here for his blind fosterage. Oh, we knew—she'd been trying to arrange a noble husband for her future use, someone she could mold to her liking while he was young, and then marry to legitimize a claim to the modern power structure of the Westlands—but it was disgusting from every possible angle, and so we did our best to pretend we didn't.

Massive age gaps are common in Faerie. Not as much among changelings, since most of us only have a few centuries to play around with, which is a lot by human standards, and nothing when compared to the literal eternities the purebloods have access to, but fae reach adulthood at roughly the same rate humans do, which means there's a lot of time for a few decades not to feel like they matter as much. Quentin wouldn't be considered an adult in fae society until he was in his thirties, which gave him plenty of time to grow up and figure himself out before he had to worry about getting married and ensuring the lines of succession.

I had to admit, though, that I'm human enough to be glad he wasn't going to be marrying a woman old enough to have personally witnessed continental drift. It would be like me getting into a romantic relationship with the Luidaeg. Not technically illegal, but imbalanced as all hell, and probably bad for both of us.

The lights were off as we approached the mortal side of Muir Woods, the state park having closed at sundown and all the rangers having long since gone home. Even the streetlights were off, presumably to dissuade local teens from breaking into the parking lot to sit in their cars and make out. I slowed down as we approached the chained-shut gates. Tybalt hopped out of the car as soon as it was safe to do so, trotting over and muttering quietly at the lock.

They used to use sturdy cast-iron padlocks on their chains, probably because the parks department has no budget to speak of, rather than out of any sincere desire to keep the fae away. Shortly after Arden reopened the knowe, the local office received a healthy security upgrade in the form of more modern materials. Chrome and stainless steel are iron derivatives. They don't mess with fae magic or poison us nearly as dramatically as the pure stuff does. In a very short period of time, the lock clicked open and Tybalt swung the gates wide, gesturing for me to pull through.

I did so, laughing. Magic and people who are willing to use it on your behalf can make life so much simpler. I should have learned about having friends and allies sooner than I did. It would have made things easier, if not always as overdramatic and violent.

There were a few cars already present, Danny's among them, all concealed by simple charms designed to repel human eyes while leaving them visible to the fae, presumably because their owners didn't want to play bumper cars in the parking lot. It was good to know that we weren't going to be the only ones suffering tonight.

Once we were parked and Quentin and I were out of the car, Tybalt strolled over and calmly offered me his arm. "Ready to change the world again, milady?" he asked, tone mild.

"As long as you're doing it with me, always ready," I said, smiling, and the three of us walked on.

TWENTY-THREE

THE FOREST WAS ONLY DARK to mortal eyes. Globes of witch-light bobbed among the trees, while swarms of bright-winged pixies flitted from bough to bough, chiming like bells, sending trails of glittering dust to drift down over everything they passed. I held Tybalt's arm as we walked, not quite trusting my balance on the slippery walkways. Arden's knowe is accessed through the public side of Muir Woods, something I have to assume was by design; otherwise why would the patch of forest adjacent to the royal seat of the Mists be one of the only stretches not sliced down during the human expansion through the state, when settlers decided that clear-cutting California's redwoods to make room for their European ideas of home and community was a really great idea?

Humans don't like falling into streams or gullies any more than I do, and like me, they lack the preternatural grace of pureblood fae. So they cut trails into the hillsides and built wooden boardwalks over the wetlands, doing their best to make as little impact as possible on the slivers of nature that they chose to preserve. It was a small kindness on top of a huge cruelty, and enough to make me think that there was less difference between them and the fae than anyone wanted to pretend. But Muir Woods was still a healthy riparian woodland, near the beach, and dampness was one of the many great gifts to which it was absolutely heir. The wood was slippery with dew and the paths were slippery with mud, and even holding onto Tybalt, he still had to catch me several times to keep me from spoiling all May's hard work.

"You could have worn more sensible shoes," he murmured, after the third time he had to set me back on my feet.

"Oh, and you would have let me leave the house in this dress and a pair of sneakers?"

"He might have, but I wouldn't," said Quentin, from the path just ahead of us. Primly, he added, "There are standards in this world, even if you think they mostly apply to other people. They need to be respected."

"See? I'm doing the best I can."

"Indeed you are, milady," said Tybalt, and lifted me off my feet to keep my skirt clear of a particularly squishy-looking patch of ground. "You have my sincere apologies for the inconveniences of fashion."

"I hold you personally responsible." I took my hand away from his arm in order to grasp the handrail along the stairway cut into the side of the hill that would take us to the next hiking trail. It wouldn't get us all the way to the door to Arden's knowe—that required a much less dignified ascent, using a series of tree roots in place of a stairway—but it would get us close enough that if I had to be carried, I wouldn't feel too bad about it.

The pixies were getting more frequent, the globes of witch-light brighter. Arden had pulled out all the stops for tonight, or as many as she could on the mortal side of the knowe. I wondered briefly whether the Luidaeg had warned her about her potential bonus guest, or whether this was just a reaction to the idea of hosting two Firstborn at the same time. Then we reached the top of the stairs and confronted the climb up the ladder of tree roots, and I no longer had time to worry about Arden's hospitality.

Sometimes, surrender is the better part of valor. I turned to Tybalt and spread my arms. "Get me to the top?" I asked.

He laughed as he swept me off my feet and braced me against his hip. It was a little awkward, but not as bad as a bridal carry would have been. "As milady wishes," he said, and started nimbly up the side of the hill, Quentin now following close behind us, presumably to step in if Tybalt slipped.

The day when a Cait Sidhe slips and falls on their way up a muddy hillside will probably come—I've seen my cats do clumsier—but it wasn't going to be tonight. When we reached the top, Tybalt set me back on my feet, waiting while I smoothed my dress with the heels of my hands, then offered me his arm. I took it decorously, and the three of us walked slowly forward.

The doors to Arden's knowe were already visible and open, set into the body of an ancient redwood tree that could probably have accommodated my first apartment within the interior of its trunk, if we'd been willing to damage the tree by carving it out. Guards in her livery stood to either side of the door, one an unfamiliar Bridge Troll whose massive shoulders strained against his uniform, the other a petite Glastig who smiled at the sight of us.

"I wondered when you'd be showing up," she said brightly, her Welsh accent stronger than usual, either because she was pushing it forward, or—more likely—because she'd stopped trying to hide it since shifting her fealty to Arden. "Fashionably late, as always."

"The command to appear said the declaration wasn't going to happen until midnight, and I really didn't feel like mingling and eating canapes while my mother glared at me from the other side of the room." I smiled at her. "Hi, Lowri. Still enjoying the Queen's guard?"

"More than I will if you linger out here and cause your mum to take offense at your absence," she said. "I don't want to be called to intervene. Get in there." She stomped one delicate cloven hoof for emphasis, and I swallowed my laughter.

"We're getting," I said, and waved for the boys to follow me as I made my way through the doors into the knowe.

The entry hall was paneled in redwood bas reliefs, each piece carved to show some significant event in the Kingdom's history. Much of the knowe had been conceived and crafted by actual artisans, but this section was solely the knowe itself, making its opinions about what did and did not matter known. The panels changed on a regular basis, even the oldest ones; now, when I looked at them, I could see Simon among the carven crowds with much more frequency than had been the case when the knowe was first reopened. I paused, smiling, at a panel that showed what I assumed was Patrick and Dianda's wedding: they were standing in front of a man whose carved face looked enough like Nolan Windermere to be the late, much-mourned King Gilad.

Simon was there, among the carved figures in the crowd. My

mother was not. Surprisingly, the Luidaeg *was*, and I wondered whether Dianda realized the sea witch had been at her wedding.

The sound of music drifted down the hall from the main ballroom. This felt more like a party than I'd expected, possibly because so many people had to attend to make what was supposedly a fairly simple process as legal as possible. We walked in that direction and were hit about halfway there with the smell of roast meat and mulled wine. There was a strong undercurrent of sugar, implying the presence of at least one dessert table.

An implication that was proven when we stepped through the door into the crowded room. If someone had told me this was a ball, my only question would have been why there was a fiddle player standing next to a harpist on the dais, rather than a full band. The fiddle player was a plump, blue-haired Daoine Sidhe, dressed in long skirt and leather corset, while the harpist was clearly Merrow, due to her current lack of legs. Her fins were tucked under her chair, well out of the way of the fiddler's feet and her own harp, and she looked blissful as she played.

People crowded the room, not so densely as to be remarkable, but enough so as to make me suspect something else was going on here tonight. Arden was near her throne, speaking with Dianda and Patrick, both of whom were dressed with utter formality. So was Arden. She was even wearing her crown, a narrow-banded concoction of braided metal and shining jewels, which I almost never saw outside of its protective case.

I started in that direction. Quentin peeled off almost immediately, presumably because he'd spotted Dean or one of his other friends in the crowd. Tybalt paced me, and together we approached the Queen, pausing about five feet away. I bowed. Tybalt did not. Arden looked amused.

"You realize that once you've set your own crown aside and married one of my subjects, you'll be expected to bow to me like a normal person," she said.

"Yes, but in the moment, I remain a King of Cats, and we do not bow to anyone," he said primly. They both grinned, clearly amused by what had long since become a familiar interplay.

I am never going to understand the relationship they have with one another, and that's fine. They get along, which is more than can be said of most monarchs of the Divided Courts and Kings or Queens of Cats.

"It's almost midnight," said Dianda.

Arden nodded. "I know. Are you sure about this?"

It was an odd question for her to ask, given that Dianda wasn't one of the people getting divorced. Dianda nodded anyway, expression determined.

"We've discussed it at length, and we're certain," she said.

"Very well, then." Arden turned and began making her way up the shallow steps to her throne. The room quieted, everyone turning to map her progress with their eyes. The musicians stopped playing. She ignored them all, settling on the cushion, looking every inch the queen.

Gone were the days when she felt comfortable receiving her court in sweatshirt and jeans, and I couldn't decide whether that was a good thing or a bad one. Her dress was form-fitting and flawless, crafted from spider-silk the deep blue-black of the night sky, fading into rose around her hips and finally a pure, clean gold at her knees. The dark portion of the dress glittered with captive, impossible stars, forming constellations across her bodice and midriff. It was stunning and eye-catching and not at all what a bookstore clerk from San Francisco would wear to something like this. The dark waves of her hair blended with the fabric at her shoulders, and she was a Faerie Queen: there could be no question of that. In a room filled with nobles and luminaries, Arden *shone*.

Tilting her head toward the few people still speaking, Arden snapped her fingers. The sound was impossibly loud in the hush of the room. They stopped immediately, and everything was silence.

"We are here tonight to discuss the marriage of Simon Torquill, landless Baron, most recently in service to the Court of Countess Evening Winterrose, who is unable to be with us tonight due to her untimely death," Arden's expression was a challenge for anyone who knew the truth about Evening to contradict her, "and Amandine, called the Liar by her siblings and descendants. Simon has requested an end to their union, and as both their daughters are present tonight, the marriage is hereby declared eligible to be dissolved. Does anyone object?"

"I do," shouted a familiar voice. I turned. Mom was standing near the courtyard doors, her cheeks flushed with unusually hectic color, her lips set into a hard, indignant line. August was beside and a little bit behind her, head bowed. Both of them wore bone-white gowns that wouldn't have looked out of place in a Waterhouse painting, although Mom's was at least embroidered in gold and belted below her breasts. It didn't do much for her. It did nothing for August, who looked like a child who'd been raiding her mother's closet.

I remembered feeling that way when I was Amandine's shadow. For the first time, I actually felt bad for my sister, who didn't have my options for getting away.

"My *husband* was stolen from me by a woman who made him impossible promises, and twisted his thinking out of true," Mom continued, stepping forward. The light struck prismatic gleams off her near-white hair. She was beautiful, even in her ill-chosen dress, and she knew it well enough to use it to her advantage. "I did nothing to betray his faith while he was running around in her service, bedding Oleander de Merelands, and behaving like a common ruffian."

"You lay with a human," drawled an insouciant voice. I glanced to my left. Raj was standing on the edge of the crowd, arms folded, looking annoyed.

"Humans don't count," snapped Amandine. "I lay with a human because I was lonely, and because I didn't want to betray my husband as he had betrayed me. I never banned him from my bed. He could have come home at any time."

"So you object to this divorce on the basis that you did nothing wrong, and so your husband should not be allowed to change his mind?" asked Arden.

"Yes," said Mom. "And on the basis that my father is Oberon himself, and I do not choose to let Simon Torquill go."

A gasp ran through the room. A surprising number of people didn't know that Mom was Firstborn. Well, that cat was well and truly out of the bag now. Mom would never be able to go back to pretending to be just another Daoine Sidhe. August shot her a look, seemingly torn between horrified and surprised. It wasn't just a matter of Mom outing herself, after all. Both of us were marked now as a Firstborn's daughters.

"That isn't the etiquette we all stood witness over when first a marriage was dissolved, Amy," said a familiar voice. The Luidaeg stepped forward, the crowd parting before her. She was wearing her surging sea dress again, and it broke around her feet like the ocean crashing on the rocks. She lifted her chin, looking down the length of her nose at Mom. "What you want matters not at all.

What he wants matters, and the choice your children make today. They're both here. That means the divorce proceeds, whether you agree with it or not." She turned to look imperiously at Arden. "There are no valid objections. Continue."

Arden looked for a moment like she wanted to argue, then thought better of the impulse. People who argue with the Luidaeg once don't usually get to make a habit of it, assuming the word "people" even applies once they're done. Instead, she cleared her throat, and said, "There are no valid objections to this divorce proceeding. The two named children of Amandine the Liar and Simon Torquill are August Torquill and October Daye. Will August and October please step forward?"

So they weren't going to force May to declare. That was a good thing. I moved to the center of the floor. August moved to meet me, and we shared a brief glance that was still the longest interaction we'd had since I refused her request to bring Simon home. She twisted the skirt of her ill-fitting dress between her fingers, honey-colored eyes filled with weary shadows. Not for the first time, I wondered what it was like bearing the full weight of our mother's attention. From the way August's shoulders drooped, I had to assume it wasn't much fun.

"Before a marriage can be dissolved, all living children must choose which line of descent and inheritance they will belong to," said Arden. "They must declare for one parent over the other. This isn't a question of love or of compassion; it's a question of who inherits what in the unfortunate circumstance that someone stops their dancing. It's a question of where you will belong. October Christine Daye, daughter of Amandine the Liar, for whom do you declare?"

"My father," I said, picturing my father, my *real* father, with as much clarity as I could. I'd been so young the last time I'd seen him, and I had no pictures. But he had loved me completely and without judging how strong my blood was, and I knew that if he were here, he would have forgiven me for choosing Simon over Mom. "I declare my line for Simon Torquill. I shall only ever be of his descent, and Oberon's, for I cannot set my blood aside." That part of the declaration had been dictated to me by May, a serious expression on her face and a mascara wand in her hand. I couldn't refute Oberon, even if I'd wanted to. Mom was another story.

Mom scoffed. "No great loss," she said. "Let Simon found his dynasty on a mongrel child, if that's what he wishes. I release my claim on her."

I didn't look in her direction, just dipped a shallow bow toward Arden and walked back to my original place.

Now for the hard one. "August Torquill, daughter of Amandine the Liar and Simon Torquill, for whom do you declare?" asked Arden.

August looked at me, and then at Mom, before scanning the crowd, presumably searching for Simon. He had to be present. As one of the people involved in the divorce, he was required to be here for it to move forward. I didn't see him. After a few seconds, it became apparent that she didn't either. Her face fell, and she returned her attention to Arden.

"Am I allowed to ask to face my father as I declare my choice?" she asked.

Arden blinked before glancing to the Luidaeg, who was, I supposed, the closest thing we had to an arbiter of the custom's intent available to us. She was older than Amandine, enough so that she would presumably know. She was also, technically, a neutral party in this endeavor.

The murmurs that had spread through the room when Mom was declared as Firstborn were starting to die down. The Luidaeg nodded. "The girl is allowed to face her father," she said.

The crowd to her left parted, and Simon Torquill stepped to the front.

He was looking better than he had been. His clothes were still shabby, the cuffs carefully mended; given that he'd been a guest in Saltmist for the past week, I had to assume that was by choice, rather than by necessity. The hollows of his cheeks had filled out somewhat, and the dark circles under his eyes were virtually gone. He'd been sleeping and eating for once, and he looked more like his brother than ever.

"I'm here," he said.

August turned to him. "Daddy?" she said, in a hopeful tone.

"Yes, pigeon, it's me," he said.

"But the Luidaeg . . ." August frowned, brow furrowing. "The terms of my debt—how can you be here?"

"It was your sister," he said, sidestepping the actual question. "She found a way to settle my accounts with the Luidaeg and bring me home."

August moved then, running across the floor and throwing herself into his arms, locking her own arms around his chest in an embrace more than a hundred years in the making. "I *missed* you," she wailed. "The tower is so cold without you. Come home. Don't do this. Come home."

"Oh, pigeon." He ran his thumb down the slope of her cheek, pulling her attention to his face. "You know I can't do that. Your mother doesn't want me there, or she would have been the one to bring me home. She would at least have tried. I'm tired. I want to be away from all this fuss and bother. I'm finished with Firstborn."

"Well, then I—"

"Will declare for your mother, as we both know you must," he said firmly. "She'd follow you forever if you tried to go with me. She'd never leave either of us in peace. And if you want to learn everything your bloodline is capable of, you need to stay with your First. The beginning of a line has always remained with its First. Be her daughter, my dearest, as you've always been, and let me love you from afar."

"Is this normal?" asked Arden, sotto voce.

"What?" I murmured back.

"A parent trying to convince one of the kids *not* to choose them."

"I don't know. I've never seen a pureblood divorce before." I paused. "Wait, haven't you done this before?"

"No." Arden shook her head. "They're rare, and I was a child. I don't even remember my father conducting a divorce."

"Huh," I said.

August was still clinging to Simon. "I know enough, and you've taught me more about blood magic than she ever bothered," she said. "I don't think she understands everything I can do. I don't think she *cares*. Daddy, I'm lonely. She doesn't know how to be a mother. She only knows how to be an owner. I can't do this. I can't lose you."

Simon closed his eyes, looking pained. "Are you asking me to stay with your mother?"

"Well, he can't," said Dianda, not bothering to keep her voice low. Heads turned toward her. She glared at them all, the expression unfettered and all-encompassing. Dianda had plenty of irritation to share with the world, and she didn't care who claimed a portion. "He's made promises, and he's going to keep them, or he's going to have to answer to me."

Simon opened his eyes, looking briefly, miserably amused, which was a neat trick. "Yes, dear," he said, not letting go of August. "I can't stay with your mother, dearest. Duchess Lorden is correct: I *have* made promises. Even if I hadn't, your mother would never forgive me for embarrassing her here today. She'd make me miserable forever if I tried to come back. What's done is done. I've made my choice."

"Well, so have I," said August, and pulled away from her father. She kept her eyes on him as she straightened, and said loudly, "I declare my line for Simon Torquill. I shall only ever be of his descent, and Oberon's, for I cannot set my blood aside."

Amandine made an unspeakable screeching noise, starting to rush forward. She stopped as a pair of strong arms closed around her from behind, leaving her unable to move forward.

The man who had stepped out of the crowd behind her was nondescript, ordinary-looking to the point of becoming extraordinary. When I glanced away from him, his face immediately slipped my mind, so that he seemed to be someone new when I looked back. Only the antlers on his brow kept him from being entirely forgettable. That, and the fact that hard as Amandine fought against him, she couldn't break away.

"Peace," he said, and his voice was a command none of us could resist. All around the room, people calmed. Even Dianda lost her glare. The Luidaeg smiled at him beatifically and walked toward Amandine.

"This is yours," she said. "You planted it and nurtured it, and now it's come to harvest. Your daughters reject you because you never learned to love anyone who wasn't yourself, and maybe that's partially on us, your siblings, for trusting you to find your own way, but that's how our parents raised us, and we didn't make the same choices you did. The rituals of divorce were laid out long ago, and August has the right to make her own decision."

August was clinging to Simon again, sobbing like her heart was broken as he stroked her hair. The Luidaeg made a small gesture with her hand. The man, who I had to assume was Oberon, let Mom go and melted back into the crowd, vanishing without a ripple. Mom snarled but didn't try to lunge again, just stood where she'd been left and glared at her older sister.

"I won't forget this," she spat. "She's *my* daughter. *Mine.*"

"Not anymore she's not," said the Luidaeg. "The children have chosen; the divorce is done. This marriage is no longer recognized in the eyes of Oberon and will not be reestablished without full consent of all parties involved. Even if it were to be, the lines now sundered will not be restored. Done is done. The lines stand as drawn. Amy, you're free to go. We're finished with you, and what comes next is not for your eyes."

Mom straightened and stomped her foot. "*I* have not forsaken my heritage," she said. "I am Oberon's own daughter, and I will not be expelled from this place against my will."

"Funny," said the Luidaeg. "I'm also Oberon's own daughter, and I say you should go. You're not wanted, Amy. You have no descendant line to stand for you, and my power is in transformation—your blood's weakness. Unless you want to be a fern for a while, which might improve your disposition, but probably wouldn't be great for your mental stability. Go home, Amy. Lick your wounds and try to figure out why this happened to you. Something's wrong when all your children choose their father, even the ones who aren't actually related to him."

Mom looked at her for a long moment, squeezing her hands into fists, looking mulish and angry. Then she spun on her heel and marched away, the crowd opening before her to let her pass. I glimpsed the man with the antlers watching sadly as she walked away. Then he faded into the background, and she was gone.

The Luidaeg clapped her hands, pulling everyone's attention back to her. Not that she could lose it for long. All these people might know that Mom was a Firstborn now, but they weren't used to it, not the way they were used to fearing and respecting the sea witch. She beamed, showing teeth that were closer to a barracuda's than a human woman's.

"As for the rest of you, please remain where you are," she said brightly. "I am Antigone of Albany, better known as the sea witch, or the Luidaeg, and it is my honor to stand before you now and conduct a wedding that has been a very long time in the coming."

I shot an alarmed glance at Tybalt. He shook his head. This hadn't been his doing.

"Will Patrick Twycross-Lorden, late of Tremont, currently of Saltmist, please step forward?"

Patrick did so, his simple tunic and trousers melting into something more formal as he moved. It wasn't quite a tuxedo—that's a tradition that hasn't caught on with the purebloods, sadly—but it was a well-fitted suit that was probably an ancestor of the modern formal option. The arms of Saltmist were stitched above his heart, the only splash of real color against the burgundy and brown.

"Will Dianda Lorden, Duchess of Saltmist, please step forward?"

Dianda moved to stand beside her husband, taking his hand, and together, they walked to stand in front of the Luidaeg. Both were smiling, both utterly relaxed.

The Luidaeg smiled at them. "Will Simon Torquill, once of Londinium, once of Shadowed Hills, please step forward?"

Simon extricated himself from August, who watched with confusion as he approached the Luidaeg. His own clothing shifted to match Patrick's, minus the arms of Saltmist. He stopped on Patrick's free side, and the two of them joined hands.

Dean moved closer to Quentin, leaning his head on the other teen's shoulder. I guess that answered the question of whether he was okay with this.

"Land and sea are not often joined," said the Luidaeg, addressing the three people in front of her. "Shipwrecks are more common than survivors. Why should Faerie honor your request to expand your bridal bed?"

"Simon Torquill is the only person in this world I've loved longer than I've loved my wife. She has never had the whole of my heart, nor has she pursued it," said Patrick. "We would have included him when we were first wed, had he not been married to a woman who didn't share."

"I knew when I allowed Patrick to court me that he came as a package deal with the man he called 'brother' only because Amandine forbade him to use the word 'lover,'" said Dianda. "I've survived a century in the Undersea with a Daoine Sidhe by my side. I can handle a few centuries more with two of them."

"I don't have a good argument for you," said Simon. "I can only tell you that I've loved Patrick Lorden longer than I've loved anyone else, except for Amy and August, and I can't be with Amy anymore. I need a place to rest. I need peace. Dianda and I may not love each other yet, but I have faith that we will. Just give us the time we need."

"Are your sons in attendance today?" asked the Luidaeg.

Dianda nodded. "They are."

Dean lifted his head from Quentin's shoulder, and called, "I'm here."

From the crowd behind me, another voice called, "I'm here as well." Peter Lorden stepped forward.

"Do you think I should allow your parents to wed another?"

"I do," said Dean. "As the one with a right to claim offense against the man, I think the punishment he deserves is my mother."

"If they want to, I don't see why it's up to me," said Peter.

The Luidaeg nodded. "Very well." She turned to Simon. "Your daughters are here. Do you think they'll agree to your remarriage when your divorce still hangs in the air?"

"I already agreed," I called.

"I . . . I can't," said August. "But I can't say no, either. I just want my father to be happy."

"This will be a harder one to end," said the Luidaeg warningly. "Divorce is complicated when there are three lines to choose between. The children you each already have will be bound only to the parents they've known; the children yet to come will have hard decisions to make."

"This marriage isn't ending," said Dianda. "Now will you marry us or not?"

While the idea of Dianda Lorden deciding to assault the Luidaeg was an entertaining one, it wasn't anything I wanted to watch today. Tybalt slid his arms around my waist. I folded my hands over his, holding him in place as he rested his chin on my shoulder.

"I will," said the Luidaeg, and smiled. "The three of you have presented a compelling case for why this should be permitted, and love is rare enough in Faerie that I trust you to nurture and care for it. Dianda, if you'd lied and claimed to already love him, I would have denied you, but you want to tend a garden as yet fallow, and I respect your ambition. Patrick, you have been faithful to two people for over a hundred years. Simon, beloved failure . . . you deserve the chance to rest. By the power once granted to me by my father and never yet rescinded, I now declare you husbands and wife."

Patrick actually cheered before turning to kiss first Dianda and then Simon. All three of them seemed to stand a little straighter.

Amandine was furious. Oberon was back, and no one knew it yet but a handful of people who understood the scope of the secret we were keeping. Evening was too powerful asleep and too powerful awake and not as isolated as we wanted her to be. Dianda and Patrick were going to have to contend with an unexpected stepdaughter now that August had chosen the Torquill line over the Carter one.

But those were all problems for tomorrow. Right now, we watched and clapped as Cassandra oversaw the wheeling out of a massive six-tiered wedding cake, and while things were still terribly broken, they were a little bit better than they had been before I'd gone looking for the man who was now, in the eyes of Faerie, my only legal parent.

Tybalt slipped his hands into mine, pulling me onto the dance floor, and I smiled at him. Sometimes you just have to take the win.

Sometimes a little bit better is enough.

Read on for
a brand-new novella
by Seanan McGuire:

SHINE IN PEARL

I will be bright, and shine in pearl and gold.
— William Shakespeare, *Titus Andronicus*

PATRICK

October 23, 1901

SIXTY YEARS IS NOT such a long time, as measured by the immortal, but it can be the better part of forever, as measured by the human world. Since my courtship of Dianda had properly begun, the city of San Francisco had exploded around me in a riot of new growth, buildings springing up virtually overnight, streets established where anyone reasonable would have been loath to cut a channel. The humans seemed to have no sense of restraint when it came to stacking their homes, one atop the next, or slicing their thoroughfares into the sides of hills steep enough to stop the stoutest heart.

When an architect warned against their choices—which was surprisingly rarely; the boldness of human planners was only exceeded by the brazen bravery of their builders—they were as like to be dismissed from their position and replaced by someone with less of a sense of the possible. There was no advantage to speaking against the plans of someone with the money to support their wild notions.

I am the son of a land where clouds, water, notes of music, and airy shadows are considered reasonable building materials, and even I was quite sure that these people were teetering on the verge of madness.

Sixty years had transformed the city into something vaster and crueler and more tamed, forcing many of the nobility to relocate the entrances to their knowes to less accessible places. The maturing park at the city's center had been declared neutral ground, allowing the common people and changelings to have a place they could call their own, while the nobility agreed to keep their distance. Rumor was that an Undine who had been close to Amandine during her misguided youth—if she could ever be said to have had a "misguided youth," having met and married Simon far too young to be seemly—was intending to root a knowe there to offer them additional safety and succor.

My own reputation was in tatters already, thanks to my "inappropriate" choices and habits, or I would have offered her any aid she desired. I might do so anyway, assuming she was able to negotiate the land grant required. Before she had the King's approval, my intervention would do naught but harm her chances, and I preferred not to be a millstone around another's throat. I had been enough of a millstone around my own.

At least I knew my lady's chances and choices had been in no way hampered by my presence. I had spent too many nights on the edge of the dock, the wind tying knots in the unfashionably short strands of my hair, with my eyes fixed on the horizon, which once seemed so fair and aspirational, and now seemed so utterly inescapable.

It always came back to the sea.

It has always, for me, come back to the sea. All the days that I can remember, even down to my childhood in the gilded halls of distant Tremont, have been haunted by the rushing of the water and the crashing of the waves. My mother used to take me to the shore to play among the driftwood and spindrift debris of the tide, laughing at the sight of me chasing after the waves as if I could catch them and keep them captive in my hands.

I had been disabused of such childish habits as I grew, taught to better behave myself and sit properly decorous among the halls of my social superiors—which was almost all of my own kind, as most Daoine Sidhe pursue power at the expense of all other things, making my status as a landless Baron barely better than common in their eyes. I had taken little of value from my time in those halls. Only a stiffened spine, a tendency to begin twitching when someone mentioned the proper pairing of wine and cheese, and Simon.

His value was enough to balance the rest of it. I had suffered in those horrible halls solely to put myself into the path of the best friend I would ever be fortunate enough to have. Simon Torquill was the finest of men and the closest of companions, and like me, had been born into a family with less power to grant than he deserved, although unlike me, he had desired more than he was given.

While I had always been more than happy to be a quiet afterthought, shadowed by my parents until my presence became a burden and then removing myself to a Kingdom as far from their halls as the geography of the continent allowed, Simon yearned to shine. His brother, the hero, cast a long shadow, and his sister, who I had gleaned offered him some light during their childhood, had remained in Europe with her husband when her brothers immigrated to the new world. He never spoke of his parents. Whoever they were, or perhaps had been, they were but a mystery to me.

In one place, at least, his ambitions had borne the intended fruit: in his marriage to the lady Amandine, whose title was a courtesy, not nobly granted, as the Countess Winterrose was swift to remind the nobility of the Mists when the topic of her graces arose. She was a beautiful woman, for to be anything else would be to have been less than Daoine Sidhe, and Amandine's priority had always been bent toward proving herself the best of us. If Treasa showed herself to be well-mannered, Amandine must find an opportunity to show her own manners to be twice as fine. If Dawn shunned the King's halls for their disarray and unruliness, Amandine must shun the King himself. And so it went, and had always gone, and Simon, with his eyes all full of her reflected light, never saw how her brightness forced him to remain dimmer, unable to find the traction he yearned for in the halls of the nobility.

Their daughter, August, was a joy when kept apart from her mother, full of the same bright wit and cunning choices that made her father such a delight to be around. Put near Amandine, however, she would rapidly acquire and emulate her mother's supposed graces, her small cruelties and her dismissal of anyone she saw as standing below her station. And Simon seemed oblivious to it all, unable to see any flaws in his lady, or to comprehend those same flaws when they came mirrored in his child.

It was almost enough to put a man off the idea of marriage, for all that it had its temptations, and its compensations. Unmarried, I was landless, with nothing to offer any who might wish to lie with me: I had a workshop, and my hands, and the flock of pixies who danced willing attendance upon both. Pixies are not considered an asset by the greater majority of Faerie. Married, I would at least have whatever halls and home my wife possessed. Had my heart been wiser, I might have made a decent match among the maidens of the Mists. Treasa Riordan was lovely to look upon, if rancid to the core of her, and Dawn Winterrose was a sweet soul to hang one's time upon.

Of her sister, the less said, the better. Evening Winterrose would never love a man, but she would freeze him solid and leave him for the sun to steal.

Other bloodlines of Faerie are freer to follow their desires than the Daoine Sidhe are bid to be. Sylvester Torquill's greatest shame, in the eyes of many, is not the reprehensible way he has treated his twin brother, who loves him yet, despite his coldness, but his taking of a Kitsune maid to wife. And as the purpose of marriage is the begetting of a new lineage, unquestionable and uncontested, I could not have married Simon even had he been unwed and interested in someone as unsuited to assist his elevation as myself. I was beneath notice and without value, and always had been. I had long since resigned myself to a life devoid of love, for my traitorous heart had never once found a woman of acceptable breeding worthy of attention.

For again, it always comes back to the sea.

The Duchess Dianda Lorden tumbled into my life at the most inopportune of times: I had become comfortable with the thought of perpetual bachelorhood, centuries of working alone in my lab or dogging Simon's steps as he ambled through the blessed sunshine of his daily life. I had found my peace with it, even a flavor of contentment. I was no longer looking for any deeper affection from the world than the sweet, untroubled attention of my friends.

As for Dianda, well. She had only just been elevated to her position, heir to her father, who had chosen to swim away from his sunken demesne, seeking his fortune in warmer waters. The manner of succession in the Undersea was still a mystery to me, for all that it had been more a mystery when first I met her, me a man who had never thought himself likely to meet a mermaid, her a mermaid who had never considered herself inclined to favor the company of a man of the land.

But I did meet her, and she did favor my company, and now, some sixty years later, we were as closely cleaved to one another as any pair I knew. She accompanied me when King Gilad sent summons to one of his infrequent social gatherings, slipping her feet into satin slippers and her hand into the crook of my arm and smiling politely at even the most minor of dignitaries, for all the world as if her station were not so far above my own as to be a mountain's summit. My only regret was that circumstance and biology forbade me to do the same for her; she had known a ball when first she attended one, had found no mystery in a dinner party, so surely they held such events in the Undersea. Surely, they had ballrooms of pearl and coral through which mermaids danced whatever strange dances were meant for fins in place of feet, surely, they played such music as could be carried on the waves. Surely.

I dreamt of it most days. The palaces beneath the sea, the palaces where my ladylove belonged, where she went when she was not in my arms. The palaces she was born to inherit, while I stood to inherit only Twycross, and that only if both my parents were gone to the night-haunts, leaving me an orphan evermore. Her riches outstripped my own by any measure, and that would have bothered me not at all, had I not feared that my company kept her from her birthright.

Even as I was forbidden to consider a more permanent arrangement between us by the order of my absent Firstborn, she was kept from my full company by biology, that cruel mistress which deemed her born to the water, while I was born to the land. She could no more share my bed from dawn until dusk without suffocating than I could go with her below the waves, and would one day have to leave me for a more suitable mate, one who could help her to secure her lineage and legacy.

Sixty years was longer than I had spent in another's company, save for Simon's, in all my life, and if I were going to be kind to her, that needed to be the whole of it. It was time for me to tell her that she deserved better than a landless baron from Tremont, and to make her heed the words as my own, and not some cruel trick of sorcery played by the Countess Winterrose, who had perhaps taken our Firstborn's command to cleave only to our own kind more deeply to heart than most of us, and who had tried on one wicked occasion to separate us with a blade made entirely of magic.

Simon had interceded on my behalf after that event, sparing me the need to face her presence a second time, and that kindness had cost him dear. Since that day my friend had grown paler and thinner, as if he dwindled before my eyes, until his melancholy seemed at times to be as deep as his Amy's, and as her black moods were all but legendary, that was a terrible comparison to draw. But when the light broke through, he was still my Simon, still scintillating and irreverent as the night is long, still one of the sweetest and dearest stars in my sky. He had spared me from the Countess, and if it meant he now danced attendance upon her, he did so willingly, without a murmur of complaint upon his lips. He insisted there were as yet no debts between us, and because I loved him and my doubt caused him pain, I chose to believe him. But oh, how it sometimes burned.

And now it was all to be for naught. I looked one last time at myself in the mirror, knowing that when I returned to my workshop, it would be as a changed man, before I turned away. My coat hung as always on the peg beside the door, and when I lifted it, two motes of colored light detached themselves from the rafters and came to flit around my shoulders, wings chiming like distant bells.

I smiled. It didn't matter what else was happening, or how far down the road of my own self-pity I had traveled, my pixies could always coax a smile from me. And after sixty years of cohabitation, I felt I could safely call them my own. I was their friend and their protector and their provider; I filled their larders and provided them with the weapons in their hands and the bangles around their wrists. In exchange, they assisted me with the finer details of my work, adjusting mechanisms too minutely built for the manipulations of my hands, which were sized to a man near six feet in stature, and not to a delicate creature barely scraping six inches, and they provided me with the companionship I would otherwise have dearly lacked.

Many of the local nobles and courtiers who frequented the various courts thought me mad for dallying with vermin. It was a fair judgment, no doubt fairer than my own, as I thought them cruel for treating the least of us as barely more than mortal, designed to be exploited and swatted carelessly away. Perhaps we were both right. Perhaps I *was* mad, a son of the Daoine Sidhe who had come to keep company with mermaids and with pixies. Perhaps I had strayed so far from my Firstborn's wishes that I deserved to be lost in whatever wood might have me, wandering forever with no light nor compass to guide me home.

As to them, they were definitely cruel.

The larger of the two pixies hung in front of my face, her arms folded across her chest, her pretty, if diminutive face set into a scowl. She rang her wings imperiously at me. I afforded her a smile.

"I am aware, Daffodil, that I'm meant to be making a stew for the colony tonight, and I fully intend to discharge my duties as soon as I return." Even a sad and broken man can chop carrots and dice chicken into a pot. The pixies would see to the spicing. They were too small to make effective use of even my kitchen, which had been adapted as far as was possible to their use, but they were dab hands with an herb garden, and under their care mine had grown almost lush enough to rival Luna Torquill's.

The pixie rang again. I sighed and raised my hand, allowing her to land upon it. The smaller pixie did the same, the glow of her wings dimming as she settled. Lilac had been brought to me as a very small child, with one wing crumpled to the point of unusability by one of the larger fae. It had taken me years of corrective devices such as no one in Faerie had ever built before to restore that wing to functionality, and while she could now fly as well as any of her kind, she tired easily, and needed to rest at frequent intervals.

She would never have survived on her own. My workshop, as much as my actions, had saved her life. Not only hers; many members of my flock would surely have been captured and pressed into service as decorative lights, left to suffocate or starve inside glass cages, had they not been able to escape to the safety of my company. I might have no kingdom of my own or land to speak to, but

I had served as their benefactor, all the same. My parents would be proud.

"I must go out," I informed the two of them. "I will be back to-night. I promise."

Lilac chimed inquisitively. I smiled at her.

"Yes, I'm seeing Dianda. She's expecting me at the pier in very short order, and you know how I do hate to disappoint my lady." Not that she would be my lady any longer when this night's work was done. She would be well within her rights to shun me, to become once more a stranger in the sea, and it would be—in all honesty—no less than I deserved.

Lilac chimed again. My smile gave way to laughter.

"I am sure she'll have remembered to bring you some bits of pretty glass for your collection, and if not, it will be a small thing to find some."

Humans were forever throwing broken bits of glass to the waves, like they believed the sea to be some great beast that could be placated with tasty scraps and trinkets. The sea, not being anything so tamable as a beast, would roll them in its depths for what seemed like eons and then spit them back onto the shore, softened and refined into colorful jewels that resembled nothing else in the world. "Driftglass," they were called. I made jewelry of the larger stones, and brought chips and pebbles for Lilac to stuff her pockets with and glory in.

Truly, my pixies were rich by the standards of their own kind, and if that richness came at the expense of my own place in polite fae society, who was to say that the ledgers between us did not balance? One life selfishly lived in exchange for over a hundred lives of peace and plenty in my rafters.

The thought somewhat eased the sting of what I was about to do. I began to lower my hand. Lilac and Daffodil, taking the cue from my motion, launched themselves into the air and began to fly a lazy loop around me.

Fortunately for us all, I have long since mastered the art of conversing with a pixie in motion. If I had not, my life would be even more confusing than it already is, and far less pleasant. "I will be back, and I'll stop for some of that bread you like so much," I said. Daffodil's answering ring was imperious. She grabbed Lilac by the hand, sweeping her away into the rafters and leaving me to finally shrug my coat over my shoulders and open the door.

The night was cool, the sidewalk washed in fog rolled off the bay, like a soft gray cloak wiping away all the world's petty imperfections. I pushed my hands down into my pockets, pulling the denser cloak of a human illusion around myself with a thought, the scent of my magic briefly sparking in the air. There are times I'm tempted to waste magic needlessly just for that moment where it wraps around me and I smell the mayflowers that were so common in my youth. California has a different set of scents to carry, and I sometimes wonder what perfumes the children born here will spin when they do their own casting.

August was born in the Mists, her magic tied to this land from her first breath, but when she spins spells, they smell of smoke and roses. Nothing to connect her to the land of her birth, only roses in mirror of her mother, and smoke, like a shadow of Simon's own, wound through her mother's floral sweetness until they could never be picked apart.

It occurred to me, as thoughts sometimes do when one walks along in the fog, with nothing to provide distraction, that I couldn't remember the last time Simon had spun or released an enchantment in my presence. He seemed always to arrive at the workshop door with his masks already in place and tailored just *so*, and kept them on until our evening ended, or, when that evening included waiting upon King Gilad's court, would remove them outside my presence. It was a jarring thought. We had always donned and doffed the illusions that allowed us to move undetected through the human world as casually as we might remove a pair of shoes, and for him to be hiding his magic from me seemed . . .

Strange. It seemed strange because it *was* strange, and it was strange because it wasn't happening. It was a ridiculous thought, brought on by my unavoidable melancholy over what I was about to do. Entertaining it for even a moment more would be a grave unkindness toward my friend, and even if he never knew of it, I would know, and I would not forgive myself. With what felt like a physical act of force, I shoved the idea aside and, driving my hands deeper into my pockets, walked onward into the fog, which spread its arms to gather me into a lover's embrace.

Fae eyesight is far keener than its mortal counterpart. While we prefer the soothing moonlight's glow to the harsh beaming of the sun, we can see equally well by either night or day, and twilight is no barrier to us. That does not mean our eyes can pierce through fog. The sound of the sea was my only beacon, a cold reminder of how many times it had been the only thing to lead me home. I no longer deserved its assistance, but I was grateful for it all the same. If I wandered lost through the streets of San Francisco until my pixies had to come and find me, Simon would never let me hear the end of it.

The fog cleared somewhat as I grew closer to the water, whipped away by the wind that chased it from the sea. Soon enough, I could see great dark patches of wave, their surfaces as smooth and shining as glass, their peaks tipped with froths of white. I walked to the pier's end and sat, pulling a small white shell from my pocket and turning it over in my hand. I could delay this. One more night, I could delay this, if I so desired.

I skipped the shell across the surface of the waves as hard as I could, refusing to allow myself any further hesitation. If this were to be done, it were better that it be done quickly. As it should have been years ago, before I became a weight around her neck.

The shell left a glittering trail behind it as it skipped across the water, striking seven times before it sank. Seven leagues away, then, a distance she could travel in a twinkling. She would never be a runner, but in the water, Dianda was faster than any fish, capable of crossing great distances faster than should have been possible. Maybe faster than *was* possible; it wouldn't make her the only person in Faerie to speed her travel through magical means, even if unconscious ones. Did the Silene put magic to their hooves when they wanted to outrun the wind, or did they simply do it? Perhaps it was the same for Merrow wishing to outswim the tides. Whatever the cause, she was close. She would be with me soon.

I closed my eyes, indulging in a brief moment of imagining that when she arrived, it would be only to wrap her arms around my shoulders and gather me close, her fins brushing my ankles as she sat beside me on the pier. Even in her natural form, her body was built along a biped's lines, with hips designed for bending and a posterior that was beautifully shaped, whether scaled or not. I was a comedy in the water, and her endurance on the land was brief, but we could sit together for hours without end, or so I had allowed myself to think once, when the world had been younger and sweeter.

Nothing truly vast had changed. The mortals bred, and expanded on their city, a hive of ever-industrious ants building their towers toward the sky. Evening and Treasa plotted and schemed, perfect ladies of the Daoine Sidhe, doubtless bent on eventual domination of the Kingdom. Simon wore himself to nothing attending on both Evening and his lady wife while Sylvester shirked his duties as often as he could manage, as if by taking another child of Faerie to his bed where tradition dictated a Daoine Sidhe woman should have lain, he had shrugged off all responsibilities laid upon him by our Firstborn when she abandoned us.

"Keep your bloodlines pure, and gather power like roses in the spring, for when I return, I will expect a hearty crop of crowns and children." Those had been Eira Rosynhwyr's last recorded words, as reported by her eldest living daughter, Rhew of the Glass Shadow. The mother of the Daoine Sidhe had raised her children to bend toward obedience, and so we had done our best to create the mandated crop.

If she were to return tomorrow, I would provide her with neither. Nor would Sylvester, and there was some succor in that, that the man who had treated my beloved friend as a failure would be the failure in our Firstborn's eyes, while only Simon had a Daoine Sidhe child to present as proof of his obedience.

The water's surface shimmered and broke as a head poked through the waves. Her dark hair was plastered down against the sides of her face, pointed ears poking through the sleek sheets of it, and her eyes were open much too wide to have just emerged from the stinging spray. The salt did not bother her the way it did me, or any other not born to the sea.

I should have raised my hand. I should have waved, have let her approach while everything seemed normal. Instead I sat as a man frozen, looking on the face of my lady one last time while I could yet call her mine without breaking any confidences or betraying any rules.

She was beautiful, my Dianda, not the pale, sculpted beauty of the Daoine Sidhe, but a rougher, more imperfect perfection. She was like the driftglass stones, rolled into a new shape by the deep water, and all the better for it. Her skin was the tawny shade of beach sand in the sunlight, darker than my own by several shades; her hair was black when not so weighted down with water as to make its color irrelevant, and her eyes were a deep and drowning blue. Compared to the Daoine Sidhe, most of whom are painted in fantastic colors, with hair in every color of the rainbow and some the rainbow has yet to conceive, she was ordinary, even drab, until she showed her scales.

They gleamed in blue and purple, green and mother-of-pearl, iridescent and flawless, like the whole of the sea was painted on her tail, that she might never forget where she came from. When she wrapped that tail around my ankles to anchor me, when her flukes stroked the line of my calf in the night . . . I could believe the stories of sailors who had flung themselves from the side of ships for the privilege of drowning. I am told it is an unpleasant way to die. It might still be worth it . . . if one were to do so in her arms.

"Patrick!" She waved, webs stretched tight between her fingers. I was here to spare her, not insult her, and so I waved back, watching as she swam closer.

When she was close enough, the webs between her fingers disappeared, withered into nothing, and she grasped the wooden handholds I had long since carved into the body of the pylon supporting the pier, using them to pull herself bodily up onto the pier. She sat herself beside me, legs dangling, a shirt she hadn't been wearing before transforming stretched down to her knees. Unlike the rest of her, it was perfectly dry, a piece of magic I had yet to understand, but was always willing to admire.

She leaned in and bumped her shoulder against mine. "Hey. Why so gloomy and glum? You called; I came. I always come when you call."

"I know," I said, and looked down at the water. It has always, always come back to the sea. "I was at Court the night before last. That dreadful King of Cats was in attendance, making cheeky comments to the house servants and insinuating that they had ideas above their stations because they allowed their children to roam the knowe as if they were born to it." How smug he had sounded, how sanctimonious, as if he knew some deep secret the rest of us were to be denied.

"Patrick? You're making me nervous. I would appreciate it if you would look at me."

It went against all rules of civility to refuse such a reasonable request, but I could no more turn to face her in that moment than I could have turned my gaze directly to the sun. "I'm sorry. I cannot."

"I see." The toes brushing my ankle disappeared, gone between one breath and the next, replaced by the slowly unfurling flag of a great, glossy fin. Sweet Oberon, but she was beautiful when she dropped her disguises. She was beautiful with them, but she was breathtaking without.

I kept my eyes turned down though I slanted my gaze to the side so that I could see the sinuous sweep of her, serpentine and also . . . not, sea serpent and siren and mistress of the deeps.

I was going to miss her so very badly.

"He saw my disapproval of his censure written in my eyes," I said. "Arden and Nolan are kindly children, for all that only their mother has ever claimed them, and I wonder, at times, if they might not favor their father, whomever he is."

Dianda scoffed. "Are you still allowing that pretty fiction that Gilad is *not* their father? They have his eyes, not their mother's, and the boy carries his grandmother's name with only the addition of a letter to obscure it, while the girl tucks her grandfather's name inside her own. They're the heirs to your Kingdom, and he allows you to treat them as if they were foundlings."

"After what happened to his parents, I can understand if the King is loath to claim them openly," I said. "The fiction of their missing father protects them."

"You landers and your rules," said Dianda. She sounded almost angry. "A lie is still a lie when it's dressed in lace and presented for the ball. We don't do things that way in the sea."

"No? How do you do them?"

"Honestly, and in the open. I told you when we met that I went to a very violent school, and that I was extremely reasonable by the standards I was raised to. My patience is legendary beneath the waves. I'm considered the most even-tempered of the coastal rulers. I almost never kill anyone." At my shocked look, she laughed. "Oberon's Law only forbids us murder. It allows us war, and anyone who claims a high enough station can declare a war begun. The Undersea has been at war since before my grandparents were born. We're always allowed to kill each other, and we do, because we're honestly remarkably annoying. You haven't spent time with very many of us, but the ones you do know, well, we're troublesome."

"You have never been troublesome to *me*," I protested.

"That would sound sweeter if you hadn't called me here because some mewling moggy who would have been better off drowned at birth somehow managed to convince you that you should stop keeping company with me."

Her words were like a slap, startling enough that for the first time I fully turned and faced her. She was looking at me, expression calm, eyes wide and bright in the moonlight, and she was so beautiful, and I loved her so much, and that was why I had to go through with this, little as I desired it.

"I . . . I can never marry you."

She blinked. "Who said I would want to marry *anyone*? I'm Duchess of my own fiefdom. I answer to no one save the King in Leucothea, who never asks anything of me as long as his spies report that I'm continuing to do my job. No one shares my coronet or title, no one sits upon my consort's throne. I never spoke of marriage because I have no need of it."

"You speak of your lands with love," I said.

"Yes."

"But you'll one day need an heir."

"So I'll throw a grand brawl and all the eligible Merrow-maids and Merrow-men for leagues will swim to my halls, eat my food, and beat each other to the verge of death until the strongest rises up to challenge me." She looked at me defiantly. "I have no need of a husband to protect me."

"Did your Firstborn not command you to tithe children to her?" My head was starting to spin.

Dianda scoffed again. "If she had, we would have swarmed her and struck her dead, Firstborn or no. Before Amphitrite set her sails against the western wind, she bid that we follow our natures and find happiness. That was all. And as we are a naturally blood-thirsty lot, we've found happiness in war eternal, and in the keeping of the ones too shy or soft to fight. We protect what's ours. It's part of what makes us so aggressive toward anything or anyone that might present a threat."

The idea of raising hands against a Firstborn—or of a Firstborn who loved her children well enough to bid them happiness—was foreign to me. I stared at her, speechless.

"And whether you like it or not, Patrick Twycross, you're mine. You offered yourself to me like a rare jewel the night you fed me cake and treated me like a person, not a princess, and you kept offering, over and over again, until I accepted. You have two paths leading from this moment, and I always knew we'd walk one of them eventually, but thought we'd have more time. Remember that you brought us here."

I said nothing. It didn't seem my place to speak, as yet.

"I dive back into the sea, an enemy, and the waters are set evermore against you; or you accept my proposal as you feel unable to make your own."

Slowly, I blinked at her.

"Proposal?"

"You say you cannot marry me. Fine. I never asked to be a wife to any man, or any woman, for that matter. But your failings are not mine. So rather than you marrying me, allow me to marry you, and make of you my husband and consort—although not, I should be clear, my co-regent. The Undersea would never stand for a descendant of Eira Rosynhwyr leading one of our domains. We're both children of Titania, so there would be no issues with reproduction." I must have looked confused, because she shook her head and said, "Sometimes children of Titania and children of Maeve, when they lie together, beget monsters. I would prefer my descendants be the ordinary sort of monster, and nothing that requires the intervention of a hero."

"Custom—"

"I could not leave my home for you even if I wished it, so you will have to come and live with me. That Andersen man did us no favors with his little 'fairy tale.' A mermaid may leave the water long enough to dance at a ball or court a man too foolish to understand that she matters more than the careless words of a King he doesn't serve, but she cannot live on land. I would suffocate in my sleep."

"I can't breathe water," I protested. If this was a marriage proposal—and I was fairly sure it was, in its own twisting way—this was the way to end it.

"Of course, you can." Dianda reached into the pocket of her shirt, which had remained, although shorter, when she transformed, and withdrew a glass bulb, small and tightly corked and filled with a golden liquid that writhed like a thing living and glittered like starlight on the sea. "Sixty years of courtship, and you think I hadn't set my court alchemists to finding a way to let you come home with me? But there are limitations. You'll be able to breathe the water as I do, for an hour, and I can easily pull you along with me to Saltmist in that time. It's not perfect. It won't protect you from the cold or make your skin suited to the water as mine is. You'll have to wait several hours between doses, and of course, once you're in my chambers below, you won't be able to leave on your own. You'll have to trust me in a way I don't know if you can." She set the bottle on the dock between us, a trace of hurt coming into her expression for the first time. "I love you. I have loved you for years, have let you set the pace of this swim, when I would have raced to the finish long ago. But if your love for me is not enough to let you stand against what you still perceive as the wishes of your lost and unlamented Firstborn, who has no place in our relationship, and no right to dictate how we love each other, then you don't trust me. You don't trust me to protect you, to partner you, to defend the walls of our home and the hearts of our children against the world. And if you can't trust me, then we may as well do what you desire, and part tonight, as enemies."

She touched my cheek, then leaned over and kissed me, delicately. Her lips were sweet as salt, either from the sea or from her unfettered tears.

"You are the love of my life, Patrick Twycross. I know I may not be the love of yours, but please allow me a little more time to harbor hope."

Then she slid off the pier, striking the surface of the water with little more than a ripple, and was gone.

I stared foolishly after her for several precious seconds—seconds which she could, I knew, use to carry herself far away from me, never to return. I had come here with the intention of ending things, not to be proposed to and then fled from as if I were some sort of monster. I stood, grabbing the bottle from where she had left it, and turned to walk away from the pier's edge.

Every inch of me was screaming that I was wasting time as I walked to the nearest building, a masonry shop that had closed at sundown, following the patterns of mortal-owned businesses. I began to load my pockets with bricks, fitting two into each side of my coat, and several handfuls of broken bits into my trousers. For the final touch I grabbed the largest stone I could hold in one hand and held it close to my body as I strode back down the pier.

When I reached the end, I pulled the cork from the bottle with my teeth and downed its contents in a single long gulp. It tasted like salted strawberries. I had no idea whether it had worked. I could still breathe, after all.

Then I stepped off the edge and let the rocks in my pockets and under my arm drag me down, toward the bottom of the bay.

DIANDA

My father would be so disappointed in me. "Never fall in love, Dianda," he warned me, more than once, when I was still small enough to float on his flukes and be called his little pearl without any chance that it would undermine my authority with those who would be my subjects. Even in the Undersea, children are allowed to be pampered, at least for a time. "Never fall in love. Men will only break your heart, and women will only desert you. The sea is changeable, and so are anyone's affections."

His were, certainly. In the end, he left me even as my mother had, although with less purpose. Both of them swam to find waters they preferred to those of Saltmist, which were sometimes cold, and always too close to the coastal kingdoms, with their unbearable assortment of land fae, whose concerns were alien and petty. And the humans! No one chooses a home near humans if they have another option. I wouldn't love Saltmist as I do if I hadn't been born to her and raised in the expectation that one day she would be mine.

My father swam away and left me behind. My mother divorced him and untethered me from her family line long before that, taking my only living brother with her into distant waters. Loving someone has never once in my life been enough to make them stay.

Foolishly, I had believed that things might be different for people of the land, that perhaps the reason so much of Faerie was centered there was because they were more skilled at loving one another without being cruel. And for a short time, it had seemed like that might be true. I had met a man who loved me for who

I was, who didn't care that our natures would always dictate a certain measure of separation, and somehow that had translated into loving me too much not to let me go. I didn't want to be released. I had swum to his net willingly, and I had done so with every intention of staying there. Letting me go was a deeper cruelty than I had thought him capable of, and I did not approve.

I swam away from the pier slowly, letting the kelp tangle around my flukes, resisting the urge to look back. If he was going to follow me, he would have done it already. He knew how fast I could move and had no reason to expect me to wait for him. No: his choice was made, and by making it, mine was made as well.

I could stay in Saltmist for a few decades, until the Selkies carried news of his departure. We would be enemies after this, both because I had promised him so, and because to be anything else would be to harm my position in a way far worse than his mewling concerns about his Firstborn's good regard. For me to love a man so far below my station was forgivable, and perhaps a sign that I was not as cold and heartless as rulers in the Undersea are often assumed to be. I could be reasoned with. See? I had found love with one of their own, had taken him to my bed and to my confidence. For me to be spurned by that same man? Unforgivable.

It would mark me as weak and taint all my further dealings with the nobility of the Mists. I liked them little enough to begin with, I had no need to treat with them from a perceived position of inferiority, the one who'd been rejected, the one who had brought an entire Duchy to the table and still not been good enough to hold one of their precious sons of Eira.

I breathed in deep, letting the cool waters of the Pacific soothe my throat even as they accepted my tears, and swam, still too slowly, but ever in the direction of home.

There was a splash from behind me, as of something falling into the water. It was quiet compared to the sounding of the sea. It was loud enough to cause me to stop swimming and whip around, hair briefly clouding my vision before the tide tucked it once again behind me.

And there was Patrick, falling gracelessly through the water, still dressed in his heavy, ridiculous clothing, which might have been suitable on the land, but was in no way suited for the water. It was dragging him down, as was the large rock he was holding. He had gambled that I'd been telling the truth when I told him I loved him, and that the potion I'd left behind on the pier would protect him. Foolish man. Foolish, foolish, wonderful man.

I flipped about in the water and swam back toward him as he continued to sink, making no effort to dawdle now. There was nothing keeping me from going as fast as I could, and I slammed into him shortly before his feet brushed the bottom. His eyes widened in clear surprise. The man had followed me into the ocean, and not expected me to be there when he arrived. Fool. Darling, dearest fool.

I closed my own eyes as I kissed him, wrapping my tail around his legs and holding him to me, keeping him from sinking into the muck at the bottom of the bay. He was heavier than I expected him to be. His pockets must have been deeper than I thought they were, and he had packed every inch of them with stones.

He kissed me back, kissed me like he was drowning, and I was all he knew of air. I pulled back a little, studying him as he blinked and then frowned, looking at me as if he was afraid he'd done something wrong. No; he wasn't drowning. This wasn't a disrupted suicide. He was a sensible man and had consumed my potion before consigning himself to the sea.

I should probably have taken the time to warn him that the potion had yet to be tested on an actual land-dweller, and that we would need to be careful in our first trials, but I had been furious with him, and brokenhearted, and unwilling to explain. As it had worked out for the best, I might wait to tell him for a hundred years or so. Long enough for "I'm sorry I nearly got you killed" to pass into the distance and become amusing.

Maybe longer than a hundred years.

I reached out and brushed my fingers against his cheek. He relaxed immediately, frown fading. No one has ever taken so much comfort in my touch. No one has ever wanted to. Was it any wonder, then, that I would cleave to him, if only to see that acceptance in his eyes.

Not moving away for fear of bringing back the frown, I pointed upward, at the surface of the water, then turned and pointed behind myself, into the distance, in the direction of Saltmist. I returned my attention to Patrick.

He bit his lip for a moment before nodding once, firmly, and pointing in the direction of my home. I must have looked as surprised as I felt, because his expression softened into a smile, besotted and fond, as he nodded again and kept pointing toward Saltmist.

He had thrown himself to the sea for me. It seemed he was willing to follow that commitment all the way down into the depths.

I unwound my tail from around his legs and grasped both his hands in my own, tugging him free of the bottom. Carefully, I flicked my fins against the dragging resistance of the water and towed him a few feet farther from the shore. It was awkward, trying to pull someone along without buffeting him with my tail, but I was sure I would get the knack of it in time. And we would have time. We would have so much time! I could show him all the wonders and dangers of the sea, and I could protect him when those dangers drew too close, and he would be there with me, someone who looked at me with wonder instead of fear.

That might be a flimsy hook to hang a heart upon, but I've seen stronger fish that I caught on far less when the bait was right.

Patrick tugged his left hand free of mine, holding up one finger in a signal for me to wait a moment, and proceeded to dump what seemed like an entire stone yard's worth of bricks and small rocks from his pockets, sending them to rest on the ocean floor. I raised my eyebrows. He shrugged sheepishly. He must have *very* much wanted to sink.

With the stones gone, he was lighter, although not measurably so, but as it was clear that he was doing his best to make this easier on me, I made a show of pulling him more smoothly, as if he had completely changed the measure of my efforts. I found that by positioning myself slightly behind him, so that his back was against my chest and our joined hands were braced one to the side and one behind his left shoulder, I could hit him less frequently with the motion of my tail. He leaned against me and let me drive us both forward, into the depths.

The transitions between the mortal and fae world on the land are usually clear-cut and obvious. One moment one world, the next moment, another. It's tidy and dishonest, because there is always blurring around the edges. There's never a point where two things meet that maintains the possibility to separate them entirely. They have to separate on their own, over time, and cut the mingled parts away, for that to ever become possible.

As we dove, the water darkened, light fading into memory. Fortunately, I had no need of sight to know where we were going;

I had swum this path so many times before that I already knew the way. The water chilled, Patrick pressing himself against me and shivering, then warmed again, returning almost to its original temperature. That made the second chill all the more shocking, as the water around us abruptly felt like it had been replaced by a sheet of liquid ice. It burned my throat and eyes, so cold that it made breathing difficult. I pushed forward, and in a few more hard strokes of my tail we were through, breaking into a different ocean.

Breaking into the seas that were my true and only home.

The water here was filled with light. Not sunlight or moonlight; sealight, which was brighter and dimmer all at the same time, swimming with crystalline streaks like rainbows caught in the current. It was rosy and golden and sweeter than the water itself, which tasted cleaner than anything in the mortal sea. Patrick kicked his legs, pushing himself up and somewhat beside me, although still leaving his hands in mine. He wanted to see this with me, and I wanted to allow it, so I slowed, and together we swam toward Saltmist. Toward my home.

I tried to see it with his eyes as we approached. The palace rose from the sea floor like a shell balanced on its end, all elegant curves and spirals, too unbalanced to have stood without the water supporting it. There were no doors, but countless wide windows with graceful balconies in front of them, allowing my subjects to swim inside whenever they desired. The walls were adorned with silver and mother-of-pearl, studded with patches of kelp and growing sea flowers, which bloomed regardless of the season. All around it were rings of gloriously multicolored coral, vast from centuries of growth, playing host to countless fish and sea creatures, some of which had been gone from mortal seas since before Oberon's departure, some of which had never swum there to begin with.

Below us spread the fields of my people, the farmland planted and heavy with the coming harvest, the homes built for those who had no desire or need to live within the palace. Some reached my chambers, an audience emerged from their home to point and wave as we swam by, and I knew that by the time we arrived, they would have assembled, ready to meet the land's man who had stolen their lady's heart.

One thing that seems to be common throughout all the realms of Faerie, whether land or sea or higher above, is that everyone loves a story. And a mermaid in love with a man of the land would always be a story good enough to catch attention. Ah, well. It couldn't be helped, and if anyone bothered us about it, I'd simply remind them that I was in charge here. Possibly with the hard side of my hand.

I pulled Patrick closer to the palace, and then through one of the larger windows. We'd need to reach one of the chambers set aside for use by the Selkies, and soon; his time under the influence of the potion would be coming to an end, and I hadn't brought him this far just to drown him, not when I could easily have done that at the pier. I pulled us through the room on the other side and toward one of the rising tunnels, only realizing my mistake as I swam into it, still pulling him in my wake.

I had chosen this tunnel because it was on the larger side, intended for the movement of goods through the palace, often used by those who were caring for children and needed the extra space. There were tunnels too narrow for even me to use, designed for use by the Cephali, whose bones were more a matter of convenience than necessity. We would both fit, if not comfortably so.

But I knew where we were going and what was going on. For Patrick, I had just pulled him into a dark, enclosed space, where the walls brushed against us as we swam upward, seemingly endlessly. I could feel him tensing against me, the first stages of panic setting in. I swam faster, unwilling to linger and risk him starting to thrash. He wasn't drowning; he could breathe. But we were surrounded by water, and his body's instincts could resume control at any time. We're all animals in the end.

We swam for no more than a few minutes before breaking into the light, airy space of the Selkies' receiving room. Some of the skinshifters were in residence, lounging on the low couches set against the wall, their skins tied around their waists or shoulders, their bodies otherwise bare. They turned toward the sound of our breaking the surface with expressions of evident surprise. Surprise which faded into shock when they recognized me, and then into dismay when they saw me haul the gasping Patrick above the surface, his sodden clothes hanging around him like a shroud.

The arrival pools are never very large, to keep the rooms they feed from flooding. I guided Patrick to the edge and let go before boosting myself out of the water and shifting back into a two-legged form. Out of respect for the Selkies and their respect for me, I garbed myself in a long blue-green dress at the same time, floor-length and concealing enough to prevent them from becoming uncomfortable with my closeness. One of them gasped as I stood. Another rose, shakily forcing a deeply awkward bow. I inclined my head, more curtly than I had intended to, and turned my attention back to Patrick.

He was still in the water, gripping the edge of the pool tightly with both hands, as if he were afraid it was going to disappear and drop him back into the depths. He opened his mouth to speak, then stopped, choking, as it filled with water.

"You have no gills to drain; you need to spit it all out," I said. Possibly more than spit; he would have both swallowed and inhaled a great deal of seawater during our swim, and his body wasn't as suited to handling it as mine was, having been created to live on land and not in the depths of the sea.

Patrick spat the mouthful of water out as decorously as he could, and I resisted the urge to laugh at him. "I didn't expect that," he managed, although his words had a deep bubbling quality to them that was going to catch up with him in a moment—and be deeply unpleasant when it did.

Ah, well. I had tried to warn him.

"Which part?" I asked. "You pointed here. I thought you were asking to come and see my home."

"I was. I am. I did. I mean—" He froze mid-sentence before whipping around and violently vomiting a remarkable quantity of water onto the floor, where it ran immediately back into the entrance pool.

And there it was.

"The potion's efficacy has ended," I said, and knelt to offer him my hands. "You'll feel better if you get out of those wet clothes. Come, let me help you. It seems like we have much to discuss, you and I, or you'd never have followed me into the water."

"I couldn't let you leave me as an enemy," he said, taking my hands and allowing me to pull him from the sea. His clothes remained stubbornly sodden, clinging to his skin. I glanced at the Selkies who were still gathered, staring at us in dismay. There are no rules against bringing land fae into the palaces of the sea, and even if there were, they wouldn't apply to me; those who make the rules have little need to follow them. Still, few land fae can survive the journey, and so this was a virtually unprecedented occurrence. I turned to the nearest of them.

"You," I said. "I don't know your name."

"H-Henry," he said.

Selkies are often more cavalier about the tradition that calls for no name to be reused. They can afford to be; their lives are so short as to make their choices virtually irrelevant to the rest of us. He was the third Selkie of his name I'd met, and I had to swallow the urge to sniff at the impropriety of it all, instead saying mildly, "Go and find Helmi. Tell her I need one of the Naiads. She should be able to bring them here."

"Yes, ma'am," he said, and flung himself into the entry pool that Patrick had so recently befouled without so much as a twitch. Either he had no sense of cleanliness, or I was frightening them worse than I realized.

And now we couldn't leave, as I had asked him to bring me Helmi, and she would expect to find me where he said I would be. Ah, well. I kept hold of Patrick's hands, pulling him with me toward one of the couches. The Selkies watched us uncertainly, clearly unsure of whether they should stay or go.

Selkies are an essential part of any functional Undersea demesne. The land courts accept them, allowing them to serve as courtiers and observe the tenor of the political situation. They make for poor spies, being too honest by nature and too clumsy on the land to successfully infiltrate most situations, but it's useful to have members of our households welcome wherever they choose to go. That doesn't mean they're comfortable here, fathoms below the sea, cut off from light and air, any more than they would be truly comfortable in the middle of a desert, feeling dry winds against their faces and shifting sands beneath their feet.

They're liminal creatures, the Selkies are, part of both worlds and fully belonging to neither, and my heart would break for them if they were not so useful as they are.

I sat, pulling Patrick down with me, and looked to the remaining Selkies, who continued to watch us in wide-eyed silence. I couldn't remember ever seeing any of them before, although they were clearly familiar enough with me to know who I was. Or maybe they were simply smart enough to assume that when a Merrow hauled a Daoine Sidhe through a hole in the floor, she was someone not to be interfered with. Either way, I was tired of their staring.

"We would like a moment's privacy, if you don't mind," I said. They didn't move. I raised an eyebrow. "*Now.*"

They scattered, not for the pool, but for the doors that would take them deeper into the air-filled complex of rooms kept for their use. In a matter of moments, we were alone, and I was leagues away, my thoughts on the interior of the palace, trying to decide which rooms would need to be drained and converted for Patrick's use. I couldn't ask the Selkies to leave, would have to keep the amount of space they were accustomed to available for them, or the whole rookery might desert me, moving down the coast to the next amenable demesne. I would never forgive myself if I dealt the defenses of Saltmist such a terrible, if accidental, blow, so I would have to find or open another space—yes, that might be the best answer. Opening new rooms would mean I wasn't taking anything away from anyone.

Beside me, Patrick took a deep breath, only coughing a little, and said, "I didn't expect you to have air-filled rooms at the bottom of the sea."

I snapped my attention back to him and smiled. "Many of my subjects *can* breathe air, even if it's not our default environment, and the Selkies require it if they're to live. We use them to send messages to the land courts, and they come here to rest and hunt in the bosom of the sea. The air is a favor to them and has been since Amphitrite's day. Before she left us, she bid us be kind to the Selkies."

"Really? Are they her descendants?"

I frowned. "I don't believe so, no. So far as I'm aware, her only children are the Merrow. I've never heard a Firstborn named for the Selkies, but Amphitrite was worried for them, and she asked us to be kind, and while I don't feel obeying our Firstborn is required with her so long gone and us left to our own devices, I see no cost in kindness."

Patrick nodded slowly. "As you were kind to me when you had no cause to be." He started to look away.

I was *not* going to have a replay of the pier, not here in my own halls, not when that nonsense should be well finished and far behind us. I grabbed his chin and wrenched his face back around toward me, taking note of his shocked expression before jerking guiltily away. He knew what I was. He knew I came from a culture more violent than his own. That didn't make it right for me to treat with him as if he had been raised in these halls, all knowing of our ways. He was of the land. I had to be more gentle, or I would risk bruising him.

"I have always had cause to be kind where you were concerned," I snapped, and he flinched, apparently startled by the harshness of my tone as he had been by the harshness of my hand. This, I made no effort to adjust. I could soften myself for his sake. I couldn't become someone entirely new. "You didn't see me as the Duke's daughter, or as a Duchess in waiting. You didn't see me as a Merrow warrior, trained and honed to a killer's edge. You saw me as a woman who wanted something more than fancy mouthfuls for her supper, and you showed me kindness first, if you recall. You fed me and saw to it that I was more comfortable in an unfamiliar, unforgiving place. Now you're the one in the unfamiliar place, and of course that will move me to as much kindness as my nature has to show, because it is a balance. This is my home, as those halls were yours. I hope . . . I very much wish that this should be a home to you, in time."

For the first time, Patrick looked alarmed. Not extremely so; his was the face of a man who had just heard that his tea might be spoilt, or his trousers might be stained, and not the face of a man who thought his life in danger. "Are you intending to keep me here?" he asked.

"Only for as long as you desire to stay." The question was reasonable enough, given the circumstances, and still it stung. I shrank a bit away from him, certain the hurt must be showing in my face, and asked, "Do you truly think I would keep you against your will?"

"N—no! I'm sorry. I don't know what I think right now." He looked slowly around the room, eyes terribly wide. "I always wondered where you went when you had to leave me. I hoped it was beautiful. This is more than I could have dreamt it would be."

I looked around the room, trying to see it with new eyes. I couldn't. It was still one of the lesser rooms in the knowe, however hard I tried, a little shabby, a little ordinary, very much in need of a deep cleaning, although I would never have said that where Helmi could hear. I may be Duchess and my word may be law, but that doesn't make me foolish enough to risk antagonizing my staff. They control too much of my nightly comfort, and I have never swept a floor or clarified water in my life.

I returned my attention to Patrick, who was still looking at his surroundings with dazed wonder. Catching my movement out of the corner of his eye, he turned back to me, and smiled. "I . . . I'm sorry. This has been a rather longer and more exciting evening than I had thought to experience. You have my sincere apologies if my attention seems elsewhere."

"Did you ask me to meet you tonight solely so you could break my heart?"

He glanced down and away but met my eyes bravely before he answered: "Yes. I thought I had played too long and carelessly with your heart, although I swear, it was not out of any ill intent. The temperature in the Mists is shifting. The kingdom grows larger, and the expectations Eira placed on all her children grow harder to shoulder. Silences to the North grows in strength and standing. I have little doubt there would be war already, were Gilad not so skilled at brokering peace. It seemed . . . unkind . . . to keep you tied as tightly to the land as I have striven to do when we could never stay together always. And once I realized our story had an ending, it felt cruel to the two of us to draw it out simply because I did not desire that end."

"If you had been born to the sea, I would slap you across your pretty face right now," I said, allowing my voice to chill. "No one— no man—makes my decisions for me, Patrick Twycross. No man says that my ties to the land are too tight, or that they have the right to spare me a cruelty I have dearly sought. I don't care what Eira wanted. A pox on that broken-down old mare, who never saw a good thing that she didn't wish to see destroyed! She may have been your First, but she's dead and gone and you've never known her, by her own choice. Amphitrite was smart enough to know that her children and their children were not toys she could play with and discard. I refuse to let my own life be disrupted by a woman too foolish to understand the same simple idea about her own descendants."

I glared at him, my hands balled to fists and my knees aching to vanish, as they often did when I was angry. The only reason the Merrow haven't swarmed the land to slap the smug smiles off the faces of the Daoine Sidhe is our tendency to revert to a finned form when angry. It makes a land war difficult for us.

Patrick stared at me, clearly startled by my outburst. Then, to my surprise, he laughed.

"You're right, aren't you? No, of course, you're right. Eira *left* us. She walked away and she left us, with only a handful of instructions as to how she wanted us to conduct our lives, and none of them suited to the child I was, or the man I would become. I have no yen for crowns or conquests. I would like children, eventually ..." He paused, cheeks flushing red. " ... but not with the bride she would have preferred for me, or as the transaction I am quite sure she would have brokered, given opportunity and time. I want to live for myself, and not for the Firstborn who deserted me."

"Well, that makes you the cleverest of your kind I've ever heard speak, although that's a shallow dive to make, and no mistake," said a familiar voice, accompanied by the distinctive slapping sound of suckers clinging to and releasing from a solid surface. I turned, already smiling, to see Helmi approaching us. As was her wont, she was halfway up the wall, "walking" in a straight line that simply happened to put her in opposition to gravity.

Patrick gasped softly. I suppose he'd never seen a Cephali before. Unlike Merrow and Selkies, they have little cause to visit the land, and Helmi had never accompanied me on one of our outings.

From the waist up, she was indistinguishable from one of the Daoine Sidhe, even down to the points of her ears. She lacked my gills and other outward signifiers of her aquatic nature, and even had something of their coloring, with her cherry-red hair and rose-pink eyes; none of them would have rejected her as belonging to another company if she'd appeared among them wearing a dress of sufficient volume. For all the trouble, from that perspective, began at her navel and extended downward from there, as her lower body was that of a giant Pacific octopus, normally and naturally colored a shade of red that matched her hair. Her tentacles seemed to all move independently of each other, but they worked together sufficiently to drive her steadily forward.

A woman walked behind her, blue-haired and clad in a simple white dress so soaked-through with seawater that she left a gleaming trail behind her as she walked. Her hair was equally sodden, rivulets running down her chest and arms where it touched. There was no possible way she could still be so wet after walking all the way through the air chambers to reach us unless she was generating the water herself. Which, of course, she was.

I rose gracefully, extending my hands toward Helmi, forearms as flat and exposed to her as my anatomy allowed. She responded by lowering herself to floor level, clasping her own hands to her sternum, and winding her two lead tentacles around my arms in a damp embrace. The Cephali have their own ways of doing many

things, and more loyal, more reliable courtiers are not to be found
in all the Undersea.

Helmi had been with me since my girlhood, and she would likely
be with me until one or both of us had gone to bones rolling across
the bottom of the sea. That is the way of things, with Cephali and
Merrow. We prize loyalty, and we prize it well enough to stake our
lives on it.

"Good fishing and kind tides, Helmi," I said. "Who have you
brought me?"

"This is one of the Naiads, as you requested," she said. The
blue-haired woman raised a hand in languid greeting but did not
offer a name. That is also the way of things with Naiads. They
come into their lives with the singing of the sea ringing in their
ears, and at times it can be all they hear or know. They tend to
gather around noble households, less out of a desire to serve or to
be protected from the more violent elements of the Undersea, but
because they like the way the presence of others changes the song
They speak rarely to the rest of us, not because they wish to kee
their secrets but because it takes so much effort for something
be worthy of being said.

"It is deeply appreciated," I said, and lowered my arms, sign
ing her to release them.

She did not, instead cocking her head and sending a glance
ward Patrick. "And who have *you* brought *me*, your Grace?"
asked.

I flushed. My manners are not normally so lacking. "My sir
apologies, dear friend. This is Patrick Twycross, Baron of F
ered Stones, late of Tremont, now of the Mists, and my cons
be. Patrick, this is Helmi, courtier of my halls and my per
lady's maid since childhood. This place wouldn't function w
her, and neither would I."

Helmi finally unwound one tentacle from around my fo
waving it at Patrick in what seemed like a jaunty mann
which I recognized as being just shy of a rude gesture. "At
suitor deigns to visit our hallowed halls. What brings yo
from the safety of your shore, air-breather?"

"My lady does," said Patrick, staying wisely seated.
view height as a form of dominance. The highest pers
room is the one with the superior position. I was taller
Helmi and the Naiad, and Helmi trusted me. As long as

highest, she had no need to go on the defensive. If Patrick placed himself above me, something he could do simply by standing, she might climb to the ceiling on instinct alone.

Cephali do not tell tales of their Firstborn. I regret that. The story of their lineage must be a *fascinating* one.

Helmi snorted. "And you allowed yourself to be brought, like a trinket or a treasure?"

"My lady is a treasure to me, and I would hope that I am a treasure to her, for if I am not, I am clearly wasting her time. So yes, exactly so."

Thoughtfully, Helmi lowered her first tentacle, and unwound the second from around my arm. "There are some who would think ill of my lady for courting a man of the land."

"There are some who think ill of me for falling in love with a mermaid. We all have our burdens to carry."

"She swims faster unburdened."

"Then I will remain here and wait for her to come back to me." Oddly enough, Patrick seemed to be *relaxing*. He was being challenged by a type of fae he had never seen before, whose quirks and abilities were unknown to him, and somehow, that was comforting. I will never understand Daoine Sidhe.

Meanwhile, the Naiad had wandered aimlessly from behind Helmi and was drifting toward Patrick, humming tunelessly. The water she left in her wake glittered silver and did not dry. He glanced at her, suddenly nervous again.

A Naiad, harmless unless threatened, was unnerving him, and Helmi was not? We were going to have to have a lot of conversations if he was going to be safe in the Undersea. I realized with a start that I was already thinking of his time here as a lasting thing; of course, he would need to be safe because he was staying. We needed to finish our conversation, so I could know for certain whether our troubles were over or simply taking a moment to reflect before they continued.

"What makes you think you're worthy of her time?" asked Helmi, more brusquely.

"Nothing," said Patrick, and spread his hands. "I am entirely unworthy of her time. I have no idea what she sees in me or why she bothers to humor my affections. But I also feel that I am unworthy to question her. If she wishes to be so foolish as to attach herself to me, I can only be grateful for her good regard, stand

back, and allow the error in hopes that I'll amuse her too much for her to think of correcting it. Were I worth more, I might have the authority to argue. Lacking that happy circumstance, I shall stay where and as I am, and love my lady, and wed her if she'll have me, that none save Oberon himself will sunder me from her side."

As marriage proposals went, it was somehow both the best and worst I'd ever heard. My ears burned red as I cleared my throat and said, "Helmi, my relationship is not up for debate at the moment. I bade you to bring me a Naiad, and you've done so; your duty is discharged, and you are free to go."

Helmi and I have been together long enough that she knew she'd have the opportunity to speak her piece later, when we were alone together. She glared at me briefly, tentacles twitching, before she turned and trundled back down the hall, this time moving at floor level, as if that alone would be sufficient to demonstrate how seriously she took this situation. I watched her go until she vanished behind a doorway and continued to watch until the slap-suck-release sound of her tentacles pulling her forward faded. Then I turned to face the Naiad.

She had moved closer to Patrick during my silence, and was standing only a few feet away from him, heavy-lidded blue eyes fixed on a point just above his collarbone. "Er, hello," he said. "I'm Patrick. And you are?"

"Naiads don't talk much," I said, just as she sighed and said, "Hydor."

I jumped a little, startled. She tipped her chin up, meeting Patrick's eyes for the first time.

"My sisters and I are all Hydor," she said, in a lilting, dreamy tone as if that was some profound explanation. "You're very wet. It isn't in your nature. May I have the water?"

This was what I'd called her for, and yet I hurried to say, "The water *outside* his body, if you please. The water *inside* his body is happy where it is."

Patrick looked alarmed. The Naiad sighed.

"As you say," she said, and raised her hands in a politely beckoning gesture.

The water still weighing down Patrick's clothing and hair began streaming off of him immediately, first pooling at his feet, then shaping itself into a long, sinuous shape, closely akin to an eel, and slithering across the floor to wind itself around the Naiad's legs.

She smiled, clearly charmed. It grew larger as Patrick grew drier, until it extended to her knees. Then she lowered her hands, and the liquid eel splashed into a formless puddle that was quickly absorbed by the hem of her dress.

"Shore water," she said thoughtfully. "Shore water and tears, and all the distance between. You'll be happy here, if you allow yourself to be. You'll drown if you don't." She turned to me then, offering a polite nod, before wandering seemingly aimlessly down the hall after Helmi, leaving us alone.

The silence remained unbroken for several seconds. Then Patrick said ponderously, "What was *that*?"

"That was Hydor," I said. "Congratulations on getting a name out of her. Naiads don't habitually speak much or give personal names. Although given that she said all her sisters were Hydor as well, it may be a family name. Naiads sculpt water. It's one of their talents. We have several living here in the palace. They help to keep the dry rooms dry and prevent cracks from forming in the walls."

"There's much here that I don't know," he said. "I'll seem very foolish to you for a time, I'm sure. I may slow you down."

"I could stand to go a little slower," I said, and moved to sit beside him again. "Did you mean what you said to Helmi?"

"The woman with the octopus arms?"

I nodded. He shook his head, seemingly less in negation than dismay. "I've never seen anyone like her before," he said, before admitting sheepishly, "I had no idea there were people like her in the sea."

"The sea holds all manner of wonders you have yet to discover or explore," I said. "There will be time to learn them all. But I do have to know—did you mean what you said to Helmi?"

He reddened but kept his eyes on mine as he said, "If a landless Baron from a nowhere County is good enough for you, if you would have me, knowing I bring nothing of value save myself . . . then yes. I meant every word and syllable. I would wed you, if you'd have me. I would be the father of your children. I would spend the rest of my life with you."

"Even knowing that it would have to be here?" I spread my arms, indicating the palace around us and, by greater extension, the sea outside. "I could give up my Duchy for love, given time to find myself an heir, but a Merrow who willingly forsakes the only shell they have to hide in is a Merrow not long for the sea. I would be hunted down by my own kind, viewed as weak, and driven to the beaches and beyond. I must stay here."

"Saltmist is beautiful," said Patrick. "As long as I could visit the land from time to time, for the sake of those I'd be leaving behind, I could be happy here."

"And where is the man who sat on the pier and told me he couldn't love me enough to hold me to him?" I cocked my head. "Where is the man who was ready and willing to leave me?"

"He drowned," said Patrick, and wrapped his arms around me, pulling me close as his lips found mine, and he kissed me like I was the only thing left in the entire world. I was all that mattered. I wrapped my arms around him in turn, returning the kiss with equal fervor.

I had not gone to the first ball, or even our first outing, with the intention of finding a husband. I had expected to do it in the normal way: to make a political alliance, or to be bested on the field of battle by someone who was willing to consider my bed better than my beheading. I certainly hadn't been expecting to find my heart in a man who couldn't breathe water without the aid of a potion, who could barely swim, but sometimes the sea has her own ideas of how a life will go.

I pulled back, looking at him seriously, and said, "We shall have to find a place to hold the wedding."

Patrick smiled, a little besotted. "What do you think of Muir Woods?" he asked.

I laughed.

SIMON

The garden grew lush and green around me, as it always did. Amy's command over her tower grounds took all the chance and chaos out of agriculture, resulting in a garden where it was always the height of spring and summer, at the very same time, save for the few plants that thrived best in fall and seemed to exist in their own private bubble of time. The beds she had set aside for my use, where I grew the herbs I would use in my potions and tinctures, were the only ones that had any respect for the natural cycles of fruit and flower, passing through the stages of growth at the customary pace, rather than refreshing themselves overnight.

My Amy is far from unique among our kind. We have all of eternity as a plaything, assuming we're wise enough to stay away from certain danger, and yet we have the patience of mortal children. If a thing is desired, it is desired right now, and no amount of pleading or argument will change that desire one bit. My need to grow things at their natural pace is often viewed as strange and even stupid by all save other herbalists and the occasional alchemist of my acquaintance.

I have to think that we were better once, when Oberon was here and the wheel of the seasons more tightly bound our motions, that we understood patience and planning and waiting for what we wanted. How else could we have built kingdoms, constructed dynasties, or composed the beautiful spells and elegant workings of our past? Even my own work, petty and primitive as it is, had to be intuited from foundations crafted from time and care and research. How we can have eternity on our sides and still have less patience than is innate to mortal children?

It is a mystery for greater minds than mine to solve, I fear. I knelt in my herb bed, golden scissors in my hand, carefully snipping the leaves and blooms I needed to craft another batch of protective tonic. I was consuming more and more these days, fighting the cumulative effects of the potion I drank to keep my lady's will from entirely overwhelming my own. The tonic I brewed now was five times stronger than I had brewed in the beginning, and even that had been a strain on my system, too potent to consume safely, and yet safer than the alternative.

I was playing a losing game, and I knew it. The longer I spent in my lady's company, the more of the potion to protect me from her will and wishes I would need to consume, lest my choices cease to be my own, as I suspected they already had. The more of the potion I consumed, the more of the tonic I would need to keep myself from dying by my own hand—but if it passed a certain quantity, the protection would become the poison, and I would die anyway.

None of this was right or reasonable. All of this was by my own choice, for I had sold myself into my lady's service to protect my dearest friend in all the world, the only person I cared for as much as I did my Amy or my daughter. Patrick Twycross was the best of what the Daoine Sidhe could be: measured, kind, protective of those with less than himself. He thought himself a failure, for he craved no crown, but he had become a king among pixies without a second thought. He had fulfilled the commands we all must live by admirably, save for the children, and many older than he—my own twin brother, even—have failed to fulfill that commandment. We can control many things with magic and with wanting. Our own biology is not among them.

But Eira's first commandment, when she left her own face behind and went into hiding as one of her own children, had been to keep the bloodlines pure. She wanted an army of Daoine Sidhe waiting for her when she shrugged off the mask of Evening Winterrose and moved to claim her rightful place.

I didn't know why one of the First would want an army, and to be honest, I try not to let my thoughts bend in that direction. With Oberon and the Queens absent, no good can come of a Firstborn with an army at her command. And few words can describe her fury at the cavalier way her descendants have been ignoring her first request. My brother, married to a Kitsune. Myself, married to a woman whose line has, so far as I am aware, no name, but who is not of Titania's blood in any way, with a daughter whose veins are entirely clear of Eira's influence. Patrick's insistence on courting a Merrow-maid had been a stroke too far for her, and she had done her best to drown their fledgling relationship at the beginning of their courtship.

She would have succeeded in turning Patrick into a murder weapon set against his own love had I not been able to intervene, not quickly enough to stop her first attempt, but before she could make a second. The cost of his freedom had been my servitude, and to my shame and dismay, it had not chafed. Not then, and not now.

Serving my lady satisfied a need in me that had always been there, but which had been all too often set aside. I was happy to dance attendance on Amy, but her role was wife, not regent, and she was rarely pleased to set me the type of tasks that my lady was. In Eira's eyes, I was a useful tool, not a partner. In Amy's eyes, which were the most beautiful jewels ever to grace our world, I was . . .

Well, I was not a partner to her, either. The more time I spent with Eira, the easier it became to see that my love, my heart, my treasure had never been able to care for me as I did for her. The distance between us was too great. It was as if Patrick had fallen in love with one of his pixies, and not with a woman who was at the very least his equal and might arguably be his superior.

I was a pet.

That was a grim understanding to reach about the mother of one's child, and each time my thoughts led me inexorably back to it, I set it firmly aside. I love my wife. August was as yet too young to allow us to divorce, even if I had wished it; to be Amy's pet, cared for and cosseted and disregarded, was better than to be without her, cast off and alone. I had no illusions about which parent our child would choose, in that unhappy future where we were no longer together. No. My life was as I wished it. I had a wife to love and a daughter to raise, a lady to serve and a garden to tend, while Patrick drifted ever farther away from me, finding safe harbor in his own lady's arms.

Might that she would be kinder to him than my own keepers had ever seen fit to be to me.

I clipped a stalk of new rhubarb, adding it to my basket. Like many of the herbs and simples I would be brewing, it was poisonous when raw, tempering to something safer as it cooked. The effort of brewing the tonic would occupy the rest of my day, well into the night, and provide the distraction necessary to keep myself from dwelling on the aspects of my life I would rather set aside.

I was reaching for the basil when a swirl of light and color raced into the garden, ringing like a klaxon bell, and proceeded to loop several times around my head. I am ashamed to admit that my first instinct was to swat at the motion, and I only stopped myself when I recognized the lights. One yellow, one orange. These were Patrick's pixies.

Carefully, I set my scissors into the basket and motioned toward the berry bush in front of me. "Please, land," I said. "You know I get dizzy when you try to communicate and move at the same time."

The pixies settled at once, tiny faces drawn in clear consternation, wings still vibrating with barely suppressed anxiety. They chimed more softly now that they were no longer moving, but still they chimed, uncomfortable and anxious.

"You also know," I said, trying to swallow my own sudden concern, "that you aren't permitted to visit me here. I enjoy your company, and my daughter finds you charming, but my wife is less easily endeared. She was raised to consider you as vermin, and vermin are not welcome in her garden."

Poppy snapped her wings shut and glared at me, before making a rude gesture with her hands. I smiled.

"Fair enough; that is a rude word to use for one's friends, although I might argue it less rude when it is in echo of someone who truly holds that opinion, and is inclined to express her desires with occasionally violent vigor. But still, you should not be here."

Daffodil made an inquisitive chiming sound.

I picked up my scissors, holding them out for her to see. "I need to finish gathering herbs. The specific tonic I'm attempting to brew requires that all ingredients be collected within an hour's time, or they fall out of synchronization with one another, and the effect is not as potent as desired." I needed it to be as potent as possible. Anything else would expose me to the effects of my own poison, and while I am not the most talented or subtle potion-maker in the Mists, I am *very* good at brewing poisons. Call it a sometimes inconvenient natural gift or call it the reason I am no longer allowed to make jam; the outcome is the same either way.

Daffodil chimed again. I cocked my head to the side.

"Please flare your wings twice if that meant what I think it meant, and you're offering to finish my harvest for me," I said politely.

She flared her wings twice, while Poppy looked silently on. Both of them had worried, drawn expressions, something which was not encumbered by our language barrier.

I nodded. "Excellent. Everything I need is in this area of the garden." I gestured to the herb bed in front of me, flanked with berry bushes, and to the ones on either side. "If you're not sure what a plant is, bring me a leaf and I'll tell you if you've got the right thing. Agreed?"

Both pixies nodded vigorously and launched themselves into the air. I sat back on my heels and began naming off herbs and simples, watching as they zipped from plant to plant and collected the pieces I had requested. Leaves, stems, flowers, seedpods, even the occasional root, they gathered them all with the quick efficiency of long-time scavengers, zipping over and holding them up for my inspection before dropping them into the basket. In a matter of minutes, they had completed a task that had been set to take me the bulk of the allotted hour. I dropped my scissors into the basket atop the gathered greenery and clapped my hands.

"Oh, *well* done!" I said. "Well done, indeed, both of you!" The prohibition against thanking someone for their service doesn't extend to pixies, of course, but as Patrick had always treated them as if they were full members of Faerie, deserving of the civility and respect we afforded one another, it seemed right to speak to them as I would have to any other who helped me in my tasks.

They landed, one on each shoulder, and rang imperiously. Poppy went so far as to grab my ear and pull, trying to guide me in her chosen direction. I coughed.

"One moment, if you please." Stasis spells are among the first any potion-maker is taught; without them, half our workings would curdle in the pot, misbrewed from the beginning. I waved my hands above the basket, murmuring a line of cradle poetry that my mother used to recite to me. The smell of smoke and rotting oranges flared in the air around us. I somehow managed not to wrinkle my nose or gag.

I first noticed that my magic was changing in character some fourteen years ago, when the mulled cider scent I had been born with and had lived with all my life began to twist and decay, first becoming the sweet scent of oranges, and then yielding, as if inevitably, to rot. My lady was unconcerned by the change, saying only that it might be spurred by the magic I borrowed from her, the magic that allowed me to do such wonderful, impossible, essential things. The blood of the Firstborn is powerful, too powerful for their descendants, much like the poisons I used to resist yielding entirely to her will. If there was a tonic that would have protected me from the damage done by her blood, she had not as yet seen fit to reveal it to me.

The pixies were the only ones I could freely cast in front of. My wife, my daughter, my best friend—all of them would have been shocked and horrified by the change in me, and would have demanded to know its source, meaning they would have demanded I reveal my lady's true identity. That would destroy me.

Or worse, my wife might not be surprised at all, might only smile her small and terrible smile and say that she had been wondering how long it would take me to tell her what was going on, and then I would know that she had allowed me to sell myself into service to her sister, and that she had not interceded on my behalf. There is some knowledge too terrible for a sane man to carry, and so I did my best to obscure what was becoming of me.

But the pixies couldn't tell anyone what they smelled, if indeed they could detect magic at all. Their own magic was visual; perhaps they thought all larger fae to be great wizards who could somehow suppress the manifestation of our magic.

The stasis spell settled into place, and I returned my attention to the pixie as yet yanking on my ear. "Only lead the way and I will follow," I said. "And if you could endeavor not to rip my ear from my head in the process, I would be most grateful for your restraint."

They both rang, then, and threw themselves back into the air, racing away—but far more slowly than I knew they were capable of moving. They were allowing me the time I needed to catch up with them, and I appreciated it, even as I worried about what it might mean.

Amy's tower is rooted in a semi-fluid spot in the Summerlands, untethered from the mortal world save in its set distance from other domains. Shadowed Hills is never more than a day's walk away, for example, but there are paths, if one is clever and familiar with the land, that can let out almost anywhere in the environs of the bay when followed. The pixies knew them even better than I did. They zipped through a short stretch of marshland that I had only ever visited in passing, banking hard to avoid collision with a door set into a crumbling wall that had probably once been part of some larger dwelling. I matched their pace as best I could, slowing when they crossed a patch of swampy grasses or skirted over a thicket of brambles. Each time, they slowed and looped back, allowing me to catch up. Their wings never stopped ringing alarm.

Whatever the trouble was, something was really and truly wrong, and so I was less surprised than perhaps I should have been when they dove into a dark den in the side of a hill, something that might have held a large badger or small bear, and I followed them to find myself climbing through a window into Patrick's workshop.

The rafters were a glittering sea of jewel-toned pixies. Patrick was nowhere to be seen.

Still, better to be sure than to be sorry. I tugged my vest into place, not pulling a human disguise over myself, and cupped my mouth in order to call, "Pat! I do say, Pat! Are you present?"

The pixies rang, scolding me. I blinked at them.

"There's no need for such language," I said. "I simply wanted to be sure. Lead, and I'll follow."

Daffodil and Poppy darted toward the door. I followed them, filling my hands with shadows and throwing a disguise over myself as we moved. This was leading to the human world, where they would be invisible, and I would not. Pointed ears were simply *not* the done thing in San Francisco.

They led me out of the workshop and along the row of shop-fronts to the pier where Patrick had often gone to meet Dianda. I was not customarily invited on those outings, nor did I attempt to insert myself, as it would have been less friendly than it was inappropriate.

At the end of the pier there were several handfuls of broken masonry, and no signs of Patrick. I stopped dead, eyes going wide, and looked at the debris, trying to deny the story it was telling me. I have always been very, very good at denial.

"Daffodil," I said, and was proud of how calm my voice stayed. "Did you bring me here because Patrick was here?"

She chimed confirmation.

"And did he go into the water?"

Yes.

"With Dianda?" That, at least, would be normal; would be something I could understand.

No.

That was more concerning. "Did they argue?"

Yes.

That was the most concerning thing of all. I rushed to the pier's end and knelt, scanning the water for signs of a half-drowned engineer who had foolishly leapt into the sea. There was no sign of him. It was the crumbs of masonry that caused me the most distress; if he and Dianda had decided to end their courtship, and the decision had not been mutual, could he have been so foolish as to do something that would cause him harm?

I would never forgive him if he had drowned. I would go to my lady and demand a means of reaching the night-haunts, beg a boon from them, and find his spirit among their wandering shades, put it into a bottle, and shake it vigorously. Perhaps then he would understand what he had done to me . . .

. . . and it wouldn't matter, as no one short of Oberon himself has ever been able to call back the dead. I turned to the pixies, my voice dull and leaden as I asked, "Did he go into the water a very long time before you came to get me?"

Yes.

Yes. So he would already have been drowned before I delayed things further with my herbs and simples and my arbitrary time-lines. I might have arrived in time to find his body. I could never have arrived in time to save him.

I sat on the pier's edge, covering my face with my hands, and tried to think beyond the cloud of grief that swirled around me, surging in to overwhelm my senses. I had been prepared to lose him to the sea, but not in so final a manner. What was worst, of the three most important women in my life, only my daughter would understand and respect my sorrow. Amy would dismiss it as a temporary thing; might even be pleased to have one of the distractions removed from my life, making more room for her to fill. She has never been overly fond of sharing when she didn't have to. My lady had already all but disowned him, claiming that when he rejected her commandments in order to love a woman of the sea, he had rejected her as well, and she had no need to care or concern herself with his comfort or well-being. I would mourn the dearest friend I had ever known all but alone.

No: not entirely alone. A pixie landed on each of my shoulders, their drooping wings still chiming faintly. I uncovered my face, taking only a moment to swipe my tears away, and looked first at Poppy, then at Daffodil.

"You are his legacy," I said solemnly. "You are a healthy, thriving flock of pixies because of his interventions. I was there when first you came to him, your damaged daughter in your arms, and trusted him with caring for her. He has loved and tended to you with a compassion that is all too rare among my own people, and for that I am sorry, and because I loved him as much as you did, I promise that you will remain safe."

Between my two ladies, both of whom considered pixies to be little more than pests, there was no way I could take them to the tower. Nor could they remain in Patrick's workshop; even if it was not seized and reclaimed by the space-hungry humans who swarmed through San Francisco, it would be a haunted house, too filled with the memory of him to render any comfort unto us. Relocation was an inevitability.

He would want me to see them settled as comfortably as possible, safe and secure and near nothing of any danger—ah. I smiled, despite the tears still running down my face. Solutions have always been pleasing to me.

"We will build you a new paradise, in the marsh beyond my wife's tower," I said. "The land is unclaimed. You shall claim it. I have the size necessary to move your homes, your worldly possessions, all the things Patrick built for you, and to assist in the construction of whatever large structures you might require. Bridges and boardwalks and support beams for additional homes. The things that will make this transition easier for you."

Daffodil rang cautiously. I shook my head.

The voices of pixies are too small and high-pitched for human-sized fae to comprehend, but I have learned more of the tones and meanings of their chimes than I would ever have believed possible, through osmosis if nothing else. "No, I will not tell my wife. You will be a secret from all save myself, and those who might wander through the marshlands—and I can set warding spells such as my lady lays around Goldengreen, to keep random strangers from wandering into your territory." It would be a complicated working, but not outside my capability. I might even be able to do it without using my lady's borrowed magic.

That would be a good way to remember my friend. He deserved the truest heart of me, and not whatever I was becoming, one stolen spell after another. He deserved the world.

Daffodil rang again, this time less cautious than sorrowful.

"I knew we would lose him to the sea, but I didn't expect it to happen so soon, or so completely." I had expected to have time. To be able to grill Dianda on her expectations—who knew what the Undersea considered to be a marriage, or how they treated their spouses?—and to reassure Patrick that he could always come home if he wanted to. I had expected visits, and long days designing wedding finery, and to see them stand before King Gilad, unaware that one of the Firstborn was there and could have officiated their marriage, had she been willing to agree. Not that she would have been. My lady might be willing to let Patrick pollute his family line with a Merrow-maid, but she would never have agreed to formalize their union, however much they might desire it.

I had expected more time.

Laboriously, I stood, pixies still on my shoulders, and began to make my plodding way back along the pier toward the shore. I would have to go to my lady. I would have to tell her that Patrick Twycross, son of her lines, had stopped his dancing. Her fury would be beyond measure. She had still been holding out hope, however frail, that he might see the error of his ways and take up the company of a good Daoine Sidhe partner. I paused.

I would have to go to her without protection of the poisons that shielded me from the sheer force of her will. The man I was when I walked into her presence might not be the man who left, depending on how angry she became. But if I delayed telling her what had happened, her anger would only grow, and the protections I needed would only become greater. There was no escaping from the fate I had crafted for myself, one small decision at a time.

I closed my eyes. It was an ending I had long seen approaching, but which I had hoped to postpone a little longer. Long enough, perhaps, to see my daughter strike out in the world and find a home and family of her own, one that would serve her better than a mother who could not truly love and a father who had sold his soul to save another.

If there was one gift I had received from my lady, it was this: I had learned through my time with her that the love of the First-born is not something their descendants were ever built to bear. It would burn us to a crisp if ever we felt it. Amy had never loved me. I wouldn't have survived. And Amy's love for our child was less the affection of a parent and more the pride of an owner. August would be the captive of her mother's love for all the days of her life, and I might not be there to shelter her.

It hurt. It felt like I was losing my entire family in one moment, and all for the sake of a man too clumsy to stay out of the sea.

There was a splashing sound from behind me. As I was already standing still, I did not outwardly freeze, but inwardly, it felt as if everything I was had been replaced by a sudden block of ice. My heart did not beat; my lungs did not move.

"Simon? Why are you here?"

The voice was Patrick's; the question was sincere. I whipped around, dislodging the pixies from both shoulders as they slung themselves into the air and raced for him, ringing and sobbing at the same time, shedding glitter like tears as they spun through the air around him. And Patrick, who was dry as a bone despite his recent drowning, actually laughed, spreading his arms to let them swirl more freely around him.

I stalked toward him, my grief washed clean away by my anger, which was a roaring fire extinguishing all in its path. "I'm *here*," I spat, "because you fell into the sea after an argument with your lover, the *mermaid*, and were gone long enough that the pixies panicked. They came for me. They thought you were dead and drowned. And so did I."

He did not laugh, but he was smiling as he spread his hands and said, "As you can see, I'm not." His smile faded. "I am sorry to have worried you. I had no sense of how long I would be gone."

There was a second splash as Dianda's head broke the surface, followed by the rest of her, already on two legs as a column of gleaming, seemingly solid water. It lifted her to the level of the pier, and she stepped off to stand next to Patrick, looking at me with wide, guileless eyes.

"Is something wrong?" she asked.

The taste of rotten oranges was heavy on my tongue. I wanted to yell. I wanted to spit every profanity I knew, to tell her that she had dragged my heart down into the deeps as if it were nothing.

But the Daoine Sidhe are meant to be elegant and composed. To stand above when all others would drag us below. I squared my shoulders and replied, as calmly as I could, "The pixies thought Patrick had been drowned. They conveyed their impressions to me."

Unlike Patrick, she looked genuinely startled and unhappy at this declaration. The taste of oranges receded. "I am so . . . I didn't know they had followed him, I'm so sorry. I would have brought him back sooner if I'd been aware that anyone had noticed his absence."

Even the ghost of Patrick's smile was gone, replaced by the dawning understanding of how badly he had frightened me—how badly he had frightened *us*. The pixies were still circling his head, ringing furiously. I sighed.

"I was on my way to tell the Countess Winterrose that you had stopped your dancing when you saw fit to return, you utter brute. I hope you're pleased with yourself."

"I am," he said. "I shouldn't be—I would rather not be, for it was never my intent to hurt you in any way—but I am." He glanced to Dianda, and then back to me. "My lady has agreed to become my lady wife. It is an honor I will spend my nights fighting to deserve from now until the night-haunts come to claim me."

"Stop," said Dianda. "None will speak ill of my husband in my hearing, and that includes my husband." The fondness in her voice was bald and unfettered, and it made the taste of oranges rise in my throat again, for my own wife had never once sounded so in love with me.

It was not a realization that any man should have to suffer, nor was it one I welcomed, not even as my time with my lady caused my eyes to become more and more open to the casual cruelty of the Firstborn, and how little they thought of those they believed to be beneath them. It was impressive that I had believed for so long that Amy could actually care for me, but now, with poison burning holes in my stomach on a weekly basis, such self-deception was increasingly beyond me.

And Patrick was to leave me, to marry his *mermaid* and go down into the depths by her side, dependent on her love if he was to stave off drowning. He would be a kept man, even more than I had been, with no hope of escaping.

Love is a lie. There are only varying stages of indenture holding people in their places. I should have learned that lesson when my parents and my sister left me, but alas, I have never been a quick study.

"My apologies," said Patrick. He turned his attention back to me. "I would that you had been elsewhere when my pixies went looking. This is a joyous occasion. Please be happy with me?"

I have always been an excellent liar. Since the days when I ran wild through my parents' halls and had to cover for both myself and my brother in times of trouble, and even into the present, I have always been an excellent liar. Marriage to Amandine and service to my lady have only honed my natural skills to a razor's edge, leaving me prepared to slice the throat of the world with a word if such is demanded of me. I reached down deep, past the part of me that wanted to wail that he wasn't allowed to leave me, that *someone* should love me enough, just once, to stay, past the part of me that wanted to parrot my lady's words despite my pro-tections and tell him that he was tainting his bloodline forever—a

thought which I knew was not my own, but the potions which protect me can only do so much when set against a will as great and
unyielding as my lady's. I could not trust that part of myself, and
if I couldn't trust it, how could I trust any other part of me? I was
a broken mirror reflecting pieces of two Firstborn, and neither of
them played gently with their toys.

I forced a smile to my face, despite the turmoil I contained, and
said, "Of course I will be happy for you. You have finally done as
I've bid you on so many occasions and met a woman foolish enough
to have you. I assume, as she is landed and you are not, that you
will be retiring to live in her demesne, down full fathom five below
the sea?"

Patrick's smile flickered. "I will still come to see you, my friend,
and the pixies. I could never leave any of you completely."

"The pixies and I have already made such arrangements as are
necessary for their continued safety. I will see them settled, and
well out of the path of any who would do them harm."

"And yourself, my friend?"

I shrugged. "I have my Amy, and my service to the Countess
Winterrose, and I'm to see my best friend married to the woman
he loves. What more could I ask the world to give me? What more
could I even desire?"

Patrick slipped his hand from Dianda's, and she let him go willingly, looking at me with odd concern as he crossed the pier between us and took my hands in his own. His fingers were cold from
the seawater, and slightly sticky with salt. He held me tightly—
more tightly than anyone had held me for years—and looked anxiously into my eyes, his smile entirely lost now, washed out to sea
with my hopes for the night, even if I couldn't have said what those
hopes were.

"Simon," he said. "You know I love you more than almost anyone, yes? If not for the timing of our first acquaintance, our lives
could have followed very different paths."

"I know that you are the best friend I've ever had, and I'm going
to miss you as I'd miss air," I said, and pulled my hands free. "Go
with your lady. Go to the depths of the sea. I will care for your
pixies."

"We're to wed on the land," said Dianda, stepping up behind
him. "If your king will marry us, we're to wed on the land."

One more break with tradition, then, if they were asking Gilad and not the highest-ranking Daoine Sidhe in the fiefdom to perform their marriage. But then, that might be for the best, considering the couple in question. I nodded.

"Then we'll move the pixies together, and I'll welcome a new sister into my heart, as the man you are marrying is as dear to me as family."

And when they left, I would be alone with the two Firstborn who waged their silent war for my soul, and with the daughter I had already failed to save. As Dianda laughed and folded me into her arms in a sister's embrace, I closed my eyes.

It was better this way. I could never have been worthy of him, even if I were not already a married man.

I could never have been worthy of either of them.